THE HIGHLY UN[...]
OF THE H[...]
MAD

AYFER TUNÇ

THE HIGHLY UNRELIABLE ACCOUNT OF THE HISTORY OF A MADHOUSE

Translated from the Turkish by
Feyza Howell

istrosbooks

L *ove: Self-sacrifice or Self-preservation?* queried the title as a tribute to the date; for it was Valentine's Day. The lecture was being given in the conference hall on the top floor of a small city mental health hospital that evoked an immediate and inexplicable sense of resentment, situated as it was with its back facing the Black Sea.

Guest speaker Ülkü Birinci, associate professor of psychology at an undistinguished private Istanbul university, had lifted the title from a quote by Nietzsche. This academic, saddled with a name that translated as *Ideal First*, spoke in the high-tension style normally reserved for his mostly moronic students.

Ülkü no longer spent ages preparing for these lectures underwritten by pharmaceutical companies. It was enough to reel off stuff that would please the sponsors and sound impressive. He used to agonise for days in search of truly meaningful messages, back when his dreams were still fresh. But he'd let that go a long time ago; now all he cared for was his fee. He didn't see any need for a decent speech in some provincial town. Keeping the audience's interest level up was enough, not that anyone asked for much more. So he sprinkled his lectures with illustrations of women's legs and large breasts – nipples discreetly concealed; slightly risqué for the provinces, but not bad enough to enrage the conservatives.

And now, every time he directed the laser pointer to the woman's breast on the screen, the medical students, who'd been dragged here by lecturers from their school at the other end of the town, and the neuropsychiatry patients, who'd sneaked into the conference hall – the perfect place for a snooze before their appointments – gawped. Ülkü knew all too well that sex was the way to revive flagging audience interest, and he put this knowledge to good use.

The cheap Formica-laminate lectern where he rested his palms wobbled, one leg being shorter than the others, which was driving him to distraction. In a foul temper, after a restless night and stressful morning, he was silently swearing to himself *How can I* focus *on my speech with this fucking lectern?*

The verb *to focus*, a construct from English, was a recent adoption. Ülkü used to say *to concentrate*. He'd seized on *focus* as soon as he'd noticed its use *ad nauseam* by **Professor Altay Çamur**, author of a third-rate book in English that had crowned his psychotherapy research in the US; so now Ülkü also said *focus* whether the occasion called for it or not.

Thanks to this penchant for snapping up neologisms, he had cultivated a rich vocabulary. Yet he was equally quick to eschew words and idioms that, in his opinion, were widely misused. One afternoon when **School Secretary Şenay** – whose holidays abroad on her pittance of a salary beggared belief – exclaimed, *I relish these biscuits!* He was instantly appalled by the verb *to relish*, which needled him no matter who uttered it.

Şenay's command of language was, as it happens, very poor; she made every mistake in the book. Worse still, she thought this was cool. Aping the private school brats she loved hobnobbing with, but who only flirted with her for sport, she'd translated the English verb *to feel* verbatim and loved asking, *How do you feel?* instead of the more conventional *How are you?* One day in the café, Ülkü overheard Şenay remarking to the waitress about the Chancellor, *He made me feel really bad!* and fumed silently, *How I'd love to punch her!*

Needless to say, he did nothing of the sort; he made another huge mistake instead. Şenay was pondering her choice of dish in the café, in front of the endless choices intended for the spoilt students, when Ülkü insinuated that the slick-haired male undergraduates only pretended to chat her up to smooth their administrative procedures and that this was little more than self-interest on their part. Ever eager to misconstrue any sexual implication, Şenay thought the handsome assistant professor was hitting on her.

It was an utterly unwarranted comment. *Whatever tempted me to utter such nonsense,* he seethed back in his office. Ülkü identified the cause of his irritation: Şenay's undaunted capacity to exude good cheer despite the Chancellor's rebuke.

This pointless remark backfired, not on his career, but on his love life. Renowned for his preference for good-looking – and wherever possible – trophy sexual partners in this community whose definition of appropriate relationships was constantly expanding, Ülkü's prestige took an untimely blow.

He'd just secured a date with the **young researcher Selcen Akbaş**, a recent addition to the faculty, whom the handsome final year students swiftly nicknamed *Obliging Selcen*. He had booked a table at the trendiest restaurant in Istanbul, sent her champagne and flowers on Facebook, and, convinced of imminent success, instructed the cleaner to change the bed using the pricey sheets reserved exclusively for special occasions.

The pretty researcher, who had been deliberating, *Which one should I sleep with to further my career?* marked Ülkü as an undiscriminating dirty old man instead of the distinguished associate professor she had mistaken him for, and, citing a flimsy excuse, cancelled the date he'd been looking forward to for days. Less than fussy in her choice of one-night stands she might be, but thanks to the simpering school secretary she'd gone off the bloke. *Reduced me to the same level as this obese creature!* she simmered, and slept instead with Altay Çamur, whose higher standing in the faculty couldn't hide the fact that he was nowhere near as hot (and totally devoid of charm, if truth be told). Since his return from the States sporting an invisible crown of glory that in his opinion empowered him to look down on his colleagues, Altay Çamur as a rule ignored the greetings of his academic inferiors. However, when it came to Ülkü, who despite clearly meriting a full professorship had yet to make it, Altay was in two minds. Until, that is, he landed on a solution that required an inordinate amount of skill: he'd pretend to greet someone located behind Ülkü. And so, despite acknowledging Altay's greeting each time, Ülkü couldn't avoid the niggling idea that he'd misread the arrogant professor's intention.

Altay, who spelt his surname *Chamur* in international correspondence and his e-mail address (to distance himself from any connection with its Turkish meaning of *mud*), was presently occupied with the translation of his one and only book into his mother tongue. He would somehow engineer to sit with the Chancellor or Vice-Chancellor at every lunch break, banging on about the ineptitude of translators and editors in our country.

Ülkü resisted the temptation to say *focus* on home ground, anxious to avoid the certain ridicule that would ensue given its conspicuous source. Just as well he did: he'd heard the student body dubbing the man *Focus Altay* the moment that American-trained mouth first opened.

But he made up for it on his travels: Ülkü was a seasoned traveller, albeit only inland. He rarely ventured abroad. He had leapt for joy two years previously when he was invited to a symposium at Tirana University – his most recent opportunity for foreign travel. Three days before he was due to fly, however, an emergency haemorrhoid operation scuppered those plans. But Şenay, well, *she* seemed to have been everywhere: Dubai, Mexico City, St Petersburg and Venice! It was puzzling. Her looks couldn't possibly justify the obvious explanation: *Someone must be taking her.* She wasn't much of a looker, surely? Had he known that those holidays (when she'd stuff napkins full of thickly buttered salami sandwiches pilfered from the breakfast bars of half-board hotels and gobble them throughout the day, and pose for snapshots in straw hats and XXL shorts above her plump knees) were funded by shedloads of consumer credit and it was only a matter of time before the banks in question took action, he would have been relieved. But he didn't. And so he wasn't.

Right now, his head was crammed full. In fairness, he did know that most of his mental accumulation was fluff. He wasn't foolish enough to overestimate his shallow intellect, something he'd come to terms with a while back, so, unable to make ends meet on the salary paid by his cheapskate university, he'd turned to easy public speaking – for a consideration, of course. Gobsmacked at first by the enthusiastic reception for his predictably cheesy speeches, he soon got used to it. But that was all. He wasn't going to fall into the trap of admiring his own hackneyed ideas. He knew who he was, yes, and what he had become, where he wanted to go and what his limitations were; yet he was tempted to deliver ever more reckless speeches devoid of any rational thought process.

Since no one bothered with lucidity anyway, those speeches – enlivened by a colourful delivery, small anecdotes and artless visuals downloaded from the internet – proved quite popular, enabling him to carry on as a paid speaker, visiting one town after another. Unless he continued lecturing, he could never meet the maintenance payments for a marriage he'd regretted even at the Register Office. He had bided his time for fifteen years – *Well, now we have a baby… now is not the time for a divorce… the potential repercussions on my career…* – but his wife and daughter-cum-self-styled solicitor had taken him to the cleaner's without blinking an eye.

The lectern rattled again. Ülkü's blue Stabilo rolled and fell to the floor. It took enormous self-control to stop himself from swinging a hefty kick at the wobbly lectern. His fuse had become much shorter of late, but he still avoided letting rip, knowing just where to stop before causing real harm.

The last time he flew into a rage was three years ago, the day he realised he no longer could avoid reading glasses. Still simmering at the wheel, he ran a red light and crashed into a taxi. As if he wasn't the guilty party, he then attacked the taxi driver, gave him a black eye, with the end result that they were both run in. *The wages of rage!* he mused when, at the inspector's bidding, they had to kiss and make up: the taxi driver he'd nearly throttled had evidently lunched on onion-rich white bean salad.

His fury was actually a vain attempt to disguise his own powerlessness before the march of time and not because he had anything against glasses *per se.* No matter how much he denied it, this fear of ageing stemmed from the instantaneous and incontrovertible recognition that he had missed the boat of his dreams, having postponed this, that and the other: *I'll start tomorrow, I'll do it soon, there's still time, today, tomorrow…*

The day he felt his age – not that he'd admit it – was the day he was unable to decipher the prospectus of the latest antioxidant vitamin supplement, no matter how far away he held it, and then convinced himself to see someone for a new prescription, only to be shocked to learn that it wasn't astigmatism after all.

He was hugely annoyed with his **ophthalmologist, Berkay Özberk** – whose walls were emblazoned with enlarged colour photocopies of a gigantic diploma attesting to his successful completion of the Hacettepe Medical School, a certificate of consultancy and a plethora of other medical qualifications from a second-rate American university – for having the temerity to snigger *It's high time you wore reading glasses.* It wouldn't have been that bad if the young doctor hadn't been quite so patronising; if he'd made a much more tactful suggestion, along the lines of *It's not really* *critical, but you might consider a pair of reading glasses.* It was his silver-tongued mocking reference to ageing that had hacked Ülkü off.

Berkay didn't make a habit of rubbing his patients up the wrong way. But he lost his cool at Ülkü's sarcastic remark on how trendy bald heads had become – uttered waving a leonine thatch barely tinged with silver at the temples. To be fair, Ülkü had meant no offence; he'd simply spotted a poster on the wall and blurted something out, as he so often did. But it caused sparks to fly. For in the colossal poster, the entire body of the ophthalmology service of this new, swanky and pricey hospital had posed side by side, and by some strange coincidence, they were all male, all with similar outfits and postures, similar gazes and smiles sparkling with healthy teeth, all handsome, fit, and glowing with self-confidence – and all with shaved heads. This poster of bald pates all in a row, some shaved due to premature greying, others to conceal a thinning top, emanated a disturbing authority, an upper-class superiority.

Ülkü had recently been suffering from a feeling of inadequacy, of powerlessness, and refused to acknowledge that he was growing older; the realisation that these young doctors bursting with self-confidence might actually be prone to a touch of baldness caused him to run a hand through his hair with a chuckle. Which didn't escape Berkay's attention: neither the sarcastic laugh, nor the gesture betraying the idea behind it.

If Ülkü had only kept shtum and not responded to the querying stare, things would have simmered down on their own. But unwilling to concede to this handsome guy with neck muscles that testified to a minimum of three mornings a week at the gym, Ülkü openly mocked, *Since shaved heads came into fashion, you can't tell who's bald, and who's not.* The young doctor, who came from a long line of alopecia sufferers, wasn't going to take this lying down, and so, with equal sarcasm, intimated that Ülkü's young days were behind him.

What ensued was a tremendously tense sight test. The fit young doctor, bedecked with certificates in every imaginable size, seriously annoyed his patient, who not only had never been to medical school, he had never even set foot on the American continent, despite his willingness to settle for a bog-standard three-month seminar programme at the most inferior of universities. And the patient's mane and unwarranted haughtiness had the same effect on the doctor.

That idiotic lectern had been placed to the right of the stage at a slight angle in the conference hall of the venerable mental health hospital in this Black Sea town, a position that enabled Ülkü to keep an eye on both his audience and the white screen that covered the entire back wall. That screen was a particular object of hatred for **caretaker Earless Ziya**, whose responsibilities included the maintenance and cleaning of the hall; unrolling it before each conference and rolling it back up afterwards he regarded as the bane of his life.

The screen was of enormous importance for Ülkü Birinci. That's where he projected his PowerPoint presentation, which, simplistic to begin with, was dumbed down even further by the bullet points in Comic Sans and illustrated with images rarely pertinent to the topic. He also had the habit of marking his subheads with clichéd symbols. And he loved sending simple emoticons, like winks and kisses during erotic exchanges with secretive chat room frequenters of indeterminate sex. Totally au fait with chatspeak, he belonged to several bizarre groups where virtual friends with blatantly suggestive handles, on receiving a fake photo, would insist *LMIRL – Let's Meet In Real Life.*

It wasn't like he hadn't been tempted by at least a couple of these requests since his divorce. He might have missed Selcen Akbaş by a hair's breadth, but he never failed to turn a few heads in his circles, amongst weary women who were nearly past it. He didn't need the ambiguous sexual denizens of the mysterious internet world. Still, a demon had sneaked inside him whose fantasies would not be slaked by the attention of the women around him. The demon awakened the moment he sat down at the computer screen – but despite the relentless temptation, he hesitated to take the next step, preferring instead to keep his interlocutors confined to the virtual world, as he chatted with abandon through the night, amazed at his own imagination.

This virtual universe, which he wandered through as **Zebb** – not the most inventive handle, true, but it did help him shed his inhibitions – was a magical land where, on nights when he was tormented by spiritual loneliness, he discovered a brand new Ülkü indulging in suppressed desires light years from his actual personality. Those night-time orgies would occasionally pop into his mind during the day, especially in formal company, and he would cringe at the memory of the vulgar chats, which surely showed on his face. It had happened again this morning: his shirt was drenched in sweat, which poured down his back because he was scared. Crazy-scared of coming face to face with these professional chatmates – whose pictures surely bore no relation to reality and whose real identities he couldn't even begin to guess. What if he couldn't stuff his suppressed desires back where they came from, and was never able to revert to his real identity as a trustworthy academic of unimpeachable gravitas?

The stage with the wobbly lectern faced a door far too narrow for this conference hall with its old, dusty loudspeaker, an age-darkened pennant sporting the logo of this hospital without a single window facing the sea, cloth banners of local sponsors and a Turkish flag threadbare from too many washes. A cheap knotty-parquet-style vinyl covered the floorboards, rotting here and there. Splinters piercing the lumpy vinyl added to the overall effect.

Earless Ziya detested wiping the vinyl, which had been laid on the orders of **Medical Director Demir Demir** – who basked in his name's unusual reduplication, which meant *Iron Iron* – after he had been forced to concede that replacing the floorboards was out of their reach for the foreseeable future. The diluted detergent rarely had time to dry, since Ziya never remembered to wipe the floor until five minutes before each conference, thereby putting the Medical Director and guest speakers at risk of slipping. And true enough, both **Metropolitan Mayor Tacettin Başusta** and **Deputy Governor Hikmet Keleşoğlu**, who'd been falling over themselves to patronise these conferences ever since the local TV stations started taping every imaginable event, had nearly slipped on the wet flooring, and a few others actually did fall.

On one occasion, the guest speaker was **Erdem Bakırcıoğlu, the Medical Director's schoolmate** from Istanbul's renowned Galatasaray Lycée, where they had regularly sneaked out of the dormitory at night and run riot in Beyoğlu. Ever since, at every opportunity, Demir Demir would repeat the well-worn phrase: *You couldn't go to Beyoğlu without a hat!* Many in this town hundreds of miles from Istanbul had heard the tales of his young years: how no one ventured into Beyoğlu without a hat, how the luminaries of the cultural and artistic milieu would debate intellectual topics at the Löbon and Markiz patisseries, and how at the latter the Medical Director had once had the honour of shaking the hand of the literary master Yahya Kemal, spotted the story writer Sait Faik coming out of the Elhamra Cinema the very same day, and on another day, he had followed Ayhan Işık as the actor walked all the way down the road, and he was indeed a right *gentil* gentleman – not that any of this meant anything to anyone any more.

Not a word of it was true anyway; he'd made it all up.

He had invited his schoolmate Erdem, a retired civil servant who for many years had served as assistant general manager of the State Railways, to deliver a ludicrous lecture on *The Benefits of Train Travel on Mental Health*. What these benefits might be had never crossed the Medical Director's mind, even if he suggested the topic. He simply wanted to do a favour for his old friend, his loyal schoolmate who often rang for a chat, never forgot to send a New Year's card and was an impeccable host whenever Demir happened to be in Istanbul. Taking advantage of the hospital's surplus budget would give them the opportunity to indulge in a bit of reminiscence: *Oh, the good old days, old chap; you couldn't go to Beyoğlu without a hat!*

The Medical Director, of course, could have invited Erdem and his gracious wife to stay with him, but **his own wife, Sevim Demir**, wouldn't hear of entertaining houseguests. Sevim, who had met and married Demir whilst still at nursing college and promptly abandoned her career before it even began, suffered from an obsessive-compulsive disorder. She couldn't rest until everything in the house touched by any outsider was wiped with bleach (which, being an Ankara girl, she called *ozone water*) and wanted neither overnight guests nor even people dropping by. Her husband's standing in society, however, as well as her own large circle of friends and acquaintances, obliged them to entertain – and frequently. So they bit the bullet and invited their guests out, knowing full well this flew in the face of tradition in the small city. Important guests they entertained at the Sultan Restaurant, the pride of the five-star seafront Diamond Hotel, whilst less important ones they took to the Three

Brothers Patisserie, the most elegant venue on the Atatürk Boulevard along the seafront and famed for its pudding served with a sprinkle of rosewater and grated coconut.

Sevim's condition was severe and her obsession with hygiene had gradually worsened. Every evening on his return home, Demir Demir stripped at the entrance hall and proceeded directly to the bathroom in his underwear. He'd got so used to this that even when she was out he never took a single step inside – never mind go to the bedroom – in his clothes. As relaxed as he was with hygiene standards outside, the moment he stepped inside, he acted just like her. Sadly, even he failed to see this as a problem, so it never crossed his mind to recommend treatment.

As the senior administrator of a mental health hospital (one of a handful in the land), he had once participated in a psychiatry congress in Istanbul. During those three days, Sevim left no stone unturned. Alcohol wipe glued to her hand, she scoured the Grand Bazaar and Ulus Market. She might have felt the irresistible urge to wash her hands whenever she touched something, but shopping had proved a far stronger addiction. She purchased a heap of clothes, which she held by her fingertips and threw into the washing machine the moment she returned home, as well as piles of shoes, handbags, belts, costume jewellery and the like, which she gave away as soon as she lost interest in them. Demir, meanwhile, dozed during the lectures and chatted with old friends during the breaks. Sevim went to an İnci Arcade shop in Pangaltı to buy a fake Louis Vuitton bag on the third day of the congress, which the Medical Director had set aside for his schoolmate. Erdem picked him up at the entrance to the Lütfi Kırdar Congress Centre, apologised on behalf of his wife, whose health had prevented her from joining them, and the two men strolled to a smart restaurant at the Hilton. The respect enjoyed by the retired civil servant did not escape the Medical Director's attention. Feeling obliged to repay him for years of truly impeccable hospitality, and desirous of displaying his own power and grace, Demir booked him a suite at the Diamond Hotel, personally paying for the upgrade, wrote *To My Dear Friend, I can't wait to see you* in black fountain pen on the return ticket, which had been purchased from a travel agency (e-tickets then still being something of a rarity) and posted it.

The invitation had *naturally included* **Erdem Bakırcıoğlu's wife, Bedia**, but she had been forced to decline. Now in her seventies, she was some sixteen years her husband's senior, and had a morbid fear of dying on the road. That's why she couldn't leave their Tarabya *yalı*, the seafront mansion where they'd lived for the past two decades, or cross the Bosphorus – not even to visit dear old Kanlıca, where she'd grown up, or the Bülbülderesi mansion known as the Rambling Rose Yalı (named for the extraordinary rose framing the door), where the most dramatic moments of her life had occurred. She very rarely ventured out. Unable to accompany Erdem, therefore, she had contented herself with conveying *her kindest wishes to Medical Director Demir Demir and his esteemed wife Sevim Hanım* and sending a present *in the hope they might find it acceptable.*

The Medical Director collected Erdem at the airport and drove him to the hotel in his gleaming official car, which the office boy had washed. The retired civil servant presented his wife's gift to Sevim at the Sultan Restaurant (dinner would be reimbursed later). Misled by the shape of the parcel to expect a silver photo frame, Sevim was far less impressed by the faded, unframed icon of *The Virgin Mary Holding the Infant Jesus*, but she was too polite to let on.

Bedia loved antiques, as evidenced by her exquisite gift. A subscriber to auction catalogues, what she didn't know about antiques and yalıs wasn't worth knowing – a passion cultivated from a very young age.

She was the daughter of the **dairy magnate Hulki**, one of Kanlıca's celebrated yogurt suppliers, who had a fifteen-cow dairy barn and yogurt and cheese factories in a street leading to the seafront. Hulki, barely out of childhood when he started his career during the British occupation, had provided the snootiest of Ottoman families with an uninterrupted supply of milk, yogurt and cheese even when Anatolia was in flames, made a tidy sum, and grabbed the **Sephardic Jew Rıfat Mustaki's** small but charming yalı when the latter, an importer of all manner of unremarkable items, such as gum mastic, door hinges, pesticides and lace bobbins, from a single-room office in the Sirkeci Nemlizade Han, was forced to auction his assets to pay the Wealth Tax, one of the thousands of minorities to have been similarly hit.[1]

Rıfat's prudence verged on parsimoniousness. The building, popularly known in the neighbourhood as Bijou Yalı, was one of the rare seafront houses to be equipped with central heating. Not that he would ever turn it on, even when snow lay knee deep: *Why heat unused rooms in vain?* All five members of his family would huddle throughout the winter in a poky room with a wood stove, and in the summer, all hell would break loose if the sliver of a quay in front of the yalı was barely dampened by tap water instead of sea water. It wasn't that he didn't have the funds to pay the tax, but due to an ancient habit from his forebears, he had been regularly sending his money abroad, so only had a modest amount of the readies.

Confident of the eventual repeal of this calamitous and unjust levy – *They'll have to drop it, sooner or later!* – he had taken no precautions and held out until the very last moment. But when the deadline came, he realised he needed an urgent solution. He would either go to the Aşkale railway construction camp in the frozen East, or pay his debt.

As it proved impossible to bring in the funds from abroad at such short notice, he sold the yalı to Hulki on the condition that it was a temporary arrangement: they agreed that the Mustaki family would continue to live there in exchange for a reasonable rent, and that Rıfat would pay a considerable amount in interest when the time came to purchase it back.

And indeed, a few months later, money that had been languishing in a Swiss bank did arrive. Except not only did Hulki refuse to sell back the yalı, he also threatened Rıfat with the courts if it wasn't vacated within the month. The tearful family left helter-skelter. Unable to stomach such terrible trickery by his yogurt man of so many years, Rıfat Mustaki sold everything he owned, grabbed his family and joined his relations who had emigrated to Haifa.

Hulki promptly moved his wife and daughters from the two-storey stone house behind the cheese factory into the yalı. Bedia was nine. She spent her first night unable to believe her luck at living in such a place! But she soon got used to it. To the extent that she completely forgot she'd been born in a sagging timber house that groaned at every footstep, with flattened kerosene tins reinforcing the window frames, and not this compact yet exquisite yalı, with windows sprinkled with sea spray by the south-westerly. She even forgot the two-storey stone house they'd moved into three years earlier, which at the time she'd mistaken for a palace.

It was a strange situation, though. They lived in a yalı, yet her father came home reeking of cheese every evening, and – in the absence of a son – sent his daughter to deliver milk and yogurt to the mansions and yalıs that staunchly and nonchalantly sustained the dominance of the Duchy of Istanbul in politics, the economy and social life, in total defiance of the new life arising in Ankara, the capital of the young republic. Well aware that she was still an outsider, Bedia put her silver tongue and sharp wit to use by cultivating upper-class friends whose politesse, good manners and refinements she adopted; this circle of friends and her knowledge of French were owed to her countless tantrums which had eventually persuaded her father to send her to the Lycée Notre Dame de Sion.

She was pretty and charming enough to double as a catwalk model at haute couture events during her time as an undergraduate in French philology. During one such show at the Hilton, she met the **stationer Tarık**. Twenty years her senior he might have been, but he was highly charismatic and handsome, a genuine man-about-town extremely popular with society ladies thanks to his sophisticated demeanour and magnetic black eyes. It didn't take long for him to sweep her off her feet, this girl with an obvious love of all things beautiful. They married within months.

But a huge shock awaited her that very same week. His sisters, who dropped in night and day, kids and all (and just wouldn't leave), told her about Tarık's six-year-old son. And that wasn't all. Tarık was neither the proprietor of a famous desk diaries brand, nor the big boss of the stationer's on Green Crescent Road – no, not even of the Piyalepaşa notebook workshop. He was nothing more than a junior partner. And the worst of it concerned the yalı with the eponymous rambling rose doorframe in Bülbülderesi: he was merely a tenant.

They had a massive row on their return from their honeymoon. Tarık claimed that he had had no intention of concealing the existence of a son: his first wife had denied him access to the boy ever since their divorce, so he'd never really felt like a father. As for the yalı: *All I said was I live in a yalı; I never said it was mine, did I?*

Next morning, although still seething at him for failing to mention his son, Bedia had to concede that Tarık had indeed never uttered a single lie; it was she who had assumed a fortune. At any rate, she worshipped the ground he walked on, and so decided to put it all behind them and enjoy life with this handsome hedonist. At any rate – again – it all turned out as he said: the son and ex-wife stayed out of their way. With no desire to see his son, or become a father again, he was scared stiff at the thought that Bedia might want to start a family.

Thankfully, it wasn't long before Bedia declared she had no intention of having children, and Tarık was able to relax. She might feel broody for half an hour or so when she saw plump, beaming, adorable babies, but the idea of pregnancy she found too distasteful. They had a wonderful life anyway. All right, so the yalı wasn't his, but he earned a decent crust, didn't he? And theirs was a match made in heaven. For nearly two decades, they lived it up in Istanbul's exclusive spots. But the whole thing came to a sudden, acrimonious and totally unexpected end, which left Bedia without a penny but with a taste for a dazzling middle-class lifestyle.

So this elegant connoisseur of antiques, searching for a suitable present for the Medical Director's wife, had come across *The Virgin Mary Holding the Infant Jesus* in a catalogue and taken a taxi to all the way to Nişantaşı's Bronze Street. Once Erdem Bakırcıoğlu handed his host the gift, he discussed the icon with him. Sevim stayed out of the conversation even as the Medical Director waxed lyrical about Bedia's refined taste. The rest of the evening passed just as the Medical Director had wanted it to, with the two men repeating their dormitory memories: *What good old days they were, old chap, you couldn't go to Beyoğlu without a hat!*

Later that night at home, having silently fretted all evening at the thought of that icon teeming with germs, Sevim scrubbed it with bleach over and over. She had no idea what to do with the gift. She hung it on one wall – no. On another – absolutely not. She laid it aside. The next morning, in her haste to prepare breakfast, she broke the china teapot rest and plonked the hot teapot on the icon instead. The circular scorch mark on Mary's face and the infant Jesus on her lap obscured their haloes. From that moment forth, Sevim used the precious icon as a pot rest, taking comfort at the thought that germs were dying by the thousands every time she placed a hot pan on it.

On the Medical Director's express instructions, a large contingent of hospital staff had been seated in the conference hall to spare Erdem's blushes – he would never allow his dear old friend to face an empty hall! The apathetic audience, however, were soon rewarded when, after being introduced by an emotional Medical Director, the retired civil servant mounted the stage to start a speech along the lines of *A Railway Man's Memoirs* rather than the benefits of train travel on mental health.

Erdem cut quite a dash in his smoke-grey suit, the creation of a top Istanbul tailor. He took a couple of steps, slipped on an undiluted blob of floor cleaner and slid on his arse all the way from one end of the vinyl-covered stage to the other; at the same time, his trouser hems with razor sharp creases rode up to his knees, leaving the audience gasping – not at the way the Medical Director's boarding-school mate had slipped, but at the suspenders holding up his silk socks.

No one in the audience had ever seen such a peculiar accessory. A few erroneously attributed a disability to the retired civil servant, having mistaken the suspenders for some medical device. This was largely due to the **elderly physician Nurettin Kozanlı's** insistence that the bizarre item on view was a newly invented orthopaedic instrument for straightening curvature of the shinbone. Nurettin wasn't kidding. He vaguely recalled reading the claim, *You Can Be Free of Bow Legs!* in a tabloid aimed at the barely literate and thought *This must be the device in the paper*.

A curious sixty-something, Nurettin was the owner of a naturally poignant face. His eyebrows drooped at the ends as if in resignation to fate, and his mouth curled up at the corners in an incongruous blend of the unbearably tragic and overly childish. The resulting melancholy expression never failed to sink the Medical Director's heart.

No softie by any stretch of the imagination, Medical Director Demir Demir still liked Nurettin of the poignant mien, for whom he felt genuine pity and so referred insignificant medical conditions to him. He'd have referred more serious cases if only he could have trusted the fellow as a physician, but Nurettin was incapable of diagnosing even the simplest strep throat or bowel infection. It was only the lower-class patients, who followed the Medical Director's advice, that had kept the old doctor's surgery going all this time.

Regrettably, the two were no longer friends. They'd fallen out in a big way. It happened at the Nation Tea Garden one Sunday five months before Erdem's speech (which despite him falling was delivered in full). The Medical Director had been on his own that day since Sevim had stayed behind to scrub the greasy kitchen tiles after frying eggy bread for breakfast. He had sat down to a game of snap with a few friends in the gentle autumn breeze. At Nurettin's approach, the Medical Director again succumbed to that feeling of pity, and genial as ever, invited him to join them. Not one to be asked twice, Nurettin sat down to watch the final rubber. Then they chatted about this and that, including, for instance, the subsidence of the coastal road after the repeated disastrous floods of recent years, so much that one of its lanes had reclaimed by the sea.

Then talk turned to **Councillor Latif Tibuk's** refusal to resign, despite days of constant re-runs on Channel SS, the local TV station, that showed his capture *in flagrante* with the **Moldovan natural blonde Anya** (five foot ten with legs to match) in a hotel right in the middle of town; both the raid and the tip-off were the doing of **his wife, Asiye**, who was filmed dragging the half-naked girl by the hair up and down the hallway.

Nearly twenty days later, tongues were still wagging about how he had had the temerity to insist, *That's not me!* even though his face was circled in every freeze-frame. At long last he was forced to admit that *That* was indeed *him*, but not without attempting to dupe the public with the theory that this was *a conspiracy by my political rivals*.

Inspired by Asiye, other wives sharpened their claws in the direction of innocent Russian women and watched their own husbands like hawks. Meanwhile, husbands with Anyas, Tanyas, Natashas, Veras, Elenas, Olgas, Lubas or Tatyanas of their own (Black Sea men, every last one of them) sneered at Latif Tibuk for getting caught, positive *they* would never be, and even if they were, their wives would never turn out to be as fearsome as Asiye Tibuk: *If ya walks in snow, ya never leaves a trace, they chortled conclusively.*

Anya, far more brazen-faced than her eighteen years might warrant, waved and blew kisses at the cameras until her capture. Transfixed by those three-foot-long legs, one of the cameramen moved heaven and earth to keep her in the frame during this cat-and-mouse game with Asiye (as if the local men didn't see enough beautiful blondes), but his incompetence showed in the footage as the hands of the hotel staff tried to obscure the view – and the long skirt and blouse in clashing patterns which covered Asiye's formidable frame.

The foxy cameraman Tolga, cousin of **the town's famous florist Önder**, on the other hand, was a much smarter cookie; instead of chasing the blonde Moldovan, he'd focused on the fifty-something councillor – white chest hair, unwieldy belly and all – who had holed up in the undersized wardrobe in that seedy room. The unrepentant councillor swung a kick at Tolga's crotch, and the man, collapsing in agony, dropped his camera, which nevertheless kept running. An astonishingly hairless pair of legs scrambling into trousers to the soundtrack of the cameraman's screams became one of the most memorable images on TV. Soon, once the gossip machine had chewed all the juice out the main incidents, attention turned to the councillor's limbs; those milk-white legs, smooth as if carefully waxed, were attributed to a circulatory condition.

Forty-seven and the mother of four (including a daughter), Asiye Tibuk stood at not quite five feet (four feet eleven and a smidge, to be precise) and weighed eleven stone nine; thanks to months of harvesting tea on their plantations in Kalkandere, Rize, and picking hazelnuts from the trees clinging to the slopes, she hadn't been the slightest bit short of breath throughout the chase. Anya was about to make the victory sign at the cameras when Asiye grabbed her long blonde tresses and felled the Moldovan, whom she then set about yanking across the floor. The hotel staff didn't half have a job rescuing the girl.

Superimposed with the faint double-S logo, the scandal filled airtime on Channel SS (named for the owner **Soner Sarıkaya's** initials) and reverberated in coffee houses, offices and homes across the city. Now a documented prostitute and an illegal immigrant to boot, Anya was deported. The Istanbul-born cameraman Tolga – whose determination to document the councillor holed up in the wardrobe had been rewarded with a kick in the goolies – was dismissed.

Soner Sarıkaya had moved up in the world from his beginnings as a grocer – first to a supermarket, and later, as fortune continued to smile and relatives proved ever ready with advice, to the TV station, whereupon he affected a new phrase, *As a visionary businessman...* He fired Tolga even though he had at first sung the cameraman's praises for videoing the hairless legs of the cowering councillor.

The station was a money pit and the cut-rate local ads were no help at all. This incident firmly established Soner, man of vision and pretension, as an unreserved scumbag. Having invited Latif Tibuk to discuss a news blackout, Soner instead blackmailed him shamelessly. The councillor, who had inherited a local newspaper from his father, and which was tottering on the brink, paid a whopping sum to become a partner in the TV station in exchange for an immediate end to the reruns that showed him in such an unfavourable light, and the first thing he did was to have Tolga fired.

Tolga, who had originally come to the town to do his national service, had settled here at the insistence of his cousin, the florist, and got a job at Channel SS. Convinced that he could now turn this setback into an opportunity, he made straight for Istanbul with a videocassette copy of the footage. Here, he thought, was solid evidence of his talent, one that would surely open the doors to one of the countless paparazzi shows broadcast on national stations; it would be a breeze.

But joining this clan wasn't a breeze; it was impossible. Istanbul was teeming with the big boys of the paparazzi world. He wasn't needed. What he knew about Istanbul's nightlife and glitterati was sketchy at best; so, tail between his legs, he returned to the town that had sacked him. Yes, he was still a cameraman, but now he had no intention of working for television.

What shall we do? What shall we do? the two cousins brainstormed. The florist shop just didn't cut it for Önder, a self-styled brainbox; he was looking for an initiative that would *make a difference*, something he was forever banging on about. Pondering over what Tolga could shoot beyond weddings, birthdays and social gatherings, he hit upon a truly ingenious solution validating his Black Sea credentials. The town was thick with wedding videographers, yes, but Tolga could shoot funerals instead.

Inspiration had come from the two factors funerals and weddings had in common: 1. The general tendency to get a high turnout, and

2. The custom of sending flowers. Despite the rising popularity of donations to charities championing education or the environment – which really got on Önder's nerves – a not inconsiderable number of mourners still sent flowers and wreaths and showed up at the funerals of local dignitaries.

The duo rolled up their sleeves. Önder announced far and wide that his cousin was a funeral videographer. At first they were quite successful. The leading lights of the town, who liked to boast of the crowds at their family's funerals, started queuing up, and some were even prepared to delay their final duties to their nearest and dearest by a day or two in order to allow Tolga to do his job properly. Still not satisfied, however, the cousins set up *MayGodgivepeace.com.tr*, where they published funeral videos and death notices and even sold advertising space.

It didn't last long. Funeral videos failed to become an established custom. Quick to notice that crying flattered no one, women were reluctant to be videoed in that state. Then the wiser minds of the town lambasted this attempt to use funerals to create a social divide; bookings petered out and soon ceased altogether. But the canny duo had made hay whilst the sun shone, and made a successful leap into weddings.

Latif, meanwhile, having failed to dupe his wife or the public, first with denials and later with conspiracy theories, eventually saved his skin with a couple of statements along the lines of *I was tempted by the Devil*, and returned home. He posed as the head of a happy family with his children and still-glowering wife, and then, buckling under Soner Sarıkaya's blackmail, invested in Channel SS.

Latif had yet another feather in his cap though: as the biggest local distributor of MoonGas LPG bottles, Beko white goods and Future Furniture, he was no stranger to the media. His twelve-page colour offset daily, *Popular News*, enjoyed a circulation of six hundred in the town and its vicinity. The newspaper's ludicrous political commentary, liberally sprinkled with misspellings and grammatical errors came from his pen alone. He had styled himself an anchorman the moment he bought the partnership in the TV station, but after one evening gave up when the teleprompter proved too difficult to follow.

So the Medical Director and the ageing physician were discussing the councillor's latest commentary; after the incident with the Moldovan

Anya, his articles had taken an excessively aggressive turn in an effort to conceal his own transgression. This led to an unwarranted debate. The Medical Director disapproved of Latif's choice of the term *bloodsuckers* in relation to his political rivals, all of whom were locals. Nurettin's glaring, *Well, aren't they?* was an inappropriate question, which at any other time would have been brushed off. But his spiteful insistence on a response placed the Medical Director in a difficult position before his friends. The debate grew nastier. It really didn't suit that melancholy face with the bitter smile.

The Medical Director bit his tongue at the annoying hostility which had replaced Nurettin's usual pathetic gloom. Mistaking his silence for capitulation, Nurettin laid it on even more thickly, rubbishing Latif's political rivals and every once in a while taking a swipe at the Medical Director too. As he did so, he grew uglier in the other's view; the stained lower teeth peeking between those lips with upturned corners seemed to become more pointed.

Nurettin's zeal for fanning the flames wasn't shared; with a disappointed *Excuse me*, addressed to his other friends, the Medical Director stood up and left. As he strolled home in the fresh air, his initial disillusionment was replaced by relief. At long last, he was free of the crushing affection elicited by that meek face; now, with no compunction prompting him to feel sorry for the old physician, a huge weight lifted off his mind. Meanwhile, Nurettin was delighted at having bested the Medical Director so thoroughly for the first time after all these years.

Yet he was still in desperate need of the Medical Director's sympathy. The last time he'd read a scientific article was the summer of 1965, around the time he qualified at medical school, and even then it hadn't really registered much. Lacking the will to study another five years just so he could specialise, he remained a general practitioner, a fate to which he eventually resigned himself.

He never read a line of scientific text other than the brochures that his sister-in-law's son, the **pharmaceutical rep İlhami**, regularly left for him. He would flick through them in a desultory fashion when he'd run out of things to do on days no patient rang the doorbell, after he'd read the tabloids, solved the crosswords and, peering in the hand mirror propped against the window, trimmed his nostril hairs with the dressing scissors.

Feeling no less sorry for his uncle than the Medical Director, İlhami frequently dropped in with samples of analgesics, vitamins, antibiotics, and give-aways like note blocks and vinyl document cases for Nurettin to impress the patients with. Then, pointing to his spot baldness, İlhami bemoaned his bane: the back of his skull had been clearing in coin-sized patches for years and years. Not a single one of the dermatologists he visited regularly for his work had been able to find a cure. Not that they were falling over themselves either: *I'd better find a solution to İlhami's alopecia areata!* Every time he dropped in, İlhami mentioned the good news of an impending partnership with a pharmaceutical distributor within a couple of months – but with no further development all these years.

Nurettin lived alone. Four years ago, on her way back from the market, his wife, the midwife Mualla, was knocked down and died on the spot. The poor woman had had both hands full. The road was strewn with her shopping, which had spilled from the carrier bags: oranges, lettuce, low-fat white cheese and a kilo and a half of filleted anchovies.

That was just after **their only daughter, Nergis Şeker**, returned home after breaking up with her husband, the **Non-Commissioned Officer Talat Şeker**, who had been having an affair with a chemist's wife. Midwife Mualla was deeply troubled.

Nergis and Talat had been living in the married quarters in Oltu, Erzurum. Despite being named after the charismatic Ottoman Empire pasha in the Committee of Union and Progress, Talat couldn't make even his knee-high kids do his bidding. So Nergis just laughed off any gossip about his lechery. She shouldn't have. The wussy husband she had thought incapable of rising to a dozen bombshells stripping right before his eyes, from brunette to blonde, redhead to chestnut, actually enjoyed quite a lively nightlife.

The **Oltu chemist Ruhi** (who had doubled his business by purchasing the shop next door and stuffing it with stock funded by the smuggled drugs and psychotropics he'd been selling to pill poppers in nearby towns) had also heard increasingly serious rumours about his wife's loose morals.

One night, when he was duty chemist, he closed the shop and turned up at home unannounced.

His promiscuous wife Nilgün was suffocating in this provincial town, where women rarely ventured out and then only if covered to their eyes; she was more used to the relaxed atmosphere of Marmaris, her hometown, where she'd slept around to her heart's content. She whiled away the entire day at the pharmacy, drinking coffee, puffing at a cigarette and tossing back her highlighted locks as she chatted with the customers, and the moment her husband went away on business, she'd seduce the occasional officer, policeman or some visiting civil servant in the blink of an eye. She was alarmed, if not exactly panicked, when she heard footsteps on the staircase the night she'd taken in Non-Commissioned Officer Talat, and just as they were getting down to business; it had to be her husband about to catch her in the act.

At the rattling of the door, Talat scrambled out of bed and into his briefs, tucked his clothes under his arm, grabbed his shoes, climbed onto the neighbour's balcony and leapt to the roof of the building next door, and then to the next one over.

It was twenty below. Ruhi's moustache was frozen solid by the time he'd got home. At the sight of his wife naked in bed with the bedroom window wide open, he pulled out his gun and started chasing Talat across the roofs, but to no avail.

Ruhi's haphazard shots roused the entire town that night. Talat got dressed in some hidden corner and returned home gasping for breath. Nergis was puzzled by his unexpected return – she thought he was on duty – and he was missing a sock too. But the following day the town was talking of nothing else; her good-for-nothing husband was frozen to the bone, and not even a pair of duvets had stopped his teeth from chattering. She finally put two and two together, grabbed the children and made straight for her parents' home.

Unable to bring himself to kill his faithless wife, Ruhi claimed he'd been chasing a burglar. But he was sick of being cuckolded; this time he was determined to shoot her. Try as he might to bear up, he couldn't ignore the rumours entirely, and once a month or so would make up his mind to blow her brains out.

But somehow Nilgün always cottoned on and burst into heart-rending sobs that twisted him round her little finger: every time he managed to point his gun at her, he ended up making long, passionate love to the woman he had met two years earlier on a camping trip with a childhood friend, the woman he had fallen head over heels in love with, from her dimpled cheeks down to the hollow in her back.

So after loosing off those rounds, Ruhi came to his senses and made up the story about a burglar. He'd come home with medicine for his wife, who was down with the flu – yes he had – and that's when he found the burglar in the living room and he followed him onto the roof, but the villain got away. To lend credence to his story, Ruhi even heel-kicked the balcony door glass before he rang the police so he could claim, *And that's how he got in, an' all!* Once a highly promising undergraduate at the Faculty of Pharmacology (who sorely disappointed his lecturers by spurning an academic career in favour of earning money straightaway) Ruhi's genius clearly did not extend to criminology: he had broken the glass from the inside.

He made a list of the items he was going to claim had been stolen: the burglar had taken the portable stereo, the camera and a silk rug, indeed he had, but because he hadn't managed to get into the bedroom, he'd not got round to stealing Nilgün's solitaire ring, mobile phone or purse. They had actually never owned a silk rug or anything; he'd just added it on the spur of the moment.

Earlier that day, with his love for his wife surging and still buzzing from an unexpected bout of morning sex just as he was about to leave for work, he had decided to buy the navy-and-purple rug she'd mentioned a while back. But on noticing his neighbours' stares and whispers as he rolled up the shutters, he had realised they were talking about his wife and with ill-judged audacity tried to confront them.

His popularity in the area prevented all but a tactful *Errm, Ruhi, your missus might like to, like, watch her behaviour; you know this is a small place…* but their eyes spoke volumes. So that inner monster of suspicion once again raised its head. Remembering that he was on duty that night, the troubled chemist decided to catch his wife out.

During the day he had forgotten about being cuckolded and made sure everything ran smoothly in his bustling shop, but his mind had been strangely fixated on that lovely silk rug he'd wanted to buy for Nilgün. Its magnificent design would pop into mind at the most inopportune moments, and the memory of Nilgün would pierce his chest like a knife. That's why he'd added the rug to the list without even noticing, and then decided against rubbing it out since that was just the sort of item the police would find convincing. He was quite wealthy, after all, and no burglar in his right mind would leave behind such a valuable – and lightweight – silk rug.

Nilgün enjoyed a sensational reputation amongst the coppers who turned up; one, in fact, had already spent several unforgettable hours here one night when Ruhi was on duty. When the call came, **the young police constable Şenol from Düzce**, who'd been spinning partly fabricated tales of his sexual exploits by the blazing wood stove at the station, twigged at once that the location was in fact Nilgün's place, which he remembered with such fondness, so he grabbed his parka and joined the squad.

This Nilgün, though, was nothing like the woman who'd given Şenol such a wonderful night in her black undies. She didn't look that hot in greying, saggy-kneed tracksuit bottoms and an old cardigan with drooping sleeves. The fact that her otherwise beautiful eyes were swollen from all that crying didn't help either.

Momentarily taken aback at seeing Şenol, Nilgün managed to keep calm. Then, whilst her hapless husband was still in full flow, she sent him a fiery gaze that reminded him of that unforgettable night. Stunned by the strength of his rekindled desire for the frump he'd just found so repulsive, Şenol adopted that faintly crooked smile women adored. He took stock of the living room he'd barely glanced at during their tryst. The state-of-the-art stereo, which the fictitious burglar had left behind as too big to carry, the loudspeakers, the gigantic TV set and expensive suite: it all said that the chemist had to be rolling in it. His blood boiled at this whoremonger who, despite selling smuggled medicines like hot cakes, had shown far less charity towards the police benevolent fund than he should have.

Şenol was as handsome as he was short-tempered. All his attempts to blag some pricey toiletries had foundered on this stingy bastard's thousand and one excuses; Şenol would have run him in and given him a good hiding. But he decided against it; if he made trouble here, in the home of the woman he'd been bragging about in full detail, he might end up paying for it. His card was marked when it came to womanising, at any rate; it was best to postpone his showdown with Ruhi to some indeterminate time in the future. He'd soon find a way to lure Nilgün to a mate's third-class hotel in Trabzon.

Ruhi had broken the windowpane to lend credence to his story, but he hadn't considered the consequences. It was freezing inside. A light sprinkling of snow fell onto the rug, melting as it did so. Much more relaxed now that she'd bent Ruhi to her will once again, Nilgün kept smouldering at the young copper; Şenol, meanwhile, remembering how he'd been frozen to the marrow on the way back from that night of passion, was blowing on his fingers and shivering in the cold, whilst murmuring *Better hot than cold any day, mate!*

He recalled the brain-sizzling heat of Mardin during his temporary posting before coming to Oltu; the mercury never fell below thirty-five even in the shade. All summer long, he had moaned about the heat under the leafless tree in the station yard, whenever he'd finished tormenting Kurds, making them wish they'd never been born, after they'd been nicked on some pretext or other; he had made passes at loose women, and treated others as if they were, and was taken to task by his chief after announcing at every opportunity how he hated to keep his pants on.

The problem was his big mouth, not his pants. With troops battling the PKK in the mountains, the governor, the chief constable and high-ranking police officers were far too busy to remember their way home; at a time like this, Şenol's vulgar sexploit tales were beyond the pale. **Chief Inspector Rıfat (from Konya)** lost it one day when, worn out with hotfooting it between the military and the police, giving a report to this commander and that chief inspector day in, day out, he heard Şenol sniggering whilst telling the same old stories. Roaring, *Like I don't know to brag about the women I've fucked! Dickhead!* the Chief Inspector knocked Şenol off his perch.

Rıfat, who loved screwing standing up (old hags with rotting teeth and saggy tits were his choice, rather than nice, decent women), in the Mersin-Antakya roadside lorry-driver brothels, makeshift latrines or petrol depots stacked high with discarded lorry tyres, might have initially turned a blind eye to Şenol as a charmer, whose escapades he silently applauded.

Except you give him an inch, he takes a mile. *If I ever catch you bullshitting on watch again, you're fucked, and don't think I've not warned you!* he said. Şenol pulled himself together at once.

When he eventually did get into trouble, it had nothing to do with any blatant disregard of rules and regulations, mistreatment or torture of Mardin's Kurds or anything like that – since none of his superiors cared anyway. It was the flimsy pretext on which he ran in a young girl and her uncle's son from a prominent Kurdish tribe that had regularly been providing Members of Parliament.

Tensions had been high in the city for some time. Chief Inspector Rıfat, already exhausted from maintaining a fine balance, discovered in the course of a brief telephone conversation with Ankara that the girl's maternal uncle was a Member of Parliament and there were village guards in her family. The youth, bristling at the wrongful arrest, was rewarded with an powerful slap by rookie copper Şenol, who, on Rıfat's advice, had been taking a break from his whoremongering. At the sight of the staggering young man Chief Inspector Rıfat paled. He took Şenol inside for a good whipping.

If the Kurdish youth had been less well connected, that slap would have gone unremarked, nay, even met with Rıfat's approval. But Rıfat was vastly experienced in the consequences of mistreating anyone with any high connections in Ankara, especially in such tense times; so he did his utmost to smooth things over, spending hours to placate the young man and grabbing Şenol by the scruff of the neck and ordering him to apologise. To no avail. The Kurd wouldn't simmer down. Rıfat's hand was forced by no less than three calls from Ankara – from the Parliament line even! – whilst he was trying to cool down in the evening with a wet towel wrapped around his neck, and Şenol was sent packing to Oltu.

Having initially paid no attention to locals' warnings – *Mind you don't walk under the eaves!* – Şenol was wandering idly one day when a chunk of ice the size of a suitcase skimmed past his neck and shattered into smithereens on the ground, frightening him nearly to death; he was already fed up with having to light a diesel fire under the engine every morning just to get the frozen patrol car started. He needed a diversion, and a diversion he soon found. The handsome copper met Ruhi's wife at the pharmacy one day when he popped in for something for his lips cracked by the cold; he marked her as a wanton spirit when she tossed her highlighted hair whilst puffing on a cigarette and saw whatever time he'd have to spend to get into her bed as a worthy investment.

As Ruhi told his account of the supposed break-in, not a single one of Nilgün's sultry gazes missed their target. Now the dutiful policeman, Şenol asked, *Sister, mind describing the burglar if you've seen him?* He didn't miss Ruhi's aching gaze at Nilgün who replied, *I was sleeping inside, never saw no one.* That arsehole couldn't keep his eyes off his wife. The other coppers, too, tipped by the direction of the broken glass that the burglar story was fake and that the bloke had chased his wife's bit on the side, were biting their cheeks; still, they held their tongues, thinking *Ya never know... 'E might cause trouble, this bloke.* They took down his statement, a mere formality, buzzed off with *We'll let you know*, and were never heard from again.

Needless to say, that's not how things carried on for Ruhi and Nilgün. Soon after the incident – which after the police had gone ended with a passionate bout of lovemaking and Nilgün swearing herself blind, her sparkling tears adorning her endless oaths – she left her husband; she was fed up with Oltu's bitter winters, the days that just wouldn't pass, and Ruhi's dull company.

Şenol was partly to blame. Nilgün had cottoned on to her reputation as a whore and was miserable. No one greeted her. Even the neighbour opposite slammed the door in her face. One Friday, when Ruhi was in Tercan visiting his mother who'd slipped on the ice and broken her arm, Şenol dropped into the pharmacy wearing his uniform. He swaggered, looked well fit and flashed his crooked smile, as every so often, his hand seemed to seek the barrel of his service pistol of its own accord. *Make up some story for your husband and I'll take you to Trabzon, to a proper brill hotel right on the seafront*, he said, all the while inspecting himself in a hand mirror on the eyewear counter. He had no doubt that he was an irresistible specimen of manhood. But that smile which had once turned her to jelly really got on her nerves this time. Already in a foul mood, she bit his head off: *What bloody hotel are y'on about? Think I'm a whore just because we once had a shag?*

Şenol thought she was playing hard to get. His beady eyes on the lookout, he tried to cop a feel and slip his hand under her skirt whilst attempting to sweet-talk her, but he finally lost his temper at the coy act. He snapped, *You were putting out with your eyes that night, bitch, what's the matter now?* Nilgün replied, *That's what you think, darling! Go on, bugger off!* Undeterred, he persisted; she grew more foul-mouthed, and soon it was a full-on bust-up.

Nilgün had had it up to here with his pestering, but when – instead of stringing him along with, *OK, we'll see…* – she screamed, *I'm not going nowhere! Go find yourself some whore to fuck!* the besotted copper went mental. *I'll kill you, bitch!* he said, digging his pistol into her temple, his furious eyes popping out, scaring her witless. He threatened her with whatever crime he could think of if one more time she dared to say no – she'd wish she was never born, he'd expose her husband for selling drugs, he'd have her house raided for prostitution. *Get ready to go to Trabzon at the weekend,* he ordered and strode off. Terrified by the handsome – and suddenly maniacal – policeman, terrified that he'd do what he said, Nilgün realised her time here was up.

That same night she announced to Ruhi that she missed Marmaris desperately and wanted to go home for a spell. Ruhi was down in the dumps. His mother's arm just wasn't healing and the doctor said there was no alternative but to operate. Nilgün's desire to go away was irritating just when he was thinking, *I'd better take mother in after the op; she can stay with us until she gets better.* **His mother, Emeti** (who saw good housekeeping as the measure of a good daughter-in-law), would raise hell and make him wish *he'd* never been born if she knew that Nilgün had swanned off to Marmaris instead of saying, *My mother-in-law's poorly; she'd better come over here so I can look after her.* Worse still, the house would descend into a shambles in her absence and he'd struggle to find a clean pair of trousers. Nilgün of the roving eye was actually a great housewife; her cooking was delicious, the house was immaculate and she made sure Ruhi was always impeccably dressed. Whenever some snippet of gossip led him to think, *Now pull your socks up,* he'd forget everything the moment he sat down at a magnificent spread of several courses from savouries to sweets, and the following day pretended to have heard nothing.

Still vexed at the prospect of his mother's operation, Ruhi tried the tough husband approach of, *You can go in the summer, stay right here for now!* But he hadn't even finished his sentence before Nilgün had a right fit. Screaming, *I've had it with my life!* she burst into tears, flinging herself from wall to wall. So terrified was she of Şenol that she started tearing her clothes and choking on her screams. Scared that she might go off her rocker, Ruhi not only said, *All right, go then*, but also promised to send her by air from Erzurum to Dalaman with a transfer at Ankara.

Nilgün wanted to stay in Marmaris for a couple of months. Time enough for Şenol to simmer down, gossip to blow over, and the hoo-ha of her mother-in-law's operation to settle before she returned. But when Ruhi (who'd been making a shitload of money from under-the-counter drugs) went and bought her a coach ticket from a lousy firm, and an aisle seat at that, Nilgün tripped her fuses. She was originally from Izmir, and Izmirians never *lost their temper*; they *tripped their fuses*. Grabbing all her lightweight valuables – including the jewellery she was given at the wedding – she returned to Marmaris. Anyway, this drab conservative town had killed her love for Ruhi. *Why am I still married to this bloke?* she wondered and failed to find a single reason. Too weary to face the gossip any longer, Ruhi only snapped, *Well, bugger off then!* without the least attempt to change her mind.

Snap though he might, living without Nilgün wasn't that easy. He tried desperately to forget the wife who'd made a cuckold out of him several times over. He wanted to believe he could live very well without her, thank you very much. Entrusting the shop to a new assistant, he stayed out for days, idling here and there, squandering handfuls of banknotes at sleazy joints tucked away in office-block basements, drinking rakı until he was sick, and even popping pills from his stock. He did all he could to purge Nilgün's sultry gaze from his mind – to no avail.

Just as he'd guessed, unable to bear the long nights in his (now that she was gone) increasingly grubby home, he would gather his single friends, set up boozy meals, get drunk out of his mind and talk about how he'd made the greatest mistake of his life by marrying someone who'd left him over a coach ticket, yell himself hoarse – *Fuck me in the town square if I ever mention her name again!* – and make a right racket swearing nine kinds of curses at Nilgün and himself. So convincing was his rage that his mates were sure this thing was over, once and for all. They set about looking for a suitable girl, but this time, a truly virtuous one.

Accountant Dilaver had put his mind to fixing Ruhi up with his **sister-in-law Fulya**. His tremendous enthusiasm owed much more to self-interest than a desire to do his mate a favour. Dilaver's business had been going downhill since the arrival of a sizeable supermarket in town, and the subsequent closure of smaller traders, such as the grocers and butchers whose books he'd been keeping. If they became brothers-in-law, he could close down the office with the increasingly unaffordable rent, make a beeline for the second chemist shop Ruhi was about to open, sit indoors in the warmth all day on the pretext of working as an assistant and every month draw a salary like clockwork.

At least that's what he told his wife. But his real problem was with Nilgün. He hated Ruhi's uppity wife. It went back to the day when Ruhi had gone to Erzurum to stock up for the second pharmacy he was planning to open. Knowing he was away, Dilaver had gone straight to the pharmacy, clutching the gold bracelet he'd bought on instalment from **jeweller Müfit**. Drowning in debt as he was, it was quite the wrong time to buy gold in order to have it off with his mate's wife. But he was infatuated with the skin under Nilgün's chin, which quivered imperceptibly every time she tossed her head, and the ample breasts, which defied all those layers she wore against the cold.

At first he was only smitten – all right, in lust with – but in time, Nilgün became the object of his love. The gormless accountant thought of nothing else day or night. His dreaminess didn't escape his wife's notice. **One of only three female civil servants at the District Village Affairs Directorate, Feriha** was a smart cookie who single-handedly ran the office. A resourceful woman who worked hard all day long, suffered no fool gladly, spent her evenings maintaining an immaculate house and counted every last penny that came into the family so she could send her son, who was in his final year at school, to the one and only, and highly unsuccessful, university cramming course in the district – she toiled, she slaved, she cooked, she baked; in short, she did all she could to make sure everything ran smoothly. When she remarked on her husband's absent-mindedness, unhappiness and loss of appetite, he blamed it all on troubles at work, grumbling, *Fuck this life… Cobbler Topbaş closed his shop, there's another account gone!* Innocent of his wicked intentions, Feriha, as kind-hearted as she was sharp, not only believed but even consoled her husband, *Don't worry; things will get better.*

Müfit had just opened the shop, *in God's name*, when that pest Dilaver turned up, no doubt to bang on again, *Give me your books! Bugger me if I don't get you a tax rebate!* Müfit had no complaints about his accountant but Dilaver just wouldn't take no for an answer. But astonishingly, instead of hustling, Dilaver straightaway enquired about the price of a stylish gold bracelet. Well aware that Müfit knew everything about everyone in the district and was sure to wonder who the skint accountant intended to impress by spending a fortune, bright spark Dilaver had come prepared with a cover story.

He was a bastard who had never bought anything, not even a pin, for his selfless, loyal and long-suffering darling wife. But you need to treasure your family and keep the lady wife happy with some little trinket, however small, every once in a while. Age teaches you that. Happiness doesn't just rain down from heaven; you have to work at it. Müfit swallowed the story hook, line and sinker (since he'd never heard of Dilaver playing around), including these golden tips for matrimonial bliss. The penniless account-ant thus pocketed the bracelet, on which he'd shelled out a quarter of his wife's salary in one fell swoop, and left.

Not that it did him any good. Dorky Dilaver hit on Nilgün, subtly at first, then quite openly, and finally held out his expensive offering; he was quite put out when she didn't even glance at the box emblazoned with the logo of Özkoçak Jewellery. Believing she'd underestimated the gift, he was seething silently *Ya can tell it's gold, can't you, you bitch; just open it and see!* When Nilgün added insult to injury by flicking the box away with a fingertip, he was gutted; the passion that had turned him into a wraith for days burst like a balloon; his pride hurt, he sounded more cross than upset as he said, *So you put out to everyone else, but nothing for me, eh?*

Blasé and brazen, Nilgün didn't blink. She and Şenol had just begun ogling each other, so she only had eyes for the copper with the crooked smile. Instead of responding to this minger, who was floundering to conjure up a smile to hide the rising fury, she merely picked up the hand mirror at the eyewear counter and held it to his face. His grin froze as then and there he began sharpening the knife for her.

It wasn't enough that Nilgün had thoroughly humiliated him that day. That bastard jeweller Müfit had lost no time blabbing to Feriha about the gold bracelet, which led to a right ding-dong at home. Feriha, it turned out, had popped into the jeweller's during her lunch break to enquire about the price of a quarter-gold coin for a friend's newborn baby, and Müfit had blurted out, as it was any of his business, *Sister, your good man's bought you a bracelet, you'll love it when you see it… Just don't say I told you though*, thereby scuppering Dilaver's plans to return the item (*The Missus didn't like it.*) Feriha gave him both barrels the moment he stepped in, *We've got nothing to wear, the children are in rags, it's not a festival or anything, so whatever made you buy me a gold bracelet?*

Dilaver had nearly jumped out of his skin when he saw his sulking wife, but breathed a sigh of relief at her innocence, nay, her naïvety even. Just as he was about to reply, *You're right, darling, I'm such an ass…* he flew into a rage. So if he really had bought it for her, she'd have torn him off a strip then, instead of being grateful? He picked a row, shouted, *Will I ever be good enough for you, eh! Ever?* and slapped her as a matter of form. No one's fool herself, Feriha grabbed their daughter's maths book and flung it at his head, and they had a bit of a tussle. Their son yelled, *Cut it out, some of us are trying to revise here!* moaning about not having his own room despite being a grown-up now, their daughter was scared and cried, etc., and eventually they all calmed down.

After grovelling for quite a while behind the bedroom door, Dilaver finally managed to get into Feriha's bed. The next day he returned the bracelet, ticking Müfit off for not holding his tongue. So Dilaver's Nilgün venture came to an end without causing much damage to his family.

But his wounded pride was still raw. His passion, extinguished by the mirror in Nilgün's hand as a silent *Just look at yourself first before hitting on me*, he was now burning to make her pay. He, who before that day had never said a single word against her, started blabbing here and there about what a whore she was, and even raked up the past in an effort to turn Ruhi against his wife.

Nilgün's departure for Marmaris played right into Dilaver's hands; ostensibly the best mate, he took Ruhi drinking, pretended to beat about the bush for a bit, and finally swore on a slice of bread, *I never dared open my mouth till now, in case you misunderstood… but your wife even hit on me, Ruhi; 'ere, strike me down if I'm lying.*

Devastated, miserable, and realising he couldn't take any more humiliation, Ruhi joined in the chorus ranting and raving against his wife. Now set on a divorce, he consulted one solicitor after another. Not that anyone in town believed the cuckolded chemist would ever divorce his wife. He was too soft, putty in that slut's hands. All Nilgün had to do was return home and cry a little, and he'd forget all about it and embrace that whore with all his heart.

So Dilaver knew he couldn't rest until he'd married Ruhi off. Nilgün was a dangerous bitch; you never knew with her. She'd given him such a look as he scuttled out of the pharmacy, tail between his legs, after tempting her with gold that he hadn't been able to sleep for days – *What if she told Ruhi?* If Nilgün were ever to change her mind about splitting up and reappeared, Ruhi would be sure to confront her, *You even hit on Dilaver!* How could he be sure Nilgün wouldn't give as good as she got? Of course she'd insist, *It was him what hit on me actually; shameless bastard went and bought me some gold, go ask Müfit if you don't believe me!* No amount of protesting would help; Ruhi would believe his wife. It wouldn't stop there either. If Nilgün returned, the matter of the gold bracelet would do the rounds and reach Feriha's ears. Ruhi might buy his wife's lies, but Feriha would never buy Dilaver's, who'd end up trapped in a hole with no shovel.

Ruhi was on the lookout for a wife to outshine Nilgün when he received an invitation to dinner, arranged by Dilaver who wanted him to meet his sister-in-law. Fulya, who normally wouldn't hear of hosting a stranger unaccompanied by his mum, wife or sister, was asked to prepare yogurt and meatball soup. The invitation came after Dilaver and Feriha had discussed the matter at length, with protracted deliberations on how the match would benefit the family.

Feriha had at first been violently opposed to the idea, furious at the suggestion that a divorcé was a suitable match for her lovely sister. But the rational Dilaver talked her round. So long as the bloke had no children, what difference did it make, divorced or single? He was wealthy, educated, well turned out and *handsome, too*, which was true: next to Dilaver, Ruhi was a veritable Brad Pitt.

Fulya had been to Ruhi's pharmacy, but she didn't really know him; she had never given him a second look since the guy was married and all, and just couldn't remember what he looked like. Her big sister kept singing his praises, *Where're you gonna find a better prospect? He's rich, you'll never want for anything!* Fulya didn't say *yes* to the idea of marrying Ruhi, but she didn't object either.

Fulya, who had no intention of changing her style just because Ruhi wanted a modest wife, greeted him in a pair of jeans and snug red handknit; she was no less pretty than Nilgün. So what if she was a little short? She did have naturally playful dark eyes and an hourglass figure with a tiny waist. They eyed each other throughout the meal. Ruhi was smitten by her physique and warmth. Fulya was pleased too; the more she looked at him, the more he grew on her. She decided she couldn't find anyone better. They got deeper and deeper into conversation as they drank their tea Erzurum style – through a hard lump of sugar clenched between the teeth. Dilaver knew it was in the bag. Ruhi sent Fulya a text message the moment he went home and was instantly rewarded with a playful reply. They texted each other all night until her pay-as-you-go account ran out. The next day they met at Dilaver's office, ostensibly by chance, and things took their natural course. It was time for the betrothal.

Ruhi's mother Emeti, impressed by Nilgün's spotless house and snow-white laundry, had always boasted about he daughter-in-law's fantastic housekeeping. *And you should taste her baklava … forty layers, every one a tender feast for the mouth!* Mystified why her son should wish to divorce this competent, house-proud, beautiful – in other words, perfect – wife instead of producing a grandchild, Emeti was violently opposed to the idea. But Ruhi stuck to his guns. He made up a bunch of conflicting tales to convince his mother that they didn't get on: Nilgün was bad-tempered, quarrelsome and a spendthrift to boot. But as one lie followed another, it suddenly dawned on him that he missed Nilgün like crazy. His eyes welled up.

Appreciative as she was of her house-proud daughter-in-law, Emeti had nevertheless found Nilgün somewhat too frivolous for this part of the world from the off – behaviour she had attributed to Nilgün's Aegean background rather than wantonness. The penny finally dropped when Ruhi studiously avoided her gaze. Whilst he was crying himself to sleep on the guest bed, the heavy woollen quilt pulled over his head, she rang several acquaintances in Oltu. The consensus (tactful yet unmistakable) was that Nilgün had a reputation as a whore; Emeti had a fit and never again wanted to hear the name of the daughter-in-law who had brought such shame upon their honour.

The moment Ruhi announced that he wanted to marry Fulya, Emeti rolled up her sleeves and gathered copious information on the accountant's sister-in-law, to prevent her son repeating the same mistake. Praise for bright Feriha, the prospective bride's big sister *(Cool and composed, she's very big on honour, etc.)* set the poor woman's heart somewhat at ease.

Of course her son could have found someone better. But Emeti was as keen to see Ruhi married off as Dilaver was. You never knew, Nilgün might still decide to return, even after the divorce, and make a right scene. Gathering her close relatives and ignoring the pain of her arm, back in plaster despite two unsuccessful operations, she left Tercan to ask for Fulya's hand. In addition to the diamond betrothal ring, she bought her prospective new daughter-in-law a gold chain that was even thicker than the one she'd bought Nilgün (and twice as long too), and made a vow: the day she heard news of her new daughter-in-law's pregnancy, she would sacrifice two rams to feed the poor and needy.

A great uncle, two aunts, the mother and Ruhi would all go to ask for Fulya's hand, and since they were already on the spot, they would conduct the betrothal at the same time. Having collected the chocolates he'd ordered, Ruhi was parked outside the bottled gas dealership waiting for the betrothal bouquet. His eye caught the fancy wrapping on the chocolate box and instantly remembered the day they'd driven to Marmaris to ask for Nilgün's hand. It was such a long way they'd decided to buy the chocolates in Aydın so they wouldn't melt. But when Emeti got food poisoning from the shish kebab they'd had at some roadside spot near Selçuk, all thoughts of chocolates and flowers had flown their mind. Ruhi had taken his mother to a private hospital in Selçuk, where the poor woman was kept overnight on a drip, so their arrival at their prospective in-laws' had been quite late. Thankfully it had been to a very warm welcome; Emeti had liked Nilgün at first sight and the two mothers-in-law had got on like a house on fire. Memories that broke Ruhi's heart. He just couldn't forget Nilgün no matter what he did.

At once, he threw it all away: his mother, his relatives getting ready at home, the new marriage that awaited him, Fulya, work, everything. He turned the key in the ignition and zoomed off to Marmaris.

In the meanwhile, everyone was waiting for him at home. **His aunt's grumpy, impatient husband, Uncle Şevket**, growled, *If he's not here in ten minutes, I'll jump into my car and make straight home for Tercan!* Emeti was just beginning to worry – *Where's the boy got to?* – when Ruhi rang. Blurting out, *I'm on my way to Marmaris, to Nilgün. I can't forget her. Don't wait for me. And tell Fulya to forgive me…* he rang off. Emeti collapsed in a faint.

By the time he knocked on Nilgün's door, which was veiled by a profusion of bougainvillea, his eyes were bloodshot with lack of sleep. He was dizzy, barely able to stand, looked awful, stank to high heaven and was starving. Falling at his wife's feet, he burst into tears, *It's just no good without you, Nilgün!* It didn't take ages to talk her round. At the sight of the dark shadows under the eyes of this new, thin-as-a-rake Ruhi, Nilgün's heart filled with genuine love for the first time; she regretted having repeatedly cheated on him.

Given his wife's reputation, Ruhi couldn't face living in Oltu. For a start, none of his family would have anything to do with him. Ruhi gave power of attorney to his **brother-in-law Kubilay (a self-styled wide boy)** and despatched him to Oltu to sell everything off: the two pharmacies, their home and whatever else he held the deed to. He intended to carry on as a chemist in Marmaris. But when all his attempts to open a shop in Marmaris – even in the remotest corner of the town – foundered due to his lack of a licence, of this, that and the other, Nilgün's hardened brothers (led by Kubilay) lured the chemist into their own field: tourism. Ruhi plonked down his money, took over a crappy bar frequented by beer-guzzling British hooligans and once again began selling – in addition to barrels of beer – narcotics under the counter. Soon he was making money hand over fist, and expanded the illicit trade.

Starving and sleepless after driving a thousand miles from Oltu to Marmaris, his stomach had been the first thing on Ruhi's mind the moment he and his wife made up, and Nilgün duly obliged her renewed passion with a panful of pasta in mince sauce. Then they dashed off into the bedroom. Nilgün, who whilst they were married and together had surreptitiously been on the pill *just in case*, was caught off guard and fell pregnant then and there.

As her last paramour, Talat Şeker – now posted to Kırkağaç, Manisa – was reconciled with his wife, Nergis, who threw herself into all sorts of courses, from macramé to drawing, from English to baking, Nilgün suffered the worst kind of misfortune. During a particularly difficult birth, when she produced **Dila, a daughter that was the spitting image of her father**, the rookie GP slashed through the wrong muscle, bungled the correction and eventually left Nilgün faecally incontinent.

Her roving eye had begun to stray even before the renewed passion for her husband fizzled out, but cheating on Ruhi was now no longer an option. She sought a cure. She consulted numerous surgeons and gynaecologists at the Ninth of September University, the Aegean Medical School, and even as far away as the Antalya University Hospitals. All to no avail. So frequently did she disgrace herself that she virtually stopped eating and drinking, just so her bowels wouldn't work and she wouldn't soil herself whenever and wherever. All that was left of that clear-eyed beauty was a bag of bones and a bundle of nerves. If only that was her only problem though! Much worse was yet to come.

Secure in Nilgün's love, his self-confidence replenished, and more than content in the tourism sector, Ruhi was no longer the old Ruhi. An entirely new man in appearance and dress, he shaved off the moustache he used to trim with Nilgün's manicure scissors every morning in Oltu. But the greatest change was in his character. He hit the nightspots in a big way, leaving his brother-in-law to deal with Nilgün's medical issues and his mother-in-law to care for Dila. He lived it up with the Scandinavian bombshells sprawling on the beaches; with his family far from his thoughts, he would stay away for ten days at a time. No amount of tears or pleas enticed him back; Nilgün was already thinking *He's got it coming*, when she was proved right.

Ruhi, it turned out, had made a fourteen-year-old girl pregnant. By the time her parents (**Gunnar**, a conductor on the Malmö-Copenhagen line, and **Sybille Promberger**, who had moved to her native Berlin after divorcing Gunnar two years previously) twigged, **Astrid Edström from Malmö** was five months gone. *Too late*, said the Swedish gynaecologists familiar with holiday mishaps of this sort; Astrid had no choice but to carry the pregnancy to term.

Gunnar Edström – whose super-package holiday had been too much of a whirlwind of ageing British divorcées and swarthy waiters for him to worry about his daughter – not only raised hell through the good offices of the consulate, but also landed in Marmaris with a horde of solicitors. Shocked at the way it all blew up, Ruhi scrambled to defend himself. To be fair, you could have knocked him over with a feather when he discovered that Astrid was a virgin, but he'd been so sure she was of age (she looked at least eighteen) and so flattered by her corny, *I'd been waiting for someone like you to be my first man*, he hadn't dwelled upon the matter.

Ruhi was denied bail as he awaited sentencing, whilst headlines in both countries blared *PEDOFIL!* and *SÜBYANCI* over his photo. Meanwhile, back in Malmö, Astrid gave birth to a son she named **Jakob**. Nilgün, now the laughing stock of Marmaris, began shuttling between Muğla Prison and medical schools.

She visited Ruhi every week. They'd start off chatting politely. Nilgün would moan about the latest consultant's prognosis, and Ruhi would cuddle his daughter, *Who's my tiny daughter then; how you've grown!* But the moment he brought up Astrid, Nilgün lost her temper and started yelling, *Don't make me trip my fuses again!* Ruhi, whose love for his wife had fizzled the moment he regained hers, would counter – *Don't get me started on your fuses, ya bitch!* – and Nilgün would burst into tears – *Bugger the day I met you! God damn a husband like you!* – and push off before the guards could intervene; but she always returned a week later with clean laundry.

In the meanwhile, Kubilay took over the bar, went bust within a few months, and vanished into thin air, up to his eyes in debt. So Nilgün had to live on charity: they'd have starved if she didn't call in on **Ruhi's partner Ercan** regularly for pocket money.

Ruhi had bought shares in a seafood restaurant, and his partner Ercan turned out to be a decent sort. Unlike the no-good brother-in-law, Ercan didn't pocket Ruhi's share the moment the latter was banged up. Having escaped by the skin of his teeth the underage tourist girl trap, he was full of sympathy. With a bribe here and there, he secreted a mobile phone into prison, checked Ruhi's e-mails regularly, and regularly brought him printouts of Jakob's latest photos sent by Astrid.

Ruhi was strangely missing Astrid, who in defiance of her red-nosed father's ban was determined to communicate with the father of her child. She'd been surreptitiously studying a *Turkish for Foreigners* book obtained from a Kurdish friend in Malmö and sent Ruhi a text message: *I send a new picture from our son to thine email.*

Every time she returned from a visit, the wife of her last paramour would pop into Nilgün's mind and she'd lament *Her curse has worked!* After that night when Ruhi had rained bullets left, right and centre, and that filthy maniac Şenol had pushed his luck, Nilgün had laughed off the news that Talat's wife had left him. But now she was tormenting herself with the idea that she was paying for being a homewrecker.

She needn't have. True, she had been at fault. But Talat was such an incorrigible letch he would have found someone else if Nilgün hadn't been around, and Nergis would have left him sooner or later.

And sure enough, too proud to stay, she did leave him; she moved to her father Nurettin Kozanlı's poky home in which you couldn't swing a cat. Nergis was sobbing, *Oh, Talat, how could you do that to me?* as her mother, Midwife Mualla, was on her way back from the market, worrying over this catastrophe just when they were desperate to make ends meet. Nergis was in a terrible state, but her mother was in an even worse one.

The times had changed; no one gave birth at home any more. The midwife was called out only once in a blue moon, and then only to a village where she was paid a couple of live hens, a jar of honey or a basketful of fruit and vegetables, but at the end of the month the landlord wanted his rent and the grocer and butcher would take nothing less than cash to settle their accounts. Her husband's occasional injection, blood pressure reading and IV drip replacement no longer fed the family. Nurettin had virtually no patients left. If it weren't for the Medical Director's referrals, he couldn't even pay the rent on the surgery. It was only the midwife's pension that kept the wolf from the door, and now suddenly the ageing couple, barely able to feed themselves, were saddled with two greedy grandchildren and a daughter who just wouldn't stop crying. Poor Mualla was so preoccupied as she crossed the street that she forgot to look both ways and so failed to see the approaching black Mercedes. She died on the spot.

The driver of the Mercedes worked for **Türkan Kaymakoğlu, one of the first female judges in the country**, who also happened to be one of the oldest of the town's leading citizens. The retired long-distance driver, **Hamdi Tutuş**, a devout father to grown-up children – he had never hurt so much as a fly or had a single accident all his life – was for once speeding that day, a gentle soul somehow led astray by the devil. The car came to a stop forty or fifty metres later and he went off his rocker when he saw the brains he'd spilled all over the road.

Thank God Türkan wasn't in the car. She had been collecting archive material on the town's history for years and had sent her driver to a close friend to collect the panoramic photograph *The Clock Tower and the Town on a Snowy Day* by the **Armenian photographer Karnik Sabuncuyan**, who had lived in the Black Sea region in the late nineteenth century. It was quite out of character for the otherwise impeccably behaved Türkan to send her driver instead of personally paying a visit to the **retired headmistress of the Girls' Institute, Huma İpekören**. It was just that the previous day she had sat outside in the garden of the Three Brothers Patisserie far too long and caught a chill; she had a runny nose and a rattle in her chest. At the time of the accident, she was waiting for her driver to return with the legendary hoto as she sipped linden tea with honey at the **Kaymakoğlu Mansion**, best known for the loquat tree in the garden. If she had been in the car, the horrible scene might have – God forbid! – given her a heart attack, and she already had one foot in the grave.

The police arrived at once. But they couldn't calm Hamdi down, neither there nor back at the station. He kept making weird gestures and bellowing, *Allaaaah! Allaaaah!* Whenever he calmed down a little, he spouted the most bizarre religious tales and burst into tears when he realised no one was paying any attention. His state was attributed to traumatic shock by the eyewitnesses as well as the policemen at the station. But when his strange behaviour continued unabated throughout the court hearing and Türkan's simplest, *Thank you, Hamdi*, elicited a stream of blessings running to no less than a score of *salaams*, Hamdi Tutuş was packed off to the Mental Health Hospital for assessment.

For a time, tongues in the city wagged that this influential, superannuated republican had pulled strings to send her driver to the mental hospital instead of prison. But Hamdi was truly sick. At the initial assessment, **Âlim Kâhkeci, Senior Psychiatrist at the Mental Health Hospital**, recommended a period of observation for suspected *neurotic guilt emotion syndrome* – findings validated by Hamdi's attempt to hang himself with his shoelaces that night. Severe emotions of guilt dating back to childhood lay at the root of his universal deference, constant well-wishing and exasperating obsequiousness. With little prospect of a quick cure, Hamdi was sectioned.

In the meanwhile, court experts apportioned fault equally to the driver and the victim. If Hamdi had been wholly responsible, Türkan, who had served on the bench for years, would not have hesitated to personally hand him over to the law. Devastated as she was by Nurettin's loss, she offered him a substantial sum in compensation, despite having no legal or ethical obligation to do so. She had no children of her own and was quite well off in both property and funds; she didn't bat an eye as she handed over the money to the old sad-faced physician.

Mualla had been an excellent midwife, a veritable angel who gave injections to the poor without charge and minded the neighbours' children in an emergency. Nurettin's grief was therefore shared by all. For a long time, food was sent every night to feed the widower, his daughter and grandchildren. Nergis had no intention of finding a job; all she did since her mother's death was cry twice as many rivers. She cursed her husband, mourned her mother and made life hell for her children and herself. Türkan's generous settlement arrived just as Nurettin was about to scrape the bottom of the barrel. A little prudence, and he might have lived comfortably on that money for the rest of his days without ever worrying *What're we gonna eat tomorrow?*

Instead he turned into a spendthrift. His pesky grandchildren – who were accustomed to getting their way with their father – were bought a bicycle here and an Atari there, just to keep them quiet; he piled so much food on the table that it went to waste, and he showered money on his daughter, heartsick from betrayal, just to cheer her up. So freely did he splash it about that one Saturday morning he said, *C'mon, I'll take you to Atatürk's Mausoleum*, to *Anıtkabir*, just to distract his grandchildren, who were squabbling over some petty toy. Nergis thought they'd make for the coach station when the old man hailed a cab outside the house; the penny dropped when he instructed the driver, *To Ankara!* – but she failed to prevent the extravagance. And go to Ankara they did! Nor did it end there: Nurettin got along so well with the driver after chatting with him for hours on the road that he booked the fellow into their hotel for the whole three days. So the same taxi took them to the mausoleum, the Ethnography Museum and Ankara Fortress.

A fool and his money are soon parted. The children would fight in their grandpa's cramped home. Nurettin yelled at them all the time. It got to be too much for Nergis. At long last she made up with Talat, who'd been sucking up to her ever since he'd heard of Türkan's largesse, but was as yet unaware that the money was gone. The NCO placed his hand on his service pistol and swore on his honour he'd never stray again – disappointed though he was at discovering that the money was gone, he still wanted his family back.

He had recently earned a new stripe and was posted to the gendarme-training brigade at Kırkağaç in Manisa. The family settled into married quarters. His eye never stopped roving, but now he played his cards close to his chest, covered his tracks well, and made sure to dance attendance on Nergis – *Darling wifey, sweetheart!* Not that she was fooled. She did, however, turn a blind eye, since the alternative was her father's cockroach-infested, stuffy two-bedroom flat that faced a dark street.

Forced reconciliation with her no-good husband, however, only aggravated Nergis's depression. Following the advice of friends and family to *find a hobby*, she signed up for several courses and made herself take the minibus day in, day out, to the Public Education Centre. As for Nurettin, who never could bear the heat, he slept with the window wide open summer and winter; he may have been hard up, but he was very happy. Since the departure of his daughter and grandchildren, he'd reverted to wandering around the house in his undies and farting to his heart's content.

Every morning in the grimy flat – regular cleaning now being a thing of the past – he greeted with a cigarette and a cup of tea as strong as tar; he then proceeded to while away the rest of the day. He used to regret never having specialised, but not for the past ten years; more accurately, he was sick of regretting the same thing for years. Still, his lifelong lack of success would cross his mind every so often; that's when he got maudlin and blamed fate, felt his years and broke into murmuring a mournful Musa Eroğlu song that made him even sadder: *I've passed over the world / Life's but a deep breath / Look how the circle of destiny / Shows the end of the road is nigh.*

He had never stuck at anything; to this day he was still amazed at having finished medical school. That being said, he had time and again cut off his nose to spite his face. At the start of his career, for instance, he had been a young state physician in Azdavay, Kastamonu. Cushy job: a civil servant with a salary paid on the dot. But he resigned after losing his temper when some bigwig asked for a prescription without an examination. Later he got a job as a factory physician, but when he was allocated a sunless basement room, he made a scene and left.

He'd never quite appreciated that it was his naturally melancholy face which had elicited the Medical Director's compassion. What he saw in the mirror whenever he looked was a guileless, even charming countenance. A tendency to attribute Demir Demir's friendship to little more than the arrogance of a more highly positioned specialist would plague his thoughts whenever he returned from spending a little time with him. Gazing at the receding back of the Medical Director leaving the Nation Tea Garden, therefore, Nurettin felt no less relieved at the severance of this friendship of unequals. It was only the following morning, as he mounted the five flights of fag-end- and spit-stained stairs that led to his top-floor, single-room surgery (equipped with the simplest of medical instruments dating back to the seventies) that the penny dropped: unless he made up to the Medical Director without delay, there'd be no new referral knocking on his door.

At first he sent greetings through intermediaries, but received none in return. Then he rang the Medical Director's secretary, requesting an appointment; it was declined. The Medical Director no longer had any wish to see Nurettin. The prospect of again having to shoulder that burden of pitying affection was too dreadful; what if the look that had flashed across the old physician's face during their absurd argument, the look of a dog about to bite the hand that fed it, had given way to the usual heartbreaking subservience? No amount of vigils at the door helped; Nurettin never got the chance to talk to the Medical Director to make things right.

Then he read in the conference announcements published for free in The Black Sea Herald that the venerable high-ranking official Erdem Bakırcıoğlu, the esteemed Medical Director's friend, would be honouring the hospital with a speech on *The Benefits of Train Travel on Mental Health*. He would engineer an encounter at the conference, take the Medical Director by the arm to say, *It doesn't become us to stay cross like this, old chap* and if all else failed, grovel.

He locked up, went to the hospital, and sat down in the middle of the third row from the front. He had planned to sit at the front to catch the Medical Director's eye, but that idea was so popular there wasn't a single free seat in the first two rows.

Nurettin was the only person in the entire hall who didn't laugh at the retired bureaucrat's sock suspenders. Recalling that newspaper item, and hoping the Medical Director would hear, he rebuked those around him, *What's so funny? It's a medical device used to straighten curvature of the shinbone!* But although the headline had been, *You Can be Free of Bow Legs!* the old physician hadn't bothered to read the article. If he had, he would have known that the report concerned, not a medical device, but a cosmetic solution involving a combination of liposuction and silicon injections.

His comment backfired horribly. Instead of making an impression on his former friend, it only broadcast his cluelessness to the world. The Medical Director knew perfectly well what this accessory was good for, having once or twice used a pair himself at his wife's insistence, and then discarded them as being inconvenient; he never wore silk socks anyway. Grumbling aloud, *Good God, such ignorance! The geezer's never seen sock suspenders!* he at once corrected the glaring *faux pas*.

He had no intention of making peace. He pretended not to have seen the fellow when they nearly collided in the hallway. He was relieved to note that the unprovoked aggression of the disloyal dog remained in full force. He was more than relieved: just as he had liked Nurettin all these years for no reason, he now hated him for no reason. Deeply dejected, Nurettin now thought the Medical Director much too arrogant, conceited and cruel. *Shame, what a shame…* he murmured, staring pitifully at the former friend who had begrudged him a greeting.

The sock suspenders occupied hospital staff for days and spilled into the town. Even to the extent that the crass shopkeepers of the Arcade Market (popular with nearby villages for their trousseaux and similar requisites) began ragging **'Girl' İsmet, the purveyor of sexy lingerie** as well as more traditional underwear, in his tiny shop beneath the stairs, *Show'uz a suspender belt, mate, make it right racy though!*

Girlie İsmet failed to convince them that suspenders weren't some sort of homosexual accessory. He wasn't sure, but he had a feeling they were something else entirely. His neighbours sniggered, hinting at his nickname and naïvety in these matters. İsmet, cringing as he hid his rising temper, insisted, *No, it's not like you think.* Finally, the **umbrella seller Remzi** (a regular at the STD clinic of State Hospital, since he laid every woman that came his way) threw down the gauntlet, *Wanna bet on it mate?* İsmet accepted in a flash of fury. If sock suspenders turned out to be something only real men wore, as İsmet claimed, Remzi would tour the arcade in women's knickers; but if, on the other hand, they turned out to be *gayboy pants*, then it would be İsmet parading in suspenders. İsmet asked his wholesale supplier to send him one sock suspender. She misunderstood. When the woman's suspenders of black lace trimmed with red feathers arrived a few days later, neither man won. They were still no clearer on whether a sock suspender was a homosexual accessory or not.

Despite Remzi's pestering, İsmet refused to tour the arcade with the suspender belt over his trousers. His eyes filled, he went bright red. *No!* he said, and nearly passed out. He looked so pathetic that a couple of conscience-stricken shopkeepers made the malicious umbrella seller stop. The suspender belt with red feathers passed from hand to hand in the chortling crowd outside the shop. At long last, Remzi – who regarded each urological examination as an opportunity to verify his manhood to the entire arcade – placed the suspender belt on his head, ostensibly to show he had nothing to prove when it came to manliness, and mimicked the famous drag queen Grumpy Virginia; his neighbours in the arcade all died laughing as they snapped him on their mobiles.

A right cheeky bunch, with only a couple of exceptions, they didn't think twice about calling the unassuming, harmless lingerie seller *Girlie İsmet* to his face. But just so the doleful lad wouldn't take offence, pack up and leave – thereby denying them their fun – they claimed it was his long locks and pale hands, as shapely as a woman's, that made them say it. To convince him, they even teased, *C'mon lad, get that hair cut... What real man would grow his hair like a tart?*

But there was no sincerity in this half-macho, half-friendly behaviour. They sounded him out at every opportunity, puzzled by his lack of interest in any of them – especially the umbrella seller who thought he deserved the glad eye. They pissed themselves laughing at Remzi's antics, like when he held one of his umbrellas like a penis every time some Natasha came to the arcade, and gossiped about Girlie İsmet – *What kind of a gayboy is he? He doesn't put out to anyone!* – as they peed on the squat toilet stone in the nearby mosque's loos, the arcade being singularly lacking in such conveniences.

İsmet placed the red-feather-trimmed suspender belt in the shopwindow, hoping some Natasha might buy it. Just as he was about to shut up shop for the night, the **handsome Paediatric Psychiatrist Faik Abacı** – who thanks to a passing resemblance styled himself after George Clooney of *ER* fame – passed by on his way to the trousseau boutique, intending to exchange a bathmat for a longer one, and the suspender belt caught his eye. There was no one else around. He sneaked into the shop, lest he was seen, and asked, *Is that a thingy?* A couple of prying questions established that the handsome doctor was interested in the garment, not for some secret mistress, but for his **demure wife, Gülümser**, whom he'd married in a splendid wedding last summer, and Girlie İsmet's world came crashing upon his head.

Despite his occupation, the lingerie seller was too shy to look women in the eye; he blushed bright red, his palms dripped with sweat and he could only address them with the most respectful *Sister* no matter what their age. His clientele not only saw no harm in shopping there, but also happily crowded into the nook under the stairs – barely wide enough to hold three – to chatter about all manner of intimate matters, from their husbands' premature ejaculations to their fruitless fantasies, or to brazenly interrogate İsmet about edible knickers and perfumed bras. And Girlie İsmet replied patiently and courteously to each and every one.

Just like his neighbours in the arcade, his female clientele had no doubt that İsmet was homosexual. Which in their eyes, if truth be told, was strangely comforting and droll. Some turned up just to see what a homosexual bloke looked like. Although nearing thirty, İsmet had, indeed, not slept with any woman, not even a prostitute, but the reason for this apparent lack of virility was his puny frame, which signalled a misleading message. He might not look masculine, but he liked only women, and was in fact besotted with Gülümser Abacı. Whenever the sweet young thing walked primly past on her way to the trousseau, china and jewellery shops, eyes modestly downcast and clearly with no intention of stepping into his shop, an aching İsmet stared after her shapely figure, barely discernible under the long, loose ecru coat.

Hands trembling at having to gift-wrap the suspender belt for the woman of his dreams, the pure angel he couldn't bear to visualise making love with her husband, certainly not wearing anything like this, his blood boiled. All right, he'd have to accept that she slept with her husband – he was her spouse before God, after all – but what was all this about, this fantasy of the suspender belt and all?

Seething, he quoted a price five times its value, hoping to elicit the objection *Whoa! What the bloody hell? I'm not buying gold here!* – which would have allowed İsmet to replace the offending article in the shop window with a dismissive *Suit yourself!* Instead, the handsome doctor bought the red-feather-trimmed black suspender belt and left without a peep.

İsmet was normally the soul of discretion about his clientele's preferences, but he was so enraged that the very next day he told Remzi he'd sold the suspender belt to the doctor, that the man had a Russian mistress with legs that went on for ever and that he'd spotted the couple entering a hotel that was more brothel than respectable. He just couldn't bring himself to discredit Gülümser. Remzi told the owner of the trousseau boutique, who passed it on to the jeweller, who in turn told everyone, and they all whooped, *Phwoar! Well done, doctor!* This short-lived gossip raised Faik's prestige in the male world but made no impact at home. No, it was even worse: shy Gülümser dug her heels in – *I'll never wear it, never, you hear?* – and flung the suspender belt into a corner, with the result that the doctor's fantasy fizzled out.

Tongues wagged for days about the Erdem's sock suspenders, which so tickled the shopkeepers of the Arcade Market. Soon after his friend's return to Istanbul, the Medical Director, chatting with someone at the 14 March Medicine Day Dinner at the Diamond Hotel ballroom, twigged that these suspenders had elicited universal derision and, rather than admitting having dabbled with them once or twice, or even rising to his old schoolmate's defence, fell in with the general consensus at the table and scoffed at the ludicrous accessory.

Meanwhile, Erdem was waxing lyrical about his friend's hospitality, *which was beyond reproach*, mentioning for the nth time the glory of the sea view from the balcony of the flower-bedecked suite the Medical Director had so thoughtfully booked for him – as if the Bakırcıoğlu home didn't have its own view of the shimmering waters of the Bosphorus. These praises were sung in a shout for the benefit of his wife, Bedia, so she could hear him above the all-night din of the taverna on the ground floor.

The retired bureaucrat was not only younger, but also much more vigorous than his wife. If he had stuck to his usual crisp linen shirts and delicate cashmere jumpers – instead of adopting an elderly man's style – and merely gone for a brisk stroll along the Bosphorus, he'd have turned many young heads, never mind women his age. Instead, slowing down deliberately to stay in step with his wife, who had gone downhill the past few years, he happily withdrew into their home and, worst of all, quite needlessly resigned himself to old age. Still deeply in love, he wasn't going to let the small matter of their age difference come between them.

Their lives were now so bland, insular and repetitive that weeks went by without them having anything worth talking about. Erdem was therefore determined to recount his visit, the most noteworthy event of recent months, over and over, starting with the Medical Director's warm greeting – a tight hug! – at the airport. There were a couple of minor details he'd forgotten to mention... but again he never got round to finishing his tale.

The revelry of the taverna patrons downstairs – until then a fairly continuous rumble – rose a few notches when they started smashing plates and took to the floor in a sirtaki dance. Increasingly louder footsteps were boom-boom-booming in the retired civil servant's head. When the windowpanes started to rattle with the intolerable noise, which began at the same time every night, Bedia literally switched off. After all, she had been listening to the same story for ten days. So she turned off her hearing aid and went to bed.

By dawn, when the taverna's patrons finally dispersed, she would stretch in the eiderdown bed that she would never swap for an orthopaedic mattress, pop in her hearing aid and begin the day savouring a cup of frothy Turkish coffee as she gazed at the Bosphorus. Erdem, on the other hand, wasn't as fortunate, having been blessed with hearing well above average for his age.

As a child, Bedia had caught a chill that led to a massive ear infection during their first winter at the Bijou Yalı in Kanlıca. The central heating had proved far too expensive to use, so her father had set up a wood stove in the sitting room of the mansion he'd swindled out of the original owners. And just like the Mustakis, his family, too, were crammed into a single room. As luck would have it, winter was particularly harsh that year, with three-foot-long icicles that refused to melt hanging from the eaves. The rest of the yalı was freezing. Moving from hot to cold and back again soon took its toll on little Bedia and she began complaining of earache, cupping her aching ear; the poor child couldn't get a wink of sleep.

Hulki brushed it off: *She's just a kid, it'll get better.* But when her temperature shot up to 40 Celsius the following week, she was rushed to the Model Hospital. *What took you so long?* asked a testy doctor with snow-white hair, tearing a strip off the father. Dozens of injections and jarfuls of pills later, Bedia was left with major hearing loss in her left ear.

Knowing how Hulki had cheated the Mustakis, his wife had tormented herself with the idea of ill-gotten gains. When her daughter went deaf, she panicked; she pleaded with her husband to return the yalı: *They must have cursed us! We're enjoying the fruits of sin!* The dairy-man, knee-deep in debt and trying to grow the business, snapped at her, *What sin, ya silly cow!* All the same, with that thought of sin preying on his mind, he took to the prayer rug for two cycles before God.

When the sirtaki started, Erdem opened a book he'd picked at random, put in his earplugs, which were useless before the infuriating noise, and traced the lines with his eyes. His petition to evict the taverna had been dragging in the courts for years. He'd even faced the odd threat or two. The proprietor of the taverna, **Reşat Özyılmazel (a.k.a. Maserati Reşat)**, after the second-hand wheels he boasted about left and right – *Cost two hundred thou yuuroos!* – despite being worth no more than sixty thousand) was the neighbourhood's hard man, the bloke whose protection every shopkeeper was bending over backwards for – from the hairdresser to the roastery, greengrocer and TV repairman. Whenever they met – *How's the court case goin', chief?* – Reşat would smirk if he was in a good mood, and if he wasn't, he'd pull his jacket back just far enough to display the butt of the pistol tucked in his waist. Erdem might have happily taken a reasonable offer for this sea-view flat, which would have been priceless before the taverna opened downstairs, but his wife had no intention of leaving their home: not a single peep was heard during the day, and she was stone deaf anyway once she turned her hearing aid off.

The fabulous view was its sole distinction, but Bedia loved this flat far more than the Rambling Rose Yalı in Bülbülderesi, which she'd enjoyed for two decades. Yet she used to think – before Erdem entered her life – that she could never live anywhere else. Every May, the door to that wonderful house was framed by hundreds of perfumed pink roses, and she would signal to her guests to listen to the glorious chorus of myriad nightingales in their woodland nests in the hills, bringing her own hand to her ear as if she, too, could hear them.

She and her first husband had lived in the rented yalı for twenty years. When their landlord died and his children put the yalı up for sale, she pleaded with Tarık for days, *I could never live anywhere else, can we please oh please buy it?* But he wouldn't hear of it; after all, he'd always said that a good merchant never tied up his money in property. The heirs held out at first, determined to sell in a hurry and divvy up the proceeds, but they wouldn't drop the price either. But after months and months, not a single offer came at the asking price, and they slashed it well below market value. Which is precisely what Tarık was waiting for, even if he pretended that it was her pleading and not his intention to snap a bargain that had changed his mind, *Seeing as you love this place so much, let's buy it!*

The day he got down to bargaining – *Could I beat the heirs down a little more for the house?* – was the day Bedia's happiness there came to an end. Tragedy would for ever tarnish the memory of that lovely place. It was ironic that Rambling Rose was the place where the agony of sin and the bliss of love came together, two halves of one apple.

That was where Bedia and Erdem died once and were reborn.

Tarık Bakırcıoğlu's son, Erdem, who had his father's magnetic dark eyes, had grown up without ever seeing his face or stepping into the yalı that was a veritable Garden of Eden. After finishing the lycée, Erdem enrolled in political sciences in Ankara – partly to avoid ever meeting this man who was no closer to him than the strangers in society pages. And there he'd stayed once he obtained his degree, a highly qualified civil servant with a bright future.

But the real reason had been to escape his mother, not his father, as he later admitted to his former stepmother / new wife one summer night as they sat on the terrace. The besotted new husband was well in his cups at the time. Silence descended once his tale was told.

Tarık, having sworn to spend his not inconsiderable fortune to the last penny so as not to leave his son even a pin, had upped sticks and moved to Switzerland to be near his stash. Unable to sell the Bijou Yalı in a hurry, newlyweds Bedia and Erdem, who just couldn't manage without a view of the Bosphorus ferry line, were living in a cosy flat – the terrace was larger than the interior – on the Vaniköy slopes, were in love and were suffering faint pangs of remorse. That was when stone-deaf Bedia (her right eardrum had burst as a result of Tarık's awful slap when she admitted to being in love with her stepson) learnt the real reason for the irreparable breach between Erdem and Tarık (who after they betrayed him referred to her as *Cursia*).

Erdem's account sadly lacked punch, delivered time and again with shouted repetitions, which, indeed, reduced this tragedy to preposterous comedy: *A chant?... No, my aunt, my aunt!... Taught them?... No, Bedia, caught them – who said anything about teaching?* as Bedia complained about the humming in her latest hearing aid. Thus the tale that formed the essence of Erdem's life was deprived of its fairy dust.

Since no amount of her asking Tarık, *Why did you split with your first wife?* had elicited anything more than the standard nonsense of *We couldn't get along, couldn't make it work…* Bedia had long suspected a secret tragedy. The truth, when at last she heard it, prompted her to regard total deafness as penance for falling in love with the poor fellow's own son – the last straw in this tragedy. She frequently asked herself, *I wonder if this is divine justice?* Comparing Tarık's transgression with her own, however, she was relieved to note that hers was based on true love. So she carried on, shrugging off the occasional pangs of conscience.

The past was even more tragic than she had supposed. **Erdem's mother, Aydanur**, had expected to catch her husband (a high society personage) in the box room with the maid or cleaner, or even one of her friends. She didn't trust Tarık as far as she could throw him. But when she caught him with **Yurdanur, her own sister**, and in Yurdanur's bedroom too, her already fragile sanity snapped.

That night, the new bride Yurdanur, who had moved to the flat opposite to be near her big sister and her nephew, Erdem, had despatched her husband of one month off on a business trip; thinking his wife was playing cards at the Equestrian Club, and having told her he had a business dinner, Tarık had dashed to his sister-in-law's bedroom.

Aydanur was indeed at the club. Twice a week she left Erdem with the nanny to play cards with her friends from the Üsküdar American College until three in the morning. They'd not even finished the first rubber when one of the girls learned that her father had had a heart attack. Aydanur accompanied her to American Hospital, which happened to be two streets behind hers. Thankfully, it was nothing. The father in question had been suffering, not from a coronary infarction, but from the three bowls of pasta he'd consumed for supper, polished off with a dozen *tulumba* doughballs dripping with syrup; the spasm had cleared by the time they'd reached the hospital.

Being so close to home, Aydanur couldn't be bothered to go back to the club. Instead, she thought she'd drop in on Yurdanur for a chat, since her brother-in-law had just that morning flown to America. Then the devil tempted. Instead of ringing the bell, she used her sister's spare key. And the moment she did, she caught her husband's heady blend of tobacco and bay, but couldn't believe them capable of such a betrayal. Stopping herself from shouting, *Yurdanuuur!* she proceeded towards the bedroom, the source of indistinct sounds, and struggled briefly with the devil, who was now insisting, *Open this door!* It would prey on her mind for the rest of her life if she turned back now. With shaking hands she pushed the door open to reveal the treachery that would poison her to her dying breath. Her husband and her sister were stark naked in the bed, framed by rows of candles. Light from even more candles on the dressing table flickered on their bare skin.

Aydanur took her son and left home within the hour. She swore undying hatred for the husband she would never see again – nor would her son if she had anything to do with it. The shame was far more unbearable than the pain. Erdem only learnt the real reason when he was old enough to understand; everyone else was told, *We just didn't get along on the spiritual level.* Humiliated, Aydanur carried on seeing her sister in order to conceal the real reason, but whenever the two were alone, she made Yurdanur's life hell with curses that alleviated her heart as they tore out of her lungs.

But that pleasure proved short lived. Yurdanur had fallen out with her own husband, received no support from her brother-in-law and, with her own mental health declining, no longer had the strength to stomach her big sister's bile. On one such occasion, she simply threw herself out of the window. Aydanur was devastated. She never completely recovered after the suicide that had taken place right before her eyes. Now both victim and culprit at the same time, she, too, flipped.

She couldn't imagine a greater sin than the deceit she had suffered. Tarık would pay, she decided, and for years brainwashed Erdem against his father.

Only the risky excesses of her sick mind backfired: Erdem eventually had enough of her rancour, which went back to when he was a mere infant, and distanced himself from the unhinged mother who had made him so miserable. Helped by a sizeable inheritance from his grandfather, and now an adult, he entrusted his mother to an army of doctors and carers. One day, he gathered his courage and rang the doorbell of the Rambling Rose Yalı to settle accounts with his father.

And fell head over heels in love the moment Bedia opened the door.

Much later, after finally opening up to his wife about his father's affair with his aunt, Erdem sat for a while in guilty silence on the geranium-bedecked Vaniköy terrace. He was perturbed, convinced that happiness had its price, and worried that he would eventually pay for taking his stepmother away from his father. Some great catastrophe would strike and he would lose his Bedia. The years that passed, however, would prove those fears to be unfounded.

In actual fact, Erdem was Tarık's nemesis; this was the sole purpose of his existence in the universe. Divine justice had punished everyone else. Tarık, who'd slept with his sister-in-law, couldn't hack it in Switzerland and moved to France – where most of his money was swindled by a young Frenchwoman and the rest won by Turks at gaming tables on the Riviera. He died on the streets, a penniless wretch who never found peace. Bedia, who'd fallen for the stepson sixteen years her junior, was left stone deaf after Tarık's violent slap and spent years traipsing from one doctor to another in pursuit of new hearing aids. Yurdanur, who'd seduced her brother-in-law, committed suicide at a young age. Aydanur, who'd poisoned her son against his father, never forgave herself for her sister's suicide and died from a simple bout of flu due to an immune system exhausted by antidepressants. Yet Erdem – his faintly guilty conscience notwithstanding – lived happily with a wife who was old enough to be his mother and whose fabulousness he never once doubted. So when he slipped and fell in the conference hall of the Mental Health Hospital, one of the many things that popped into his mind was *Divine justice!*

The slip and fall that reverberated around the town didn't end with the sock suspenders. As Erdem Bakırcıoğlu, who had inherited his father's sartorial elegance and that magnetic gaze which made him the centre of attention everywhere, slid along the stage on his arse, his patent-leather-shod foot slammed into a floral arrangement made up of shrivelled carnations, gladioli that would never open and some pointless foliage, all in an earthenware pot (recycled from a betrothal order from the previous day that had remained uncollected; the florist Önder was renowned for scouring wedding halls at turn-out time to collect the bouquets he'd already sold and palming them off on someone else the following day), which had been shamelessly foisted upon the Medical Director, who had wanted to present his friend with a welcoming gesture. This precariously balanced floral arrangement shot off to smash against the right little toe of a neuropsychiatrist in the front row, who had been listening to the speaker with her legs slightly parted, flat shoes slipped off her swollen feet, heels resting on the ground.

This minor mishap turned into a bit of a performance and caused a major crisis in the hospital. The **unstable Neuropsychiatrist Nebahat Özdamar**, given to bursting into tears at the most inopportune moments due to her weak nerves, freed her foot from the mess of faded flowers and foliage, raised it into the air, broke into wails and promptly fainted.

That's when Erdem espied the long knickers visible between her parted legs; sitting on the stage in a daze until someone helped him up, musing – amongst other things – about his love for Bedia, whom he could never even visualise in such a garment, and ladies' underwear in general.

Bedia had always worn exquisite lacy delicates in silver, old rose or ivory; she would never leave the house without tucking her boobs – now little more than hardened strips of leather – into padded bras, and she always tottered on heels even around the house. Not even in her advanced years did she abandon worrying her skirt, now tugging it down grace-fully and then tugging it up, like a young thirty-something as she crossed and uncrossed her legs. Until his mind was thrown into turmoil by the outsized boobs of **Psychologist Gülnazmiye Görgün**, also in the front row, Erdem had never queried his unabated lust for Bedia, although the undying love had been taken for granted.

In the meanwhile, orderlies rushed the now unconscious neuropsy-chiatrist to A&E at State Hospital. The X-ray revealed a hairline fracture; instead of a plaster cast, the foot was tightly bound, and a pair of crutches were procured. The damage wasn't great, but as Nebahat was constantly on the lookout for a reason to cry, she sobbed for hours over the accident.

Once Erdem's long-winded lecture (delivered notwithstanding his befuddled state after that ignominious slide in front of some seventy or eighty people, mostly hospital staff at that) was over, the Medical Director went to Nebahat's room to wish her a speedy recovery. Exhausted by crying, she'd just fallen silent, but the moment she saw him, she burst into tears with renewed vigour. The more she cried, the more she wound him up. He couldn't stand her, but bit his tongue to avoid a scene.

The stumpy neuropsychiatrist's crying attacks were due to a nervous condition that emerged after her **radiologist husband, Kahraman İnal**, walked out, and only got worse over time. She had surprised everyone by giving up her fifty red Winstons the day after the divorce. Her behaviour had always been somewhat erratic, but still… The Medical Director was delighted at the insufferable Kahraman İnal's departure, not only from Nebahat's life, but from the hospital at large, since the bloke had always been kicking up a fuss over something or other.

One morning, when Nebahat turned up at work with her hair (she'd stopped colouring the roots long since) shaved to a grade-three buzz, she gave everyone a fright – staff as well as the seriously deranged patients who were kept from self-harm only by the strongest of tranquillisers.

Once considered quite pretty, Nebahat had forgotten how to smile a long time ago. Her mental balance had been hanging on a knife edge anyway, well before she was jilted; it echoed on her face as her misshapen jaws clicked and the sudden twitches of her facial muscles created an erratic character out of the doctor. The new haircut was the icing on the cake that transformed her into an ogress. She developed bizarre habits such as popping up at the hospital at the strangest of times, occasionally staying there for days on end without sleeping, and wandering around the dangerous patient wards at night even when she wasn't on duty. She had attached a door handle to her wrist with a long chain – it was the type orderlies used to access the rooms in the secure unit. She entered and left those rooms recklessly, occasionally walking out with the doors unlocked, in flagrant disregard of the mandatory security procedures in this section, leaving nurses scrambling in her wake to lock up.

Troubled at the gravity of the situation, the Medical Director asked the psychiatrist Âlim Kâhkeci to keep an eye on her. Âlim showed her to a chair and advised her not to bottle things up – it was far better to give vent to her troubles – and above all to strengthen her morale; a strong morale could cure all her mental problems. He also recommended a hobby, just for something to say, before he plied her with a heap of medication including a potent antidepressant.

He wasn't the least bit confident that she'd actually paid any attention, although he didn't think she presented a danger to anyone other than herself. He told the Medical Director that with tactful handling she'd get better in time. The poor thing was undergoing a traumatic loss; divorce, after all, was a major upheaval. The grieving that normally followed such situations had merely lasted for a little longer, that was all. Sympathy would help, as would making her feel that she wasn't alone. Otherwise – God forbid! – they might be forced to section their colleague of so many years in the very same hospital. Taking his advice, the Medical Director looked after her like a sister; the man who unfailingly turned a deaf ear to other doctors' requests for larger rooms conceded at once when Nebahat asked for a more spacious room on the ground floor.

Thankfully, he'd been worrying needlessly; Nebahat seemed on an even keel. She was very good at her job. Although her eccentricity had noticeably grown over time, no one minded much since she was harmless.

One day she decided she wanted a cabinet for her office, whose walls she'd already had painted a brick red, and she would pay for it out of her own pocket. She placed the order with **Odd-Eyes Sipahi (who had one blue eye and one hazel eye)**. Despite full payment in advance, and after a reassuring, *Don't you worry now Miss Doctor; I'll deliver it in ten days flat*, the carpenter, who handled all similar jobs for the hospital, took three and a half months and delivered the cabinet half-finished at that. He did, however, pay a price for causing her such distress over a simple cabinet – in screams when his hand (which had got caught in the bench planer when he was cleaning it) was stitched up without adequate anaesthesia.

At the sight of the blood pumping out of the deep cut between his thumb and index finger, Odd-Eyes Sipahi had wrapped his hand in his shirt and dashed off to the Mental Health Hospital two streets away. The orderlies had just received their *sucuklu pide* and invited the popular, unassuming doctor, Faik Abacı, to join them in demolishing the spicy sausage flatbreads. They'd have been in seventh heaven if Nebahat hadn't popped up with a chocolate drop cake like a jack-in-the-box, as was her wont.

She managed to ruin their meal anyway, whingeing that they were stinking the place out with their sucuk instead of her delicious chocolate cake.

Odd-Eyes Sipahi fetched up gasping for breath, bawling his eyes out, and yelling, *Lost me 'and! Lost me 'and!* – asking for help just as the doctor was tucking in. At the sight of the bright red shirt wrapped around the carpenter's hand, Faik said, *Hold on, I'll stitch it in no time at all,* stuffed the last morsel into his mouth, cleaned his hands with an alcohol wipe and stood up. The *Serves you right!* expression on Nebahat's face didn't escape Odd-Eyes Sipahi's notice; meanwhile, the tut-tutting orderlies asked how he'd slashed his hand. The handsome doctor led the carpenter back to his office, made him scream as he stitched the hand and sent him home with an analgaesic.

But his throbbing hand kept Odd-Eyes awake all night. His stash of dope had run out. The first thing he did in the morning was to cadge some here and there and get stoned; next, he accused the doctors of breaking the Hippocratic oath, which hung on the wall behind the information counter and which he couldn't help reading every time he came to the hospital; it ended, *that I will fulfil according to my ability and judgment this oath and this covenant,* which somehow sounded hugely impressive. Odd-Eyes was well high by now; he accused the neuropsychiatrist of vengefulness just because her cabinet was a little late and said she'd colluded with Dr Faik Abacı with the express purpose of causing him insufferable pain; he wasn't letting them get away with it, oh no; he was going to sue.

But the doctor wasn't having any of it, given how he'd stepped in even though it wasn't even his job, just to spare the carpenter more blood loss – which would have been certain if he'd had to schlep over to State Hospital instead. Pointing out that the hand had been properly anaesthetised, he explained that, if Odd-Eyes had not been a junkie, the local anaesthesia would have been perfectly effective; all the doctor had to do was inform the Medical Director, and the carpenter could wave goodbye to any future work from the hospital. Odd-Eyes shut up at once.

Faik would have merrily given him hell if the bloke had persisted. He was already well pissed off with Odd-Eyes for taking so long over the alterations to his new place overlooking the rocks where the wild Black

Sea waves crashed in a white foam. As a consequence, the Abacıs were still stuck in rented property and his bashful young wife, Gülümser, was niggling and nagging at a surprising level of cantankerousness.

The neuropsychiatrist Nebahat promptly filled the belated cabinet with a simple kettle, a jar of Turkish coffee and a few varieties of tea bags. In time, this paltry offering for hospital staff grew to a fully equipped tea-and-coffee cabinet with a teasmade reminiscent of a samovar, a couple of coffee makers (filter and Turkish), as well as a vast selection of teas (from green to orange-flavoured varieties) and coffees (decaf to espresso).

Her generosity wasn't restricted to hot drinks, either. She might have turned a deaf ear to the psychiatrist's recommendation to strengthen her morale, but the idea of a hobby had struck a chord. Thereafter she baked nearly every night, concocting a vast variety of cakes in the cramped kitchen of her flat in one of the most recent developments in town. The products were taken to work, at every opportunity hospital staff (Âlim Kâhkeci in particular) were invited to her office for a cuppa and a bite, and she personally carried her offerings to anyone who wouldn't come. Her visitors, whilst enjoying a delicious cup of coffee or tea and sampling those wonderful cakes that simply melted in the mouth, had to listen yet again to her interminable tale of betrayal, which after all these years the unstable lady doctor just couldn't stop talking about.

They wouldn't have minded quite so much if there were anything original about the tale. It was just one of thousands: a rat of a husband had upped and left his wife of fourteen years (who'd crammed two miscarriages and an ectopic pregnancy into that time) for someone he'd been having an affair with for five years. He'd married his mistress and was very happy. That was it. As might be expected, Nebahat was utterly blameless; it was all *his* fault.

The only interesting angle in this tale, which she believed unique, was that for five years no one had noticed that Kahraman was carrying on (and at the hospital too!) with a married mother of three. **Hercai Sekban, the hospital's accounting manager**, was thirty-four at the time she began having it off with Kahraman; she was nearly three stone overweight even then, and **her husband, the market police officer Şaban Sekban**, hadn't yet been promoted to deputy inspector.

The affair had started on the heels of Nebahat's ectopic pregnancy operation, when Kahraman complained that his life had become hell. Nebahat, who since they'd got married had never let even a single day pass without grumbling, was making mountains out of molehills again, ranting and raving day and night with the usual grumbles directed at his family, such as *Was it too much to expect your mum to make a bowl of soup for her sick daughter-in-law?* or *Your sister would've endangered her mortal soul, would she, if she'd stayed one night to look after me?*

Kahraman was chatting with Hercai in the hallway when he felt an overwhelming desire to rest his head on her vast, white bosom. And the moment he did – in Radiology, in one of those universally avoided radioactive rooms behind doors marked with the skull and bones – his life and outlook changed irreversibly. Each time they neatened up after a quickie (first thing in the morning, as the rest of the staff were still tucking into their muffins, or during their lunch break or even just before they clocked off), Hercai would giggle, *Quick as a flash!* and Kahraman harped on, *We can't go on meeting like this, Hercai; either we split up or you leave your husband.*

When they finally did ran away together, they saw no need to clear the decks first. Leaving behind a letter each, they zoomed off to Istanbul. Give her credit, though: Hercai had felt quite guilty, even shedding a few tears as she wrote *You see, Şaban, our love is gone, and there's no respect either, and anyways, I love someone else. Forgive me for the sake of the children…* etc. In contrast, Kahraman had made no effort to offer a long explanation or cite a cause or anything; it was enough to dash off *I've taken my personal belongings, you keep the rest. I'll file for divorce within the month. Don't make things difficult!*

Everything was ready for their life together. Kahraman had been going frequently to Istanbul on the pretext of attending congresses, seminars and what have you, interviewed with several hospitals, agreed terms with a small private institution in Zuhuratbaba, in Bakırköy, rented a two-storey house at Halkalı Houses and forked out to furnish their new home. The house had been expecting its new residents for days; it even had French windows that opened out to a wide lawn from the living room.

There was a general election in the offing, and since the Prime Minister was due to hold a rally in the town on Friday, the town council was on high alert. Şaban Sekban, who once couldn't say boo to a goose, had assumed a swagger since his promotion to deputy inspector – but there was a price. Work kept him away from home. On Thursday, Kahraman claimed he was moonlighting at a private hospital, pulled up behind the Nation Tea Garden and waited until the dead of the night. Once the townsfolk were asleep, he drove up to Hercai's door, where she, her daughter and two sons piled into the car, and they set off for Istanbul. The boot was stuffed with Hercai's and her children's belongings. Kahraman had packed only a small suitcase as if for a short break.

The accounting manager who ran away with the radiologist wasn't entirely sure who had fathered her youngest, her second son. She might not have made love to her husband that frequently, but there were a couple of quickies she could recall. Once she'd realised she was pregnant, she kept her thoughts to herself, and even insisted on naming the child after her mother-in-law if it was a girl. To be honest, Şaban wasn't over the moon at the news of a third child on the way. He'd been up to his eyes in work ever since his promotion, and never mind a decent session with his wife, their paths barely crossed. He couldn't quite remember when he last managed to do the deed, but chose not to dwell on it. So busy were his days that he'd forget what he had for supper the night before.

The next morning, Nebahat flew into a rage after reading the letter propped on the dining table. She had no idea whom Kahraman had run away with, which made her even madder. Apoplectic, she charged over to the hospital and announced what had happened. Strangely, the accounting manager's absence had gone unnoticed although it was close to noon. Hercai was in the habit of swanning in late, citing *the kids' school, the baby's doctor, this and that*. In the meanwhile, having taken jobsworthiness to another level entirely, Şaban had tormented his squad all night long with his insistence on inspecting every single restaurant, nightclub, bakery and patisserie in town – as if he hadn't showed off enough during the day – just because he was dying to shake the Prime Minister's hand.

Nebahat was having a fit at the hospital when the Prime Minister arrived in town. He held a pointless rally, sat down for a short while in the mayor's office, ate Black Sea pide with a veal sauté filling, washed it down with *ayran*, and took off without inspecting a single spot. The entourage was so large that, never mind shake the his hand, the Deputy Inspector of Market Police couldn't get anywhere near the PM.

It had been hours by the time Şaban realised his wife had run away, taking the children, all the gold, and everything of value that was portable. By the time he was reading the letter (more like a bucket of cold water), Kahraman and Hercai had already unpacked in their new home and were about to light the barbecue in their flower-filled garden to celebrate their new life.

Neither of the abandoned spouses knew whom their partners had run off with. One was in hysterics – *My husband's left me!* – as the other, in an effort to save his honour, was ringing his wife's family, pretending nothing was wrong and hoping to learn where she might have gone.

It eventually dawned on hospital staff that Hercai had been absent for three days running. Şaban, who couldn't bring himself to admit that his wife had run off, brushed away the queries of the accountants worried about their boss, which prompted the question *I wonder if those two have run off together?* A probability quickly discarded since no one considered Hercai (whose looks surely disqualified her in the femininity stakes?) and the strapping Kahraman a suitable match.

Nebahat seemed to twig, though; she scuttled off to her office, rang the town council, asked to be put through to Şaban and, once they established that his wife had run away at the same time as her husband, taking the kids and leaving a letter behind, they got the picture.

She managed to wind him up during that call. The poor husband had no recourse but to scramble over to the hospital. As he swore at the top of his voice, *Fuck my mother if I don't bump off the pair o' them with a bullet right in the forehead!* the neuropsychiatrist – now well and truly off her rocker – was egging him on, *Yes, bump'em off, yes, yes!*, jawbones clicking non-stop.

Unable to stomach the fact that Hercai had run off with someone else, and with the children too (rather than the fact that she'd just run away, full stop), Şaban's rage seemed to seethe for a time. He kicked chairs, upended a table and punched the walls. In the end, he sobbed on the neck of the young **Psychiatrist Aydemir Güzeldere** in the Medical Director's office as the latter skimmed through regulations for clues on what procedures he could use against the doctor and the accounting manager, who had behaved so inappropriately with regard to their standing as civil servants. Appalled at such unaccustomed physical contact, Aydemir tried to unlock the arms of the Deputy Inspector of the Market Police, his eyes locked with those of his cousin, the Medical Director. At the silent *Go on, console him; so what?* in his cousin's eyes, Aydemir patted Şaban on the back.

Aydemir was second cousin to Sevim, the Medical Director's wife. Intending to pursue an academic career in alcohol and substance abuse, he had stopped by to show the Medical Director his latest paper. He felt really sorry for Şaban, who was sobbing and yelling, *I'll either shoot them or myself! No two ways about it, none!* and at long last managed to calm the poor fellow down and talk him out of doing something crazy.

That's how Şaban Sekban became Aydemir's patient. The psychiatrist who'd been set on a specialisation found himself as a practising therapist. Şaban's mental state offered Aydemir years of close observation, which would prove very useful. As it turned out, this did them both good; at the very least, it prevented suicide or murder. Despite his lack of experience, Aydemir took to therapy like a duck to water and abandoned the idea of an academic career.

The affair of the radiologist and the accounting manager who vanished into thin air kept tongues wagging in the town for months. In the meanwhile, Kahraman retained a tough lawyer and filed for divorce, giving a fictitious address. Nebahat's attempts to contest the petition failed. On the day the decree absolute was granted, she indulged in her most spectacular nervous breakdown yet, one of many that would later become routine. She rolled on the floor twitching in a quasi-epileptic fit, fell in a faint into the arms of the **dinner lady Hacer**, banged her head against the walls… It was quite a performance. Which is how she elicited genuine universal sympathy for her and condemnation for Kahraman.

Herself a victim of desertion and thus unable to stop herself from identifying with *any woman thrown over for another*, Hacer decided to keep Nebahat company on her first night as a divorced woman. Hacer – who referred to her ex-husband as *Man* – might spend her life in institutional kitchens chopping onions, peeling potatoes, washing gigantic cauldrons and scrubbing trays, but she was still pretty, still attractive, and truly feminine – and she knew it. So she dived in straightaway: beauty. It wasn't just that she'd been dumped, she'd been thrown over for someone uglier. Within minutes of arriving at the freshly divorced Nebahat's flat, she seemed to forget completely about the doctor's need for consolation and, in graphic detail and colourful language, launched into her own tale. Her bloke had *left for a scrawny minger, swarthy too* – to be honest, she had mentioned him at least once daily for the past twenty years. She was so cut up over losing to a scrawny, swarthy plug-ugly tart that she never give Nebahat a chance to open her mouth – never mind offer a sympathetic ear.

May your beard be soaped on the morgue table, man! And may centipedes eat your bollocks, man! Hacer cursed as if he were there, cadged half of Nebahat's new pack of Winstons, blew smoke out of her nostrils like a chimney and thoroughly put her hostess off smoking. Nebahat found neither peace nor consolation that night; but she did give up smoking once and for all.

The neuropsychiatrist noticed that she felt better so long as the tale of how badly she'd been wronged stayed on the agenda. The moment it looked like it was cooling down, she brought her husband's debauchery back onto the front burner with a new fit of hysterics, and wouldn't let the staff forget the event that had ruined her life. For the first two years she didn't have a shadow of a doubt that one day, a desperately remorseful and unhappy Kahraman would throw himself back at her feet. In time, though, those hopes faded, dwindled, and eventually vanished. Lacking all self-control, she gradually broke down altogether.

There had to be something else behind it, she thought, especially since the hospital staff viewed the lovers as such an unlikely match. Yet this seemingly incongruous couple were happy. They read each other like a book. Hercai never nagged, for a start, and she loved having fun besides. She never let anything trouble her, and never stifled Kahraman, making sure instead that he had a good time. Kahraman's inheritance from his father (who died of a cerebral haemorrhage after dropping a barbell on his own head – weightlifting at his age!) allowed them to purchase, redecorate and refurbish the two-storey house they'd originally rented and to send the children to private schools. After the birth of a fourth child (definitely Kahraman's this time) Hercai left her job at the paint factory, which was being repeatedly fined by the Environment Directorate for polluting the Ayamama Stream, and dedicated herself to her children and husband. Kahraman adored his upbeat, merry, light-hearted wife and all their children, whether step- or his own.

Şaban may have lost face, but he did save his mental health thanks to Aydemir Güzeldere's kindly, helpful therapy; so despite Nebahat's relentless taunts, he not only refused to contest Hercai's petition for divorce, but also wished her happiness and agreed to give up custody of the children provided he could see them frequently. He resigned his new position at the town council, which he considered beneath him, having been put out to grass at the Parks and Gardens Directorate by the new mayor after the elections, found a job at the glue factory and accepted his wife's new life.

Now a weekly regular at his therapist's, the idea of marrying again never crossed his mind. He stayed with the İnals in Istanbul for a fortnight every summer so he could spend time with his children to his heart's content. None of them seemed bothered by this unconventional situation. Şaban was treated like an old friend, even a visiting brother, rather than Kahraman's wife's former husband. Every night Kahraman came home from work, arms laden with food, and lit the barbecue in the garden to look after the father of two (possibly three) of the children that he had taken to his bosom as his own.

Hercai couldn't even imagine that she was once married to this polite guest who bent over backwards to avoid troubling his hosts. The eldest of the three children called Şaban *Dad*; her youngest – a girl, as it happens – sometimes called him *Uncle*, and sometimes *Dad*, which made them all laugh. The woman, her ex-husband, her new husband, and the children made up a family of sorts, gallivanting about Istanbul for a fortnight, at the end of which time Kahraman drove his wife's ex-husband to the coach station and sent him on his way with a hug and a kiss. It got so bizarre at Şaban's latest visit that when the radiologist proposed going to a holiday village together the following year, Hercai clapped her hands in approval.

The İnals were happy enough, but Şaban had been a little down in the dumps of late – in fact ever since Aydemir Güzeldere resigned his post at the hospital and opened a surgery in Istanbul. On the Medical Director's recommendation, Şaban was now seeing **Psychotherapist Gamze Berberoğlu**, whose surgery, rather unfortunately, was in the busiest part of town. Scared of being seen going to a *crazy doctor* (a fact he'd been hiding from his friends all these years), Şaban had taken up window shopping before his appointments, ostensibly to explain why he was in the area – a pointless, not to mention enervating effort, it turned out. It was no secret that the former Deputy Inspector of Market Police went to a *crazy doctor*, not that anyone gave two hoots. The sad reality was that no one did.

At first Gamze couldn't figure out what Şaban's problem was. A few sessions later, she decided it wasn't due to a serious mental issue; he was simply addicted to therapy. She wasn't best pleased. She held no truck with people who were their own worst enemies and so sought therapy. She was on the verge of palming him off on another colleague when she heard of Şaban's holidays with his ex-wife and her new family, and in their home no less; all at once, this dull patient presented a far more fascinating case.

She probed him with questions along the lines of *Was it your choice to go to them, rather than have your children come to you?* Şaban cringed, *I mean… There's no choice nor nothing here…* He wasn't such an arse; of course he'd stayed in a hotel the first time. But the moment his Kahraman Abi realised that Şaban wasn't happy in that cheap and nasty place, he'd said, *C'mon, stay here with us; it's no trouble!* The offer was readily accepted. At the doctor's astonished gaze, Şaban added, *Not like there's nothin' untoward or anythin'…*

She was barking up the wrong tree. Kahraman had twigged straightaway how harmless the lonely wretch was, taken pity on the bloke he'd deprived of a family, and so feigned a degree of hospitality to alleviate his twinge of conscience. But within half an hour he'd grown genuinely fond of Şaban.

It had been at a *kebab* restaurant on the Bakırköy shore. Hercai was dishing out the salad, and it was Şaban's turn. The gesture elicited such a meek *Thanks, sister…* to his former wife of nine years that Kahraman's heart broke. Şaban's helpless acceptance of his new status plagued Kahraman for the rest of the day. Not like the bloke was exactly well off either; Kahraman discussed it with his wife, and they agreed, *Of course! He might as well save himself the hotel costs so he can have spending money…* That was how Şaban moved from father to uncle in the eyes of his children, a far more comfortable position for him.

He also knew that his family and friends wouldn't take kindly to this friendship with his ex-wife's new husband, so he kept shtum and asked the doctor to keep it between the two of them. Gamze may have sympathised to a degree with Şaban, in view of his natural desire to see his children, but Kahraman's condition she decided was grave. What kind of husband would give such a warm welcome to his wife's ex? She churned out theory after theory, querying their validity, but the psychological reasons she'd suspected of underpinning this weird relationship kept eluding her. All the same, she couldn't resist the temptation to stress that this situation was a bit much in light of the recommendations on how to maintain civil relations with the new families of former spouses.

Such civility was a bit too much, a bit too little, he should form a different relationship with his children, otherwise they'd never accept him as their father, etc., etc., etc... Şaban didn't care a fig. Thanks to this excessive civility, he didn't have to spend money to see his children, his Kahraman Abi treated him really well, and that was all he needed. When Gamze tried to throw a spanner into works that had been running like clockwork, he dropped her. On a New Year's break when he was again visiting Istanbul on his Kahraman Abi's invitation – his mate had even wired him the coach fare, and the crazy cow had the gall to say, *Don't see him!* Still eternally grateful to his former therapist, Şaban looked up Aydemir Güzeldere, in vain, as it turned out. Having cut his teeth on Şaban, Aydemir had joined the ranks of the most celebrated psychiatrists in Istanbul, prospered thanks to hourly fees in goodness knew how many dollars, and was just then celebrating New Year's Eve abroad. The haughty secretary nearly tipped Şaban into a breakdown. Thankfully, however, he received a great job offer upon his return. Leaving the security hut at the glue factory, he settled into the administration manager's chair at the sulphuric acid plant, a position that flattered him considerably.

Whilst the former Deputy Inspector of Market Police was regaining his mental health thanks to the ministrations of his therapist Aydemir, Nebahat, who'd shared his fate, completely lost hers.

Having blown out of all proportion the incident that had resulted in the fracture of her little toe, and discovering how much she enjoyed playing the victim, Nebahat hobbled around, quite unnecessarily, on crutches for a whole month, after which time she adopted slippers on the pretext of her bandaged foot. Once she realised that she really liked how roomy slippers were, how comfortable, and how easy it was to fling them off the feet whenever she had a mind to, she took to wearing them around the hospital all the time. This had a major benefit on the staff. At the first sound of those shuffling slippers they would all sneak off, thereby sparing themselves her endless tales of woe.

Not satisfied with her role as victim in the sock suspenders incident, Nebahat also demanded an official enquiry into caretaker Ziya, on grounds of him failing to clean the stage properly and thereby causing her injury; to this end, she had gone to the Medical Director in a hissy (and very tearful) fit, *Punish him!* Whilst her ludicrous insistence did have the potential to make a scapegoat out of Ziya, the perfunctory enquiry into his dereliction of duty was inconclusive. She tried to appeal, but the Medical Director, whose patience had finally snapped after all these years, tore her off a strip and the matter was closed. Earless Ziya carried on as before, scratching the scar tissue where his ear once was.

Ziya had lost his *pinna* (external ear, to the layman) at the age of twelve or thirteen, when he lived in a village perched on a steep slope. Once, on a scramble uphill to reach the wild beehives, he'd slipped on a loose, mossy stone and plummeted to the stream fifteen feet below as rocks and bushes tore at his left ear. Bleeding profusely, he was taken to State Hospital, where the **Istanbul-born surgeon Hilmi Ziya Ötüken** – a lifelong moaner *(I'm wasted here, I don't deserve to be rotting in this place!)* – regretfully informed little Ziya's mother that it was impossible to reconstruct the shredded pinna waving like ribbons, and proceeded to amputate his little namesake's external ear.

The tired and lonely surgeon (a bachelor who refused to even look for a wife) regularly sank into a bout of *Blast this fate!* depression whenever he had to undertake such irreversible procedures. He blamed their frequency on the chronic shortages of equipment, materials and drugs in a hospital that, despite its massive *State Hospital* sign at the door, was permanently neglected by the state, its demands always declined with or without explanation. But there were several rumours concerning his recurrent attacks of depression and his operations. Whilst the charitable view blamed his depression on his inability to save otherwise viable organs due to the lack of materials and medical supplies, the cynics claimed that the surgeon was amputating yet another arm, leg or pinna precisely because he'd slumped into depression again, and that most of these organs could have been saved.

As a matter of fact, despite their apparent contradiction, both views had a degree of truth in them – like the chicken-and-egg conundrum. Hilmi Ziya was actually one of those obsessives who were destined to be unhappy to their dying day, needing only the flimsiest of excuses to sink into depression. But never had he lopped off a single viable organ, nor deliberately harmed a patient. What triggered his breakdowns was the inevitability of cutting off a gangrenous arm or a thrombophlebitic leg using instruments long past their best-before date in a country that denied its people a viable solution, cure or medication. Those were the years of hardship, inadequate funding, import restrictions and shortages of medical supplies: never mind restocking, even keeping the hospital warm in winter was a challenge. This was the environment in which the two opposing views battled constantly and pointlessly, since Hilmi Ziya's nervous breakdowns defied any diagnosis. The poor chap did his utmost to cope with life's ups and downs, and slumped into the arms of melancholia each time he divested a patient of an organ.

At such times he would curse fate, rant and rave, get signed off for a few days, withdraw home, mope in pyjamas, hardly eat or drink (and rapidly lose weight) and listen from morning till night to the same old Seçil Heper single on the portable record player – never mind that the entire world had moved on to tape decks and cassettes: *Bouquet of light, smile so spring bemoans its fate / You are another light, another dream, another time.*

The sentimental lyrics, which for him contained a pun (since his name meant *light*), illuminated the thwarted Hilmi Ziya, he thought, absolutely convinced that he'd have turned out to be *another light*, a different Ziya, if only fortune had smiled upon him… But life had begrudged him even the tiniest happiness.

In a fresh bout of depression after removing little Ziya's pinna, Hilmi Ziya had fetched up once again at the door of **Neurologist Adnan Çolakoğlu**, no less a pessimist than himself. Adnan would much rather *sign him off and be done with it!* subscribing as he did to the *Nothing ever changes* school. Certainly not in the health service at any rate. Consequently, he would sign off any colleague without question. He held no opinion one way or the other on the surgeon (who had long since fallen out with his own lot). Whenever Hilmi Ziya turned up, Adnan would send him home for a rest without giving the chap a chance to whinge. So with a signature quick as a flash, the mournful surgeon – who'd topped his class at Cerrahpaşa Medical School, but was now languishing in late middle age at the state hospital of a provincial city, having singularly failed to live up to his own former great expectations – was sent home for ten days.

Hilmi Ziya Ötüken bemoaned the family misfortune that had dogged him all his life: **Kalemkâri Beardless Kasım Pasha**, his great-great-grandfather on his mother's side, was an illustrious statesman under Sultan Abdülaziz, no less. This master of the fine art of *kalemişi*, or decorative painting (hence the appellation *Kalemkâri*), had the smooth cheeks and scant moustache typical of a hormonal deficiency (thus *Beardless*). His fiery gaze, powerful broad shoulders and stentorian tones amply compensated for the gentle, mirror-smooth face; he had a fearsome presence that commanded respect. His single greatest characteristic, however, was staunch loyalty. To the extent that when his beloved emperor was deposed and a few days later found dead with his wrists slashed, the devoted pasha mourned in the palace for a week without eating a single morsel, thereby dropping fifteen pounds; after reciting the entire Koran and praying for his emperor's soul on the seventh day, he returned home to a household that barely recognised him.

Beardless Kasım – as he was known at the time, the overthrow of Abdülaziz having predated his passion for *kalemişi* – led the contingent that embraced the conspiracy theory that his beloved sultan had been assassinated by wrestlers to prevent a fight for the throne. Thankfully, he was intelligent enough to figure out that speaking his mind, especially in this part of the world, was not the most advisable course of action.

Hurriedly burying his pain deep in his heart, he offered allegiance to his new emperor and continued to ascend the steps of imperial favour.

Kasım lived in a resplendent timber mansion; the painted decorations in the men's quarters had impressed so many that he willingly laid aside his sombre statesman's hat to adorn the interiors of his nearest and dearest in similar fashion. And during his tenure in Budapest, the vaults and ceilings of the ambassador's residence also received their share of this artistic attention.

Kalemkâri Beardless Kasım, acclaimed for his personal charity to others (regardless of language, faith or sex), especially on the Pest side of this city divided by the Danube, and so remembered with great affection for many years after his death, shot himself in the heart with his service pistol in a famous spa hotel dating from the 14th century. The suicide, occurring a mere week before the end of his term, came as a profound shock to both his family and the Foreign Ministry.

Official sources remained mute on the reason; reports (unfounded or otherwise) did, however, reach his family through official/unofficial channels. This family consisted of Kasım's five daughters by previous wives, five sons-in-law, and his **fortune-hunting third wife, Hürmüz**, whose capricious refusal to accompany her husband to Budapest backfired on her when she was left to stew in her own juice in the finely decorated mansion, attended by her husband's faithful servants, who couldn't stand her. Kalemkâri Kasım Pasha was alleged to have committed suicide out of love for a lady married to a prominent rich Hungarian. There was a degree of truth in these rumours. The pasha had indeed shot himself for love. But it wasn't the love of a Hungarian woman that sent him to his death, but rather, his obsession with **golden-haired Zoltan**, a seventeen-year-old lad with legs as white and smooth as alabaster.

Until his arrival unfamiliar with Budapest's wealth of spas, the fastidious pasha had been fretting over the prospect of missing his favourite Tiled Hamam, accustomed as he was since childhood to going to a Turkish bath three times a week – one of which always fell on a Friday. Not only was he pleasantly surprised by the finest of baths in this Central European city, but he also lost his heart to the golden-haired Zoltan. They fell head over heels in love. Or rather, the pasha did. As for Zoltan, more pulchritudinous than the comeliest belle: he shared Kasım's jaw-dropping generosity with his own boyfriend, the **blacksmith Sandor**, who prudently kept out of sight.

Immediately appointed by the spa manager to serve Kasım, Zoltan would wrap his charge in towels after each bath, lead him up to his room and help him stretch out on the vast eiderdown bed for a session of scented oil massage of this powerful body that exuded masculinity, lack of facial hair notwithstanding; after a sleepless night with his pasha, Zoltan would then return to the bosom of Sandor, he of the darling ginger moustaches.

The lad, since the age of seven, had been no stranger to lascivious interest. But no amount of ardent declarations could tempt him away from that morbid passion for Sandor, which was nothing less than a slave's unconditional devotion to his master. He had been at this coarse black-smith's beck and call for the past three years. Sandor, though, was no different from a useless husband. To be fair, the handsome blacksmith – with his iron biceps, tempered by all that hammering, peeking a *Hello!* from under his sleeves and his ginger moustaches, on which the sun's rays danced – he, too, was madly in love with Zoltan, and desperately possessive to boot. Except he never missed a single opportunity to hurt Zoltan or bring him to tears.

The course of their love never did run smooth. Sandor loved to make a scene, at times just to verify that his power on Zoltan was as strong as ever, and at others, out of sheer jealousy; he adored wounding his boyfriend, cutting him down to size, making him cry, and even, unable to stop himself, giving him six of the best with his belt. Zoltan didn't object. If he had, he'd have said yes to one of his countless suitors in high places and, the moment he did, Sandor would have rued the day he was born. The fact was that, as much as Sandor enjoyed hurting Zoltan, Zoltan adored how the conscience-stricken Sandor would torment himself after each of these crises – the passionate embrace, the kisses covering his damp eyelids and the rough and lusty lovemaking that ensued. In short, Zoltan adored every moment of this intense passion.

It had taken a good deal of convincing Sandor that Zoltan's relationship with the pasha was part of the job. Austrian on his mother's side, Sandor had grown up with tales of Ottoman horrors handed down from one generation to the next; he couldn't stand hearing the pasha's name, which is what caused their biggest row. Zoltan's tearful (with real tears for once, not flirtatious dewdrops) question *Who could possibly refuse a genuine Ottoman pasha?* elicited a stream of invective aimed at seven generations of the pasha's antecedents.

Each time, however, ruffled feathers were smoothed by what Zoltan brought back from the hotel: purses of gold bringing the dream of a stud farm in Bohemia ever closer to reality. In time, Sandor learnt not to care about his boyfriend's relationship with the pasha.

But whilst Zoltan made no secret of his attraction to Kasım – who was a considerate lover, both romantically and physically – and frequently intimated his delight in the pasha's sweet smell and broken Hungarian, he wasn't in love. Sadly, Kasım thought otherwise whenever he ran his graceful hands over the younger man's shoulder blades, mistakenly attributing the lad's shivers to love.

All hell broke loose when the time came for Kasım to return. Zoltan, who, every time they retired to the room after Kasım's bath, was forced to dress up like a Hungarian woman and then undress – from stockings to petticoats – was pestered to go to Istanbul. He had come to loathe these tulle-and-velvet fantasies and the cloying love that was no longer so gentle, and had absolutely no intention of dumping Sandor in favour of being locked up in some Istanbul mansion.

There was a storm that night. Thick clouds obscured the full moon. A ferocious rain lashed the deserted streets of Budapest, and the wind banged together such shutters as were left open. Kasım and Zoltan were in the largest and most luxurious suite of the hotel. As far as the youngster was concerned, the relationship had got completely out of hand. He wore a heavy, gold-embroidered maroon velvet dress and a wide-brimmed hat in old rose with a net veil. His plan was to please Kasım one last night, pocket the purse of gold and run to Sandor, and then never go anywhere near this fellow again. Kasım, however, was babbling in broken Hungarian about a mansion, a skiff, a four-horse carriage and countless servants; Zoltan would be living in the lap of luxury. Drowned out by the roar of the storm, his booming voice failed to wake the sleeping hotel guests unwound by the hot, therapeutic waters.

Zoltan's refusal to go to Istanbul was what invited disaster. It was nearly morning. Kasım was relentless: in Hungarian he pleaded, in florid Ottoman he recited ardent couplets, in French he promised the sky and the stars along with all the jewels of the world, all that he was going to lay at Zoltan's feet, and in Turkish he waxed lyrical about the life that awaited in Istanbul; the only thing in this volley of words that the golden-haired youth with the cloud-coloured eyes picked up were the pleas in Hungarian.

Zoltan wanted to leave, but the door was blocked by Kasım's burly figure, which threw itself at the exquisite ladies' heels – yet another present. Hopping away, the youth was desperate to free his feet and convince his benefactor that the affair was over. At last he said he had a boyfriend. Kasım paused briefly, then suddenly reached for his pistol. Zoltan was petrified. Abandoning all hope in his elementary Hungarian and fluent French, the pasha stared him in the eye and uttered in Turkish, *I'll kill myself if you go!* Although in the two years they'd spent together Zoltan had taught the pasha a little Hungarian, he himself hadn't picked up a word of Turkish. Seeing the gun, he thought Kasım was about to kill him and so threw open the door and bolted out as the gun fired.

He was still wearing the maroon velvet dress, his face veiled by two layers of netting when he reached the street, still terrified for his life. The rain was hammering down now; the wet netting stuck to his face and the heavy velvet was weighing him down. He ran in a lurching hop until he finally paused in a dark, filthy street to kick off the remaining shoe; then in bare feet he resumed his run. He was scared shitless. Scared of being blamed for shooting the pasha, worried about the notorious dungeons of Budapest, which he'd never seen, sure that his delicate body would never survive even a week in those mouldy cells. He vanished into the dark streets, desperate to snuggle into the ginger thatch on Sandor's warm chest and cry in his arms until he forgot this horrific night.

He needn't have been so terrified and worried. No one suspected him. A few guests who heard the gunshot despite the raging storm had noticed an elegant lady in a maroon dress hopping down the hallway, but no one had followed that figure since no one knew quite what had taken place. Hotel staff entered the room to find the pasha lying in a pool of blood, gun in his hand, index finger still gripping the trigger; by his head lay a ladies' shoe.

It was new and expensive. It resembled those favoured by the wife of a Hungarian merchant who had frequently entertained the pasha at his home: **the lovely Helen was evidently infatuated** with the charming, haughty diplomat. Despite the more conventional clothes left behind by Zoltan, the consensus of opinion attributed the pasha's death to a passionate affair with the owner of those full lips that beckoned like ripe fruit on her porcelain-white face. Thus was born the rumour of the pasha's hopeless love for a married Hungarian lady.

Kasım's young wife, Hürmüz, went practically berserk at losing her husband before she'd managed to fall pregnant. Entering widowhood without so much as a male child to assure her status had shattered all her dreams. She had earlier advanced one flimsy objection after another, hoping her husband would ply her with a yalı, a mansion or, at the very least, some magnificent jewellery to coax her to accompany him to Buda-pest. Up to his ears in state affairs, however, he didn't even have time to scratch his own head, never mind talk to his wife face to face, so when she received his terse, *Tell her to suit herself*, she'd realised that, A., retreat would cause her a tremendous loss of face, and, B., he wasn't so easy to twist around her little finger after all. Regretting her confidence in her youth, beauty and feminine wiles, Hürmüz had been fervently awaiting her hus-band's return, impatient to bear him a son so she could attain the rank of *valide* – mother – thereby cutting her arrogant step-daughters down to size.

Now, with her hopes dashed to the ground yet determined to secure her future, she was not going to let propriety to stand in her way. Imme-diately after the funeral, she sat down to a bellowing negotiation with the pasha's ageing sons-in-law in the antechamber between the harem and the male visitors' quarters. The louder she screeched, the worse her voice cracked, echoing in the finely painted ceilings of the mansion; her shameless words, reaching the harem on one side and the men's quarters on the other, made the pasha's relatives and friends blush to their ears. The mansion was brimming with visitors who had come to offer their condolences. The grieving daughters, sons-in-law and grandchildren were shocked by this wicked stepmother's attitude, this bottomless pit of avarice demanding the yalı for starters, as well as enough property and money to feed not only herself but seven generations to come and threatening the dignified, high-ranking sons-in-law that she would reveal to all and sundry the truth behind the pasha's death, which had so far been described as the result of an *accidental bullet*. She didn't need to carry out this threat. The visitors sipping their coffee in silence heard her every word and so learnt about the pasha's suicide as well as the fictitious love affair… as did the whole of the Seat of the Empire before sunset.

The sons-in-law bit their tongues, restraining the urge to rip apart that fishwife mouth as she ranted and raved at the top of her voice, mollified her with promises of discussing the matter later, had their father-in-law's seventh day prayers recited at the Aksaray Valide Mosque, killed the fatted calf for their visitors, waved good-bye to their houseguests and promptly threw her out without a penny.

This being the last thing she'd have expected of the daughters and sons-in-law of such a venerable personage as Kalemkâri Beardless Kasım Pasha, Hürmüz was so badly caught off guard that all she could sneak into her bundle was a **portrait of Kalemkâri Beardless Kasım Pasha taken by the photographer Cosmi Sébah** along with a ruby ring that had belonged to her husband.

The wispy moustache in the portrait (which defied his beardlessness) had been artfully touched up to approximate a much more distinctive shape. Oblivious to the curse he left behind, the pasha's frowning image still exuded an intimidating air of authority. Hürmüz placed this charismatic portrait inside the illuminated hand-written Koran he had presented to her on their wedding night.

The family might well have been cursed after the suicide, which shook the Seat of the Empire to its core. First to go was the exquisite mansion that had escaped Hürmüz's clutches: it burnt to a cinder when the furnace for the bath collapsed during the 1894 earthquake. Then one of the sons-in-law was sent into exile on charges of political conspiracy and the family were plagued with ailments. Many years before Hilmi Ziya Ötüken's birth, his mother's maternal uncle and two aunts died one after the other. The children of some of his surviving relations were diagnosed with mental deficiency, diabetes and even manic-depressive psychosis. A diabetic cousin on his mother's side went blind; another committed suicide by jumping from the cliffs of Antalya. Family members incapable of looking after their finances were swindled by the pasha's loyal servants. His wealth had been squandered even before the victorious end of the War of Independence and the proclamation of the Republic.[2]

By the time Hilmi Ziya started school (his father begrudged him a single penny, having been divorced by Hilmi Ziya's mother, who defied convention by filing the petition), all that remained of that magnificent fortune was a poky little flat in a narrow four-storey block in Fatih Nişanca, a few properties that brought no income at all and a modest pension from his maternal grandfather, who'd received his civil service job thanks to the reputation of Kalemkâri Beardless Kasım Pasha.

The important American scholarship Hilmi Ziya won after his specialty training – and he'd felt the pinch every single day – convinced him that he had finally triumphed over the misfortune that had blighted his youth, that curse handed down on from one generation to the next. True, fate had shafted his family, but so far it had spared Hilmi Ziya. He might have been seriously short of money, but otherwise everything went swimmingly. Finishing medical school with high honours had been a doddle, and he'd just become engaged to a pretty and intelligent classmate.

Fate had not shafted him, quite the opposite: it might have blighted the whole family, but it had favoured him. Still, Hilmi Ziya liked living under a bane. He chose to believe that the curse lying in ambush for him finally revealed itself when he missed his flight to the US, which he and **his beautiful fiancée Nesteren** were due to take.

He'd just gone to Bursa to sell off the last remaining piece of family property for pocket money for their stay in the US – and thus save his blushes before Nesteren, who was used to spending money like it was going out of style, since her father had made a killing on the black market during the war.

The surprising news about the property had come far too late. The solicitor acting on behalf of a silk manufacturer who wanted to build a modern yarn factory on the land had been tracking down every one of the hundred-plus shareholders. Hilmi Ziya's mother was the last one. By the time the solicitor contacted her and explained the situation, the newly qualified doctor was three days away from flying to America.

Hilmi Ziya, who had been sinking into ever deeper self-pity as the day of departure loomed closer – *I'm so skint that in America I'll be mortified before my fiancée* – leapt for joy and charged off to Bursa. But the Land Registry procedures dragged on and on, with one hitch after another, and it took ages to close the sale. As if that wasn't enough, the rattling, long-bonneted coach broke down on the return journey. Stuck near Yalova with no alternative means of transport at that ungodly hour, he knew he would miss the flight.

The next day, just as he was hopping on yet another wreck for Istanbul, his fiancée, Nesteren, was pacing back and forth in her father's enormous flat opposite Teşvikiye Mosque; the oak parquet floor in the double-door reception room, glazed to a mirror shine, squeaked under her stomping. Her incessant *I'm not going anywhere without Hilmi Ziya!* only further enraged her father, who was thinking of all the money he'd shelled out on the airfare; her mother, eyes fixed on the clock, insisted, *If you don't, your ticket's burnt. Why don't you go? Hilmi Ziya will follow you later.*

A few hours before the scheduled departure, Nesteren finally allowed herself to be convinced. Her gigantic shiny leather suitcases were loaded onto her father's latest-model black Packard, and the beautiful fiancée caught her flight at the last moment. If only she hadn't. The aircraft plunged into the Atlantic. There were no survivors.

Hilmi Ziya's world came crashing down. His devastation was perfectly understandable. But instead of grieving to his heart's content and then taking comfort in the thought *Fortune favoured me, I was spared*, he embraced sackcloth and ashes. He was convinced that the family curse had finally shown its face, starting by taking away his sweetheart, his beautiful fiancée, his one and only Nesteren, whom he'd loved more than his own life. He had no idea how wrong he was. Fate was actually firmly on his side.

Nesteren had been one of God's fortunate creatures, blessed with both remarkable beauty and shedloads of intelligence. *Lucky bastard,* thought Hilmi Ziya's envious classmates, *to have pulled such a lovely, smart girl, a dead cert to be a highly successful doctor – and the daughter of a rich man to boot!* as they indulged in hopeless dreams of luring her away. If only they'd had the slightest idea of her ambition and wickedness (in addition to her beauty and intelligence), of how she enjoyed crushing and tormenting others, they would have pitied the poor chap instead.

Utterly devoid of compassion, Nesteren had had a capacity for harbouring endless grudges on the flimsiest of pretexts. She had also failed to identify a single worthy prospect until her final year at university. One day, chancing upon a conversation between the **Biochemistry Professor Zafer Uzunköprülü** (famed for his august lineage, being the grandson of an eminent Ottoman pasha) and Hilmi Ziya, her jaw dropped.

The professor lived in a seafront mansion commonly known as the Rabbit Yalı, after the few rabbits he raised in the garden; located in the finest spot in the prestigious Rumelihisarı neighbourhood, the place would swarm with his large family of some twenty souls whenever his children, nieces and nephews returned from their studies abroad. There this snooty aristocrat lived with countless servants – including a retired ninety-nine-year-old black woman, who, convinced that the Ottoman Empire was still a going concern, wanted to go to Çırağan Palace on every holiday and shout, *Long live my Padişah!*

The professor rarely admitted visitors to his office; only those deemed to possess superb manners and blue blood passed muster.

Nothing Nesteren did worked; none of the ruses she adopted to display her studied charm and intellectual brilliance elicited any attention from Zafer; but the moment she spotted Hilmi Ziya sitting opposite the snooty professor, one leg crossed over the other, the two men chatting merrily as equals, and smoking and drinking coffee to boot, she knew he was special. A short investigation revealed that her classmate – who, though she thought him a good student, had never really struck her as a prospect up to then – was the descendant of an important historical figure called Kalemkâri Köse Kasım Pasha. She set her sights on Hilmi Ziya that very instant; by marrying the grandson of a pasha, she would fill in the one gap in her family's credentials: aristocracy.

Had Hilmi Ziya Ötüken married Nesteren, he would never have enjoyed a day's peace: her insatiable wickedness would have left him without a single friend and made his life hell. He would have spent the rest of his days trying to free himself from this troublesome spouse. Fate had actually done him a great favour. But the obstinate young doctor refused to see that Nesteren – whose mind focused only on evil – had alienated even his closest friends, and chose instead to labour under naïve delusions.

Certain that his family's bane would never leave him, and despite the scholarship foundation's generous offer of an extended bereavement leave, he changed his mind about going to the US. In time, he lost his joy in life and gave up altogether. After years that passed by in a blur of incomprehensible pain and heartache, he found himself complaining of his fate in the state hospital of a Black Sea backwater. True, he did have to remove young Ziya's pinna, but the boy had received the best possible treatment and been spared the risk of infection. As Ziya wandered in the wards in clogs, waiting to be discharged from this place where flies swarmed and the squat toilets frequently overflowed, Hilmi Ziya had long since retreated to his home on sick leave.

Ziya kept the dressings over his ear for a time, hoping that by some miracle a new external ear would grow and replace the old one, but it didn't happen. When four or five months later the dressings, so soiled as to be indistinguishable from a scrap of thick leather, were finally removed – the village kids burst into shrill yells of *Earless! Eaaarleeessss!* And every time they did, Ziya's mother, **Crazy Three-Skirt Emine** (as a young girl, she'd been known simply as Crazy Emine; it was only when she began wearing three skirts after her marriage that the name took its final form) really did go crazy, grabbing a log, running after them, and beating to a pulp whomever she could catch. She cracked a few heads and broke one or two front teeth. But since she was crazy, no one dared to take her on; if they had, she'd have killed them, make no mistake.

Emine wasn't crazy at all; as a matter of fact, she was quite bright. Her reputation stemmed from the hiding she'd given **her own father, Ne'er-Do-Well Bolat**, with a glowing log she'd grabbed from the fireplace during supper. The villagers, who all detested the man, though they remembered **his Uncle Mamşırek** with great gratitude and affection, were shocked by this fifteen-year-old girl who'd trounced her mountain of a dad.

When she was beating him up, she had set fire to his moustache (curled daily with hazelnut oil) and greying hair, surprising even herself with the power of her rage. **His real name was Dzambolat**; he was only a year old when his mother, **Christian Alla**, brought him from Ossetia. Dzambolat eventually became just Bolat. The Ne'er-Do-Well part harked back to the time he'd left his dying mum alone in her bed to go to a friend's wedding, a three-day, three-night affair in a neighbouring county.

Whilst Ne'er-Do-Well Bolat was keeping rhythm on a piece of wood and dancing Caucasian numbers at the wedding, his Muslim uncle Mamşırek and the villagers were busy trying to get Christian Alla to bear testimony to Islam before she drew her last breath; they were desperate to see that the poor emaciated lady died a Muslim and thus be ensured a place in paradise. Alla had finally recited the shahada after a fashion, died and been laid to rest in the Muslim section by villagers, who were confident they were doing the right thing, when Bolat blew in, knackered, on a steaming, frothing bay horse, his toes torn to shreds from all that dancing. The first thing he did upon hearing of his mum's death was to visit the fresh grave to dupe blazing-eyed Uncle Mamşırek and his other relatives, playacting as he bawled, *Sod the wedding, I wish I'd broken my leg and stayed! Would I have gone if I'd known mum would die?* Then he set about looking for the gold coins Alla had hidden from him as if her life had depended upon it.

Bolat's family had come from Tli, a verdant, fertile Ossetian village on the banks of the Gizeldon, in late 1914 or early 1915, during Enver Pasha's infamous and lamentable Battle of Sarıkamış. The family belonged to one of a handful of Muslim clans in the mainly Christian country. **Mamşırek's wife, Agunde**, was Christian, as was Alla. Agunde had fallen for Mamşırek way back when and embraced Islam immediately after the wedding.

Bolat had grown up an orphan. His father **Elbeg, a local celebrity famous for his skill in playing the *fanduri***, a three-string Ossetian instrument, had died shortly before the migration: he'd ignored a splinter embedded under his nail as he was cutting wood in the forest; the wound became infected, his finger turned black and swelled up, then the blackness spread to his hand and arm, and eventually that mountain of a man died of blood poisoning, groaning in agony to his last breath.

Elbeg's fanduri rang with tunes fine enough to conquer any maiden's heart, Muslim or Christian; his charity and kindness won hearts every-where. It was after his death when Bolat's mum and uncle left their home village along with other villagers. Why, Bolat neither knew nor wondered about. The only explanation Mamşırek ever offered was *bad blood*; by then he was thoroughly assimilated into his new village, a popular fellow, hardworking and honest. Those had been dark days, days of powerful antagonism from the Christian majority. Bad blood emanating from Ottoman battlefronts on all four corners of the land had wrenched them from their homeland, just another Muslim family amongst the thousands so displaced.

Alla strapped her only son Dzambolat onto her back, stowed away her gold coins, little knick-knacks and the icon *The Virgin Mary Holding the Infant Jesus* – in her horse's feedbag, at the bottom of the cheese sacks and in the secret pockets of her underdrawers – and joined her brother-in-law Mamşırek, sister-in-law Agunde, their three beautiful daughters **Satana**, **Balseg** and **Arverashugd**, all with silken hair and green eyes, and some Muslim neighbours from Tli, as they set off on the gruelling, months-long journey that brought them to this village, which welcomed them with open arms.

Once Mamşırek settled here, he altered his daughters' names as the brand-new republic issued every citizen with an identity certificate: they would henceforth be known as **Seten**, **Balkız** and **Asude**. Alla, on the other hand, insisted on calling her son – who was noted as *Bolat, Muslim* on his ID – Dzambolat until her dying breath. She never stopped dyeing eggs with onion skins at Easter or keeping Lent to coincide with Ramadan; she continued to tend her herd of sheep and goats, which had begun with just a small scattering and flourished over the years until it spread all the way to the steep slope rising behind the village.

The last time she fed her herd was the morning before Bolat dug his heels in, *I'm gonna go to the wedding, and that's that!* She had then collapsed, never to rise from her bed again.

Unlike her sweet-natured, but somewhat slow sister-in-law Agunde, the cheerful, charming and bright Alla had picked up Turkish almost immediately, yet she flatly refused to remarry or, despite Mamşırek's insistence, to convert to Islam. As a matter of fact, every night she knelt by her bed below *The Virgin Mary Holding the Infant Jesus*, reciting a long string of prayers before she turned in.

Her brother-in-law's persistence, however, did pay off eventually: grateful for his years of care and protection, Alla recited the testimony to faith with her last breath, upon which Mamşırek took down the icon, kissed it, touched it to his forehead and locked it in the drawer. It might have made a good memento for his nephew Bolat – until the villagers gave him the nickname *Ne'er-Do-Well* for having abandoned his mother on her deathbed and Mamşırek changed his mind. Indifferent to his mum's memory, the worthless lad never even thought to enquire about the icon.

If he had any idea of its true value – more than a handful of gold coins, as it happened – he'd have cried his eyes out, pleading with his uncle to hand over his mum's memento. The cinnabar icon was the work of a nineteenth-century artist from Tbilisi, who spurned portrait commissions from the aristocracy, thereby sentencing himself to a life of toil and tears: the **Georgian painter Guram Chaliashvili remained relatively obscure**, so much so that Russian art encyclopaedias mistakenly spelt his surname Dzhugashvili, after Josef Stalin's real surname – an erratum that implied he was a cousin of Stalin's grandfather. But the only thing of value that mattered to Bolat was the clink of gold coins.

Seten, Mamşırek's eldest daughter, adored the Virgin Mary. True, she was the daughter of a Muslim father, but her body was not indifferent to the awesome power of her mother's Christian blood and her eyes welled whenever she gazed at this holy mother cradling the baby Jesus. This was due as much to the love of Mary in her heart as the harmonious colour scheme of the dazzling icon.

Mamşırek gave the icon to his daughter on the occasion of her marriage to the **stuttering Hafız Süleyman**, who sold agricultural supplies, such as chicken feed and blue vitriol, and recited the Koran in a sweet voice during the ceremonies of the notables where he lived, a full five hours' drive from Seten's village.

The icon then passed to Seten's daughter, **Henna Meryem**, as devout a Muslim as her mother wasn't and unwilling to entertain the notion that she too carried her grandmother's Christian blood. Her father's reassurances that it was no sin for women's hands and feet to be visible fell on deaf ears: Meryem not only covered up as thoroughly as possible but also applied the deepest, darkest henna on her hands and feet, to above her wrists and ankles. Nor did she share Seten's devotion to Mary, her own namesake; she ignored her father's assurances – *B-b-but ch-ch-child, M-m-mother M-m-Mary is h-h-holy in our r-r-religion t-t-too* – and placed the icon at the bottom of her hope chest, where she forgot about it.

Many years passed. Meryem's younger son, Ömer, heedless of the daily rod, just wouldn't stop drawing with pieces of charcoal on the walls. When he grew up, he won a place at the Mimar Sinan University Faculty of Fine Arts, Department of Painting. Meryem had a fit when she heard that her son would be drawing images at school and said, *I'll never give you my blessing if you go to this school.* But he didn't take a blind bit of notice and went off to study in Istanbul anyway.

There being two Ömer Çakırs in his year, he was given the name **Earring Ömer Çakır**, in reference to this audacious affectation at a time when such men were looked down on. Ömer soon recognised his own lack of talent. Resigned to the knowledge that he would never become a good painter, he turned to art as a business and instantly discovered the newly gentrifying Çukurcuma district and the potential presented by that section of society which adored the aesthetics of the past. Here he would make his fortune. He started working in an antique gallery whilst still at university, and soon learnt not only the answer to the question *What's an antique, and what is it good for?* but also *How do you schmooze with the rich?* It wasn't long before he was obsessed with opening an antique gallery that would one day be the darling of high society.

Since leaving for Istanbul, he had never until now set foot in the family home, but when he tore it apart – *I'm sure to find something for the shop in some nook or cranny* – he was hugely disappointed. His mother, who had moved to the town years before, had got rid of all her old stuff: copper pans were replaced first with aluminium, and then steel; lovely, engraved copper pitchers gave way to plastic thingamajigs, handwoven kilims to machine-made rugs, and cheap market rubbish had supplanted the fabulous mirrors with the hand-painted underglass frames.

Now a self-styled aesthete by virtue of a handful of university classes and a stint with an experienced antiques dealer, Ömer Çakır refused to lose heart. Touring the handful of mansions still left in the city and the mountain villages in the back of beyond, he knocked on doors one by one.

Whatever he could, starting with some of those carved wooden doors he'd knocked on, he gathered up for a song: cowbells, kerosene cookers, samovars with amber handles, wooden ceiling roses, cast-iron door locks, porcelain banister newel caps, cigarette cases, pocket watches, bath sheets, oil bottles, albums, old photographs, phonograph records, cloaks, velvet kaftans with gold embroidery, vintage wedding gowns, a vast variety of glass pitchers, goblets and used perfume phials… and filled his basement shop in a street where Çukurcuma met Galatasaray.

His mother, though she nearing seventy, still insisted on hennaing her hands and feet; if only he had thought of rifling through her hope chest, he'd have discovered the real treasure, and might have seized his chance to become an antiques dealer instead of the owner of a second-hand shop. Nothing suitable turned up in his old home for that junk shop he'd dressed up as an antiques gallery, not even a brooch; indifferent to the cheap Formica box that had replaced the magnificent carved rosewood hope chest with the beaten copper locks, he didn't even open the lid.

One day, during a thorough spring clean, Henna Meryem came across the long-forgotten icon. She became emotional, remembering her mum, who'd long since returned to dust, and had a bit of a cry and everything… But was there any reason to hang on to this Christian image? No. Yet it was too beautiful to chuck out. So she sold it to the **rag-and-bone man Zülfü**, who regularly passed down the street towards noon and gathered up whatever he could, scrap or still serviceable: broken TV sets, water heaters, old newspapers and copper wire.

Zülfü drove a hard bargain. He offered Meryem a melamine dining set for six, a wooden board brush, two washbowls, and, when she still wasn't convinced, even threw in thirty-six wooden clothes pegs; but once she dug her heels in *I want money!* he was left with no choice. The money she wrung out of him went to pay the first instalment on a steam iron for her granddaughter, still in primary school. It never occurred to her that by the time this granddaughter was old enough to get married, far more advanced models would be available.

This was around the time of the dissolution of the Soviet Union when the border crossing at Sarp was opened and passenger liners started criss-crossing the Black Sea. Russians flocked to every city in Turkey; the town in which the Mental Health Hospital stood, with its back to the sea, was no exception. The new visitors set up stands at the port to sell the stuff they'd brought: splinter-rich Russian cigarettes, tinned caviar well past the use-by date, bottles of vodka with labels worn out from all that schlepping, eau de cologne whose alcohol had long since evaporated, Matrushka dolls, stale chocolate tasting of margarine, Red Army caps, fur kalpaks, drill bits, military binoculars, Phillips-head screwdrivers, pincers and Zenit cameras (*a.k.a.* the Kalashnikov of cameras) along with an assortment of lenses.

As the stands sprawled out and a previously quiet section of the port mushroomed into an open market of sorts, Zülfü grabbed one for himself. The icon was placed on a purple velvet spread, next to Russian teapots, pans, enamelled buckets, old fountain pens, small boxes of indeterminate purpose and censers.

Journalist Berrak Armağan, who loathed her editors for insisting that she leave the Journalists' Union, an organisation on the brink of obsolescence and thus entering a vegetative state, was here to file a somewhat belated report on the unstoppable flow of former Soviet citizens, commonly referred to as Russians, who'd left an astoundingly vast land and crossed a sea they knew well to a shore they knew not at all – the dismal detritus of an empire manning temporary stalls, their faces brightening briefly as they chatted in their own tongue before clamming up again, a people who looked proud and doomed at the same time. But instead of talking to these people to probe the economic and social reasons that had driven them to this shore, she mooched around the open market all day long and shopped.

From these sad, tense vendors, who had sailed mostly from Black Sea towns like Sochi, Batumi and Odessa, in a few months picking up just enough Turkish to get by, she bought the following: eight hammer-and-sickle *CCCP* badges, one bronze medal of honour she was certain had been bestowed upon one of the Red Army's glorious soldiers, a shedload of Red Square, Kremlin, Lenin and Stalin postcards, a double long-playing album titled *Troika*, consisting of folk music from countries that had made up the former USSR (such as Tajikistan, Kyrgyzstan and Armenia), and another LP, this one a late-sixties recording of the Baku State Philharmonic Orchestra conducted by the famous Rostropovich before his fall from grace and the subsequent stripping of his citizenship for associating with the dissident writer Solzhenitsyn.

The total had come to less than the price of lunch in a nondescript tradesmen's restaurant nearby. The records were worn, the badges tarnished and the medal was nestled in a dusty box – and thousands more badges and dozens of medals still languished on those stalls. She would never know the hands that had revered these decorations, the chests they'd been pinned upon, or the hopes they had raised, these articles crushed by the most painful devaluation of all. Something had happened in the fabric of time, something had thundered out of the blue, history had been rent open, and a medal once worn with pride and honour on one side of the world during the Cold War was now worth less than a plate of fried cheese and a panful of anchovies in a neighbouring land.

That's enough melancholy for now, she thought, on the verge of leaving, her gaze caressing each and every article, until she noticed *The Virgin Mary Holding the Infant Jesus* on Zülfü's stand.

Since Meryem had proved to be such a tough haggler, the rag-and-bone man now had no intention of accepting anything less than his stated amount. But the icon had been lying there for days without attracting a single glance; he realised that floging an icon in a Muslim city was like trying to sell bacon there. Another buyer might take months to appear, he reasoned, and since the Istanbul journalist showed an interest… So he agreed to a quarter of his asking price and got rid of the icon, which had been taking up space anyway.

It was the time of *Excuse mes*, of *We were wrongs* for Turks, who, for decades had been inculcated in the virtues of self-sufficiency and prudence, of donning batik dresses and Bodrum sandals and sitting on pine furniture. The press was no longer the Fourth Estate, foreign investment was incentivised, and businesses with wild growth-rate targets tempted journalists with generous junkets – the same journalists who were aching to bury their venerated principles in order to keep up with the times – and a new generation of lifestyle magazine editors flooded the offices: young, leggy and beauty-obsessed.

Refusing to compromise her principles, Berrak eschewed these junkets and maintained her membership of the Union. At first, her editors tried to reward this ethical journalist. They sent her to Vienna to cover a conference of European social democrats. They also intimated subtly – too circumspect to say it out loud – that were she to leave the Union upon her return, promotion would follow – *Wherever Europe's social democrats were, Berrak would be there too!* – and she would travel around the globe as an esteemed reporter. But all their hints went over her naïve head. She would only twig once she'd been moved from foreign news to one feature after another.

After spending three days and nights with the European social democrats and filing detailed reports, Berrak set the fourth day aside for herself; after a few hours of discovering Vienna, a city big in stature but small in scale, she visited the Leopold Museum. As she was leaving, she shelled out for a beautiful Egon Schiele reproduction. She hung his nude *Self-Portrait* next to Guram Chaliashvili's devotional icon *The Virgin Mary Holding the Infant Jesus* in her living room crammed with pine furniture, cacti and knick-knacks of myriad types.

Schiele had depicted his own genitals in graphic detail, truncated his legs at the ankles, covered his face with an arm and painted the single visible eye red. The tremendous conflict between the intense sorrow that emanated from this emaciated body expressed in sharp, harsh lines and the holy mother holding God's plump son on her lap created a bizarre tension on Berrak's wall.

This tension weighed inordinately on **her live-in boyfriend and fellow journalist, Ferhat**. He objected to both works. Utterly devoid of any interest in religion or piety, his question *What's this arse-licking to Christians about anyway?* ignited a massive row whose topic soon moved away from the icon. He then trained his fury on the Schiele, exclaiming, *Call this art? You can see his bollocks an' all!*, and stormed out.

They soon made up. Ferhat came back to explain that his objection to the nude self-portrait was based on his concern for any relatives who might visit. On the other hand, his view about atheists hanging icons on their walls remained unchanged: this was nothing less than an affectation. In the end they came to an agreement, or rather, Ferhat won. The Schiele was removed and placed in a drawer, and the Virgin Mary was demoted to staring sadly from a corner of Berrak's desk instead of her earlier pride of place in the living room.

Fame had eluded Guram Chaliashvili, who had died immediately after finishing the icon for the church in the village of his birth in Georgia; the icon that then went to the pawnbroker instead of the church and was passed from hand to hand before reaching Alla, remained in Berrak's study for quite a while. Berrak and Ferhat, who had agreed to compromise on what they called *The Sacred and the Nude*, eventually split up. Since he had no intention to stop having flings with interns – *I mean, it's not like love or anything, was just a one night stand* – Ferhat was told to leave. But he didn't have the luxury of regret. Made redundant during a rationalisation drive marked by eye-watering solidarity amongst the news barons, Ferhat became editor-in-chief at a political magazine that had never dropped the Kurdish issue from its agenda. Up to his eyes in work, he had no time to cry over his ex.

Berrak, who'd immediately after his departure hung *The Sacred and the Nude* side by side, was rewarded for caving in and leaving the Journalists' Union of her own accord; her salary was doubled at once. The newspaper had lightened up considerably in the meanwhile; covering Europe's social democrats was no longer a priority. As if it were being published in a land of milk and honey with decent education and health services, instead of one whose political and economic situation was little better than chaotic, the newspaper now filled most of its pages with coverage of high flyers living it up. Berrak, quickly adjusting to the new order, started filing colourful interviews that supported the new lifestyle recommended by her paper.

One day she went to **antique dealer Haymon Yener's** new gallery in Nişantaşı's Bronze Street to interview him on the *Increasing numbers of auction houses*. Haymon's collection of icons, which she espied amongst his more valuable items (and which he was intending to put on the market presently), prompted her to mention the icon she'd bought from Zülfü – the remarkable grief in Mary's gaze and the angelic depiction of Jesus.

It was true; she really did find Mary sad and Jesus angelic. But her main reason for saying this was to avoid the disdainful scrutiny of the proprietor of this snooty, aristocratic gallery, where even the cheapest object on sale was priced at several times her salary, and to demonstrate her own intellectual and cultural credentials, that she was no bumpkin. Haymon, for his part, dreamt of being Turkey's top authority on icons;

unimpressed as he was by Berrak's vast command of terminology, he still wished to see *The Virgin Mary Holding the Infant Jesus*.

After receiving a raise in reward for abandoning her original principles, Berrak sold her unreliable 1982 champagne Murat 131, threw caution to the winds, joined the wild caravan of white-collar consumerism fuelled by bank loans of every imaginable type, and purchased a sky-blue Škoda. But the instalments, which she'd underestimated, proved hard to meet as the inflation monster kept gnawing at the doubled salary. The dealer's wish to see the icon was tempting. She'd had enough of *The Sacred and the Nude* hanging side by side, anyway, so the following day she returned and handed the icon to the master of his trade. Haymon's poker face concealed his delight. Obfuscating behind a plethora of convoluted sentences – *It's not particularly valuable. Leave it if you like; we'll sell it if anyone shows interest…* – he snapped it up for an amount that fell well short of Berrak's hopes.

The Virgin Mary Holding the Infant Jesus thus appeared in the inaugural auction at Haymon's new gallery. Ömer, whose aspirations had stalled at second-hand goods, saw it in the catalogue. It rang a bell, but he didn't dwell on it.

The icon of indeterminate provenance failed to raise any interest at the auction.

It languished in the gallery for years. Haymon showed it to experts and compared it to similar items in loads of catalogues: to no avail. Although he managed to figure out approximately when it was painted, he got no further on the identity of the artist. Eventually he gave up, and placed the *Artist unknown* item in a much less exclusive auction at a significantly reduced starting price.

Spotting it as she flicked through the catalogue looking for something for the esteemed spouse of the Medical Director, Bedia was instantly enchanted. This elite customer made enquiries, learnt that it was available, and took a taxi to the gallery. And since she was already there, she checked out the new items, sipped an unsweetened Turkish coffee, and spotted a painting by Refik Epikman – an Independent artist she particularly liked – which she also purchased before returning home.

Impressed by the icon's brushstrokes, which he found to be highly skilled, Haymon mused *Wish I hadn't sold it*. The icon that had left his inventory but not his mind must have been the work of a renowned artist. He was mistaken. *Georgian Painters of the 19th Century*, published recently in Tbilisi, devoted little more than a few lines to the biography of Guram Chaliashvili, dismissing him as one of the countless imitators of the world-famous painter Niko Pirosmanashvili. The icon might have had little in the way of artistic value, that much was true; but for Mamşırek, who never once considered its monetary value, it was his only memento of his brother's wife, the unfortunate Alla.

Ne'er-Do-Well Bolat hadn't even noticed that his uncle had stashed the icon away; all he could think about was the gold his mother must have hidden somewhere. He set upon the house that Alla had laboured to build in his uncle's garden, dismantled every single board, clawing at the corners of cupboards and rummaging inside wool mattresses. Carrying on at night so his uncle wouldn't suspect, he turned the house inside out, down to the last pinhole. But he found nothing. Not a single coin. In the end, he lost hope and decided that his mother must have spent the fortune he vaguely remembered from his childhood.

Greedy Bolat, an immoral reprobate in every sense of the word, was also a liar and partial to molesting minors. The village girls would complain only to Agunde, so as not to upset Uncle Mamşırek, but Agunde, who after years and years finally spoke Turkish, didn't dare pass these complaints on to her husband. Instead she pulled her nephew aside and merely admonished him, *Don't do it, Son; you'll get into trouble one day.* Later, however, it came to light that Bolat hadn't restricted himself to simple molestation.

With no sons of his own, Mamşırek loved Bolat, who was all he had left of Elbeg, his only brother, as if he were his own, never mind that the boy was a villain. That's why he never let his nephew go without a beating, and if that didn't work, he had no qualms about pressing his gun – lovingly disassembled and reassembled weekly – to Bolat's forehead. Bolat would have stood up to his uncle without thinking if only he could be sure that the gun held to his forehead wouldn't fire. What he did know was that if he ever really pissed off Mamşırek, who was famous for shot the feather of a bird on the wing in Tli, *his* brains would be scraped off the ground.

One day the gun was again pressed to Bolat's forehead. But this time Mamşırek's fury scared the bounder witless with the fear that the hand trembling with rage might squeeze the trigger by accident. Mamşırek said, *Marry the girl you've ruined!*

The girl in question was an **orphan named Suna**. She was only six when her parents had succumbed to an unknown disease within a week of each other; then, until the age of twelve, she lived with the skeletal **centenarian Sediye Hatun**. An ancient figure with blue eyes, Sediye never stood idle; with a staff permanently affixed to her hand, she wandered around barefoot both summer and winter, tending to her two cows, five sheep, countless chickens, beehives and a dog. Like a relic from antiquity, she rarely used cash, instead bartering milk, cheese and eggs for her daily needs. It's not that she didn't know the value of money; in fact, whatever she got for her wheels of cheese she converted into gold coins, which she carried on her person.

The orphan Suna lived in Sediye's hut, rising in the dark every God-given day to milk the cows, boil the milk, start the cheese and do the housework, all the time thinking that this living corpse would never die.

Sediye was something of a legend amongst the villagers for raising and marrying off several orphaned girls. Every once in a while one or another of them would come to visit. They got no affection or interest, nor any distress or discomfiture from her. She was neither good nor evil. All she did was live. Suna was fed well and looked after when she was ill. But Sediye never indulged the little girl, never said, *She's just a child, she's still young,* and never allowed her even a few minutes' slack.

When Sediye died, allegedly in her one hundred and seventh year, Suna was left all alone. Mamşırek and his silent wife, Agunde, now that their three daughters were married off, were just rattling around in the house; thinking it might cheer them up, they took in Suna, welcomed her, treated her like their own daughter, and made sure she could enjoy what little of her childhood she had left.

A few years later, however, they noticed that something was wrong. Suna's tears wouldn't stop and she was rubbing her belly all the time. A distinctly uneasy Agunde persuaded her to speak. Suna was pregnant with Bolat's child. Thus, Bolat was forced to marry Suna, terrified that his uncle's gun, pressed to his forehead, would go off.

Without blinking an eye, Uncle Mamşırek slaughtered seven sheep from his own flock to give his useless nephew a magnificent wedding, where he looked so happy it could have been his own son getting married, did Caucasian dances on tiptoe and threw knives at boards. For Suna, those three days would be the best time of her life.

Mamşırek survived his sister-in-law by many years. He carried on looking after the herd Alla had worked her fingers to the bone to raise, and never hesitated to threaten Bolat with his gun, as needed. By the time his uncle died, Bolat was a family man, the father of three daughters, of whom the eldest was Emine (later mother to the boy who would grow up to be Earless Ziya). But Bolat was still the same useless old bastard.

One day the hole in the garden that served as the toilet overflowed, indicating it was time to dig a new one in another spot. Bolat was busy giving an earful to the workman, who was drenched in sweat. The hole wasn't even half a metre deep when the pickaxe smashed the earthenware jar Alla had buried years earlier, and the gold coins came to light. At first, the treasure caused great excitement in the village, but the lack of any real fortune soon quashed it. The jar was stuffed with heaps of worthless baubles poor Alla had mistaken for precious items and only a few gold coins, enough to fill a small bowl. But it was enough for Bolat to ditch home altogether.

Long since graduated from useless son to useless father, it took Bolat a mere few months to squander that handful of rainy-day gold his mum had saved for years and years. Drink-fuelled orgies with infamous whores from neighbouring towns and live music and everything put paid to the stash. Next came the herd. Already depleted to a few ailing cows and mangy sheep, it lost a cow here and a sheep there, was sold for a song, and Bolat went whoring again. When the herd was down to two or three sickly sheep no one would buy, he sold the land.

Whenever he lost his temper he would beat his family until their noses bled. One evening, too broke to go out for some fun, he stayed at home. His wife, Suna – who had submitted to her fate on the day she was born – had cooked a lamb stew with shallots, stirring it for four hours; he flung it out of the window, newly tinned copper pan and all, claiming it was too salty. As the windowpanes smashed, a maddening ringing started in Emine's ears. It was like a filament had broken inside her head and was twitching. Bolat – who had no qualms about wasting his family's few pennies on whores and his own clothing, without so much as asking, *What're my wife and children gonna eat?* and then had the temerity to insist, *Make me a lamb stew with shallots!* as if he brought any money home – had not only thrown the pan out of the window but was now banging his wife's head against the wall, shouting, *What'd ya do?*

Emine saw red when she saw her mother's snow-white headscarf covered in blood. The ringing in her ears rose to a pitch high enough to snap her brain. Grabbing a log from the fireplace, one end glowing red, she attacked her father. She chased him all the way to the village square and thrashed him for all the world to see, his face and hands still spattered with the blood that had spurted from Suna's brow.

The village was shaking with the news the following day, but all Emine could recall was the strength in her body – where it had come from, she had no idea – and that infernal ringing in her ears. Yet the previous night, after she beat up her father, she had dressed the brow of her weeping mother with tobacco, retrieved the dented pan from the garden, washed it and put it away, fixed an omelette for her hungry sisters and then gone to bed as if nothing had happened.

So unpopular was the bad-tempered, deceitful and quarrelsome Bolat that when his own daughter was walloping his back with a burning log, no one had attempted to stop her; quite the opposite: whenever he had tried to run, his way was blocked. After that flaming beating at the hands of his fifteen-year-old daughter before the eyes of the entire village, he vanished, and no one ever saw hide or hair of him again. Although the corpse found a few years later in a road ditch off the beaten track was alleged to be his, none of God's children was in the least bit concerned about this bag of bones and handful of hair, the flesh having long since rotted away; defying the custom of never speaking ill of the dead, some people even said, *God willing it's him, let's hope he died a horrible death!*

The young maiden who had beat her own father up with a burning log scared off the local bachelors. Emine was a much more powerful copy of her beautiful, slender-waisted Caucasian grandmother Alla, and a couple of sizes larger too. Every man in the village (single or married, young or old) might have hankered after her, but no one had the balls to marry this madwoman. Her only suitor was a shepherd from the neighbouring village, **Memnun, king of idlers**.

Whenever he took the herd to the mountain, he'd lose a couple of animals to the wolves, yet slow-witted Memnun always returned to the village displaying all thirty-two teeth as if nothing was wrong. All that he wanted was to live without doing a stitch of work and make love to a plump woman until his dying day. Every time he dropped into the village he'd be ogling Emine, unable to keep his eyes off those long legs, which even under her skirt looked powerful. Anyways, if she had trounced her mountain of a dad, she'd surely cope with the work.

Emine fancied him in return. Memnun might be known as the king of idlers, but she wasn't one to leave work to someone else, not even her husband. Moreover, whenever she looked at the suntanned, cheerful, happy-go-lucky fella, she felt like those strong arms extending from broad shoulders could crush her bones, which gave her a lovely warm feeling inside. He didn't need to ask twice; they got married and he settled into the home where Emine lived with her mum and sisters.

Memnun, who didn't have a single tree to his name (which meant *pleased*), was proven right on all counts. Emine rolled up her sleeves, cured the two or three sickly sheep left over from the herd decimated by her father, set upon the hazelnut grove, terraced the field that had been reduced to the size of a handkerchief, lugged rocks, dug channels, repaired the roof of the house Grandma Alla had built with her own hands brick by brick, tidied up here and there, built a kitchen to the rear, kept an eye on her sisters and sorted things out in no time at all. She always put food on the table, made sure there was smoke coming out of the chimney, worked, toiled, and made a small fortune. The money she haggled for when she sold the hazelnuts and livestock she kept concealed in the secret pockets she'd sewn into the three skirts she wore on top of one another. So her young maiden nickname of Crazy became Crazy Three-Skirt. She bore Memnun five sons; two died before their fortieth day, and a third when he was seventeen months old. Ziya was her fifth.

Her periods stopped after he was born. He wasn't a tetchy child, happy to sit peacefully wherever he was placed, and she always loved him just a bit more than her other surviving son **Barhun, who was quite a handful**.

After a life lived just as he wanted – never doing a stroke of work, lying under the pear tree in the front garden in summer and by the fire Emine lit before sunrise in winter and making love to her morning and night – one summer morning Memnun dropped dead of a heart attack on his way to the stream for a ritual full bath. Emine was left with her two sons. She was upset but didn't complain about being left without a husband. She was getting on in years and getting fed up with Memnun leaping on her twice a day.

Barhun was razor sharp. The village teacher, who couldn't wait to get away from here, was exasperated by the boy who wandered up hill, down dale all day long, gathered all the rocks, logs, and bones he could find, had an insatiable curiosity about everything and pestered him with questions.

Whenever Emine had had enough of Barhun's exuberance (which unbeknownst to her, stemmed from his intelligence) she would hug her Ziya, still gaping stupidly where she'd left him; her instincts told her Barhun would be all right, but she would need to keep Ziya under her wing all his life.

Frightened by the winter, which would clearly drag on, and fed up with the boy, Barhun's teacher wangled sick leave and took to his heels; his replacement, **Zahit, a man of Adyghe origin**, was forced to teach every class on his own in this mountainside village. His interest was piqued straightaway by the boy's name, which he knew from his book of Ossetian Folk Legends; a short chat with Emine established that their ancestors had indeed come from neighbouring lands.

Zahit had been teaching himself Russian to aid his research into the peoples of the entire Caucasus, not just Adygea; he took pride in his roots, true, but he also genuinely subscribed to the concept of *ethnicity* – a term whose entry into common parlance lay long in the future – as a kind of cultural asset. In order to promote the language and traditions of his ancestors, he collected publications on the history and culture of the region and, whenever possible, contributed to magazines published by the recently established Caucasian cultural associations, which the 1980 coup would close down.

A decade later, when an unexpected twist in history opened the borders, Zahit was able to set foot in the lands of his ancestors, after dreaming for years of free and happy societies where cultural diversity flourished – attributing, as he did, a democratic dimension to the concept of ethnic origin. By then a middle-aged researcher, he had read and learnt an enormous amount about history, time and the nature of nations.

No amount of mental fortitude, however, had prepared him for the heartbreaking chasm between the reality he was seeing and the society he had visualised. It wasn't that the inhabitants of those lands were living in the present, as indicated by calendars, and not in some prosperous past dreamworld recounted by his elders. What he found so hard to acknowledge was the fact that this real time was dominated by profound poverty, pessimism and despair. During his visit to the Caucasus, he had sought out, met and stayed with several his distant relations, some of whom were philologists and doctors. Inured to hearing (and speaking) the broken Adyghe language of his village, amongst relations who enjoyed a quiet life at one with nature, Zahit was a little surprised and thoroughly delighted by how that language reverberated in the shops and restaurants and on the buses in Sochi and Maikop; even children as young as five were fluent in Adyghe, or some close relative of it.

Barhun's spectacular intelligence had caught Zahit's eye on day one. Quick on the uptake and unable to sit still, the bright-eyes lad sat, bored, having instantly solved in his head every arithmetic problem Zahit's chalk scratched on the blackboard, whilst the other kids just stared blankly. The idealistic young teacher marked him for special attention. Rolling up his sleeves, he made the boy study hard so he could pass the state boarding school bursary exams.

From a very young age, Barhun had been fascinated by rocks, metals and other natural elements; this top middle school boarder proceeded to the Science Lycée and subsequently to the Middle Eastern Technical University Department of Mining Engineering, again as a top student. His pictures were emblazoned all over the papers. Illiterate she may have been, but Emine stuck the clippings to her wall with egg white, called her neighbours over and cried as she pointed to her son's photos.

Flooded with invitations from the best universities in the world, Barhun won enough in bursaries to never need a penny from his mother's herd, hazelnut grove or vegetable patch. But over the years he did lose touch with his home; he crossed oceans and stopped speaking the language not only of his brother and mother but also the language of the village and the land of his birth. His brother Ziya, no less lazy or dim than their father, had already bagged the cushy caretaker job in the Mental Health Hospital by the time Barhun was earning enough to keep his mother in comfort and peace of mind for the rest of her days. The scholar vanished into thin air in the splendid university campuses of the New World.

Truly proud of this storybook hero of a brother he might have been, but Ziya had no wish to look him up. It was enough to know that his big brother was alive. In contrast, Barhun's eyes would well up suddenly whenever he recalled his brother's moronic stare or his own uncontrollable sobs upon hearing of the amputated ear. He often intended to write and send money, but just then his phone would ring, some fresh new data would ping into his inbox, or some lab result would arrive. And in his enthusiasm, Barhun would immediately forget about his brother.

But Barhun's kind wife, Angela, a genetic engineer from Melbourne, didn't. Never never forgot Ziya, Ziya's wife, the gentle Munise, or their children.

The last time they'd come to Turkey was seven years ago, on holiday with **Key-Chong Woon, Angela's Korean friend and colleague** on a team researching *the role of genetics in muscular dystrophy diseases*. For twenty days, the three scholars had a fabulous time all around Ölüdeniz, Göcek, Patara and Olympus.

It was the second last day of their holiday. Their dinner table, placed in a sea bathed scarlet by the setting sun, was covered with a snow-white cloth and bedecked with dozens of mezes and seafood dishes. Key-Chong was downing his rakı and digging into his samphire and *cacık*, as he rolled pebbles under his feet, cooling in the sea.

Then the sun set, a magnificent full moon rose and heralded the time when rakı loosens tongues. Out of the blue, Key-Chong became emotional at the memory of his five siblings (one in Seoul, the others dispersed to the four corners of vast America), whom he'd not seen in twelve years, and broke into tales of his childhood.

His nostalgia spread to Barhun, who had by this time downed three glasses of rakı in quick succession. The personality he'd worked for years to assimilate, which gave no outward clue to his internal world and conformed to class standards to a T, split at its weakest point – his childhood – and Barhun spilled his guts. Out came a wealth of details he'd never shared even with his wife, despite his pleasure at how they validated his success and show how far he'd come: the lowly house he was born in, the rocks he'd collected on the steep hill behind the village, his illiterate mother known as *Crazy Three-Skirt Emine* and the boarding school bursary exam he'd been forced to take by his schoolteacher Zahit.

The 70-centilitre bottle was gone. Key-Chong carried on dipping his bread into the dregs of the lemon sauce for the steamed grouper in a gigantic oval dish, as Barhun, a scientist sponsored by a shady international foundation to lead a major research project into radioactive minerals, spoke between sobs about his brother's amputated pinna.

Once Angela started niggling, *Let's go see your family*, Barhun, realising that his adopted identity was badly compromised, failed miserably in his attempt to brush her off. No fan of rakı herself, Angela was at the wheel of their hire car well before the full moon vanished behind the mountains. By the time they knocked on the door of Ziya's poor but sweet home, the sun was at its zenith.

Ziya was astonished by the sight of his big brother standing there next to a redheaded woman and a slant-eyed man. Blighted by cataracts, Emine struggled to make out her son and the daughter-in-law she'd never met, as the tiny fingers of Ziya's children reached for the tattoos on Key-Chong's upper arms.

The ginger cat-like Munise stared at Key-Chong's face as often as she could, impatient to describe to her neighbours those slanted eyes, such as she'd only ever seen on TV, tugging at her baggy trousers as she boiled a chicken, happy butterflies fluttering in her stomach at the arrival of her brother-in-law and his wife. Ziya, who never took a drop himself but wouldn't dream of being anything less than the perfect host, dashed off to the grocer for three bottles of beer.

Barhun had noticed the Diamond Hotel sign as they were entering the city, and at the time had thought *We'll leave after supper, tour the city a little and stay the night here.* But the moment he hugged his mother – at whose sight his tears had run freely – and took in her smell, he sensed painfully that this lap he'd been missing unawares for years would soon crumble into dust and that he would never be able to rest his head against her bosom. He never mentioned the hotel. They spent the night in Ziya's tiny two-room house: Key-Chong on the sofa, and Barhun and his wife on mattresses on the floor.

After their visit and all during the return journey to Wisconsin via Istanbul, Key-Chong waxed lyrical about this provincial Black Sea city he had no reason to ever set foot in again, his first cup of Turkish tea (it simply hadn't occurred to him to try it before) and the sunflower seeds he'd cracked with his teeth to keep up with the reunited family as belly dancers shimmied on the muted television all night long; Angela, for her part, praised the way the two brothers (chalk and cheese, but all the same) had gazed at their mother's beautiful face with undisguised love, and the hug and kisses Munise – whose life was clearly spent being kind to others – had given her as they took their leave.

Barhun was at the wheel of the hired Toyota, which seemed to be overflowing with unfamiliar emotions for all three. There was no air-con; a dusty wind blew in through the windows, filling the car and giving him a headache; his heart was aching as his wife and friend chattered on about his family. His over-emotional state was as much due to the genuine love offered by the murmuring Munise and his younger brother (who looked the older), as it was to Angela's kind cheerfulness.

Having left Emine behind for what he was sure was the last time and proceeding through Immigration at Istanbul Atatürk Airport, Barhun – a US citizen for many years – felt the split in his identity healing. As he set off for his second homeland, which he knew he would never fully belong to, he swore to himself never to set foot again in the land of his birth, touch another drop of rakı, or get quite so sentimental over his childhood. As he knew all too well, a wounded identity had no chance of survival in the merciless jungle that was the New World.

Relationships with their standoffish neighbours in Wisconsin and their university colleagues had never progressed beyond polite *hellos*, and Angela, a devout Catholic, had always found their social circle to be severely circumscribed: no more a handful of close friends like Key-Chong, whose roots reached to other continents, which made the

US what it was. Feeling an enormous affection for Ziya and his family, overwhelmed by their poverty and concerned about offending them if she sent any money directly, she hit upon an ingenious solution. This was the origin of the annual Christmas hamper, which went all the way from Wisconsin to the outer skirts of that Black Sea town, containing chocolates, instant coffee, toys and a few bottles of the best Californian wines – mostly without Barhun's knowledge. The children were ecstatic at the chocolates and the toys, and the first thing Munise did was to impress her neighbours with some milky coffee, and she made quite a show of it too. A swaggering Ziya presented the Medical Director with the wine sent by his sister-in-law. The Medical Director was aware that this earless fellow's big brother was an eminent scientist, an extraordinarily remote possibility in his opinion, judging by the dim-witted king of slackers known as Ziya – *Like father, like son.*

His mother's reputation as a madwoman might have spared Ziya overt taunts of *Earless!* in childhood, but he couldn't avoid the nickname in the army. In keeping with the rural tradition of minimising contact with bureaucracy, Ziya, instead of being recorded at the register office in his own name with the correct date of birth, had been given the ID certificate of the older brother who'd died at seventeenth months. Which meant that Ziya wasn't even nineteen when he was called up. Unlike Barhun, he was quite small anyway and had a baby face to boot. But not a soul remarked, *He's just a kid!* – it never occured to anyone to ask what his real age was.

The lack of an ear, however, was hardly the kind of thing that would go unnoticed at the base. Surgeon Hilmi Ziya Ötüken might have amputated the pinna quite neatly, but Ziya's fingers were constantly scratching at the non-existent scab on the smooth tissue.

Staff Sergeant Mamoş, too fat for his knees to meet, needed to join two belts to circle his midriff. It was his, *Ya' earless poofter, don't let me get started on your mother now!* that established the moniker on Ziya's very first day, with the added slur on his sexuality. At once the abuse made him long for his mother, and Ziya, barely out of childhood, broke into a stream of tears. At the sight of which Mamoş acquainted him with an army thrashing for having turned on the tap before he'd had even touched him (he'd sworn, scoffed, and guffawed at him, yes, but he hadn't yet laid a finger on the lad). Throughout the beating, Ziya dreamt of his mother breaking the Staff Sergeant's gappy buckteeth with a log – if only she were here.

The staff sergeant's moods and the humiliating nickname kept Ziya in a perpetually tearful state for the first couple of months. The lad's kindness and cheerful readiness to help, however, shamed his brothers-in-arms into dropping the *poofter* part, whilst *Earless* stuck. Mamoş was the only one who still called him *Earless poofter*, but no one took the sergeant seriously anyway.

Ziya did his national service at a time when TV was becoming more widespread around the country, and there was a set in the garrison canteen. Mamoş, who needed no excuse to beat whichever conscript caught his eye, all day long in the freezing chill of Kütahya, would summon Ziya before *Roots* began and force his own Kunta Kinte to stand beside him and watch; he would demand tea, water, coffee, hand-rolled cigarettes and a light for those cigarettes until the lad was ready to drop with exhaustion, then scold him and give him a good whipping for being too heartless to cry at the misery depicted on the screen. Sorry as fellow conscripts were at how often Ziya was beaten, there was little they could do.

One night, when Ziya had sixty-eight days to go, he was caught chuckling with a mate at something as the credits were rolling on the screen. It annoyed the hell out of the staff sergeant, who was blubbering at Kunta Kinte's woes; with nothing else to do, no family to go to, he was bored. He called Ziya over. Sniggering, he directed ridiculously random general-knowledge questions at the lad, such as *Who's the Minister of the Interior? What's the capital of Hungary?* Every wrong answer earned a slap harder than the preceding one. After a thorough thrashing, Mamoş despatched him to the canteen, saying, *Now go get me a toastie with lashings of sucuk!*

The conscript in the canteen, who had also taken his share of the staff sergeant's sadism, although not to the same extent, let out a chestful of vitriol and indulged in visions of chopping off the staff sergeant's fingers as he sliced the spicy sausage into thick rings.

That night in his quarters, Mamoş drifted off whilst munching his humongous toastie. He slept so deeply he never noticed the chunk of sucuk sticking in his throat and choking him to death. It was nearly day-break when his body was found, by which time the soles of his boots had melted on the electric heater where he'd rested his feet. The room stank of rubber.

At first Ziya was terribly offended by the nickname *Earless*, but over time he got used to it and, after starting the job in the hospital, even began to see it as a mark of distinction. Once he noticed the pity and kindness of the medical staff, he discarded his perennial yellow-and-navy beanie and had his head shaved to a grade three, as if he was still in the army.

Ziya wasn't the least bit daunted at the prospect of an enquiry into the incident in which the Medical Director's schoolmate slipped and fell and Neuropsychiatrist Nebahat Özdamar's little toe sustained a fracture. He might not have been too bright, but one thing he did know was that he was no contracted personnel without security or a future. No, he was protected by the rock-solid Civil Servants Act No. 657, and so never had to worry about being sacked. If anything, he'd have loved the enquiry to go on and on so he could enjoy his suspension, but the Medical Director refused to make a big thing of it: he closed the file, leaving Ziya no choice but to return to work.

It was always the same; the vinyl he wiped in a hurry just wouldn't dry. And he always being scolded by the Medical Director for neglecting to dry the stage after a hasty wipe with sudsy water (a handful of detergent did the trick). To be fair, the vinyl with the knotted-wood pattern was getting a bit worn, and even when wet was nowhere near as slippery as it once had been, but then, rebuking Ziya had become a habit for the Medical Director. Ziya hated this part of his job; in fact, he was constantly dreaming of retirement as the remainder of his working life loomed like a century before him. He'd have been chuffed if the Medical Director just went ahead and shut down the conference hall.

He quite liked being at the hospital actually; if only he didn't have to work. He loved crouching in the courtyard, leaning against the blind wall as he had a cigarette, staring at the sea, shooting the breeze with the nurses, who had similarly come out for a fag on the sly, and peeking out of the corner of his eye at Psychologist Gülnazmiye Görgün's boobs, which she tried to minimise with bras one size smaller. Sometimes he would dream of a day when all the patients would be discharged, the empty rooms would be bathed in sunlight, and he'd be chatting with his favourite doctors and other members of staff as they all sprawled out in the hospital garden.

Earless Ziya sometimes liked the hospital, and sometimes didn't, but Medical Director Demir Demir loved it. He couldn't live anywhere outside this labyrinthine building with its back to the sea. He loved this great occupation – being a medical director. Not that he didn't enjoy grumbling, at least for form's sake, about the workload. If he didn't stress the magnitude of his responsibility at every opportunity, he might lose his raison d'être and – horror of horrors! – even be suspected of having an easy time of it.

If truth be told, the idea of retirement did not appear entirely without attraction whenever he'd had a bellyful of dealing with over three hundred patients (a hundred and forty-two in the secure unit), over fifty substance dependants, never fewer than a score of convicts with heightened security requirements and countless others – outpatients and applications for Certificates of Mental Capacity – not to mention close to two hundred staff who fetched up at his door any time they had any sort of problem. But then he'd visualise himself staying at home instead of going to the hospital, wandering aimlessly around the town, and felt so bereft that his heart would break as if he had been given the boot. He'd then promise himself never again to grumble, a promise he couldn't keep.

Once, after they'd, thankfully, got off very lightly from a fire, he had given the prospect of retirement serious thought. But then things had worked out just fine. By which time he was hooked on the idea of writing the history of the place; there was no way he would even consider retiring until he had completed a comprehensive history of the hospital he'd been directing for years and come to regard as a second home.

The idea of writing a book was put into his head by Deputy Governor Hikmet Keleşoğlu, whom he'd met at the office of a **printer Kamer**. The Medical Director had penned an informal list of regulations in a pleasantly stern style for staff members who occasionally took things just a little bit too easy, to the extent that they could be accused of dereliction of duty, and decided to have it printed, as computer printouts would cost far too much. *But Mr Medical Director Sir, all I want to do is help our hospital in whatever* *way I can; just say the word and it'll be done,* Kamer had insisted; he wouldn't hear of taking any money from the Medical Director, who was treating his sister, the **blue-eyed Maviş, who suffered from semantic paraphasia**. The painstakingly prepared clean copy would normally have been delivered by his **secretary, Nemika (Nemişo to her colleagues)**, but the Medical Director had forgotten that she was on leave to prepare for her engagement party, and, anyway, her head had been in the clouds since she'd got engaged. It therefore fell upon him to deliver the list of rules, which he demanded *absolute and universal compliance with,* intended for everyone from the nurses to kitchen staff, social service experts and orderlies.

The Medical Director had drawn it up in response to an incident early one morning, when he had walked in on pandemonium. He wasn't in the habit of starting the workday as early as seven thirty; he usually arrived towards ten – and rarely left before eight in the evening. On this occasion, however, he had awakened early, alone, as his wife was in Ankara, and thought *I'll get a bite to eat at the hospital just this once.* He was reluctant to make his own breakfast, or more accurately to clear up afterwards and do the dishes. Of course they had a dishwasher, but since Sevim abhorred the thought of dirty dishes waiting inside it, and wouldn't dream of wasting water to run the machine for just a couple of plates and a bowl, she'd use a ton of water to wash everything squeaky clean by hand. Demir Demir consequently had no idea how to start this unfamiliar contraption.

The hospital's shambolic state was evident at the gate. Not a single guard was to be seen in the hut where Türkan Kaymakoğlu's former driver Hamdi Tutuş (who had freaked out after running over Midwife Mualla) sat on a chair, shoes and socks off, trimming the calluses on his feet with an old razor blade. So engrossed was he that he never even noticed the arrival of the Medical Director, whose hackles rose as he confiscated the filthy tool. At the sight of shabby inmates wandering unchecked in the garden, some barefoot, others in slippers, he really blew his top.

He found the guards and some of the nurses in the day room on the first floor, where inmates played backgammon, Rummikub and what-have-you under staff supervision. They'd put the tables together, covered them with newspapers, laid out a veritable feast of treats, from pine honey, butter and herb cheese to green olives, pastrami and even halva, and were cheerfully tucking into their breakfast, accompanied by Trabzon bread so fresh it was steaming. They had no idea whether the inmates had buzzed off somewhere or were climbing the walls. At the sight of the Medical Director they sprang to their feet, terrified.

How the heck does a dangerous patient get hold of a razor? he meant to yell and bring them to book. Except he noticed the butter melting inside the warm bread, smiled and said, *Enjoy.* Unaccustomed to seeing him at the hospital at that hour, the bewildered nurses immediately invited him to join them. The poor fellow hadn't had a proper meal the previous night either and was famished. He couldn't resist the mature cheese, creamy enough to smear its wrapping, the green olives glistening in oil, the last tomatoes of the season, the still tender peppers, the sour cherry jam and above all Nebahat's cake dotted with dazzling golden walnuts, so instead of giving them a good tongue lashing, he sat down and stuffed his face.

This unexpected familiarity caused some of the staff to forget themselves. One or two nearly went too far just because they were all sitting at the same table. Sensing that harsh words would have been a little hypocritical now, the Medical Director decided to draw up a *List of Basic Regulations* to remind them of their duties; a degree of semi-formality would also be in order.

A few days later, he went to Kamer, who handled print work for many factories and businesses in the area, and who, like every boss, always complained of *business being really slow now.* The shop floor was very quiet. Only the guillotine cutter was operating, with a rhythmical clatter that echoed off the high corrugated ceiling. The Medical Director thought the bloke could be right this once. Kamer might be reluctant to take his print job, moaning about the sluggishness of business – a vexing possibility indeed. Thinking he'd try his luck anyway, he ascended to the office on the mezzanine, where Kamer broke into a grin the moment he saw the Medical Director and welcomed him with *Bye!*

Startled by the absurd grin and incongruous greeting, Deputy Governor Hikmet Keleşoğlu raised his head from the proofs of his fourth volume of poetry, which were spread on the coffee table.

That questioning gaze prompted Kamer to offer an elaborate explanation of his nine-year-old sister's condition: her *semantic paraphasia* caused her to substitute a word that had a similar sense to the one she meant to use – *dish* instead of *glass*, for instance, or *table* instead of *bed* – but thanks to the Medical Director's untiring efforts, she'd shown great progress, at least everyone now understood what she meant; Kamer then rattled off the names of every type of paraphasia he'd learnt from the Medical Director – *semantic, neologistic, phonemic*, etc. – sounding just a little too jolly as he did so. He did tend to swing like a pendulum between the extremes of cheer and gloom: distress at his sister's inability to communicate gave way to pitiably overstated merriment, amusing at first, but heartrending after a while, until it fizzled out like a match.

Kamer had just ordered unsweetened coffees for the important visitors who had honoured his office when the noise that had been marking time to his words like a hidden metronome suddenly fell silent. Before long one of the workers appeared at the door, saying, *Kamer Abi? Cutter's busted again.*

Kamer's bearing changed from a man who'd won the jackpot to one who'd heard his house was on fire as he ran down to the shop floor in exaggerated panic. The metal staircase vibrated with the sound of his booming footsteps, which bounced off the walls and reached the feet of the two visitors. The junior waiter brought their coffees as in their host's absence the two men introduced themselves and, after a sip or two, were chatting like old friends.

Hikmet – whose first priority the moment he'd settled into his appointment as deputy governor was to find a local press for his latest volume of poetry – presented the Medical Director with copies of his earlier books (he always carried a few sets), signing each one then and there. So began a cordial yet superficial friendship between the two men, which led to discussions at the Nation Tea Garden on life, intelligence and the soul.

When Hikmet, who had originally appeared quite moderate in all matters, gradually aligned his viewpoint with the present government, their friendship faltered somewhat. Hikmet had expanded his remit to include checking whether officials were attending Friday prayers or not; his conversation focused a little too much on sin, virtue and the benefits of prayer, and he even persisted in recommending a plethora of religious publications to the Medical Director – his senior in years – and did so with a slightly patronising air. A palpable coolness settled between the two, and they no longer met quite so frequently. What drove the Medical Director away, was not the Deputy Governor's pious views but more the way he styled himself as a supercilious elder brother to a man who was his senior.

Of course they did chat whenever their paths crossed. The Deputy Governor carried on showing up at scientific panels in the hospital's conference hall, and he made sure to pay the Medical Director a courtesy call each time. But their friendship was now limited to these brief greetings and the standard text messages on religious occasions which the Deputy Governor sent to his entire mobile telephone directory. The Medical Director contented himself with a courteous reply each time.

The Deputy Governor landed himself in deep trouble when the press got wind of his decision to personally inspect the books donated to the county library, and burn those he'd deemed *unsuitable*. Massive headlines questioned which particular law had authorised him as a censor, and the papers demanded to know what criteria, if any, he'd used to judge as unsuitable the books he had had torched in the county hall garden. A long list of titles followed, covering everything from children's books and run-of-the-mill romances to politics and history. Some of these had indeed been burnt to ashes on his orders, but a significant proportion consisted of tomes that had been nicked from the library or borrowed and never returned.

The librarian Zeynel Canpolat, who had had a beef with the Deputy Governor on account of the several unwarranted rebukes – and to be honest, as a member of a strict religious order himself, the librarian deemed unsuitable many more books than the ones torched on the orders of the Deputy Governor – had inflated the list with everything that had been entrusted to him and that, sadly, could no longer be found on the shelves; not content with leaking it to the press, he'd also uploaded the thirty-second clip of the book burning, which he surreptitiously recorded on his mobile.

At first Hikmet brushed it all off. But when the book burning hit the local press, then the big papers, and finally the national TV channels, all thanks to the clip shared on YouTube, he scrambled to defend himself.

According to his somewhat less than credible account, the books had been burnt not because the Deputy Governor found them undesirable on political or moral grounds, but because they presented a public health hazard. *Books are sacred, I wouldn't dream of having them burnt*, he insisted. Asked how on earth books could present a public health hazard, he explained: as the press might remember, the main waste-water pipe had burst, leaving the basement knee-deep in sewage and inundating volumes intended to be returned to the shelves once the reorganisation of the library was complete. The Deputy Governor, to whom public health mattered above all else, had thus ordered the burning of any items that had likely been contaminated by sewage – *Yes, so they wouldn't threaten public health* – and had thus saved *our dear children who use the library from the risk of any potential contact with germs.*

Zeynel, who had never for a moment anticipated the repercussions of the incident and worried that he'd end up carrying the can, now volunteered to become the Deputy Governor's chief witness. He announced here and there that the burst pipe had ruined some of the archives too, and the papers burnt along with the books were largely *unimportant archival material* which had been stored in the basement for that very reason. He took it upon himself to convey to the Deputy Governor certain documents bearing official stamps, plumbers' invoices and receipts for materials. Only the latter – no flies on him – had pre-empted him; by the time the librarian turned up brandishing his receipts, pleased as punch, the Deputy Governor's secretary had long since faxed the same documents to the press.

Whilst the images on national TV showed the books, it was hard to tell if they were damp or soiled. Reporters tried to pin the Deputy Governor down: if those books had indeed been soaked in sewage, how come they caught fire so readily? Damp objects didn't, on the whole, yet the flames in the video were reaching into the sky. Hikmet replied that not all the books were damp, only some had been soiled, but since the staff – and the librarian in particular – had so carelessly piled the clean along with the contaminated, he simply couldn't take the risk of endangering public health by shelving books that looked dry. And in order to prove just how much he loved the books, which he would never dream of destroying – *A barbaric idea!* – he pointed to the pile of newly purchased replacements; he even picked out eight or ten in front of the reporteres and said he'd take them home to read – titles he would never consider reading in a month of Sundays.

Still unconvinced, the press pressed on, triggering a reluctant Interior Ministry enquiry for appearances' sake. Inspectors arrived, inspectors left, and it all ended with a resounding vindication for Hikmet and the county library. The conclusion was that the Deputy Governor had indeed acted to protect public health. Anyone would have thought the bloke was in line for a commendation next. The library's stock grew considerably with the new books purchased on the county budget. The initial controversy died down and the book burning story became a nine days' wonder as yet another incident that vanished into the black hole of public memory.

It was the self-appointed corroborator of the Deputy Governor's claims (and the man who had originated the story) who came out worst – just as he'd feared. Once an enquiry was launched, the inspectors, loath to leave without issuing a fine, sought out a scapegoat and gave Zeynel a caution for dereliction of duty. He was furious at the Deputy Governor, in whose defence he'd bent over backwards and who in return had not only stood by and watched as he was wrongfully accused, but even pointed the finger. Already cheesed off, he now had a justifiable grievance too. But the grudge nursed by an ordinary librarian had absolutely no impact whatsoever upon the life of the Deputy Governor.

But it was one thing after another: just when Hikmet thought he could breathe easy, his son ran away from school. A **cheeky and bright thirteen-year-old, Muharrem** flatly refused to return to the Istanbul boarding school, which placed undue emphasis on religious values.

Muharrem enjoyed every minute of his stay with his **uncle, a software programmer and bass guitarist named Tümay**, who had been shunned for years by Hikmet and his wife. A manager in a small yet notable business, Tümay wore a suit and tie during the working week, but on Friday and Saturday nights, he would gig with his group in a decent bar in upmarket Suadiye. The rest of the time he played every type of musical instrument – piano, tambur, violin, and even ney – at his studio-slash-home, which was equipped with the latest technology and sound systems; the boy was enchanted by tunes he was hearing for the first time.

Tümay, whose compositions were already doing the rounds on the internet, was due to record his first studio album. He was quite fond of his nephew and flattered that the kid liked him well enough to come over. But crossing swords with his brother-in-law was the last thing he wanted. He'd have handed Muharrem over to the grandparents, but the boy, clearly in the clutches of an adolescent crisis, was crying and pleading to stay with his uncle.

Muharrem had first come across his uncle on Facebook on one of those rare occasions when he was able to visit an internet café. Tümay's profile was visible to *friends only*; but Muharrem sent him a message anyway. It remained unanswered as an astonished Tümay mused *Should I respond or not? If I did, would I fall out with my big sister?* – since he'd had no contact with his big sister, brother-in-law or nephew for years. Before he had a chance to write back, however, Muharrem had googled his uncle, found out where he worked and simply turned up.

At lunch in a Baghdad Road café, the boy calmly and rationally explained that he didn't want to go to that school any more. Daunted by the responsibility, however, Tümay rang his big sister, **Tülay, who had 'covered up' five years earlier.**

The moment the school rang to say that her son had gone missing, a panicked Tülay rushed to her husband's office at County Hall; as she burst into her account in tears, her mobile rang. It was the brother whose voice she hadn't heard in years: Tümay had threatened to ring County Hall himself if Muharrem didn't give him Tülay's mobile number. Wailing, *Don't send me back to school!* the boy caved in.

It was far too brief a conversation. All Tümay could say was, *Muharrem's with me, don't worry*, before adding, *I'd say 'Come and get him,' but don't think I'm rejecting the kid. You know I'm very fond of him.* Her bright-eyed brother's distant, slightly cross, yet wistfully affectionate voice tugged at Tülay's heartstrings. How she longed to see him! She burst into sobs.

Hikmet was outraged at his son's flight to an uncle who was a man by day but a bum by night. He'd have bitched to his wife about Tümay, but bit his tongue because he felt sorry for her. Poor Tülay was falling to pieces. She cried buckets, then went away, washed up and returned. They agreed it was best to avoid spooking the boy.

Fourteen years ago, when a friend introduced her to Hikmet, Tülay never thought she might one day wish to adopt the neo-conservative dress code known as *tesettür*. Nor had it ever occurred to Hikmet that he might one day ask his wife to *cover up*, and to be fair, he never did. True, he came from a devout conservative family, where the majority of the women were covered. Then again, there were some who weren't – one of his sisters, for instance. He secretly wished his wife would cover herself, but he wasn't going to insist upon it, at least not in the short term.

That the Keleşoğlu women were generally covered up didn't escape Tülay's parents' attention when Hikmet and his family had arrived to ask for her hand. The **retired accountant Turgut Bey** and his wife, **Berat Hanım – from progressive Pendik, born and bred** – duly warned their daughter, who rounded on them with accusations of prejudice. It turned into quite an issue as uncles and aunts got involved. Eventually Hikmet promised, even solemnly swore, that he'd never force Tülay into doing something against her will; since Tülay also dug her heels in, her parents gave their consent and Tülay married Hikmet.

Tülay's decision to cover up was prompted by the varying degrees of peer pressure (at times subtle, at others more overt) in their environment dictated by Hikmet's career. But that wasn't the only factor. She'd always been somewhat devout since childhood anyway, and there was an atmosphere of piety that frequently surrounded her even as she felt lost during their tenure in the back of beyond in provincial Anatolia.

She had, at any rate, been all but covered up until then. The majority of the women in her circles wore headscarves, and practically all of them were the wives of her husband's colleagues. She'd taken to wearing a headscarf so as not to feel like an outsider, unpicked the tight trousers and below-the-knee skirts she'd been wearing up to a few years previously and made them into patchwork covers, and taken to greeting headscarved women on the street even if she didn't know them. She found a degree of belonging in this pious environment. One evening, when she announced her decision to adopt *tesettür*, Hikmet's eyes welled up with joy.

Tülay's already strained relations with her family came to a breaking point when she chose the elaborate three-layer head covering and long, baggy and shapeless garments; but instead of adopting a conciliatory style, she'd simply snapped, *Take me as I am or write me off; your call.*

Turgut and Berat were just about to move to Bostancı from Pendik, where they'd been living for fifty years, all because of this divisive controversy of covered vs. uncovered. They'd been shaking with outrage for days, still struggling to stomach what they'd gone through in their hometown. Tülay's decision came like a bucket of cold water.

They'd been aware for some time that the Tobacco and Alcohol Monopolies outlet opposite had closed down, the neighbourhood supermarket had stopped selling alcohol, some seafront restaurants whose licences had been revoked were now serving alcohol surreptitiously and the proportion of covered women in Pendik was growing fast; but they had not paid much attention to it all. The first time they recognised the threat posed to individual rights by this discrimination of covered/uncovered, or secular/religious, was when Turgut found it increasingly difficult to get his regular weekend copies of the newspaper *Cumhuriyet*. To be fair, he was more interested in the *Science and Technology* supplement and the prize crossword than the paper itself. At any rate, the grocer had either stopped stocking *Cumhuriyet* or ordered so few copies it was always sold out. Poor Turgut had to walk all the way to the newsagent at the station, and made a determined effort to ignore the dwindling number of shopkeepers who greeted him, but chafed silently all the same. But the elderly couple panicked when Berat was verbally abused one day in Pendik market by a clot of women in black çarşaf for having *one foot in the grave and still wandering around with her head uncovered.*

Unable for once to fight her corner, Berat was paralysed, powerless to open her mouth. Her blood pressure shot up to 200. She was as white as a sheet on her return home, incapable of answering her husband's questions beyond repeating over and over, *Never thought I'd live to see the day!*

Hearing about it when he dropped in, Tümay told them to move straightaway. Scared witless for the safety of his septuagenarian parents, he raised hell, *Don't let me get started on your secularist struggle!* and not long after swept them off to a spacious sea-view flat on the eighth floor of a fourteen-storey block in Bostancı.

He was still searching for a decent flat for them when Tülay, as yet was unaware of the incident, dropped in with her husband and three sons, the youngest of whom was barely one. She had come to announce that she'd adopted *tesettür* and would brook no further discussion. Although it wasn't a total surprise, Berat still couldn't believe her ears. Turgut, for his part, left his visitors in the sitting room, retreated to the bedroom in the middle of the day and shut the door firmly. His son-in-law, understanding this to mean *Leave*, took umbrage, and the couple grabbed their children and left.

Neither side had given an inch and even their mutual phone calls had come to a stop. Tülay desperately missed her father, whom she hadn't seen for five years, nor her brother for four, but she was determined to hold her ground. Berat, however, who ignored her aching knees to join every secularist demonstration waving a flag, couldn't bear not seeing her daughter, so they started meeting, however infrequently. Distraught mother and daughter at first only rang each other. They then progressed to meeting at a restaurant whose glasses Tülay made sure hadn't been contaminated by a single drop of alcohol. Her husband knew about it, but not her father.

These reunions always began with tears of joy and long hugs, but the moment Berat brought up the abuse she'd been subjected to in her lovely Pendik where she'd lived for fifty years, an argument would break out and before the meal was over mother and daughter would be going at it hammer and tongs until they finally stormed off swearing they'd never see each other again.

Muharrem's escape didn't help. That day, though, recognising that Tülay's tears were caused more by missing her brother than concern for her son, Hikmet blew his top and they had a row.

The Deputy Governor said he was going to leap into his car, go to Istanbul at once, and seize his son from his brother-in-law – *take him by force* if he had to. It was this talk of taking him by force that raised Tülay's hackles. In an icy voice, she pointed out that Tümay would never have rung if he had any intention of holding on to Muharrem, that he'd been looking after their son, and that Hikmet's *I'll take him by force* was downright ungrateful when in fact he should have felt indebted to her brother for informing them at once.

This was their first row over her family. It flashed through Hikmet's mind that his wife would never break off all relations with her family. Determined to stand his ground, he was about to ask, *Since when have you become your brother's lawyer?* when Tümay rang again. *Muharrem used to have an allergy to sausages; does he still?* The kid had asked for a hot dog, his uncle had remembered his nephew's allergy after all this time and needed confirmation even after the boy said, *Nah!* Hikmet melted and made up with his wife. At any rate he was expected at police headquarters for a meeting, so they agreed to resume their discussion at home.

There, later that evening, Tülay cried her heart out. Muharrem was an adolescent; how could they be sure he wouldn't run away again if they forced him to come home or go back to school? As for Hikmet, a profound dread over his son's future had replaced the earlier rage that had flared up during the day; he had to concede her point. They agreed to treat the boy with kid gloves and let him stay with his uncle for a bit.

During those twenty days Tülay would frequently ring her brother. Every time she did, a spark of affection glowed between the siblings before fizzling out – their true feelings remained hopelessly inarticulate and they both sounded too cold. Every time she rang, they longed to speak freely, fondly; instead they spoke with a great deal of reserve, like two complete strangers.

Tülay rang because she wanted to speak to her son. Knowing he was safe did nothing to reassure her; she couldn't sleep a wink. It was a little different for Hikmet; fretting over the potential disruption to Muharrem's carefully charted education and the risk of the boy straying from the path he'd drawn, he'd kept at Tülay to call. For the first ten days, however, the boy flatly refused to speak to either parent and Tümay let him be.

But after a while, concerned for that thin fraternal thread, his uncle gently chided him, hinting that a forced return to school could be on the cards if such behaviour carried on. So Muharrem agreed to talk to his mother. Unable to hold back any longer, Tülay burst into tears at the sound of his voice.

Hikmet appreciated this soft spot; still, worried about losing control, he hid behind a sterner and more decided tone of voice than usual, which made Muharrem freeze. That night, he and his uncle discussed at length why he should love his parents. It was the first time Muharrem had stayed up until three in the morning chatting with someone who treated him like an adult.

The distraught parents consulted the Medical Director to ask, *What should we do; how should we treat the boy?* Graciously welcoming this former companion, the Medical Director admitted he was no expert in adolescent psychiatry and recommended the handsome Paediatric Psychiatrist Faik Abacı.

The couple went to the surgery in Gazi Road. The psychiatrist – whose world view wasn't that different from Hikmet's – suggested they might temporarily remove the boy from boarding school, and that it would do him good to stay at home for a while with his brothers. They could send him back once he had come to his senses. Hikmet would have objected, worried about explaining the situation to the headmaster and his own circle, but had no choice when Tülay broke into fresh sobs.

Deciding that Muharrem had stayed away long enough, they travelled to Istanbul. He didn't really want to leave his uncle – who seemed less indulgent now – but his parents spoke to him gently and kindly, just as Faik had recommended. They'd picked a grill on Baghdad Road close to Tümay's office. Tülay had thought she'd be wracked at the sight of her brother just as she had been at his voice, but that's not what happened. Her heart still broke a little, and a natural affinity would have sprung up between them if her husband hadn't been around. But as soon as the bassist stepped into the café, Hikmet adopted a fixed, tense and somewhat less than kindly expression; soon, his mood infected her too.

Tümay's emotions weren't so different. They didn't catch each other's eye long enough to evoke childhood memories or show how much they'd missed each other. Although a little upset by this reserve, Muharrem wasn't vexed or cross. After that late night conversation, he idolised his uncle; all the same, it was obvious he had to go with his parents. Scared of the punishment that might await him at home, he kept tearing off tiny bits of bread to nibble as he listened, careful not to look anyone in the face.

Throughout the meal the adults made small talk in impeccably courteous tones devoid of terms of endearment and steered clear of controversy. The only exception came when Tümay laid his fork down as if to broach a question, began, *Punishing Muharrem or anything...* and fell silent. Tülay's locked eyes signalled *Stop right there.* Tümay would have interfered – even risked causing an incident – if he had the slightest suspicion that the boy would be chastised. Thankfully, he saw Hikmet's adoring fatherly gaze: it was all right, the boy wouldn't be bawled out. The meal ended without any awkwardness and they all stood up.

Hikmet offered a rather stiff thanks to his brother-in-law. Tümay replied that it was his duty. Then he sensed he was on the verge of upsetting Muharrem, even despite their long chat. Thinking he'd outstayed his welcome, the boy's blond eyelashes blinked rapidly and his lips were quivering. But Tümay stroked his head with a warm, open smile, instantly regaining Muharrem's affection and trust.

The bassist and the Deputy Governor merely shook hands instead of kissing each other on the cheek as was the custom. Tülay lightly brushed her brother's cheeks with her lips.

Tümay left first. As Tülay stared at her strapping, handsome brother, something totally unexpected happened: just as with the phone calls, she suddenly felt sick at heart, with aching and longing. Her hand went up to her headscarf. She asked herself, *Is it this?* Was that what had come between them, holding back the love? She was intelligent enough to know it wasn't that simple. But what was it that had driven apart these two siblings, born of the same parents and raised in the same home under the same conditions? Was this how they would carry on? How would they find a way to express their love for each other?

Although preoccupied with this and similar questions, she refused to brood on the issue: the more she did, the more it cut her to the quick. Hiding her tears from her husband, she grasped Muharrem's hand. In the meanwhile, Hikmet was grumbling over Tümay's earring. He whipped round to check Muharrem's earlobes. *You never know,* he thought, *the boy might have niggled for one himself...* No, thank God.

They flew back that same day. Muharrem wasn't punished. He was reunited with his brothers, whom he'd been missing lots, and enrolled in a different school. His father promised to get an internet connection and even let him chat to his uncle from time to time, provided Muharrem went to Faik once a week.

Once Muharrem's studies and behaviour recovered under Faik's supervision, the Deputy Governor thanked the Medical Director for the recommendation when the two men met at the Three Brothers Patisserie. The former, anticipating a promotion to governor any day now, was invited to join the Medical Director at his table. Conscious that a dry thank-you would appear discourteous, Hikmet sat down and signed his fifth volume of poetry, which despite his workload he'd found the time to write and publish. As he handed it to the Medical Director, he asked, *Have you started your book yet?* He, too, had heard of the history of the hospital the Medical Director was writing. *I'm still collecting documents*, came the reply, and no further detail was forthcoming. Not that there was any to go into.

When they had first met at Kamer's print shop, they'd talked at some length about literature and poetry. More accurately, Hikmet had done all the talking and the Medical Director had listened. He really wasn't that interested in literature or poetry or anything, but he was very impressed with this fellow – at least ten years his junior – who had three books to his name and was about to publish a fourth.

The guillotine cutter restarted and Kamer rejoined his visitors just as a heartfelt, *I'd love to write something like you've done, something to leave behind*, tumbled out of the Medical Director's mouth. How Hikmet might have replied we'll never know, since Kamer distracted them with his moaning about the trivial malfunction as though it were a major setback that would take a whole year to recover from.

That afternoon, once he was done at the printer's, the Medical Director, instead of returning to the hospital straightaway, strolled over to the Nation Tea Garden to enjoy the last of the autumn sunshine. Sipping a cold fizzy drink, he wondered *What can I write?* What type of publications had he'd come across of late? History books he'd flicked through, scientific papers he'd been sent and the latest new thing: self-help books, et cetera, et cetera. He needed to write a book, but what should it be about? He couldn't say. If he were to start now, he'd have something to leave to the institution he'd served for so long – before he retired. Retirement, however, was the last thing on his mind, since he was one of those people who'd work to their last breath.

But on a different day, he sat down in exactly the same tea garden and spent several hours seriously considering the question. The aftershocks of the fire in the hospital had indisputably played a part. But the main factor was the tension created by the **harelipped Gynaecologist Ayşe Nuran Serbest**, who had come from the Maternity Hospital to deliver a lecture on *Hygiene in Women's Health*, a dull-as-ditch-water rant that opened lyrically: *When a woman becomes a mother, her spirit blossoms.*

After her lecture (if you could call that vapid speech a lecture), the Medical Director had ordered a couple of packs of bourbon creams and, out of courtesy, as he did with all his guests, invited the gynaecologist to his office for a cup of tea. First, they exchanged tales of woe about understaffing and supply shortages. Then, with his index finger on his temple and his eyes fixed on that harelip, the Medical Director had said, *You have no idea how much I envy you, Nuran Hanım. Your job is with women, not like us with the deranged.* And a frosty wind blew through the room. The paranoid gynaecologist completely misread his intentions.

Ayşe Nuran Serbest was still a virgin; no man had ever touched her, and at this rate no man ever would, either. Her belief that her facial defect must remind men of her genitals owed something, no doubt, to the epithet *cunnylips* she'd overheard time and again. Now thirty-nine years old, Ayşe Nuran (originally from Tomarza, Kayseri) had been top of her class at the lycée and thus received a direct offer from the Gevher Nesibe Faculty of Medicine. Before the start of her medical training, she had never seen pictures of either male or female genitalia, and had no idea what they looked like. The day she saw her first patient waiting, legs spread apart, for an internal examination, Ayşe Nuran nearly fainted. Worse still were her classmates' sniggers; she was shocked, really distraught. She seriously considered dropping out. But **her mother, Faika Serbest**, whose greatest wish was to see her daughter qualify as a doctor, pestered, *I'll never give you my blessings otherwise!* So Ayşe Nuran had little choice. And managed to live perfectly normally despite her obsession – if one didn't look too closely at her, that is. She was a good doctor, she didn't hide herself or her defect, and wasn't the least bit nervous about appearing in public.

She was in the fifth year of medical school when a female lecturer loosened her tongue, got her to reveal her problem and, instead of sending her to a psychiatrist, recommended she specialise in gynaecology, precisely in order to overcome it. Though hardly intellectually superior to her classmates – if anything, a little inferior – the bookworm (more like textbookworm) Ayşe Nuran studied night and day, passing all her exams like clockwork, and so entered this highly popular branch of medicine.

In time, however, gynaecology backfired on her. Ayşe Nuran, who had seen thousands of vulvas throughout her professional career, would lately become close to tears whenever she looked in the mirror. Although at first recognising the pointlessness of this fixation, it had increasingly grown worse and now preyed on her mind. Nowadays, whenever someone stared at her face, she made a scene.

So at Medical Director's sardonic comment *Your job is with women*, coupled with him staring at her harelip, she lost her head. Hinting at the spinster's disfigurement was the last thing on the Medical Director's mind, however: he was barely aware of her sex, never mind trying to visualise her vulva. He had other things to worry about.

Just the previous night, a supposedly low-risk patient, the **schizoid Barış Bakış** – also known as BB in the hospital – had drenched his bed with eau de cologne and struck a match, yelling, *This is the bed where my wife cuckolded me!* The bed was next to a window. The foam mattress had burst into flames, which soon leapt to other beds and the window frame, as the fire threatened to spread to the other wards. The poor Medical Director was fretting over the enquiry that was likely to follow.

He had been woken by a phone call in the middle of the night, jumped out of his warm, soft bed (whose sheets his wife changed every morning), scrambled into some clothes and zoomed over to the hospital. Thank God the fire was put out quickly before it had a chance to spread anywhere beyond BB's ward.

By the time the Medical Director returned home, once the fire-fighters had finished cooling the building and the orderlies had set about tidying the scorched room, it was nearly morning, but his usual procedure of undressing in the hallway and taking a quick shower wasn't good enough. Sevim nagged and nagged, *I bet your hair and everything's absorbed all that poisonous smoke and filled your mouth and nose too!* which gave him no choice but to take an extremely long shower and gargle with an antiseptic mouthwash. A plodding dawn was breaking when he finally returned to bed, with the call to morning prayer drowned out by the rumble of the washing machine, worn out with washing several loads day in, day out.

The ensuing commotion had eaten into the morning, with telephones ringing off the hook, and the Medical Director was exhausted after discussing the fire, by now no secret, with at least a hundred people (or so it seemed). Thankfully, things had quietened down by the afternoon lecture, and the hall was packed for the first time in a while. Strictly speaking, it was filled with students from the girls' vocational school, who had been brought here en masse to learn about the importance of hygiene in women's health – a topic that held no interest for the girls, who ignored their teachers' warnings and giggled as they texted their boyfriends. All the same, the conference had attracted sufficient interest to make him happy.

The evening news on the local TV station Channel SS (now, since the Moldovan Anya incident, boasting a co-owner in the person of Councillor Latif) would certainly show a heaving conference hall, which would enable the Medical Director to dictate hire terms for staff training seminars and wangle whatever he could for the hospital – tables, chairs, TV sets, anything. Government funding was inadequate and the float just didn't stretch to soap, toothpaste, sanitary pads for female patients, and so on. That's why the Medical Director, who regarded such toiletries not as a luxury but as a vital necessity, had to cosy up to the local business community and regularly make such requests for patients without families.

He was just about to tell Ayşe Nuran about the fire, just to make conversation, and say, *Thank God no one was hurt*, when the harelipped gynaecologist splashed his face with the dregs of her tea, yelled a heap of abuse at him and charged out. Dumbfounded, he was about to follow her out to ask, *What's wrong?* but changed his mind. *What if she got her knickers in an even worse twist?* He paced in his office restlessly for a bit before deciding to take it out on Barış Bakış, the untouchable firebug who had caused this mess.

It was the afternoon. According to the floor nurse who picked up the phone, BB's doctor, Âlim Kâhkeci, was in the masjid; she said she'd last seen the patient strolling in the hallways of the open unit with a book under his arm. The Medical Director couldn't believe his ears: the patient who had made his night and morning a living nightmare was swanning around like nothing was wrong. Thundering, *Immobilise him at once!* he raised hell.

Guards in hospital gear were alerted at once, as though Barış Bakış were about to terrorise the place with a long-barrelled rifle. The patient was located in the first-floor day room, calmly re-reading *Journals of a Non-Madman* for perhaps the thousandth time. Just like the protagonist of Feyyaz Kayacan's story, BB kept a journal he'd named *Hospital Diary*; every night, he noted down whatever took place in his confused mind. Slipping a straitjacket over him as he protested, *OK, OK, don't yank, I'm coming,* the guards whisked him away.

Strictly speaking, he wasn't a difficult patient. Except for the fire, that is – but he had never hurt anyone. True, he refused to acknowledge his left hand, insisting that it belonged to someone else or was even another person. And that wasn't all. He believed his wife was cheating on him with his left hand. In actual fact he was too immature to be married. At the same time, however, neither his doctor, Âlim Kâhkeci, nor anyone else responsible for his care knew anything about the fictional character he identified with. Yet he'd given them all the clues they needed in his book – surely its title was suggestive enough? – which he never let go of.

The heartbreakingly handsome lad with the green eyes had been brought to the hospital nine months earlier by his mother and sectioned at her request. After a week's observation in the secure unit, with no evident reason to keep him there, he took his two elegant suitcases, one packed to the gills with books, and moved to the open floor where the patients weren't locked up.

Neither Âlim Kâhkeci nor the Medical Director (who, on a phone call from a high-ranking friend of BB's mother, had been told in the most judicious tones that the patient must receive the very best possible care and that there could be *absolutely no doubt that maximum care would be taken*) believed hospitalisation to be needed, never mind sectioning.

Medication could be supervised perfectly well outside. But the mother, **Veda Alkan, a Foreign Ministry political expert in a European Union negotiations workgroup**, insisted that it was impossible for her to control her son or adequately continue his treatment at home.

The Medical Director naturally enquired, *Why not place him in a hospital in Ankara?* It never occurred to him that someone who moved in high circles might wish to keep her son out of sight so as not to compromise her standing in society. No spring chicken, yet still a highly attractive platinum blonde sporting a glowing tan and a beauty spot at the corner of her mouth, Veda snapped back, inscrutably, *I see no reason to divulge my private reasons!*

She was in a hurry, incessantly fanning the generous décolleté of her ivory silk blouse with her return ticket as she spoke and filling the office with her heady scent: she had to fly back to Ankara for a very important meeting at the Foreign Ministry. So the admission procedures were rushed through. She kissed and cuddled her son, gave the Medical Director all her telephone numbers, including her mobile, and vanished, never to be seen again. The political expert had to travel constantly. Give her credit though: she never neglected her son, always ringing from four corners of the globe to ensure he received the most preferential treatment possible.

There was nothing of the crocodile about her tears as she took leave of her son with the deep green eyes, a forehead shaded by a black fringe, stunning cheekbones and a sweet voice like a burbling brook – a combination that made him the centre of attention in the hospital. But those angelic looks did more than merely turn the head of the Psychologist Gülnazmiye Görgün, a fresh and somewhat addle-brained graduate of the Ankara Faculty of Letters and History, who had arrived a few months earlier to take up her post; the hapless girl thought she'd choke unless she gazed at this wonderful face every hour, on the hour.

Secretly finding the name *Gülnazmiye* a bit common, she claimed that she actually had two first names, *Gül* and *Nazmiye*, but the registrar had accidently written them as one name; she *answered to Gül*, which meant rose. Except that she was immediately dubbed Melek Görgün by the male staff over the age of forty, on account of her large and indisputably lovely breasts; she, for her part, had never heard of the seventies sex goddess of Yeşilçam where the heart of Turkish cinema had produced such unforgettable erotic masterpieces as *The Director's Bedroom*, *Şevket the Hamam Attendant*, and *Love Your Brush, Painter*. Younger males simply called her *Big Tits*. Having missed out on the erstwhile darling of the male world and far less concerned with propriety, they had no qualms about being overheard.

The name Melek Görgün completely went over her head, but not the whispered Big Tits, which she overheard one day: realising they were talking about her, she took to wearing bras a size smaller to minimise her breasts. Once she got lost in BB's water green eyes, though, she released them in their full glory. At first she'd only fancied him; but after a long chat with him, she fell in love. Truly, madly, deeply.

A scrapped four-seater rear bench with the foam spilling out of the rips in the red vinyl stood between the overflowing wheelie bins and mountains of central heating coal, ripped off a minibus in one of the car repair workshops nearby and carelessly flung onto what had become a rubbish tip at the rear of the hospital, the side that faced the sea. Gülnazmiye Görgün was perched on its edge. This had become a favourite hideaway after learning that the Medical Director was an ardent anti-smoker. Barış Bakış arrived, carrying his customary copy of *Journals of a Non-Madman*, and sat down at the other end; his mother's VIP status had enabled – nay, even encouraged – him to wander unchecked around the hospital so as to prevent him withdrawing into himself and losing contact with the external world, albeit under close supervision so he wouldn't up and leave.

How lovely the sea looked that day. The dark clouds gathering in the sky had changed it to a deep, greenish blue and the languid waves were tipped with snow-white foam. Gülnazmiye couldn't take her eyes off the sea as she wondered why there wasn't a single window on the seaward side of the town's oldest hospital. At BB's arrival, she suddenly became flustered. Nearly had a heart attack, not knowing what to do, where to place her hands.

In a tone that suggested this gorgeous heartthrob might care for her, he said, *I've sat down, but I hope I'm not disturbing you…* as his water-green eyes bore into hers, but it was the final part of this conversation she would later recall verbatim.

After learning her name and what she did at the hospital, Barış Bakış continued, *There are two types of narcissists, Gül Hanım.* She had no idea how they'd got to narcissism, although it was very simple actually. He had complained at length about his doctor Âlim Kâhkeci, suggesting (at times in surprisingly well-formed sentences, but at other times in truncated sentences, mixed with incongruous phrases on other matters) that it was due to a narcissistic personality that the fellow never bothered listening to anyone.

Despite occasionally seeming a threat, Âlim Kâhkeci rarely worried his patient. Barış Barış was quite happy at the hospital, where he could read to his heart's content, write in a secret diary, wander at will and do whatever he wanted, provided he didn't leave. All he wanted was a little chat from time to time. But whenever they sat down to talk – and his treatment necessitated frequent conversations – Âlim Kâhkeci turned a deaf ear to what Barış had to say about books, insisting instead on raising the matter of the fictitious wife, which jangled the young man's nerves and made him wish he'd never blurted out his secret.

The red vinyl upholstery of the four-seater that Barış Barış was leaning back on threw those green eyes into stark relief. Gülnazmiye's gaze, a moment ago fixed on the sea, was now fixed on his eyes. Barış broke the heavily charged pause by saying, *The first type of narcissists believe the whole world's in love with them.* She shivered with anticipation at the phrase *in love*; they may talk of love yet. But when the owner of those green eyes continued, *They only communicate with their inferiors in order to protect their own egos from harm*, a stab of pain pierced her heart. His glamorous mother had swept through the hospital like a gust of wind, leaving in her wake not just her magnificent perfume but a tremendous fragrance of the upper classes as well.

Melting under that green gaze, Gülnazmiye felt so worthless, so inferior, that when Barış Bakış added, *The second type of narcissists think too highly of themselves. The hand that could touch that precious complexion, the lips that would kiss those divine lips or the eye that had the right to look at those deep eyes… have yet to be created*, she was devastated. Her head dropped. Was this young man (whom she fancied enough to die for just then!) trying to suggest that he's a green-eyed narcissist and she had no right to look him in the eye? Attempting an honourable retreat from this battle of love she thought she could never win, she surprised herself with her own audacity when she asked, *And which type are you? First or second?*

The moment his bright white teeth gleamed was the moment that did for Gülnazmiye Görgün. If that shambles of a four-seater could speak, it would explain how her hands, dripping with sweat, stuck to the red vinyl and how she was nearly choking with love.

Barış wasn't entirely insane… but neither was he totally sane. At any rate, sane wasn't the opposite of insane. And his sanity (or lack thereof) was no obstacle to Gülnazmiye's infatuation. The truth of the matter was, to quote that **loveable foulmouth, Sister Zerrin**: *You never knew who in this shitty world was bloody crazy and who wasn't.*

It was BB's life spent *now with one grandma, now with the other* as the child of divorced parents that, in Âlim Kâhkeci's words, *had upset the boy's balance.* The probability of a genetic predisposition couldn't be discounted either, given the many serious cases of schizophrenia on BB's paternal side. For years and years, his mother and her sisters had blamed the boy's condition on the father: the bloke had up and left his happy home to live like *Tarzan of Manisa*, in the words of **Veda's mother, Rana**. Except that had been a perfectly rational, conscious choice; it had nothing to do with schizophrenia.

Originally a civil servant with a bright future at the Foreign Ministry, **Menderes Bakış had turned into an environmentalist** and, opting for a natural lifestyle quite out of the blue, decided to leave his wife and job and settle in Datça on the southwestern tip of Anatolia. Veda was shocked. She blamed the break-up on the **Austrian environmentalist Karolin Pichler**, a colleague of his from the chemical pollution prevention project in Izmit Bay.

According to Veda, Karolin (*Karo to my friends*) – a Green from Salzburg who strung everyone along with unrealistic projects as she toured all four corners of the globe thanks to the funds lavished on environmentalists by the European Union – had tempted Menderes, the conqueror of Ankara's roads in his gas-guzzling Grand Cherokee, threats to the future of the planet being far from his mind at the time. Karo had thus toyed with a man's home and perfectly good career.

This allegation met with enthusiastic acceptance amongst those who didn't know Karo very well. The women were dying to swap places with her, due to her shapely legs that defied those artless outfits and unkempt looks as well as the fantastic breasts that she saw no reason to hide even on the most formal of occasions; and the men were dying to swap places with Menderes for precisely the same reasons. Tongues wagged about the taut figure that had swept Menderes off his feet, as this spurious allegation spread throughout Ankara's diplomatic and bureaucratic circles, which was just what Veda wanted.

These rumours had no repercussions either for Karo or the world of diplomacy. Quite the opposite; Menderes – *lucky bastard* in the men's eyes, as much for Karo as for his strikingly sexy wife Veda – became the hottest topic at leisurely lunches on wine and carpaccio. Veda, in the meanwhile, swiftly settled into the role of victim. Much solace was offered by several diplomats and high-ranking civil servants. Some even succeeded in consoling this wronged beauty whose world had come crashing down upon her head when her husband up and left.

Only she knew perfectly well that there was no such relationship. Karo was devastatingly beautiful, but she was a thoroughly professional, dedicated environmentalist whose gorgeous boyfriend back in Salzburg could run rings around Menderes. *I want to steal hearts, wreck homes, I've never tasted one before so why not have a torrid fling with a Turk whilst I'm here,* and so on – these were the last things on her mind. At any rate, given her fleeting involvement with the project in question, she had long since left for Beijing on the other side of the world; her contact with Menderes had been nothing more than a handful of official meetings and lunches.

Veda's perceptiveness in matters of the heart merits mention. She had been around long enough to tell at once when a woman was interested in any man in her vicinity, not only her husband. It actually suited her to blame the suspiciously gorgeous and overly informal Karo for the break-up of her marriage, thereby scotching any potential allegations that Veda had failed to make her husband happy, that their marriage had already been on shaky ground.

Karo's only fault was to introduce Menderes to a few of her friends from Turkey's increasingly popular environmentalist movements.

These introductions led not to a new romance but to a brand new life. Fed up with the soulless, formal atmosphere that reigned in Ankara, as it does in so many capitals, sick to the gills of politicking, of running with the fox and hunting with the hounds, and realising that he was no longer in love with his wife, Menderes Barış knew he couldn't go on living in this city with this woman and resolved to make a radical change.

Just then, at an official function at the Romanian Embassy, Veda was being introduced to **Emil Pavulescu, at the time a rather unremarkable diplomat who was yet to earn his stripes**. Their paths would cross again years later. Barış, as usual, was staying at her mother's; he had finished his chicken noodle soup and dropped off in grandma's vast walnut bed. Menderes Bakış came home. He was pouring himself a drink to relax after a particularly stressful day... when he suddenly felt he'd suffocate if he stayed here for one more minute.

Grabbing a few essentials and the bike he'd been riding on weekends to keep fit, in the Hoşebe Forest in Nallıhan or the İnözü Valley in Beypazarı, he raced over to the coach station. This would be the last time he'd ever drive the Jeep he'd been so eager to buy, his precious wheels that hurtled up and down deserted roads at mind-blowing speeds in the early hours when all Ankara was in deep sleep. Boarding a coach, he made straight for the fantastic expanse of land his father had bought for a song back in the day and later forgotten about: thick with eucalyptuses and carobs, it stretched along the seafront as far as the eye could see.

When Veda Bakış (as she still was) returned home in the early hours after the reception, which had dragged on, and after guiding her foreign guests (including Emil Pavulescu) through Ankara's dull nightlife, although now she was feeling more relaxed and mellower thanks to the alcohol, her husband was nowhere to be seen. Too exhausted to worry about his whereabouts, she just fell into bed. The next day, Menderes Bakış rang to announce that he'd left her. The ignition key was still in the car where he'd left it in the car park; she might want to retrieve it before it was stolen. He had no wish to drive a car again, but Veda probably wouldn't be too keen on letting the sizeable amount they'd paid go to waste. He sounded quite forbidding and obviously had no intention of coming back.

Veda ranted and raved but just couldn't bring herself to accept that her husband had chosen a totally new lifestyle. She knew he hadn't been deliriously happy, and in fact, he had frequently cheated on her. Not that she herself was pure as the driven snow, given the length of her own list of adulterous affairs. They had come to the brink several times in the past, but things had improved of late; they had rekindled their love and even started thinking about *perhaps a brother or sister* for their son, whom *they loved dearly*, however infrequently they saw him. The prospect had cropped up of a foreign posting for Menderes – Geneva or Strasbourg – which would be a welcome change for them both.

Consequently, Veda mistook this for a premature mid-life crisis; convinced that in a few months he would tire of the eco-friendly lifestyle and return, she did her best to stop him from resigning from a post that every young aspiring civil servant would give a right arm for. But his decision had nothing at all to do with whether he was happy in his marriage, or that he was only four years short of forty. Nor was it a momentary lapse of reason, or even a sudden falling in love. He was unhappy, full stop, and truly did intend to transform his life.

Even as she snuggled in consoling arms, waiting for him to come to his senses and return to her, Menderes filed the petition for divorce. He lived in a hut he'd built with his own hands, using only natural materials on land inaccessible to all motorised traffic. This latter-day Robinson Crusoe eschewed all synthetics, drew water from the well he had dug himself, felt no need for electricity, lived on the fruit and vegetables he grew, and the bread, milk and eggs he bought from villages nearby. The only contemporary items his natural world admitted were books and magazines.

He cycled forty kilometres to Datça several times a week, posted articles in English and French to foreign environmentalist and natural-lifestyle magazines, collected the publications he had ordered, and cycled back. The popularity of his articles on the environment and his lifestyle philosophy grew, as did the numbers of his visitors. Veda realised resistance was futile, agreed to the divorce, won custody of her son and promptly handed him over to her mother, who in her day had twisted Ankara's bureaucratic class around *her* little finger.

Over the years, Menderes turned into a sort of natural lifestyle guru and was kept extremely busy thanks to his growing reputation amongst ecologists, Greenpeace and the like; all this demanded the adoption of certain compromises on his originally unequivocal principles. At first he had used the hearth or an olive oil burner for light, and written his articles on a clapped-out old typewriter, but eventually he bowed to the necessity of connecting his home (now no longer a hut) to the grid, using a laptop, and even travelling in fossil-fuel-burning vehicles to get to seminars and other activities. But he was careful to maintain a balance. His views, in any case, were not of the utopic type that sought to hinder the ways of the world. The prudence of his articles had a wide appeal as much with strict followers of the green movement as with many sensible moderates concerned with the environment.

He also opposed most vaccines and all synthetic medicines. Yet it was his own neglect that caused the unfortunate death of this otherwise level-headed environmentalist.

He was having a shouting match in the forest with the **documentary director Çiğdem Taşpınar** – his girlfriend of six months, except he'd adamantly refused to live with her on the pretext that this would damage their relationship – when he stepped on a rusty tin can with a serrated edge that ripped into his bare foot. In his rage, he refused her suggestion to go to a health centre to have the wound dressed and get a tetanus shot. Eyes watering with the pain, he tugged the can out of his flesh, left his girlfriend alone in the forest, and cycled for nine kilometres with an injured foot.

It certainly wasn't an argument worth dying for. But because of his mood swings Menderes could easily throw the baby out with the bathwater without blinking.

Çiğdem was due to shoot *Bosnia's Weeping Women*, a documentary about the worst victims of that ongoing war. She had come to visit him before setting off for Sarajevo to make the French-Hungarian co--production. For three days, they had a wonderful time: she took countless photographs of Menderes, who'd grown even more eccentric with his long hair and beard, which made him even more handsome, and devoured his latest articles. Merrily, they baked cookies using the fruit he'd grown and dried, molasses and pure flour in the kitchen of what was now almost a mansion after the addition of various annexes and extensions. They were in seventh heaven like young lovers. Or at least, that's how they looked. Inwardly, Çiğdem had butterflies in her stomach.

Menderes had fallen out big time with **Çiğdem's co-producer, Vincent Barratier**, whose mere name was enough to piss him off. Menderes thought the bloke was a hypocritical parasite: managing somehow to wangle money out of cultural institutions and international organisations for trivial projects, getting in on all manner of social schemes, putting his nose into anything where he could smell funding, schmoozing to get to the source, and stopping at nothing to scupper the project the moment he suspected personal benefit was out of his reach.

Menderes had first met Vincent during negotiations for a multinational documentary on *Acomys cilicicus*, a threatened native species of southwest Anatolia also known as the Silifke porcupine mouse. Vincent had put his name forward as executive producer. But within thirty minutes of meeting him, having marked him as a nasty piece of work who'd happily exploit anyone and everyone, Menderes had flatly refused the parasite's request to participate in the project. The ensuing tension grew worse whenever they met. So Menderes went ballistic when he recognised Vincent's hand in the rejection of his latest application, and since then he'd been looking for an opportunity to blow the whistle on the geezer.

Vincent's lack of honesty and trustworthiness had not escaped Çiğdem's attention either; only she wasn't sure he was all bad, or even a complete parasite. Moreover, since he had a finger in every pie in so many countries, staying on his good side might open doors for her; so she took pains to avoid crossing him.

Which effectively meant that Vincent didn't know of her relationship with Menderes, and Menderes didn't know the identity of her producer on her latest project.

She'd been intending to break it to him gently during a stroll in the forest. Just as she was thinking *What's the best way of mentioning it in passing?* Menderes, his bare feet idly kicking at the mossy stones in the stream, asked, perhaps for the tenth time, who the producer was. Çiğdem had parried earlier questions with *Don't know yet.* Taken unawares this time, however, she stayed silent for just that bit too long; Menderes, who'd already smelt a rat, realised that the unmentioned name was Vincent and went ape. So she blew up, exclaimed, *Yes, it's Vincent! So what?* and they went at each other hammer and tongs. An incandescent Menderes trod on the tin can, stifled his scream and shoved away the hand reaching out to help.

Menderes fumed all the way home – *Bet the bitch's shagged this bastard and all!* – the veins in his neck swelling in his rage. The pedal, slick with blood, left a trail on the ground. Too wrapped up in his ranting and raving, he never felt the pain. And when he got home, instead of cleaning and dressing his wound, he rolled a stonking joint and fell asleep.

Seriously hacked off for being abandoned in the middle of the forest, Çiğdem resolved to break up with him at once. As if she couldn't tell that she was the one who'd been ditched. Upon reaching the house, the scene of their happy breakfast just that morning, she hurled a mouthful of invectives at the man lying in bed: he was pathetic and jealous, and a pushy blunderer to boot. Menderes carried on snoring without even rolling over.

As far as the ambitious filmmaker was concerned, the tension between Menderes and Vincent had nothing to do with her. She would make him pay for this outburst: she ripped out the film from the camera to ruin the photos she'd taken in the morning, gleefully poured wine over his writings, magazines, precious books and the laptop he'd forked out a fortune for only last month (a model that had only just been launched), and ripped out the telephone cable. Then, looking around, she wondered *What else can I destroy?* and decided she'd done enough. Grabbing her stuff, she set off for the Datça hotel to join her assistant (on a short break before filming began) and a few friends and pour her heart out in tears.

It was the start of closed season. Adopting the slogan *Fair chase!* a group of hunters, led by the **Atçalı Village headman, Uncle Nezir**, declared war on unscrupulous poachers whose use of unsporting equipment was giving hunting a bad name. Atçalı's disciplined hunters followed the rules and followed up on tip-offs.

Uncle Nezir was on his way back to the village after having finished his errands in Datça. His wreck of a Murat 124 blew a tyre. Huffing and puffing, he was changing it when he noticed the blood on the ground. He touched it; it was only just dry. The trail came out of the forest, reached the asphalt and carried on for a bit. He was curious. He followed the drops with his gaze and then started walking.

Before disappearing into the ground, the trail ran up to a path he had long since suspected led to a poacher's hideaway. Nezir didn't need to think twice; this had to be the blood of a wild boar shot illegally by **Bald Hüseyin, the black sheep of the hunting world**. Despite all the rumours, Nezir had so far been unable to prove anything against Bald Hüseyin. He raised the gendarme, the County Hunting Directorate and other officials on the CB radio he'd recently installed in the Murat 124.

Bald Hüseyin was raided that very day. He and a hotelier were nabbed haggling over some skinned beasts in a filthy barn camouflaged behind bushes, twigs and haystacks, where he slaughtered the wild boar he intended to sell on the sly. A hole had been dug in the ground to bury the useless skin and offal, coarsely chopped fat was set aside to be preserved later, and six headless carcasses with gleaming pink flesh were hanging on meat hooks, ready to be jointed. Glowering at Uncle Nezir, Bald Hüseyin asked, *Drop this blood trail bullshit, Nezir. Tell me who grassed on me?* His insistence that he had never taken the boar down the asphalt went in one ear and out the other.

If only, instead of grabbing his mike the moment he saw the blood to yell, *Gotcha now Hüseyin!*, Uncle Nezir had followed the trail a little longer, just another five or six steps, he'd have seen the size-forty-four footprint on a large, flat rock and might have saved a man's life. The injured man had cycled all that way and dismounted dog-tired with a few hundred metres left to go. Then he had stepped on a rock and left a very clear footprint in blood. If only Uncle Nezir hadn't been quite so sure!

Uncle Nezir would never know that he'd missed his opportunity to save the life of Menderes Bakış, who had supported their co-operative, offered advice, helped them source high quality seeds and organic pesticides, mobilised the lackadaisical agriculture and animal husbandry officials in the district and always helped the village and the villagers.

As for Bald Hüseyin, who was charged and heavily fined after being caught red-handed once his clandestine activities came to light: he never again sold poached game. He always maintained he'd never have been caught if someone hadn't snitched. Obsessed with finding the culprit, he dropped everything else, blamed the unlikeliest of people, fell out with practically the entire village, and never spoke to Uncle Nezir again.

They fell out so badly that when Bald Hüseyin's son and Uncle Nezir's daughter fell in love, the two men railed against each other to the tune of *I'd die before letting my daughter marry that bastard's son!* and *I'd die before letting my son marry that whistle-blowing headman's daughter!* Thankfully, their wives were too sensible to allow that sulk to interfere with the young couple's happiness. When Hüseyin was forced to go ask for the girl's hand for his son, he refused to talk to Uncle Nezir, so it fell upon his wife to pronounce the traditional opening: *By the command of Allah and the consent of the Prophet…*

At the wedding, the two fathers-in-law sat at adjacent tables without exchanging a single word. Their wives provided the only means of communication between them: *Tell that devil Uncle Nezir to do such and such,* and *Tell that shameless baldie to do such and such.* Ignoring their sulking husbands, the mothers-in-law became inseparable, always in one or the other's home, whilst Hüseyin (now called Sulky Hüseyin) and Uncle Nezir (now called Mulish Uncle Nezir) took to going to the village coffee house at different times so they wouldn't run into each other.

It wasn't until a fortnight after their row, the tin can incident and her break-up that Çiğdem realised how Vincent had shafted her – the worst rip-off she'd experienced in her career so far – and that Menderes had been right after all. She thought she could smell a rat when nothing seemed to be happening with *Bosnia's Weeping Women*, the project she'd dedicated her whole being to; the promised funds just weren't coming through, nor was there any information or interest – and her crew, who'd all this time been on starting blocks, were getting restless. Çiğdem rang the company's head office in Budapest every day, but she couldn't get hold of anyone in charge. At long last she got through to one of the female directors, who said, *I'll call you back in five minutes.* And didn't for a week.

Biting the bullet, she hopped on a flight to Budapest, where all she got was a cool *Sorry!* The director said they'd changed their minds about shooting in Bosnia due to security issues, but she hoped they'd work together on other projects in the future. Çiğdem bought the excuse at first; after all, everyone was justifiably worried about the wars still raging in Bosnia–Herzegovina and Croatia. But something tempted her to dig a little deeper, and she discovered Vincent's hand in the business. The bloke had promoted his own project instead (same premise, different script, but one he had partially co-authored) and convinced the directors that it would be far more profitable and far more *high profile*.

Depressed and disappointed, Çiğdem returned to Datça. She hired a motorbike and straightaway went to apologise to Menderes, fall at his feet and even plead if need be; they could then work out how to make Vincent pay. She had got in with a scumbag for the sake of a film she'd hoped would be a major milestone in her career, and thrown over her boyfriend. When she arrived, though, her boyfriend was drenched in sweat in a soaking wet bed, his muscles contracted, unable to swallow or speak. He was on the verge of losing consciousness and his wound looked revolting.

The landline cable having been ripped out by her own hand and the ubiquity of mobile phones being still some way off, Çiğdem had no choice but to ride to the village for help. When she got there she saw Uncle Nezir sitting under the willow outside the coffee house, sipping a freshly squeezed black mulberry juice and for the nth time recounting – with much embellishment – how he got Hüseyin nicked. Meanwhile, Hüseyin, in pre-trial detention, was quizzing every single visitor to name the snitch who'd shopped him.

Panicking and breathless, Çiğdem explained Menderes's condition and Uncle Nezir moved at once. They rang for an ambulance to take Menderes to Datça State Hospital, by which time flies were buzzing around the putrid wound. A tearful Çiğdem begged for forgiveness all the way. But Menderes was already unconscious, his pulse too low to hear her heartfelt confession or to forgive her.

By the time they reached the hospital it was too late.

Barış was ten when his father died of tetanus; earlier that summer, thinking he was Mary Poppins, the boy had leapt off his grandmother's ornate balcony. He was the only heir to the land which Menderes had earmarked for a summer school for tomorrow's ecologists. Barış was still only a minor, and his mother, on grounds of her son's unsound mind, would assume guardianship well before he came of age.

Thus Veda took control of the land. At first she was unwilling to sell it cheap – it had, after all, developed into something of a wonder of nature through the years – but it proved difficult to sell. She waited for ages, eventually lost patience, and sold it to a developer in exchange for four villas. The developer moved bulldozers into that corner of paradise, ripped out the eucalyptuses, carobs, stone pines and olive trees, as well as the organic orchards Menderes had taken such pains to establish (the almond, orange, cherry and peach trees had grown wild in the interim), and erected thirty-eight summer villas, all with a sea view thanks to a superior feat of planning. Sold them all off-plan, too, and like hot cakes.

Barış had been nine the last time he'd seen his father – at his paternal grandmother's funeral at the heaving Kocatepe Mosque in Ankara. He was led by the hand to a gigantic man with hair down to his broad shoulders and a beard down to his chest, a man he mistook for Zeus, the ruler of the gods, whose picture he'd seen in his *Mythology for Children*, an illustrated book he had read over and over.

Father and son shared the same sense of estrangement. Menderes stared at the son he hadn't seen for years without feeling much of anything, hardly able to believe that he was the father of this child with the huge emerald-green eyes. Barış, for his part, was inspecting his father, who, he was told, lived alone on an enormous piece of land in the Aegean Region. After gazing at each other silently for a spell, they both lost interest. Menderes eventually returned to his eucalyptuses and fruit trees in Datça without communicating much more with his son, and Barış carried on occupying himself in his lonely and delirious world.

It was a time when his mother was again hugely busy, one of his aunts was doing a postgraduate degree abroad, and the other had got married, so he was left with his grandmother, Rana. His strange behaviour somehow seemed to escape notice. If only they had paid attention earlier, they would have seen how he identified with Peter in *Heidi*, with Carbonel, the King of Cats, with Moby Dick and with many other fictional characters. To be fair, they did notice, but attributed it to childishness. And in fact, when he leapt off the first floor balcony holding an umbrella, he nearly gave the old woman a heart attack. Thankfully, he only sprained an ankle, and the incident remained a secret between grandmother and grandson.

Later, he identified with Pip from *Great Expectations*, Jean Valjean, Raskolnikov, Oblomov, Martin Eden and even Josef K., before latching onto Hanno Buddenbrook – the melancholic, fragile Hanno, a critical clue to the disturbance in his own mental health. He told everyone that he answered to the name Hanno, and chatted with Aunt Antonie in his room at night.

As his mother flitted between Vienna, Jeddah, Moscow and Washington, kissed, cuddled and lavished presents on Barış before buzzing off again, it was only Rana who noticed his conversations with the non-existent Antonie. But she was getting on in years and ascribed this adorable game to the intelligence and intellectual accumulation of her grandson, who was now in senior school.

His reading interest had expanded over time; when he discoveried the cream of contemporary literature, he found himself drawn much more to the secondary characters. He identified with one or several of the characters in every book he read, acted like them and spoke incessantly. It was the increasing degree of nonsense in these speeches that alerted his teachers to the gravity of his condition.

Barış, who had started reading Turkish literature the year before he was sectioned, had assumed the protagonist's identity in Feyyaz Kayacan Fergan's *Journals of a Non-Madman* to the extent that he was having heated arguments with some of the secondary characters. He, too, was hung up on doctors, and consequently did his best to stay on his own doctor's (that is, Âlim Kâhkeci's) good side, saving his *Hospital Diary* for the toilet, where he wrote squatting in the dark to avoid being seen by the other patients.

On the day he and the young female psychologist sat on either end of the discarded four-seater bench, Barış had replied to her question, *Which type are you?* with a dazzling smile, saying in an astonishingly clear-headed tone, *I'm talking about narcissists, not you or me.* Chatting her up was the last thing on his mind. He'd suddenly slipped into another reality, slipped out of his own personality, and formed an illusion-like communication with her. Her insides melting at his *you*, Gülnazmiye felt she would gladly give her life for him.

They'd talked of life, of literature, of poetry for such a long time – or rather, Barış had talked in words that went way over her head, even as she hung onto his every word – that by the time his absence was noted in the hospital, it was way past her office hours; she'd already missed the bus for the remote district where she lived. The attendants, sighing in relief at finally locating BB, approached him gently, coaxing him as if they were talking to a child – *C'mon darling, let's go in now* – and whisked away the object of her passion.

She gazed after his retreating back as he went with them obediently and realised that throughout this long lyrical chat, the love of her life had never once gazed at her breasts, which she had been conscious of for ever. It hurt for the first time in her life.

The young man's green eyes had claimed her heart, and his words had fascinated her not only emotionally but also scientifically. She dashed off an article entitled *Types of Relationships in Narcissist Personalities*, which began, *There are two types of narcissists*; it was a nonsensical essay sprinkled with romantic verses, rehashing what Barış had said down to his every last word, and despatched it to *Unnerving*, a peer-reviewed psychology magazine. Needless to say, it was rejected.

Most of the editorial board had failed to get past even the first page of her sentimental contribution, which was festooned with simplistic poems. Except for the self-styled doyen of his field, Prof Altay Çamur (*Chamur* in his preferred spelling), a regular contributor of patronising essays to virtually every issue, said essays never forgetting to herald the glad tidings of his book's imminent Turkish edition, notwithstanding the fact that his only publication to date was one single execrable volume in English – only he read her article in full. He also noted rather astutely that, although it was miles from being scientific, her article did evidence a romantic attachment on the part of the young psychologist; so Altay wrote *Tips for the Young Psychologist* for the next issue of *Unnerving*.

It started in a very gentle, low-key tone, touched on the indisputable value of emotional experience to the science of psychology, mentioned several events – *as experienced by a friend of the author* – that had happened to him personally, and recommended a psychotherapic approach for young psychologists to analyse their own experiences. Blessed with a supreme degree of self-confidence in his vast knowledge in every area of life, Altay Çamur had interjected the word *incidentally* before launching into poetry and literature (since Gülnazmiye had tucked a few verses into her article) and, referring to Shakespeare's *All the world's a stage*, rattled off numerous views on how men and women are merely players in the parts they are cast in – views in circulation since the sixteenth century – which he presented as his own discoveries.

Ostensibly a tribute to literature and the arts, despite their utter banality, his lines returned to Gülnazmiye without mentioning her by name, and continued, *My young friend, you are still at the start of the thorny path that is science. You will have plenty of time to read novels when you retire. Make time for scientific books now. My book, entitled* New Approaches in Psychotherapy, *is due for publication soon…* Helpful tips to young psychologists on how to write scientific articles followed (these were little more than platitudes), and the supercilious professor concluded his avuncular essay modestly… after a fashion.

Next month, Gülnazmiye Görgün went to the Road Bookshop to collect the issue of *Unnerving* she'd ordered. It hadn't yet arrived. Her whingeing, *But you said it would come today! And I've come all this way…* was interrupted by the **tetchy bookseller Özcan Durna**: *He was expecting a delivery; the magazine she wanted would probably arrive by noon*, and, with a snappy *Pop round in a while*, he got back to work.

The lovesick girl was so excited that she decided to wait. She looked around, couldn't see anywhere to sit, and leant back against a bookshelf. Which caused an almighty crash as a heap of books tumbled to the floor: what she had mistaken for a bookshelf was in tact a tower built out of copies of the latest Harry Potter novel, which Özcan had spent all morning to erect in alternating rows, one protruding, the next set back. The perpetually cantankerous bookseller foamed at the mouth; when the mortified girl attempted to pick up the books, her massive handbag smashed into a precariously balanced stack of Sezen Aksu CDs. So now a load of CDs tumbled to the floor, some falling open and a number of the flimsy lids breaking. Özcan really blew a gasket. Fearing that she would turn his bookshop into a battleground if she stayed another minute, he sent her packing with, *You've laid waste to the place, you silly cow! I've said it's not here yet, what part of no don't you understand? Ring and we'll tell you it's here when it is! Good God!*

She didn't mind; she had other dreams for that day. She would savour reading her article, and then engineer to leave the magazine, open to that page, somewhere Barış Bakış could see it, and her bookworm sweetheart would realise how passionately she'd referred to him.

She rang perhaps five times before noon to ask, *Has it come?* Finally realising that the only way to get rid of her was to give her the magazine, he unwrapped the parcel he'd set aside earlier, thinking *What's the hurry? I'll open it whenever…* found the copy of *Unnerving*, and rang back to say, *It's here, come and get it.* Gülnazmiye tore off, grabbed the magazine she'd been waiting for with bated breath and returned to the hospital. She didn't dare open it on the way, hoping to read it at her desk when her colleagues went to lunch.

On that particular day though, two of the three psychologists that she shared the office with, sardine-fashion, just happened be discussing last night's soap on TV as they waited for their Kayseri-style *mantı*, having ordered a take-away when they'd heard the main course at the canteen was lentils. When the breathless Gülnazmiye blew in, they offered to *order some for her, too.* Off her food since her chat with Barış, though, there was no way she'd be tempted by the high-calorie feast of mince-filled pasta parcels dripping with melted chilli butter. Clutching her handbag to her chest, she went to the office of **Matron Servinaz Ceviz** and settled at the massive, spotless desk.

Servinaz, the bane of the lower-level staff until two years ago, had become the sweetest thing since her husband had succumbed to a sudden cardiac arrest. Unfamiliar as she was with the iron-fisted draconian Matron of old, Gülnazmiye rejected the tales of *Terrible Servinaz* as fabrications by vicious, lazy nurses.

Except they were all true. In order to hide the amount of abuse she suffered from her husband, Servinaz Ceviz had stormed around the hospital for years and years, making the lives of her staff hell for even the slightest mistakes. She paid no attention to rules, regulations, cautions or warnings. Despite being a fine-looking woman herself with lovely eyes who should be enjoying her early forties, she had picked on the young nurses in particular. A hundred complaints and an incredibly high turnover of supply staff made no impression: the Medical Director, thoroughly satisfied with her discipline, which made sure the hospital ran like clockwork, turned a deaf ear to it all, dragged his heels over enquiries and only occasionally issued a half-hearted caution.

Her pervert of a husband, Ekrem Ceviz, had never laid a hand on her face; but if her friends had seen her poor body, they'd have been horrified by the marks of his sexual aberration. Servinaz could, and did, put up with numerous deviant demands (which had begun gently, at first in the heat of lust with her consent, but over the years he'd turned into a total sadist) – such as beating her up whilst they made love, burning her genitals with a cigarette or drawing a blade across her skin and forcing her to lick the blood he smeared on his finger, and more. The one thing she couldn't bear any longer was the shame of being forced to lie prone as all kinds of inconceivable objects were rammed up her back passage.

She was too embarrassed to open her mouth, scared that people would believe the angelic Ekrem – the father of her children, to boot! – and not her. What if someone asked, *What were you thinking all these years?* Pleading was no use; she just couldn't stop his vile sex games.

She left him once. Grabbing her thirteen-year-old daughter and nine-year-old son, she went to her father's. There was no way she could tell her parents what she had been putting up with. Instead, she told them that they just couldn't get along, but she didn't convince anyone. **Her father, Selman Emice**, was a shopkeeper who with his offerings for soldiers (a range of thick underwear, shoe polish, mirrors, combs, deodorant) and pilgrims (two lengths of cotton for robes, prayer beads and prayer rugs) could barely keep body and soul together; his long face said it all. More than happy with a son-in-law who rushed in whenever he needed a helping hand and never had to be asked twice for anything, Selman didn't approve of his daughter's wish to leave her husband, and he expressed his disapproval in no uncertain terms. Servinaz was more than ready to accept a life of disdain from her family so long as she wasn't forced to return to her husband. She let her father's increasingly harsher words wash over her, hinted that she'd hand over her entire salary to the last penny, was never idle but always made sure her mother didn't have to do a stitch of housework, but she couldn't elicit a smile from either parent.

Her husband turned up a week later. It was all planned. Selman Emice had shut up his shop after selling a few scraps to soldiers (eau de cologne, pointless souvenirs of the town, and long johns), dropped in on the tax office where Ekrem worked, and told him, *Come by this evening. I'll make sure you two make up, and you can take your wife and children home.* That evening Ekrem whimpered, eyes downcast, listing wistful entreaties that melted his father-in-law's heart: *Where did I failed, Dad? Did I not bring home our daily bread? Did I neglect my children? Did I play away? What have I done?* Her lips sealed, Servinaz sat still throughout. She had absolutely no intention of getting back together, but then she caught a glint in his eye. That pervert had sat his adolescent daughter on his lap and was stroking her long hair; he gave Servinaz a look that said, *It'll be her, if you don't come back! Tomorrow, if not today!* Terrified, she went back, lamb to slaughter.

And then as he was preparing for yet another sadistic act, the man who woke her every morning with kisses and cuddles after a night of perversion, made her breakfast, and sent their children off to school after fixing them a hearty breakfast (eggs and milk and all), died of a sudden cardiac arrest. Servinaz went hysterical, flung herself from wall to wall, ripped at her own clothes and played the role of her life.

It was the sight of her daughter's hairbrush in his hand that warned of yet another deviant session in the offing after three relatively calm nights; the realisation that the thing she'd been dreading was soon to happen pierced her to the quick. She knew he would ejaculate on the hairbrush and forbid her to throw it out; she would be forced to soak it in bleach with a flood of tears, then witness their daughter brushing her hair with it the following morning. The thought that the girl would be next was unbearable.

She gave him an ice cold lemonade lashed with a hefty dose of thioridazine, a neuroleptic she'd nicked from the medicines cabinet on her floor a few months earlier. Appalled at the idea of killing someone, however, she just hadn't been able to bring herself to use it, regardless of the mind-boggling abuse he'd subjected her to. The unsuspecting pervert, who'd been beating a path to cardiologists' doors of late, complaining of his heart, necked the unexpected treat.

Thioridazine had been linked to sudden cardiac arrests. A patient had died after taking it, which had resulted in heated discussions, enquiries, several reports and numerous visits from the reps of the pharmaceutical company in question as well as from Ministry of Health inspectors. In the meanwhile, Matron had taught herself as much about it as a pharmacologist, secretly poring over books and drug prospectuses.

Ekrem never got the chance to use that hairbrush he'd been carrying around for days. With butterflies in her stomach ever since she'd given him the drink, the tearful Servinaz was awaiting her fate, lying prone on the bed as ordered. Suddenly, Ekrem staggered and collapsed to the ground with a thud. An excruciating pain in his chest went all the way to his back and his whole body contracted in agony. He didn't know what was happening. His eyes bulging in fear for his life and his teeth clenched, he stared at her imploringly: *I'm dying! Take me to the hospital…* but all his vocal chords could manage was a rattle.

Her nerves shot, painfully aware that she was killing her husband, Servinaz murmured over and over to herself *I'm becoming a murderer! I'm becoming a murderer!* Just as she was on the verge of relenting and calling an ambulance – hang the risk of being exposed as a would-be murderer, of facing prison and misery – she caught sight of the hairbrush he was gripping. The risk of ruining her own life meant nothing. If Ekrem survived, however, she would be throwing her only daughter into the lap of a perverted father. Thinking of her daughter's sandy hair framing her pure face, she burst into tears.

With growing horror Ekrem realised that his naked wife, now standing by his head with tears streaming down her face, wasn't going to call an ambulance, that she was going to let him die. He convulsed on the floor, trying to grab and kiss her ankles, trying to plead. All it did was tire him out and hasten the end.

As she watched the death of the man she had married for love, who had shared her bed for fifteen years and at first made her very happy, she forced her fingers to trace the scars on her body to convince herself – still in a flood of tears – that he deserved this death. Ekrem breathed his last in the silent house. The children were sleeping soundly. Servinaz looked at her dead husband lying on the floor and then at her own naked, scarred body. She had to pull herself together. Hastily she climbed into her underwear and long-sleeved flannel nightgown, took a deep breath and started screaming.

She mourned for a month or so after he was interred (the death certificate stated *heart attack*) and she faced no enquiry. She spoke of him as a good husband; concerned about the mental health of her two children, she spoke to them about their wonderful father and made sure they never forgot him. But when she was alone in the bedroom, she would stare at her daughter's hairbrush to still the pangs of conscience for the murder she'd committed.

Her conscience and soul did not take that long to heal. One night, as she again stared at the hairbrush, she realised that she felt no sadness, no guilt, not anything; she felt utterly relieved. She binned the hairbrush, went to bed and slept like a log. In the morning, she woke up feeling at peace, as if Ekrem and all her troubles were centuries in the past.

Once over the trauma, Servinaz mellowed into sweetness personified, leaving her office door wide open, lending an ear to the troubles of the same staff she used to crush and bending over backwards to be of help. Her kindness knew no bounds. So jolly, so friendly, so happy and understanding she was that the hospital staff joked amongst themselves, *Widowhood becomes her! So it was all that greasy pig's fault... Ha ha ha!* No one suspected anything.

Gülnazmiye was one of the many who benefited from this open-door policy. Matron, before whom even doctors used to tremble, befriended the poor girl, who must be struggling to earn a crust so far away from family, all on her own, too, with no friends as yet in this town, where she was still a newcomer. Aware of the cramped conditions in that shared office, Matron had told her, *Don't be shy, little rose; come and work in my office whenever you want.*

On the day of the tennis racquet incident, a trembling Gülnazmiye had settled at Matron's desk and switched on the electric heater, having mistaken her excitement for a chill. The magazine was on the desk, but she was too tense to open it. Her eye was on the door in case someone came in. She was shaking in her boots: what if that someone were to spot the magazine, insist, *I wanna take a look too!* read her article and realise she was in love with Barış Bakış, and the matter went to her superiors and she faced an enquiry? It wasn't so much the risk of losing her job that troubled her as never being able to see him again. She got really worked up, one worry following another. Murmuring, *I'll never stop loving him – never!* she closed her eyes, thought of him and opened the magazine. She wasn't even halfway through flicking it when she heard a rattle.

It was Friday. She could see the office door of his doctor, Âlim Kâhkeci. As he stepped out to go to Friday prayers, Gülnazmiye's eye fell upon the cabinet with the patient files. She was jolted by the idea that flashed through her mind: she might lay her hands on his file if she rifled through that cabinet.

Barış had told her a heap of stuff about his mother and his mother's Romanian lover Emil Pavulescu. Gülnazmiye had absolutely no doubt that that bitch of a mother had ganged up with her lover to get Barış Bakış locked up. But the only way she could learn more than what her sweetheart was able to tell her was to read the file. *Let's see what that whore Veda has been telling his doctor!*

If she could read his medical history in detail, she would learn about all the tricks they used to drag her boyfriend here, to the Mental Health Hospital in this Black Sea city, and to extend his stay too, even though he should have been released long ago. She would be party to secrets that even Barış didn't know and could find some way of rescuing from this hellhole the young man whose love had claimed her soul. She was all eyes and ears: would the doctor – who prayed in the hospital masjid most of the week, but made a point of joining the congregation in the biggest mosque in town for Friday noon prayers – lock his door?

The latch bolt had slipped. Âlim Kâhkeci must have told Odd-Eyes Sipahi to repair it, told him ten times if he told him once, but despite his protestations – *I swear I'll sort it today, Mr Doctor, sir!* – the junkie carpenter hadn't even touched it. Giving up, Âlim now carefully pulled the door to without letting the latch bolt drop. God forbid, if it ever got stuck, they'd have to break down the door. Thinking he might go home for a half-hour snooze after prayers, the doctor vanished down the hallway.

Gülnazmiye looked right and left: there wasn't a soul in sight. It was a wonderful opportunity to peek into *his* file. The nurses were occupied with the patients whose medication time it was, which meant they wouldn't be around for at least an hour. Getting the patients to take their medicine was no easy task. Patients resisted taking their medicine for a variety of reasons, especially those who were paranoid about being poisoned; they hid the pills under their tongues and refused to swallow unless forced. Some had developed incredible methods, such as sticking the pills to the roofs of their mouths, hiding them in their throats and even breaking them up to stuff into cavities where their fillings had once been – and later spitting them out in bits.

Until very recently, no one knew who took medicines regularly and who did not. Younger nurses in particular had got into the habit of pretending to forget to check mouths – a task they found repulsive, given the patients' major issues with personal hygiene in the first place. In other words, a serious lack of discipline had been the only way to describe medication time.

But one day something happened that forced the Medical Director to gather all the nurses in the canteen, read them the riot act in a thundering fury as his hands shook with rage, and making no secret of his determination to do the needful about anyone suspected of dereliction of duty. He did not mince words when he reminded Matron that in this matter the main responsibility lay with her, and her alone.

The reason was **a twenty-two-year-old patient with bipolar affective disorder named Leyla Böğrü**, the daughter of a modest sheep farmer from a village in Çiçekdağı, in Kırşehir: she had stripped stark naked outside the Medical Director's door and sang *Oh Leyla*.

She had been committed six times in five years, staying for around three months each time. Her condition received public attention when she was a new bride of only four days. Until then, few neighbours had noticed that she'd strip stark naked when she milked the sheep in the barn, or remove her baggy trousers in front of the TV as the whole family were watching something on the box. Her parents attributed such demented and indecent acts to sexual frustration and she'd get a terrible hiding by her mother each time. Leyla was only seventeen when she was married off to **Mustafa Keklik, her first suitor** – just to prevent her from getting the family into trouble, or shaming their name.

Smitten with her beautiful long hair and baby face, the barely eighteen-year-old Mustafa, ignoring his parents' advice – *Go finish your national service first, eh?* – had dug his heels in *I wanna marry her!* **The sheep farmer, Abdıraman**, was more than happy to oblige when someone turned up asking for his daughter's hand. Not only did he not feign reluctance like all good fathers, he never even said, *Can't have a wedding between two holidays*; instead, he insisted on marrying his daughter off as soon as possible. Without a peep he sold ten of his fifty head of sheep for half their value just so he could send her off with a great trousseau.

Leyla's mother, Nazife, was less charitable. She was constantly fretting about Leyla's frequent disappearances (and her flimsy excuses upon her return, such as *I was down at the stream… I was in the field… I went to the mill…*) Once, when Leyla vanished again soon after the betrothal, returning hours later, and Nazife asked, *Where've you been?* Leyla gave one of her usual answers. Smelling a rat, Nazife pulled her aside to ask, *If they bring you back after the nuptials, saying you're defiled, I don't care if you're my child, the Koran strike me if I don't strangle you with my own hands… So tell me now, are you still a maid?* The urgency of the question went over the girl's head; with a blank stare, Leyla babbled nonsense, hopping from one topic to the next, *I want red lipstick for the wedding… A wolf throttled the Niyazis' sheep…* Failing to wrest a proper answer out of her and saying, *We'll suffer whatever fate's got in store if we must*, Nazife threw herself into the wedding preparations.

Abdıraman's immoderate eagerness put the wind up Mustafa's parents. Something fishy was going on; they wanted to turn back whilst there was still time. But the besotted lad had a right fit, screaming and yelling, *If you won't let me marry Leyla, I'll shoot meself, I swear I will!* You never knew what *he* would do next anyway. Worried – *He would, and all!* – they, too, bowed to their fate.

It was not like Nazife was going to kill her daughter if Leyla had cried and snuffled when cornered, if she'd said, *I'm no maid, so-and-so took my maidenhead.* Nazife would have been heartbroken, true, but it would have been enough just to rip the girl's hair out, beat her senseless and lock her up. Dreadfully restless, sensing something was wrong… It would have been better if she knew for sure that their daughter was defiled: then she'd have sent word to the other side, along the lines of *It's never gonna work*, then break off the betrothal, send away any other potential suitor with *Our daughter's still too young*, and try to sort it out with no public shame – and try to sort it out with whoever had taken their daughter's maidenhead.

But what with one thing and another, both families wavered between going ahead with the wedding and calling it off, and before they knew it, the big day arrived.

The wedding dinner was served on a long table set out in the garden, despite the occasional sprinkling of snow: cauldron after cauldron of meat and rice, sultana compote and yogurt. Young brides and unmarried girls on both sides adorned their hands with the copious henna provided by the generous bridegroom and joined the village girls in their crisp, fresh outfits to make music with trays and wooden spoons as they sang and danced such folk numbers as *Three Lads, Stroll On My Beauty* and the *Kıvrak Halay*.

If the wedding had taken place in the summer, the young men would have lined up facing the girls to dance the *Hasan Dağı Sekme* in the garden, but since it was freezing, they were all cooped up indoors. Not content with the opium they'd consumed beforehand, some had spiked their compote with vodka on the sly and were now well hammered. They had a great time downstairs. The drums and the *zurna* played non-stop, downstairs, upstairs, but mostly in the garden. To such an extent that a neighbour (who refused to come, having fallen out with the bridegroom's family some time earlier) wanted to complain to the headman. Except the headman was also at the wedding; he was so carried away that he kept shooting into the air. After families with young children and the elderly who'd had enough of the noise had left, the young men, now blind drunk, spilled into the garden, forced the drummer and the piper to dance in the snow, fell out over nothing, went berserk and traded punches and kicks; there were even a couple of gunshots. The girls screamed, but the older, cooler heads on the bridegroom's side rounded up the rowdiest of the young men and marched them off. Things calmed down. Finally, after all the guests had left, the bridegroom's mates banged on lad's back as they shoved him into the nuptials room. And that's how Mustafa Keklik got his heart's desire.

The next morning, a trembling Nazife heard the good news: Leyla was a pure virgin. At the sight of the bloodied sheet the bride's mother burst into tears of joy.

The festivities were still the talk of the village four days later on the morning of the Feast of Sacrifice. Prayers rang out as two hennaed rams were slaughtered – one of which was the bridegroom's offering – and the newlyweds' foreheads were smeared with blood. Leyla's blissful husband, Mustafa (still walking on air), her father and brother-in-law had skinned and jointed the carcasses, and were now weighing and separating the meat to give away. Her mother-in-law, having chopped the livers and kidneys, was now sautéing the quick-cook parts in a gigantic copper pan in the garden.

Once the sacrifice was done and dusted, the floor table was prepared downstairs, the piping hot sauté was placed in the centre and hands reached out to tear pieces out of the feast loaves, which the sisters-in-law had baked in the brick oven. Everyone present, children and all, sat down to eat.

Just after her father-in-law had, with a prayer, placed the first morsel into his mouth, Leyla Böğrü blurted out, in the most vulgar language, that her husband was impotent; then, as if that wasn't enough, she burst into unspeakably shameless acts, baring her breasts, guffawing all the while. Everyone was gobsmacked.

Mustafa leapt up and tried to restrain her, with a hand over her mouth. But when she set to ripping her clothes off and kept shouting filth, his parents realised that their daughter-in-law of four days wasn't normal at all; now they understood why Abdıraman had insisted on having the wedding *as soon as possible*, despite all their pleas to *hold it after the holiday*. Now they knew why he had been so keen on the idea.

Having spoiled their meal, Leyla played catch-me-if-you-can with her new relations as she carried on stripping in the snowy garden; she was eventually captured by Mustafa and her brothers-in-law, received a thorough thrashing and collapsed in a heap. Swearing and cursing, they dragged the unconscious girl by the arms and flung her back at her father's door.

Nazife grabbed the stove tongs to wallop the exhausted girl, who was still saying unspeakable things about Mustafa and laughing like a hyena.

Nazife came at her, screaming, *Ya little harlot!* Abdıraman stepped in and wrenched the tongs out of her hand. Nazife was still having fits: *I should have borne a rock instead of you!* But Leyla, who hadn't slept since the wedding four days ago, and was only beginning to feel the pain of the thrashing she received on this feast day, made for her old room, picked a duvet out of the linen cupboard and went to bed.

Nazife and Abdıraman had a right ding-dong. Nazife attacked him for intervening, and he yelled right back. He might have left school at year three, true, and wasn't well educated, but he was smart. He read the newspapers in the coffee house whenever he could get his hands on one, and watched the TV from time to time, too. He was aware that there was something called mental illness and realised that beating was no way to control Leyla. So he took her to the Kırşehir State Hospital, where she was declared in urgent need of sectioning. That's how the bride of four days' standing got sent to the Mental Health Hospital.

Ever since his gabby sisters-in-law tattled twelve to the dozen everywhere in the village, and even in villages nearby, claiming that Mustafa hadn't been able to penetrate Leyla, the poor lad had been too embarrassed to show his face at home or outside. His brothers' wives wracked their limited imagination to cast aspersions even on the bloodied sheet: Mustafa had nicked a finger chopping wood; in other words, they pulled out all the stops to discredit the youngest, most popular and attractive son of the family. Villagers befuddled by this peculiar tale took to calling him *Songless bird Mustafa*.

None of it was true. Mustafa, who had actually been the talk of Kırşehir's clandestine whorehouses since the age of fifteen, had kept his bride up not only on their wedding night, but through all four nights. But the truth was no help. People believed what they wanted to believe: this strapping hunk was useless in bed. His sisters-in-law, envious of Mustafa's charm and Leyla's beauty, had dished out the slurs to break his heart.

On the day his father went to the Agriculture Bank to ask for a loan, Mustafa sold the best cow to someone in the next village so he could buy a second-hand Kırıkkale pistol. By the time his father returned and raised hell at the loss of his most valuable milch cow, Mustafa was already on the way to shoot his bride.

At the Mental Health Hospital, he announced calmly that he was visiting Leyla Keklik. On hearing, *No such patient here*, he figured she must have been admitted under her maiden name. Having given satisfactory answers to such questions as *Who are you? What relation are you to her?* he was allowed upstairs.

This being when Matron's husband was at his most perverted and she was consequently at her strictest, patient medication was always scrupulously administered.

So when Mustafa Keklik located the wife who had made him a laughing stock and offended his male pride, she was in a drugged daze, barely able to stand up. He drew out the pistol without a second thought, pointed it and squeezed the trigger. But it jammed.

By the time Mustafa, who'd been fiddling with it to see why, shot himself in the calf, Leyla – too drugged to recognise her husband – had returned to her room and climbed back into the bed she never wanted to leave.

The orderlies who had run towards the gunshot found Mustafa bleeding on the floor, sobbing in pain and frustration. Despatched to the State Hospital at once, Mustafa Keklik, as soon as he'd been treated, was arrested on several charges – relevant or not – such as attempted murder, carrying an unlicensed firearm, discharging said firearm, incitement to public agitation and disturbing the peace. Convicted of carrying an unlicensed firearm and acquitted on all other charges on lack of evidence, he was sent down for a grand total of two months and ten days. Upon his release, unable to face the village, he enlisted in the army.

As for Leyla, the tranquillisers would seem to work and she would be discharged, but then she'd be brought back to the hospital the next time she made a scene. She was back in hospital for the fourth time when Mustafa finished his national service and decided to earn his living in Istanbul. After trying his hand at this, that and the other, he started working as a waiter in the Etiler restaurant owned by the gambling boss Reşat Özyılmazel, *a.k.a.* Maserati Reşat.

Tall, well-built and handsome, Mustafa was blessed with a natural charisma that turned heads – although it had failed to impress his wife or sisters-in-law. Hardened by that early humiliation, prison and the years in the army, and blessed with a formidable physique, he took no nonsense from patrons who tried to act up. It all caught Maserati Reşat's eye. The waiter was soon promoted to driver-cum-bodyguard and given his first mission that week: to scare off – *But gently, eh?* – the retired manager and his old wife in the flat above the Tarabya tavern and who had been a thorn in Reşat's side for some time.

Natty in navy blue threads and carrying a mobile phone and a Glock, thanks to his Reşat Abi's generosity, Mustafa Keklik rang the doorbell; just then, the flat's owner was hundreds of kilometres away from home, sliding on his arse, revealing a pair of sock suspenders that mystified the conference hall of the Mental Health Hospital with its back to the sea.

The door was opened by the **young cleaning woman, Kübra**, a relatively new addition to the household. And the moment she did, they fell in love. She was dumbstruck by his good looks. They held each other's gaze like they do in films. Kübra was quite a stunner herself; long, slender olive-skinned fingers holding the delicate sweep of her chin as she gazed up at him, black eyelashes a-flutter. And the handsome bodyguard devoured her with eyes.

In the lounge, Bedia was about to sit down at the tea table by the window that faced the shimmering waters of the Bosphorus. Kübra was placing a sheet of paper into the pocket of her spangled denim jacket when Mustafa said, *I need to talk to the man of the house.* It didn't sound quite as harsh as he had rehearsed; his mind was actually on how good this beautiful brunette looked in that denim jacket.

Kübra replied sweetly to the towering young man in navy blue, *Sir's out; he'll be back tomorrow, but Madam is in.* Opening the door wide, and without questioning him further, she admitted the lad who reminded her of Özcan Deniz in the TV series *Vine Mansion*.

She was dying to linger. Dying to linger here, to gaze at him, spend time with him, but she was in a hurry. Announcing, *This gentleman's here to speak to you*, she left him alone with Bedia, who was about to pop a petit-four from the Royal Worcester plate into her mouth. With a last look, Kübra left, her mind still on Mustafa, who, this being his debut in this new career on the wrong side of the law, had no idea how to make threatening speeches. At any rate, having been thrown by Kübra's beauty, he was finding it hard to look tough. So he without any preamble blurted out, *The tavern's staying right where it is, and you can just sod off if you don't like it!*

Bedia invited him to tea. The battery for her hearing aid had gone flat that morning, so she'd just despatched Kübra (with a sheet of paper bearing the brand and the model) to a medical appliance stockist in Şişli, and now she mistook the handsome young man for the insurance salesman who had earlier made an appointment.

Mustafa might not have sounded particularly tough, but when what he thought was a harsh threat was countered by an offer of tea, he dropped his guard. He sat down, musing, *So that's how these things're done*, and a true dialogue of the deaf ensued.

Having braved a family tragedy to marry her stepson with the bewitchingly smouldering dark eyes, and having dedicated her whole life to beauty, Bedia couldn't bear to have ugly people around her. She even picked the better-looking sales assistants when she was shopping and specifically asked for the most handsome driver whenever she booked a minicab. Kübra had been employed not because she was skilled or gentle, but because she was pretty. So unassailable was her confidence in her husband's love for her, and her own effect on him, that Bedia never felt threatened by the proximity of other beautiful women.

At Mustafa's nearly wild good looks, she felt for the first time the profoundly bitter pain of being very old, a pain that was curiously agreeable. Gratified that she had lived life to the full and delighted in all its wonders, she turned to Mustafa to speak. What came out was totally unexpected from someone who treasured her femininity above all else and had reigned supreme in her circle: *My bonny boy, I'm in my seventies. How much longer do you think I've got? All I want to do now is to gaze at the shimmering waters of the Bosphorus.*

She had worked hard to preserve her beauty and elegance but never done anything to live longer. The end was approaching. Hence her lack of interest in life insurance or health cover. The poor lad was only trying to sell her a policy, she thought, and she'd been ungracious, letting him come all this way. She extended the little plate of thin lemon slices in order to linger a little more with this handsome, swarthy face. Instead of the stunning allure that had swept people off their feet for years and years, her smile held the kindness of a mother, something she'd never personally experienced. She wanted nothing to do with insurance, policies or hospitals when there was so much beauty in the world that deserved to be talked about. She talked in melancholic sentences of the beauty of the Bosphorus and the magic of Istanbul. Mustafa listened in silence. Not that she could hear him should he choose to reply anyway.

His heart sank as he put a slice of lemon into his cup with a silver fork thin enough to break. *If the poor lady's so old, God knows how much older her husband must be…* There was no way he could be party to such heinousness as turning these poor people out in their last days. After having a cup of lemon tea with the graceful and kind-hearted elderly lady, he presented his compliments and went out.

Mustafa wondered what his boss wanted from these poor old folks and chided himself for his part in such wickedness. Then again, he wasn't brave enough to stand up to a bloke armed with two pistols 24/7 who kept two pit bull terriers with frothing mouths in his garden. He didn't know what to do.

In the evening, on their way to the Çatalca casino, Reşat Abi asked for a sit-rep. Mustafa took a critical decision. The face that had failed to intimidate Bedia adopted a credible expression before Maserati Reşat. He played his part beautifully. *All sorted, Abi,* he said. *Spoke with the old bird, scared her shitless… They'll clear off before the month is out.* Well impressed with this first success, Reşat said as a reward, when they reached the casino, *Go for a bit of a spin; you can come back when I call*; he knew the lad loved driving.

Mustafa gunned the two-hundred-thousand-euro (or so he thought) second-hand Maserati, several times gobbled up pointlessly the 77 km between Çatalca and Çerkezköy, and then pulled up and got out. Still thinking about Bedia, and Kübra's beauty, he drew his pistol and fired a few rounds at the motorway toll sign just to take his mind off the fix he was in.

He felt better; his mind was clear now. Astonishingly, the Glock (a make that was recently selling like hot cakes) didn't jam even once. The memory of his first pistol, his dud second-hand Kırıkkale, was galling. He'd been badly shafted! When he'd found out that the money from the cow could have bought three spanking new Glocks he'd been so angry that he'd have plugged the bloke in the middle of the forehead if he only had the face to go back.

That night, Mustafa kept firing the gun for half an hour; he remembered his Kırıkkale, but his Leyla didn't cross his mind even once. As if he hadn't shot himself instead of her with that pistol he'd been conned into buying, hadn't been banged up all that time, and hadn't been forced to leave his home and village. His mind was clear, as was his memory.

When, after quite a while, the retired bureaucrat and his wife showed no inclination to move out, Reşat twigged he'd been strung along. In the meanwhile, Mustafa had got it on with Kübra, decided to marry her, and begun to run errands for Bedia and Erdem partly to please her. But his Reşat Abi would eventually cotton on that instead of intimidating these two oldies he was serving them. He didn't really like this bodyguard business, anyways. He was a gentle soul, didn't enjoy intimidating or threatening people, not that he was that good at it in the first place. The lovers put their heads together to look for a way out. **Kübra's brother Yıldırım** had found a bar for rent in Anamur, Mersin, and proposed to run it together with his sister, who was getting ready for her engagement to Mustafa. The lovers agreed to run away with the money they'd saved up thanks to Bedia's generosity, get married there and start a new life.

By the time they were boarding the coach, Reşat Özyılmazel had finally worked out that Mustafa had been all but adopted by the oldies, and started looking for the boy to give him a lesson. Kübra and Mustafa rang Yıldırım from the motorway service station to tell him they were on their way. Mustafa then broke his SIM card and flung it away so his Reşat Abi couldn't keep ringing him non-stop.

Maserati Reşat went ape. He terrorised the entire casino, roaring, *I'll bump him off, fuck me if I don't!* He chased after Mustafa for a bit. Someone said he'd gone to Izmir. Reşat had the place checked out, but got nothing. His fury gradually abated, and a few months later he forgot about the lad.

As their coach neared the Mediterranean, the brunette bombshell Kübra was dozing on Mustafa's shoulder; in the meanwhile, in the dim ward of the Mental Health Hospital she was now in for the sixth time, his first love, Leyla Böğrü, was playing the five stones game on her bed with the pills she'd saved up instead of swallowing.

This was around the time of the death of Ekrem Ceviz and the subsequent new lease of life for his widow (and new slacker) Matron Servinaz Ceviz – instead of occupying herself with the patients, she was having a whale of a time with the nurses, chatting, laughing and exchanging jokes (Sister Zerrin, she of the foul mouth and tales of sexual exploits, had become a very good friend). Servinaz had been neglecting to supervise the young nurses who should have made sure the patients took their medication. Just when the two lovers were enjoying *tantuni*, chewing their spicy mince wraps on the Anamur seafront and dreaming about the bar they'd leased as a going concern, Leyla Böğrü, who hadn't swallowed even a single tablet went off the rails.

The Medical Director had just blurted out his intention to write a book on the history of the hospital during an interview with *The Black Sea Herald* when a stark naked Leyla appeared at the end of a neat trail of knickers, bra, vest, tights, skirt, jumper, cardigan and slippers, leading all the way back to her room. She was singing at the top of her voice when the foul-mouthed nurse clambered up the stairs, grumbling, *Whatcha howling for, woman, like the wail of a torn cunt?* And froze, not because she spotted Leyla but because she swearing in front of the Medical Director.

He would have played it down if all this hadn't taken place right before the eyes of *The Black Sea Herald* **reporter Fahrettin Daşçı**. The orderlies arrived with a straitjacket and a blanket, had the devil of a job to immobilise the girl, who was eventually shoved into the soft cell, which despite the advances in psychiatry was still being used when needed. In the meanwhile, the Medical Director sent the reporter away after extracting a promise not to write about what he had just seen, and finally allowed himself to blow his top at the nurses he had summoned to the canteen.

After reading them all the riot act, he summoned Matron to his office and asked, *What happened to that battleaxe Servinaz? What happened to you, lass?* He grumbled bitterly, blaming her recent negligence on the menopause. Servinaz promised she would enforce the strictest of checks from now on and immediately went back to her office to type, and then wait by the printer for, countless copies of *Have you checked the patient's mouth after handing out the medication?* in forty-eight-point bold.

But the printer jammed again. She had to call that **smart-arse resident nerd (*a.k.a.* IT dude) Emrah** and, unimpressed by the swaggering arc his red Marlboro pack described towards her desk, warned him, *You can't smoke here!* His only response was curling his lip, on which hung an unlit cigarette in the manner of someone doing something incredibly important. In the meanwhile, having already tattled to his colleagues about Leyla Böğrü's striptease, the reporter Fahrettin Daşçı was hurrying to the coffee house to repeat the story.

As a consequence of this episode, which was drooled over again and again in coffee houses, bars, beer joints and pool halls, the hospital noted a surprising increase in visitor numbers. The guards tightened controls once they'd realised that most of the people citing some random patient's name before they dived in were in actual fact suckers who hoped for a repeat of the Leyla Böğrü incident. These so-called visitors needn't have bothered – and after waiting in the visitors' section for hours and even sneaking into other floors, they soon gave up – no one stripped, and all the patients appeared quite calm.

Having got a tongue-lashing after the Leyla Böğrü incident and consequently watchful of her step around the Medical Director, Servinaz now had no choice but to monitor the young nurses at medication time and personally check to see that the patients actually did swallow their tablets. Since many patients needed medication several times a day, she no longer had the luxury of relaxing in her office. Which is why she'd opened her doors to Gülnazmiye, she of that cramped office for four. Servinaz spent most of her time with the patients and the rest in Neuropsychiatrist Nebahat Özdamar's office, where the two women swapped baking recipes. True, Nebahat did bang on about the story of her treacherous husband, which she peppered with the most intimate details of their married life, a story Servinaz had heard so many times she knew it by heart, but, thankfully, she had discovered how to avoid listening. As she ate her cake, she would look at the other's eyes, make appropriate noises and nod, her mind on a myriad of life's cares, such as her salary, the kids' schools and the Koran recitation she would arrange for her husband's anniversary.

Matron's new bosom buddy, the neuropsychiatrist (to whom, however, she was not close enough to discourage from that grade-three buzz), was now acting quite scary. Offering her a tempting slice of cake dotted with crushed coffee beans, Nebahat asked, *Guess what's in it?* Spotting the coffee beans, Servinaz replied smugly, *Coffeeee?* But the moment she did, she knew the neuropsychiatrist meant something else, something mysterious, even something dodgy.

Unable to swallow, she reeled off a list of random stuff like nigella seeds, aniseed, linseed and green tea. Nebahat opened her eyes terrifyingly wide and exclaimed, *Weed!* Servinaz didn't get it at first; the penny only dropped at the other's maniacal cackle. Panicking, Servinaz nearly had a heart attack: she was being fed *weed cake*, no less. She didn't dare ask where it had come from. And even if she had, the increasingly loony neuropsychiatrist was hardly going to admit that her source was in the Substance Abuse ward.

Nebahat's erratic behaviour had of late become more pronounced, to the extent that the worried Medical Director no longer put her on duty. Nevertheless, the vertically challenged doctor had been taking it into her head to go on night duty every once in a while and reward the straggling groups of patients watching TV with the cakes she hadn't been able foist on anyone during the day. On one such night, cake in hand as usual, she had entered a random room in Substance Abuse where the inmates had been well out of control for some time.

Although he had no intention of giving up drugs, **Tahir, the night watchman at the Ballıca Cigarette Factory**, had admitted himself voluntarily just to stop his new wife's nagging – *You never even tried!* A shoebox on his lap, he was rolling his second joint. The twenty-seven-year-old pothead, who had started at fifteen, wouldn't let his guard down even when spaced out: the moment the door opened, the shoebox vanished under the bed.

Nebahat might be off her rocker, but she was neither stupid nor ignorant. One sniff and she knew what the night watchman was rolling. a little too young to be a flower child, she had still got round to trying pot at the Istanbul Cerrahpaşa Medical School. Although she'd never really rolled her own, she had taken a couple of drags at friends' places, pissing off her boyfriend, Kahraman İnal, who wouldn't touch a joint with a bargepole – and whom she married the moment she qualified. One of those friends was raided by the Narcotics Squad in the final year of her specialisation; scared witless, she had never touched another joint.

She entered the room, sat down facing the pothead and extended a slice of cake with a knowing look, saying, *You'll be dying for something sweet soon – here, grab a few slices.* Tahir was gobsmacked that the doctor (who must have sniffed the pot!) seemed OK with it. Nebahat's smile might have been suggesting, *I'm on to you, but hey, fill your boots!* They grinned at each other for a bit. Then they tucked into the cake and started chatting. Nebahat offered recipes – *My labneh cake is to die for!* High as he was, Tahir soon sussed out that she was as nutty as her cake, and relaxed. He couldn't hold out much longer: retrieving the shoebox, he rolled a joint, took a drag and handed it to her. Having quit smoking years ago, she hesitated.

At that ungodly hour a bizarre intimacy – a ridiculous chumminess – arose between the junkie and the neuropsychiatrist, who were gazing at each other from facing beds. Thinking, *a single drag's not gonna make me start smoking again*, she picked up the joint and inhaled deeply. As the smoke wandered around her body, she felt a little dizzy, relaxed, and settled onto the bed, leaning against the wall. She looked content, much brighter than she'd been for a long time.

They chatted until morning. Whilst some of the addicts were sawing wood and others paced the hallways up and down, the two new chums got well and truly stoned. Nebahat related her husband's wickedness. Tahir listened, frequently interjecting, *Bloody bastard… Bugger… Son of a bitch…* as comment on Kahraman İnal, whom he'd never met. The more her new pal swore at her ex-husband, the more Nebahat cheered up, and the more she cheered up, the more she succumbed to a laughing fit.

Tahir harped on about his wife's family. His father-in-law was filthy rich. He'd erected a huge block of flats in the New District, but had he offered one to his daughter and son-in-law or said, *Come, live here?* No. Tahir had sworn at her husband; now she returned the favour, expressing her view about her new pal's father-in-law with *Arsehole! Like his shroud had a pocket!* They smoked, griped, and when they got tired of griping, they said, *Whatever!* They realised no one did anyone else a good turn in this life.

Nebahat was struggling to get up and leave as the first rays of the sun broke through; Tahir gave her a little weed wrapped in a cigarette paper cone and said, *Think of me when you smoke, Doctor Hanım...* Reluctant to start smoking again just for a bit of pot, she laid it somewhere. The following night, realising that she'd come to the end of her recipe book, she was wondering *What shall I flavour the cake with this time?* when it occurred to her to add a little weed to the coffee beans in the mortar.

The revelation that the cake contained weed made Servinaz jump out of her skin; she couldn't swallow. She stared aghast. She might never have worked in substance abuse, but she was no stranger to the harm caused by drugs. *What if she attacked me?* flitted through her mind, and she started looking for a way to push off without unnerving the neuropsychiatrist. Thank God that was just when the Medical Director's yell *Servinaaaz!* rang through the hallways. As she tumbled out of the office, she spat the mouthful into her hand.

Since then, she had been unable to shake off the image of Nebahat's eyes staring at her like a *psycho*. That had been a while ago, but she still hadn't made her mind up. She couldn't envisage what would happen if she informed the Medical Director, or how Nebahat would react if the Medical Director interrogated her. He might try to discover where Nebahat got her narcotics, home on to the substance abuse wing as the easy bet and arouse that sleeping dog, with the immediate consequence that the hospital's routine would be turned upside down and Servinaz might even be left holding the baby, however unfair it might seem. So she decided to forget the matter. The only thing she did was warn the staff: *Mind now... she's crazy; you never know, she might poison em; don't you dare eat her cakes!*

That day, Nebahat had got well and truly stoned on the cake she hadn't been able to tempt anyone else with – other than Servinaz, who had promptly spat it out. Tahir was discharged a few days later, and Nebahat's newfound enthusiasm for weed cake came to an untimely end.

But by the time guest speaker Ülkü Birinci was delivering his Valentine's Day speech on love, the neuropsychiatrist was again high as a kite. She wasn't the only one either. She had baked with Tahir's gift again, and this time her cake had found many unsuspecting takers.

Having sorely missed her newly acquired taste for weed, she rushed over the moment she'd heard Tahir was back. It was the 13 February. She chided him for failing to drop in all that time. Tahir apologised profusely, *Just never got round to it, Doctor Hanım, work and all…* etc. Then he added suggestively, *I've not come empty-handed though,* and they giggled. But it was daytime; everyone was up and about. A pot party was out of the question. Nebahat took her gift and baked when she got home, this time with chunks of chocolate and walnut instead of coffee.

Substance Abuse was the most disorderly section of the Mental Health Hospital. Ever since the Medical Director had got a bee in his bonnet about writing its history, he had stopped paying attention to the hospital; the deeper he got into it, the more the night-time traffic of joints and lumps of cannabis grew. Resident nerd Emrah and a few orderlies had set up a smooth system that ran like clockwork. The addicts, who had absolutely no intention of getting clean, were living it up; they were only there on the insistence of their nearest and dearest, testing was infrequent and reviews sporadic. All it took was a single gesture for Emrah and the orderlies to source and promptly deliver the goods.

It should have come to the Medical Director's notice: substance abusers were returning all too soon after being discharged. Their families complained that the treatment did no good; but any such complaint that reached him was dismissed due to his conviction in the near impossibility of rehabilitation in the first place.

The young Psychologist Gülnazmiye Görgün knew nothing of weeds or roots or anything; she was grateful for the opportunity to stretch out in Matron's office – who since the day of the weed cake had been changing course whenever she spotted Nebahat. Gülnazmiye was in the claws of another type of addiction altogether. Whilst Matron was checking dental cavities one by one with a toothpick, having firmly gripped the cause of her present troubles by the lower jaw, Gülnazmiye sneaked into Âlim Kâhkeci's office after he left for Friday prayers. Unaware that she was doing so, Gülnazmiye was still clutching the magazine.

Equally unaware that the latch bolt had slipped, she slammed the door to avoid being caught. The door was stuck. In her excitement, she never realised she was locked in. Noticing the magazine in her hand, she laid it down on the immaculate desktop and started yanking drawers to look for BB's file.

It took quite a while. She was opening drawers at random, with no method, and was often rifling through the same drawer more than once. Eventually she found it in the last drawer. She passed over the copy of the admission form, his prescriptions and what have you, and just as she was about to read Âlim Kâhkeci's notes, entitled *Patient History*, she jumped into the air at the sound of Odd-Eyes Sipahi's *Hold! Lift! Tug! Smash!*

Hammer in hand, the carpenter was yelling at his apprentice as he banged at the lock. Just as Gülnazmiye stuffed the file back without having read a single line and slammed the drawer into place, the door was smashed. The acne-ridden apprentice stepped in and dropped the toolbox bang in the middle as Gülnazmiye swept up the doctor's tennis racquet, which was leaning against the wall.

A leader amongst the town's handful of neo-devouts who wished to reconcile a modern life style with Islam (not that he would actually say as much out loud), Âlim Kâhkeci had just that morning unwrapped his new racquet, bought online and delivered by courier, lingered over its lines, tapped its taut strings and leant it against the wall when he saw it was time for prayers.

An active member of cinema forums online, Âlim Kâhkeci also blogged about his interest in technology and cinema practically every night. In addition to religious and political topics, he commented on acclaimed films chosen from his largely bootleg DVD collection of over 1,000, some of which even had erotic scenes, if only within certain boundaries. This huge fan of indie American cinema and the immortal sit-com *Seinfeld* had been going to the Tennis Club every weekend since the end of the summer.

His mind was on his new Wilson Fusion. Just as he was leaving, though, he saw Odd-Eyes Sipahi and his apprentice unloading a drawer cabinet from their flatbed. The Medical Director had ordered a new cabinet when his existing furniture proved inadequate for the document copies he considered essential to his proposed book; the carpenter, whose main income came from the hospital, had obligingly crafted a superb cabinet in one week flat.

Kâhkeci and the carpenter caught each other's eye. The former was enraged at the latter's grin as if the door with the slipped latch bolt had been totally forgotten. The doctor would have strode past without a greeting. But Odd-Eyes blocked his way, still grinning, to ask a favour. His sister – who had national health cover in the form of the coveted green card – was about to give birth. Would the good doctor's **gynae-cologist wife, Tuğba, who worked at the Maternity Hospital,** have her admitted?

Kâhkeci knew it actually had nothing to do with admission; the bloke was asking for privileged treatment at the oversubscribed hospital. That brazen request was dismissed with *Sort my door out first before asking for a favour!* Odd-Eyes handed his toolbox to his apprentice at once, grasped the doctor by the arm, and said, *Let's sort it out right now, Doctor Bey.* Kâhkeci tried to object, *I'm on my way to Friday prayers, some other time…* but Odd-Eyes wouldn't hear of it. He dragged the doctor back in, *Show us what's wrong with the door first – you can go after.* Kâhkeci glanced at his watch, thinking, *I can make it,* but the racquet's imminent fate would make him miss Friday prayers for only the second time in his life.

Racquet held above her head, Gülnazmiye Görgün looked ready to smash the acne-ridden apprentice. Âlim Kâhkeci swept into his office on the heels of said apprentice and the junkie carpenter, saw his precious new Wilson in Gülnazmiye's hand and, quite understandably, thundered, *What the heck are you doing?* It hadn't occurred to him to ask what she was doing in his office; all he could think of was the racquet he'd paid through the nose for. A cowering Gülnazmiye wasn't about to say, *I was reading my sweetheart's file.* Instead she blurted out, *I swear to God I wasn't poking around, Doctor Bey; I was chasing a mouse.*

The ill-considered lie caused a great commotion. The batty neuropsy-chiatrist who had come by to tempt Matron with a dried mango and almond cake (to make up for the earlier offence of weed cake) saw her bane, Odd-Eyes, with a hammer in his hand and, curious to see what he was up to, stuck her head through the smashed door. At Gülnazmiye's *I was chasing a mouse,* she broke into a run, screeching, *Mouse! Mouse!*

She ran into **the retired literature teacher Zarife Gülercan.** The poor thing – a petite fifty-something, a distant relation of the Medical

Director – had gone into shock when her son had drowned in the sea after finishing school, only the shock had soon given way to hysterical laughter, which made her family think she must have lost her marbles. She wouldn't calm down; if anything, Miss Zarife, who was once the epitome of courtesy, had lost all decency: when, not content with spraying everyone with profanities, along the lines of *Whore, Pimp*, etc, she shooed visitors away shouting, *Fuck your cunts, fuck off from my house!* she was taken to the hospital.

The initial psychiatric examination had proved inconclusive. She again broke into uncontrollable laughter upon hearing of mice in the hospital. By the time she entered the female patients' day room, where people were knitted and made dough flowers, the petite fifty-year-old was laughing so hard she was crying. *What's the matter,* people asked her; it took a while, but she eventually calmed down enough to reply, *There was a mouse in the doctor's office.*

The wave of hysteria rapidly spread. Kindled by the neuropsychiatrist and stoked by the retired literature teacher, the crisis now reached the patients' rooms; given their constant mood swings, it was only to be expected that some would climb tables and others rattle the iron bars wanting to throw themselves out of their windows. Most of the male patients had no idea what had happened. But this seemed like a perfect opportunity to fling themselves from one bed to the next or bang their heads against the wall. The Medical Director was finally informed when dozens of nurses and carers were unable to get the patients under control.

This hospital, like any other, had its regular share of rodents – perhaps even fewer than most. Regular poisoning kept the numbers down; few, if any, made it out of the basement during their abbreviated lifespan; and those that did promptly fell prey to the enormous cats fattened on food scraps in the rear garden. The rumours grew and grew: the mice became snakes; the snakes became scorpions. The Medical Director had to intervene. The patients who'd been kicking up were finally sedated. The dust settled, but only after a time, and only gradually at that. A patient who'd smashed his head in a fit needed stiches, and a few who'd ripped their own clothes were dressed again. By dinnertime most were asleep, and anyone still awake was quietly watching TV.

But the neuropsychiatrist's hysteria defied everything. Nothing the Medical Director did was of any use: neither rational explanations nor the empty mouse poison packs that were procured for her attention.

The Medical Director eventually hit upon an ingenious solution: he needed a dead mouse. Any dead mouse. So he **despatched the taxi driver-cum-caretaker Cumali** (everyone knew he moonlighted in his brother-in-law's taxi) to find one. Cumali was the man on whose head a flowerpot was broken when he'd been caught leering at Leyla as she rolled about on the floor stark naked. It wasn't enough that he'd been leering; he'd also dawdled instead of immediately covering the girl who was having a manic attack, and he even tried to cop a feel as the straitjacket was pulled over her.

That scene cut Matron Servinaz to the quick. She had been extremely lax of late, but at the memory of her perverted husband and the years of abuse, she suddenly lost it and smashed that flowerpot on Cumali's head. As the nurses and orderlies struggled to place the straitjacket on Leyla, Servinaz was trying to stab Cumali's eye with a potsherd, yelling, *I'm gonna kill you, you bastard, you pervert!* The Medical Director was tugging her off the caretaker, *You're gonna kill him, Servinaz! Let him go!* Under this onslaught, Cumali's protests were drowned out: he hadn't meant to touch Leyla, his hand had only brushed her accidentally, etc, etc.

The Black Sea Herald reporter Fahrettin Daşçı witnessed the whole scene, including Leyla's stripping. He got carried away, too, and admired Servinaz for her immediate intervention and attempt to tear the caretaker apart. If truth be told, what he saw at the hospital that day suggested a serious lack of authority. A great topic in its own right, but the risk of falling out with the Medical Director was daunting. He contented himself with embellishing his endlessly repeated Leyla tale with the bit about the brave Matron attacking the perverted caretaker.

At the Medical Director's, *You'll kill him!* Servinaz sank to the floor in uncontrollable sobs. The image of her husband in his death throes blending with memories of the torture she'd suffered at his hands were just too much. In the meanwhile, Leyla had been marched off to the soft cell and things had calmed down somewhat. The Medical Director had been worried quite a while about how to confront Servinaz for slacking off – he loved her like a sister, after all. So her apparent recovery, back into her former lioness self, was great news, except for the alarming outburst just now. He suggested she might take a few days' paid leave. Servinaz objected vehemently. Just because she'd lost control for a moment didn't mean she needed time off.

The old *Servinaz the Terrible* had returned, if only for a while, and given Cumali a proper hard time in the hallway. She swore she'd gouge out his eyes if he ever leered at the female patients again, never mind grope them. Head still throbbing, Cumali knew she would do it too; his eyes were already aching in trepidation.

He may have grumbled at the Medical Director's order to go to the basement and procure a dead mouse, but defying Servinaz was something else entirely: cowering, he traipsed down to the basement. As luck would have it, the basement had just been cleaned. There wasn't a single dead mouse anywhere. After an entire afternoon of poking in every corner, he located a tiny dead mouse behind a disgustingly filthy pipe in the boiler room. It took a good deal of manoeuvring with a broom to prise out. He popped it into a plastic bag and brought it to the Medical Director, who promptly showed the foetid corpse to the nutty neuropsychiatrist. She failed to notice that the mouse had been dead for a long time, but seeing it in the flesh, calmed down at once.

Whilst Cumali was searching for a mouse corpse, Âlim Kâhkeci (his Friday prayers now irretrievably missed) was interrogating Gülnazmiye Görgün, not so much about what she was actually doing in his office as about whether the brand new racquet he'd splashed out on had actually touched the mouse. If it had, it would have to go. No amount of her swearing that the racquet never came anywhere near the non-existent mouse, *as God is my witness!* seemed to help. Grabbing the copy of *Unnerving*, which was placed haphazardly on his desk – thereby spoiling its demented symmetry – he wrapped it around the grip, and making sure not to touch it anywhere, and flung the racquet onto the revolting pile of rubbish in one of the overflowing bins behind the hospital. Gülnazmiye was torn off a strip upon his return – and what was he supposed to do now about all that money he'd shelled out? Grateful to have so narrowly escaped (she hadn't been caught reading her boyfriend's file!) and that she wasn't in trouble, Gülnazmiye sobbed, *I'll pay whatever it cost, Doctor Bey*, as Âlim Kâhkeci wondered whether it was fair to dock the girl, who could only be drawing a pitiful salary; still, he couldn't stop lamenting about his contaminated racquet.

That day, Barış went round the back of the hospital to gaze at the sea and picked up the magazine he spied on the bin. Smoothing it out and settling into the old four-seater, he flicked through his find. The name Shakespeare in Prof Altay Çamur's article caught his eye; intrigued, he started reading. He was already engrossed in it when a couple of neighbourhood brats leapt over the wall and started rooting around in the rubbish, which should have been sorted as medical waste but wasn't. Distracted by their arrival, Barış asked what they were looking for and was told it was serum tubing, *Make the best slingshots, they do!* Barış joined them as they rummaged around, but they found nothing useful, no serum bottle, no tubes, nothing.

In the meanwhile, he told them a heap of stuff about birds, kites and clouds. *Have you read Five Weeks in a Balloon?* he asked. *Tsk!* said the boys. Then his eyes caught the Black Sea stretching like a wild terrain, its waves rising to meet the stiff wind, and he moved on to tales of pirates and the sea, speaking of *Treasure Island* and *Moby Dick*, and mixing them all up. The kids couldn't make head or tail of his speech jumping around; alarmed by his words falling like rain, the parts he was acting out, the way he changed his voice and made wild, expansive gestures, they wanted to get away. Then he showed them how to make a devil's kite: he ripped the magazine, made a kite and finally attached the tail. Saying, *Just tie a reel of cotton yarn and fly it – here you go!* he handed the jerry-built contraption to the kids, who scuttled off with it. Back in his room he lay on his bed to think about kites and talk to his left hand.

The kids flung down the kite the moment they left the hospital garden and crossed the street. Gülnazmiye's magazine was run over, crushed and scattered, and joined the great detritus of life. She ordered another copy from the grumpy bookseller Özcan Durna and made his life hell until she got it. Gutted to see that her article had not been published, she phoned the magazine straightaway. The secretary offered a standard reply: flooded as they were with contributions, they had to publish them in the order they received them. Gülnazmiye's time would come but exactly when was hard to say. Recommending patience, she mollified Gülnazmiye at once.

That night, after the terrors of day – what with tennis racquets and everything, Gülnazmiye dreamt of Barış Bakış. It was a long dream, wonderful despite everything, and very, very clear. Poking his fingers through the strings of a gigantic tennis racquet as if he was in jail, Barış was crying, tears streaming from his water-green eyes. Holding, nay, gripping her boyfriend's slender fingers, Gülnazmiye swore to him that she would sooner or later get rid of this mesh between them which kept their hearts apart. She cried a lot, whispered her love, and clutched his fingers with all the power of her love. She woke up in agony, disappointed to see she was gripping her pillow instead of those slender fingers. Her fingers had gone numb.

From that night onwards, she never stopped dreaming about their happiness. She didn't complain, only it was getting to be a little upsetting. She wanted to be happy in her boyfriend's arms, and not just in her dreams, but their love just wasn't making progress, Barış just wouldn't take her in his arms. It was impossible to be alone together at the hospital anyway, so she had to make do with dreams. Which were quite strange. Her boyfriend reached out to her every night in a different setting, whispered sweet nothings, but always suffered. Usually complaining about his mother or crying because of the obstacles between them, he would ask Gülnazmiye for help as he gazed at her from the depths of his water-green eyes. After every dream with him pleading to her, the hapless girl swore to rescue her boyfriend from the hospital.

It was a few weeks after the tennis racquet incident, round about the time Barış was soaking his bed in eau de cologne and striking a match, when she woke up in a panic. An icy breeze was licking her face; in her dream, her boyfriend stood in the hospital garden in the gently falling snow, hugging his naked upper body with his powerful arms, and imploring her through chattering teeth, *Gül, warm me up, I'm freezing!*

In actual fact, it was a much more natural and simpler dream than usual. A little digging would easily reveal the connection between his nakedness and powerful arms, and her lust for this handsome young man. But just like someone with a full bladder dreaming of standing on the edge of the precipice (associating, therefore, wetting the bed with falling), or another who's really thirsty who sees herself unable to reach the source of water, Gülnazmiye was shivering under two duvets as she was dreaming of Barış.

Her room was in fact freezing. The naughty neighbourhood kids throwing stones at the flocks of birds in the tree outside had broken her window and run away. It wasn't in her nature to raise hell, to screech, *Who did this?* especially in this neighbourhood, where people hassled her for living on her own. And since her salary had run out, she had no choice but to nail an old blanket over the window to make do until month end. But it was a very cold night, and a violent gust of the north-westerly had tugged the blanket out of the nails and turned the already chilly room (she was nothing if not cautious, having doused her bottled gas heater before turning in) into a walk-in freezer.

In the morning, still in the grip of that dream, she made for the Arcade Market first thing instead of the hospital. She would go to Girlie İsmet's shop and put her prudently hoarded credit card to good use: she'd buy her poor Barış a long-sleeved woollen vest and long johns so he wouldn't catch a cold and get sick.

Traumatised after the night before, Girlie İsmet had not opened his shop that morning. Gülnazmiye stared at the shop windows in the arcade for half an hour or so as she waited. In vain though. Poor İsmet would never open his shop again.

The previous night, after turning a deaf ear all this time to his arcade neighbours' insinuations, İsmet had finally given in and agreed to go to an orgy to prove he wasn't homosexual. The group included the umbrella-seller Remzi.

İsmet shut his shop, entered the wreck of a black Ford, and they set off. The **bug-eyed self-styled broker Hidayet** was at the wheel as the car rattled with every gear change. Bit of a wide boy, Hidayet had rented an office in Arcade Market six months earlier, seemingly to handle car sales, broker property sales and fill out tax returns etc. for a living. Except it wasn't much of a living. He was married with four kids and barely made enough to pay the rent on the office. Yet he somehow seemed to have bucketloads for nightlife, boasting that what he spent on women would have bought a block of flats. Every once in a while he'd vanish for several days, return grinning ear to ear and bang on about exaggerated tales of conquest, ninety per cent of which were downright lies, each time adorned with a new fantasy prefaced by a titillating *You know, mate, pulled a bird in Konya, banged her in a vineyard house, day and night for ten days!* thereby earning the admiration of the men in the arcade who'd never get the chance to enjoy such mouth-watering jaunts and so had to content themselves with sleazy nightclubs and ordinary whorehouses.

Remzi was in the front, arm casually draped over the back of his good mate Hidayet's seat. İsmet sat in the rear next to a **belching greengrocery wholesaler** (judging by the phone calls he made throughout the journey), who gave directions to Hidayet, who in turn was chuntering, *Bloody car's gonna fall apart in my hands!* as the car rattled and clattered. They stopped on the outskirts of the city before the conversation really got going, went into a supermarket for rakı, cigarettes, meat, bread and barbecue coal, etc. İsmet wanted to pay his share, but Remzi wouldn't dream of it, *You're our guest tonight; you can pay next time!*

It was a merry ride as everyone except İsmet related something or other. İsmet enjoyed Hidayet's colourful stories accompanied by sweeping gestures at the wheel. These amusing tales of the city's fleshpots included fond reminiscences of unforgettable prostitutes: *Ah, mate, she was something, that tart!* The belching wholesaler was too busy on his phone throughout the drive to contribute anything of his own. Whenever he began, *And me, there was this one time…* his phone would ring again, he'd leave the tale halfway, and Remzi would start another that was not much different from Hidayet's.

At one point Remzi said he'd had enough of Moldovan girls; tonight's company would be Uzbeks. He then proceeded to elaborate on far-fetched links between the almond eyes and round faces of Uzbek girls and their strange sexual tricks. Blood pressure rising in anticipation of his first sexual encounter, İsmet piped up, *Are the girls coming straight to the house?* just as Remzi turned to Hidayet, who was flicking his cigarette ash out of the window he'd opened just a crack, and asked him, *You gonna give us an imitation of that lame belly dancer at the Outer Space Nightclub tonight?* The three men who knew the dancer guffawed. İsmet's anxiety rose as his question remained unanswered.

The summer house with the paintwork blistering in the damp air was perched high, overlooking the sea, some seventy kilometres from the city. It was freezing. As the car drew to a halt outside the house and they all filed out, İsmet felt a shiver down his spine. Moonlight peeped between the clouds now and then, washing the sky in a cool blue. Seven or eight summer houses, built far too close to each other, stood with their windows dark – the set of a horror film in black outline to the soundtrack of colossal waves.

Daunted by his lack of sexual experience, İsmet was hoping for an understanding Uzbek girl; with a foolish grin pasted on his face to hide his fear, he wandered between the men as one lit the fire, the other lit the barbecue and the third necked some rakı the moment they'd stepped in.

It wasn't long before the girls arrived, accompanied by a couple more men. The girls were neither Uzbek nor Moldovan; what's worse, they were much older and much skankier than İsmet had been expecting. As these ageing prostitutes hopped from one lap to the other, swearing liberally and copping a feel here and there, a furiously blushing İsmet felt his ears ringing with embarrassment.

It was revolting. The coarse speech of the women with greasy hair and visibly dark roots, their deepened voices, the stench that emanated from the wholesaler's mouth with every belch, Hidayet's imitation of the hobbling tubercular belly dancer, the grease dripping from the chicken wings in the hands of one of the new arrivals, the atmosphere, himself – it was all revolting. But he couldn't just push off. It was late, the house was miles from anywhere, and not even a lorry passed down the deserted road. He briefly toyed with the idea of braving the cold to hike up to the main road, where he was sure to find a car to take him back to the city. But he didn't dare. His masculinity was already doubted by his mates. If he scarpered now, his reputation in the arcade would never recover. He had no choice but to join in.

A portable rakı table was laid out in front of the fireplace, where enormous logs were burning. A thick fug of cigarette smoke filled the room. İsmet sat down too and began to eat nervously. He was laughing at Hidayet's imitations, putting up with Remzi collapsing over him in bouts of laughter and trying very hard to hide his disgust at the sight of the women's filthy bra straps.

Get a couple of these down you! Here! Your world's never gonna be the same again! exclaimed Remzi, flinging some pills onto the table. İsmet, who could barely enjoy a drink of rakı, downed the pills, got quite merry, laughed non-stop, downed a couple more an hour later, and couldn't remember the rest.

The next morning, whilst Gülnazmiye was crouching by the door in the Arcade Market waiting for him to open his shop, İsmet opened an eye. The snorer beside him wasn't **Emriye from Küçükbakkalköy**, who'd kept choking him all last night every time she lowered her hefty body onto his lap and brayed as she pinched him here and there, Emriye with the stomach-churning bad breath exuding from rotten teeth. It was the umbrella-seller Remzi. İsmet was naked and ached everywhere. Suddenly the scales fell from his eyes.

When he emerged from the damp room, whose furniture consisted of an ancient bed covered in swathes of stains, a duvet without a cover and some cartons of mysterious contents, Emriye was making tea in the sitting room, a fag dangling from her lips. *Had a good night, girl?* she asked. His icy stare told her he'd been tricked, so she added, *That Remzi's a right swine, he is.* Not that she'd waste more than thirty seconds on pity; having seen such awful traps throughout her career and witnessed such pain, she didn't think İsmet's troubles merited more than that.

The hapless İsmet froze on the spot. He grabbed his clothes and dashed out of the room the moment he'd seen Remzi snoring beside him, and then got dressed outside the door, shivering with the cold and shame. Emriye stuffed her face with bread she'd toasted on the smoulder-ing embers in the fireplace before dunking it into last night's garlic-yogurt dip, sure İsmet was now heading for the same end as her. Her advice – *You'll be ruined here* – littered with examples from her own life, painted a grim picture of the future that awaited him if he carried on hanging out with Remzi.

By the time she launched into the story of her life, from the seedy nightclubs on the outskirts of Istanbul to the whorehouses on intercity roads, İsmet was out of the house, heading for the main road in the gently falling snow, as thoughts of flinging himself into the wild waves of the Black Sea passed through his mind.

This lost soul hitched a lift from a passing lorry back into the city. He didn't open his shop that day, or ever again. He had been unable to throw himself into the sea, but at home he opened the gas canister in the kitchen all the way. If his father, a **kemençe bard named Seyit**, hadn't found him quite by chance, he might have died.

The old man, famed throughout the nearby villages and towns for his risqué witticisms and colourful word-duelling, had donned his black suit – now greying from years of wear, which he'd had since the first flush of youth – and hopped on a minibus to participate in the Duelling Bards contest on Channel SS. The **driver, Beaknose Şahin**, was a right nutter. Never pausing to think *There are ladies on board, it would be rude, I'd best behave myself,* he loved tacky double entendres. He'd been beaten up countless times, to the extent that that magnificent nose of his had once been broken, but he never changed. That morning, when he stared at Seyit in the rear-view mirror and said, *Gentlemen all pay up the rear!* the old bard's instant retort, *Keep your eyes on the road / They'll hand over their load!* cracked up the passengers; thankfully, on this occasion it was all men on the minibus. He was questioned about his threads; he said he was on his way to compete on TV, in a bard duel. Everyone egged him on; the more they did, the bigger his head got. They were nearing his stop when Beaknose Şahin teased him again with a convincing *But Uncle Seyit, you have no tie, can you go on TV without one?* The passengers piped in too. Bard Seyit decided to drop in on his son to get kitted up.

He reached the Arcade Market, where Gülnazmiye Görgün was standing at the door of the shop. *Whatcha standing here for, lass?* he asked, eliciting a tense explanation that even though she'd been waiting for an hour, the shop was still not open; she then turned on her heel and left in a huff. Something had to be wrong. His quiet and unassuming yet busy-bee son not open his shop by now? It was unheard of. He went straight to İsmet's house. By the time he got there, the place was like a primed bomb filled with gas. The old man flung open every window, stuck his middle finger down his son's throat and made him vomit buckets. Flinging his son on his back, he rushed to the State Hospital.

His stomach pumped and doggedly silent before his father's persistent *Whatever made you gas yourself?* İsmet soon came round. Feeling a little relieved, Seyit decided to get to the show, tie or no tie. Only his mind was still on his son. When his turn came, he was lost in thought and failed to trounce his opponent with a belter of a ditty, as he normally would have done. Tongue-tied Seyit, a shoo-in for the trophy, lost the popular jury vote.

Something awful must be troubling İsmet. So grabbing the young man, whose eyes were blurred by a film of tears, Seyit brought him back to his village. His wife, sulking about her husband's failure on TV, was devastated when she learned of her son's attempted suicide. They both did their best to get to the truth. To no avail. Eventually, they concluded that İsmet must be pining for love.

The villagers, disappointed at Bard Seyit's first-round exit, didn't miss the opportunity rub his nose in it without so much as a hello or a gentle preliminary. Seyit objected violently, his anger momentarily overcoming concern for his son. He'd *thrashed he scoundrel who'd won* – he really did – but see, he was eliminated *'cause he had no tie*. Beaknose Şahin was his witness.

İsmet was now spending all his time sleeping late, only managing a bite or two at the insistence of his mother, who cried buckets at the state he was in; he took to wandering along the stream without speaking a word to anyone, or reflecting for hours as he sat in the tiny store where the family dried their hazelnuts and corn, the *serender* on four posts planed to a smooth finish to prevent mice from climbing up. He felt neither cold nor hunger. His devastated mother beat a path to the doors of healers for one magic talisman after another to slip into his bedclothes, which might cure him of the hopeless love she blamed for his condition.

Having failed to convince his son to reopen his shop, Bard Seyit transferred it to the **pirate DVD seller Talip**, a fan of singer Müslüm Gürses. Seyit might have been matchless at duelling with other bards in the coffee house, but he was useless when it came to money. Fed up with trundling between the village and the city to find a solution, he was more than happy to hand the shop over – lock, stock and barrel – to the cheerfully garrulous Talip for next to nothing. The first thing Talip did was inspect his new inventory. He handed out the erotic lingerie to his mates, sold the rest of the stock as a job lot to a draper, stacked his new shelves with loads of cassette tapes, a few CDs and legit DVDs of popular films and began selling pirate DVDs under the counter.

Opening this shop in the Arcade Market had two unforeseen consequences for this man, whose knowledge of the cinema was limited to the names of the stars of certain American blockbusters. The first was meeting Âlim Kâhkeci. The doctor now dropped in regularly looking for specific films – private or licensed copy – which he asked for by title and director's name. His interest thus piqued, Talip, who up to that point had been utterly unaware of the importance of a director in cinema, started watching them himself.

At first he didn't get any of it. But surely the great doctor must know a thing or two if he turned his nose up at popular movies and insisted on these? Highly impressed by this diverse array of select titles, Talip Erbaş became a surprisingly sophisticated connoisseur, beginning with *Fight Club*, *U-Turn*, *Mulholland Drive*, *Fargo*, *Barton Fink*, the *Three Colours* trilogy, *The Million Dollar Hotel*, *The Confession*, *The Lovers on the Bridge*, *Love's a Bitch* and *Straw Dogs*. Their message might escape him, but he was pleased to note that they were different. In time, he developed into one of only two people in the city who knew the winners of every single award, from the Palme d'Or of Cannes through to the Golden Bear of Berlin and the Golden Tulip of Istanbul. The other person was, as might be expected, Dr Âlim Kâhkeci.

Talip also spent twenty-seven days in prison. One day, as he was stacking legitimate DVDs on the shelves, with a new Müslüm Gürses song on his lips as was recently his habit, he felt Remzi stroke his arm (he had ostensibly come to the shop to help). He flipped at the sight of the umbrella-seller's hairy hand with sausage fingers. *I must be seeing things!* flashed through his mind. He lifted his head to see Remzi's leer.

Puny Talip saw red and delivered a punch in the nose. He beat Remzi to a pulp for mistaking him for a homosexual, just because he'd been murmuring a song and had earlier let slip that he'd enjoyed *Brokeback Mountain* (the pirated version was renamed *The Queer Cowboys*). Talip would have been spared the twenty-seven day sentence if he hadn't broken Remzi's nose, but Remzi's abominable wife wouldn't let it go. At the hearing neither man could explain what the fight was about.

All they said was, *We argued over an unpaid debt*. Despite his wife's nagging, Remzi didn't press charges and the matter was closed.

Just when Girlie İsmet had turned the gas on all the way and gone to bed, Gülnazmiye gave up. The shop wasn't going to open. She left the Arcade Market to traipse round all the underwear shops in the city until she finally bought some woollen underwear for her green-eyed Barış, who'd been complaining of the cold in her dream; it wasn't quite the quality she was looking for, but it was better than nothing. When she reached the hospital it was nearly evening; the sun would soon be setting, but it had been hidden behind thick clouds all day anyway.

The lovesick girl thought she was in for it this time with Servinaz and would have to come up with some lie. But the hospital was still in turmoil after the fire of the night before and her absence had gone unnoticed. As she strode on without looking right or left, intent on finding and warming her sweetheart as soon as possible, she crashed into harelipped Ayşe Nuran Serbest and dropped the carrier bag with the underwear. The fuming gynaecologist swept past without so much as saying sorry.

Hearing of the fire in BB's room, Gülnazmiye's heart missed a beat. She looked for her sweetheart here, there and everywhere – no luck. Finally, with a great deal of trepidation, she asked Servinaz. The whole world came crashing down upon her head when she was told that he had been restrained and sedated. Without even asking why, she swept towards the Medical Director's office.

She had no doubt that *that wicked mother of his*, Veda Alkan, who was carrying on with the Romanian chargé d'affaires Emil Pavulescu (hadn't her Barış said so?), had a hand in it. She couldn't quite figure out what was going on, except for the thought that the more she wanted to save Barış, the deeper his chances were scuppered by his mother. Risking her professional career before it had even started and blindsiding the addle-brained secretary Nemişo, who was surfing the net, she dived into the Medical Director's office.

He was having a terrible day. Just when his nerves, shot by the previous night's fire, were calming down – thankfully no one was hurt and it hadn't got out of hand – he'd been sloshed with the dregs of the gynaecologist's tea and was again on edge. Perplexed by the young psychologist's puce face and enormous assets rising and falling with each breath, he addressed her as *Melek Hanım* instead of *Gül Hanım*, referring to the sex goddess of yore.

God must have been watching out for Gülnazmiye's career that day. The phone rang as she was about to screech, accuse the Medical Director of some heinous plot, and blurt out her love for Barış, thus blotting her copybook and even attracting a formal reprimand.

Scared witless at his own slip of the tongue, which could have caused a huge incident, the Medical Director was saved by the telephone. As he picked up, saying, *Just a second*, to Gülnazmiye, Nebahat Özdamar burst in to complain about the caretaker. In floods of tears, she moaned that Earless Ziya didn't carry the boxes she'd told him to carry, didn't dust her office or mop the hallway; that no one paid her the slightest bit of notice. In an effort to drown out the sobbing neuropsychiatrist, Gülnazmiye's voice rose to a haughty, *Sir, might I enquire why you've had Barış Bakış restrained?* just as Nemişo entered to inform the Medical Director that the main vane had burst in the hamam and the basement was knee-deep in water. The Medical Director had had it up to here; flinging the earpiece in his hand, he stormed out, shouting, *Enouuugh!*

The stumpy neuropsychiatrist with the defiant buzz cut dragged Gülnazmiye, who'd yet to hear in full detail the tale of the errant husband, to her office for a cup of coffee, as the Medical Director mobilised the technicians to clear the hamam, bellowing till he was blue in the face, *This place's has to be dry as a bone tomorrow morning!* and stormed off to the Three Brothers Patisserie.

He calmed down after sipping a hot milky drink; this was around the time the city folk usually got ready to leave for home. Retirement had never looked so attractive before. Why put up with all this rubbish when he could sit at home and write his book at leisure?

Since he had no real intention of leaving the hospital, however, his thoughts began to wander and before he knew it, he was reflecting on the knotty parquet pattern vinyl, which simply didn't suit the conference hall, and the ageing seats: at the very least the front row should be replaced. He murmured, *We really need a sponsor.*

The conference hall, which regularly hosted a variety of official bodies (starting with the city council) as well as the medical school and pharmaceutical companies, was located in the remotest corner of the hospital. Just getting there was a problem. Despite the arrow signs placed throughout the hospital last year on the orders of the Medical Director, it was almost impossible for anyone to find the conference hall without taking a wrong turn or two in that labyrinth.

Yet when the plans had been drawn, the governors at the time, and **Undersecretary Cevdet Pektaş** in particular, had demanded quite the opposite: the conference hall had to be in the most spectacular location. The original foundations were laid in 1898 and the hospital was opened in 1902; this first building no longer being fit for purpose – not a single brick had been added since Turkey became a republic – a much larger and more elaborate one was commissioned. A state-of-the-art edifice featuring a stylish modern conference hall, Cevdet insisted.

The thrill of the 1961 Constitution, which had swept in a gust of liberty around the country, might have been on the wane, as were the shining stars of science and culture, but, all the same, senior bureaucrats still enjoyed the appearance of serving those twin ideals. The conference hall had to have a premium site in the hospital, he insisted, claiming that it would host lectures by the world's top scientists and so make this not just a hospital but a house of learning, which in turn would raise the prestige of the city multifold. Cevdet took personal interest in every detail, dropped everything and dedicated himself to the new hospital building. Well before the first pick-axe struck, his desk was piled high with catalogues and samples of the absolute latest in building materials, from tiles to wall sockets.

The real reason he had thrown himself so wholeheartedly into the project was, in actual fact, not his belief in science but love. His head was in the clouds. He was madly in love with the **almond-eyed teacher Şehriban**, whom he'd met in the office of a friend, a senior civil servant in the Ministry of Education.

The moment he first saw those eyes, he'd rushed into the office, sat down facing Şehriban and fixed his shapeless rheumy eyes on hers. His bureaucrat friend ordered him a cup of bitter coffee and the Undersecretary immediately drew out his flat pack of Yenice to offer round. That was a time before smoking was demonised as the peril that would end the human race, a time when everyone smoked anywhere and everywhere. Şehriban said, *No, thank you; I don't smoke.* This sentence echoed in his head for days. *No, thank you; I don't smoke.*

She was called Almond-eyed Şehriban by her family and friends, referring to her perpetual use of black kohl to disguise a tiny flaw from a childhood infection, all but invisible to the naked eye, which had left one eye slightly smaller than the other.

Many years later, sitting at her cinnamon doughnut stand in Ayvalık, the recollection of that nickname cut her to the quick as her whole life passed before her eyes. It was triggered by the actress Gülriz Sururi's memoirs, *Finer than a Hair and Sharper than a Sword*, which she'd bought from a second-hand bookstall run by a few women for the benefit of the Modern Life Support Society. Affected similiarly, the famous actress had hit upon the same solution! With a furtive glance at her own reflection in the stand's glass, Şehriban noticed with a pang that she looked quite old.

On the day the Undersecretary fell for her, she'd come to plead for a change in her posting, at the very least to a district in Ankara County – somewhere like Haymana, Ayaş or Bâlâ – instead of the back of beyond, the most remote village in some eastern county. Since she'd never be free to do what she wanted in her hometown, she couldn't wait to claim a spot in the modern atmosphere of the capital and join in its ranks of elegant ladies.

Upon learning that Şehriban was one of the first graduates of the Ladies' Teaching College in the same city as his new hospital building, and that her family still lived there, the Undersecretary used his connections to secure a posting, not to Haymana or Bâlâ, but to the most prestigious primary school in the heart of the capital: the Republic Primary School – his excuse to keep the line of communication with these almond eyes at the ready.

Now everything was about the hospital or Şehriban. He kept ringing with one idiotic question after another, *How about the entrance door? Like this, or like that? Should the outpatient clinics be sited at the front or at the back?* And every time the young teacher demurred, *I wouldn't know,* he'd insist with a syrupy *But it's gonna be built in your hometown.*

He was spending days and nights at the Development Directorate in order to commission the best possible plans, as though this were not just some public building, but instead, his wedding present to the city where his precious Şehriban was born and raised in, where his future in-laws lived and which he would therefore obviously visit often.

Nothing was too good for the hometown of his darling Şehriban, whom he took to out-of-the-way restaurants in taxis, lest they be seen in his official car together, the girl he showered gifts on (clothing such as a coat, silk blouses, shoes and slips; smuggled perfumes; a heart-shaped pendant in which he'd placed a passport photo of himself) and verses scrawled on onionskin paper, which he despatched with his office boy: *a gold ring thick / I ordered from Tokat's masters / The doc won't sign off / The lovesick* or *Want to hop on a horse / Want to dismount at the stream / Want to see that / Almond-eyed beauty once again.* He would roll up his sleeves.

And roll up his sleeves he did, but not to supervise the construction – no, the first thing he did was desert his wife, **Naime Pektaş, who all year round shuffled about in size-forty-two slippers** due to her gout and all night long groaned with joint pain, leaving her with their four daughters.

The news that her husband of so many years (with grandchildren too!) had fallen for a young teacher came like a bolt from the blue. Their daughters, the eldest married with children and the youngest still in secondary school, all fell to pieces. Cevdet turned a blind eye to the tears of his wife and daughters, and a deaf ear to the threats of his son-in-law, and brushed off the contempt and warnings of his friends. Thankfully, he wasn't shameless enough to hold a grand wedding; he settled for a plain but very elegant ceremony (even the Minister of Education sent flowers) and was finally united with his Şehriban.

It didn't take long for her to turn her back to it all, though: her hometown, the hospital building and her husband the Undersecretary. It was still many years before the new building would be ready to serve the country when she began cuckolding Cevdet with **Civan Caymaz, the PE teacher and volleyball team coach** in the girls' lycée next to her school.

The pretty daughter of a City Council tax collector, Şehriban's head had been turned by the official car, official driver, office boy, concierge, friendship with senior civil servants in the capital and the double flat in one of the finest blocks of Kavaklıdere, but sadly, on their first night together, this man twenty-five years her senior turned out to be a huge disappointment, a repulsive, abject failure in bed. The Undersecretary was unable to finish what he'd started, not even for himself; panting through his nose, he fell in an exhausted heap on top of her. The poor girl felt her stomach churning as she removed the black chest hairs sticking to her boobs. She regretted having begrudged her besotted suitor even a kiss – *Not before marriage*, she had said.

Civan was a far more satisfying lover, but the Undersecretary's failings weren't limited only to his performance in bed. The real problem was her disgust for her husband, a miserable wretch who slept in his socks, thought *Pardon me!* sufficed to excuse a belch and farted in his sleep. Now permanently tense, Şehriban needed tablets and always turned in early: *I've got a headache, Cevdet; please leave me alone!* Which, in turn, urged the Undersecretary to sell his vineyards and orchards in Tokat bit by bit to fund expensive gifts for his young wife, throw himself upon her mercy and send her on holidays and trips. Unwilling to give up the vast flat, the official car and her new class status, which included the *dear wives of senior civil servants*, Şehriban settled for sneaking off to friends' flats and cheap hotels to sleep with Civan.

One day, something else happened quite out of the blue. Without feeling any need to break up with Şehriban, Civan Caymaz fell in love with and wanted to marry the **volleyball team player and lycée II student Sedef** – every time she jumped to the net her blonde ponytail swept the nape of her neck in a way that melted his insides. Şehriban practically fainted in the teachers' room when she heard of her lover's engagement. It was only yesterday they'd met and made love at a friend's pad in Keçiören (timing their arrivals with a fifteen-minute gap), biting their lips to keep quiet, scared of the scandal if the people upstairs heard.

She attempted suicide by taking a whole pack of Diazem. The Undersecretary came home in the evening, office boy in tow – weighed down under kilos of lamb chops, air-dried beef, kalamata olives, aged kaşar and Anamur bananas – found her foaming at the mouth and rushed her off to the hospital.

She felt so awful that when she was placed in a private room after her stomach was pumped, she tearfully blurted it all out to **Nurse Emel Yanık, who, fishing for information**, had enquired, *What makes a woman living in the lap of luxury attempt suicide?* instead of, as the nurse later claimed, simply asking how she was. They might have saved her this time, sobbed Şehriban, but she couldn't live without Civan. She'd commit suicide again; she'd either belong to Civan or to the earth.

Nurse Emel Yanık was not one for keeping others' secrets. But nor would she openly announce what she'd heard; it wasn't for her to jeopardise her trustworthiness. Squirming a bit before the doctor who was checking on the Undersecretary's wife, she posed a leading question: *D'you think pumping her stomach and then discharging her is gonna be enough? Far be it from* the nurse *to take such liberties,* but she *did have a duty of care,* and *perhaps the lady needed to see a neurologist too?* Again, *far be it from her to say so,* but what Şehriban Hanım had confided to her in tears suggested that *she might make another attempt.* The Undersecretary's wife had given her serious cause for worry, see; she had said, I *'ll either belong to Never-mind-his-Name or to the earth!*

That the inquisitive doctor would grill her was inevitable the moment he heard all this. Emel Yanık related everything Şehriban had said *purely out of concern for her patient's mental health* and found herself forced to give up the name of *Never-mind-his-Name.*

The conversation had taken less than ten minutes; news of Şehriban cuckolding the Undersecretary with the handsome PE teacher (and it had been going on for months!) swept round all the floor nurses before the doctor had even left the floor, then every doctor on watch before the morning, the whole hospital the next day, and the entire capital within the week.

Every *irreproachably* virtuous housewife and family man, outraged by the way the Undersecretary had divorced his wife of twenty-seven years to marry a teacher young enough to be his daughter, was waiting for scandal – any moment now, that slut Şehriban might be shot by her husband, or at the very least thrown out in disgrace. But shockingly, the Undersecretary accused this moral community of slander. The men were envious of his young and beautiful wife, green with envy when they looked at their sagging wives, and falling over themselves to sling mud at his almond-eyed Şehriban. His wife, surely, hadn't attempted suicide over some illicit love affair; she'd been poisoned by the fish she'd had at supper.

After the Undersecretary welcomed with open arms his darling wife upon her discharge, there was a distinctly swift drop in the number of people who greeted him. Şehriban was shunned by the super-prim headmaster, assistant headmasters and teachers; some of the parents went as far as demanding a different teacher for their children. Şehriban had to ask for long-term sick leave.

The real loser in this scandal was the handsome PE teacher Civan Caymaz, once the rumours reached the ears of the **property developer Abdülkadir Çemiş, from Niğde.** Volleyball player Sedef's father had joined the ranks of Ankara's leading businessmen after erecting seventeen blocks of flats, each six storeys high, all inside of five years. He'd never taken to this artist wannabe with his hair greased to a mirror shine. He hated the guts of this shitty prospective son-in-law, whose only saving grace was his looks. When his only daughter, whom he'd spoiled rotten after her mother had died in childbirth, dug her heels in, sobbing on her nanny's lap, *If daddy won't let me marry Civan, I'll kill myself!* and did, in fact, stop eating, he had no choice but to give in, provided she first finished the lycée.

Sports, schports: he wasn't thrilled about the future son-in-law's occupation. A teacher might be acceptable, but coaching was no profession in his view; he wanted Civan to get a proper job, i.e., to work for him in his company. One morning at breakfast, when he broached this matter of sports, Sedef interrupted: she and Civan one day intended to open a sports hall.

She shared Civan's grandiose dreams of a sports complex that offered top service to the upper classes: a facility with lots of different units, from tennis courts to a gym, run by great-looking male and female instructors – funded, naturally, by a considerable amount that would be extracted from Abdülkadir. To give him credit, Abdülkadir managed to hold his tongue, even as he saw red listening to these castles in the air, and waited for her to finish before giving her a long speech.

Sports halls and what have you, these were all pipe dreams. You'd never make money this way. Plus, sports were only good for one thing: keeping youngsters like his daughter healthy at school, keeping their minds off canoodling. Not that the facts bore him out, given the present situation; sports had done nothing of the sort here, and his only daughter had fallen for some penniless creep.

Sedef froze at this outburst, her jam toast still in her mouth. The developer was about to sound off on Civan next. But when he noticed her welling eyes and trembling lips, he switched to giving advice, and in a much gentler tone. Eventually, his daughter would drop these dreams, once she had settled down in her own home. *Won't you, darling?* he asked sweetly. That he meant Civan went right over her head. Remembering how Civan had fallen for her when she was jumping up to the net, she said, *I'll never give up volleyball!* The developer didn't labour the point. *That's for your husband to say when the time comes,* he replied, shaking his head, praying for a miracle that would rescue his daughter from this pipsqueak.

It was Şehriban's attempted suicide that proved to be the answer to his prayers. Not entirely confident he could keep Civan in check even if he insisted that the young couple move in with him, Abdülkadir clutched at the scandal without bothering to enquire further. He announced that he'd changed his mind about allowing his only daughter to marry this shameless scoundrel and even pulled strings to have Civan fired from both the coaching and the teaching posts. Sedef cried her eyes out, locked herself in her room and eventually agreed to go to her aunt in Istanbul to finish her schooling. She'd gone off Civan after all this gossip anyway. Especially as he'd been two-timing her for months and months with a married woman known as Almond-eyed Şehriban; no, she could never accept that.

Prompted by the news of Civan's debauchery, Sedef's aunt hopped onto the sleeper train for Ankara. **Keriman Sevimli, who lived like a queen** thanks to the income from the properties she'd inherited from her husbands, both of whom had died prematurely, tempted her niece with *Come and stay with me, finish lycée and then go to university.* Sedef hummed and hawed, but her aunt added mouth-watering accounts of how girls her age lived in Istanbul. That did the trick. Keriman lived in a flat in the upmarket Joy Court; it had two palm trees in the garden and faced the

Lycée St Joseph, which was famed for its strapping, handsome students. Moda and its surroundings thronged with good-looking young people.

Sent off with her father's *Let her get over it first, then we'll see,* Sedef not only regained her self-confidence (and more) on her first night of flirting to her heart's content with the boys at the Moda Marine Club, but also forgot Civan at once and blossomed into a popular beauty. She had a total makeover, learnt all the new dances and broke a record by breaking up with four boyfriends before the summer was out. By the time she started university, at the Faculty of Sciences, she had gained a reputation as a Moda flirt, but she'd preserved her virginity all the same.

She met her match in year three: the sullen **law student Kenan Canıtez**, a lad with rough good looks who thought himself God's gift to women, a view sadly shared by the girls. With his airs and graces, he was nothing like the boyfriends who escorted her to dances, parties and patisseries. Her head was turned by Kenan's extraordinary affectations, tough attitude and wistful gaze, etc., but he was playing hard to get. Especially where Sedef was concerned, although he tormented all the girls.

Just when Sedef's self-confidence was about to crash, a faint sign appeared. They would gaze at each other at the second-hand book market and sit side by side in the dining hall. Then quite by chance they'd meet in the lobby of the cinema. Eventually, Sedef managed to bend him to her will, and won over this young man, whose tedious nature was as yet hidden behind his looks. They decided to marry.

As a member of Istanbul's upper crust, Keriman objected vociferously to the match on grounds of cultural disparity. But Abdülkadir Çemiş, who had been keeping an eye on his daughter – albeit at a distance – wasn't very optimistic about her future prospects if she carried on carrying on with Moda's young men for a few more years. Then no one would marry her. So he gave his consent and Keriman had to drop her objections.

The wedding took place in Rize's Arhavi, the groom's hometown: a massive affair with hundreds of rounds shot into the air and *horon* dances to the uninterrupted sound of kemençes and bagpipes. Sedef settled into a noisy life in a flat that took up an entire storey in the block where Kenan's family lived: her in-laws and unmarried sisters-in-law upstairs, married sisters-in-law with their families downstairs.

Proud of his barrister son-in-law from a leading family in Arhavi, which at the time was marginally better than a village, Abdülkadir Çemiş was convinced his daughter had married well. He visited them frequently, adored spending time with **his first grandson, Kürşat**, who was born ten months after the wedding, and enjoyed strolling in the fresh air along the shore of the crystal clear sea.

In time, however, he grew tired of the shouting that passed for conversation in that crowded family, their unbounded exaggeration with every subject, their insistent (*Eaaat, why don't you!*) offerings of kale cooked in suet, and the way they grabbed a pistol and fired it off whenever the fancy took them, so he stopped going. But he was content. His only daughter, who had grown up lonely, was happy in this big, noisy and cheerful family, where she was loved and where her sisters-in-law could be counted upon to look after her two sons. But she hadn't been married a year before she realised that Kenan's apparent sobriety stemmed as much from his imbecility as anything; once she'd had her fill of his good looks, she began to find him quite dull. Still, she really did love this plain-hearted fellow and enjoyed schooling him in the finer aspects of life; moreover, she who had grown up cheerless between a sad father and silent nannies was now cherished by this family, who had taken her to their hearts.

Many years went by. Sedef was at the Mental Health Hospital when she heard that her father had died in his sleep. Accompanied by her eldest son Kürşat (whom everyone mistook for her brother), she was taking **her hyperactive grandson Kayra** to the doctor as her daughter-in-law, heavily pregnant with her second child, was confined to the home under doctor's orders. Kayra never stopped for a second and was so naughty that the family had had enough. He was diagnosed with ADHD in Trabzon. The treatment had failed, so it was time to take him to the Paediatric Psychiatrist Faik Abacı, whose fame had reached Arhavi. As it turned out, something came up and Faik Abacı had wanted to postpone the appointment to the afternoon. Mother and son held a quick conflab: *Shall we cancel and go back to Arhavi or not?* In the end, they decided to wait; coming back another time would have been a nuisance.

Taking the boy with the scabby limbs, they went to the Sultan Restaurant. Kürşat, who was also a qualified barrister, had joined his father

Kenan Canıtez in his chambers. Kürşat always dined at the Sultan on his frequent business trips here, and earlier that morning, as they were setting off, he had promised his mother he'd take her there for a delicious grey mullet, the restaurant's speciality.

The boy wouldn't stay still, though: he toppled a gigantic flowerpot, crashed into waiters, fidgeted constantly at the table and interrupted their conversation. So that modest lunch was spoiled for the adults. Just as they were about to get up, Kürşat's mobile rang. He didn't conceal the sad news from his mother. Abdülkadir's death wasn't unexpected. Calling off their appointment with Faik Abacı, they returned to Arhavi at once and hopped into the car that very night to travel to Ankara. Abdülkadir Çemiş was interred with a grand ceremony, attended by his grandsons, his great-grandson Kayra and the entire contingent of his son-in-law's family – sisters-in-law and brothers-in-law and all their children. There was much crying, loads of flowers and prayers. Sedef might have been gutted by her first betrothed's betrayal, but she had found love – however short-lived the passion – and happiness with Kenan, and her father had died in peace.

Around the time Sedef had just moved to Istanbul, well before she'd met Kenan or even feasted her eyes on the energetic swarthy youths playing football in the Saint Joseph school garden, Şehriban returned home to her husband, the Undersecretary, after her attempted suicide, determined to love Civan to her dying day and never let him go. Swallowing her pride, she filled countless letters with such gushings as *Death is preferable to living without you; either take me back into your arms or have a fresh grave dug!* and sent messages to him through anyone and everyone.

Civan was aware that he could no longer stay in Ankara, where the developer Abdülkadir Çemiş called the shots with such resounding force. It also had to be said that he was impressed – nay, hugely flattered – by Şehriban risking death for his sake. And there was no end to the love letters from his almond-eyed paramour. Ten weeks after the attempted suicide, they had a tearful reunion in Swan Park. Şehriban grabbed her suitcase that very day and left the Undersecretary. She hadn't forgotten to take her portable record player and records, gold bangles, solitaire and the diamond earrings the Undersecretary had bought with the proceeds of the last remaining bit of his vineyard in Tokat.

Her sick leave had ended by the time they left Ankara; thankfully it was the summer holiday. Saying, *We'll be together and have a holiday too,* off they went to Ayvalık to settle into a bed and breakfast. When it became painfully clear that their salaries wouldn't stretch to this long, passionate holiday, Şehriban sold one of her bangles and realised that prudence was required if she wanted to hang on to the rest. She no longer had an undersecretary to give her the kind of life she had become accustomed to.

Its fame being still somewhere in the future, Ayvalık at the time was a charming, unassuming little town. They loved it. Şehriban applied for a posting here. Civan gave up teaching. They got married and moved into an old Greek house. Şehriban had to sell a couple more bangles to buy some decent furniture. They made do with her salary for a while. Then Civan's father died; adding that modest inheritance to the money from the last remaining bangles, diamond earrings and solitaire, the couple bought an olive grove. But they made a mess of it and frittered away all that money.

Yet defying all expectations, they stayed together and even had two children. After two births and two miscarriages, that fragile, petite woman whose eyes had once tempted the Undersecretary gained a hundred pounds over the years; her jawline vanished and her chin sagged in folds. The almond-eyed Şehriban of yore came to be known as *Turkey Neck Şehriban* amongst her neighbours. And since her eyeliner ran whenever she swam in the sea, she stopped outlining her eyes with a black kohl pencil. She let herself go.

Civan failed to make anything of himself after leaving teaching. Except for his greying hair, he didn't change much until he turned fifty. The fabulous contrast between his silver mane and bronze tan all year round only served to attract the female holidaymakers in Cunda all the more. But then overnight he grew old and for some reason looked closer to seventy.

To make ends meet in her retirement Şehriban took up selling cinnamon doughnuts in summer at a stall outside the Stone Café in Cunda. Civan, who all winter long played backgammon and shot the breeze with the townsfolk in the Mortar Coffee House until nightfall, in the summer rented canoes and pedalos to tourists. So summers were relatively more comfortable. But come winter, when all the tourists had left, money was tight again. They weren't that lucky with their children either. Neither boy did great at school. Their elder son opened a bakery in Romania and was earning a decent living. Not that he ever visited or helped his family all these years. But Şehriban wasn't going to complain, so long as he wasn't the burden their younger son was.

That son arrived every summer, complete with wife and children, settled into the parental home, and holidayed for at least a fortnight during which time his hand never strayed into his own pocket, whilst he expected fully laid rakı tables and a barbecue every night. Despite his title of marketing manager, he was a salesman in a small company of dubious reputation; a spendthrift who always lived just beyond his means, he was always in financial trouble... which troubled his mother.

Yet in spite of everything, Şehriban and Civan were happy. They never went to bed without finishing a bottle of rakı between them at the meze table, which never lacked stuffed courgette flowers or octopus salad. Except Civan's health had been quite poor of late. He needed to stop drinking but couldn't. Occasionally, when she was pouring batter into the hot oil, Şehriban agonised over her own money troubles and her younger son's debts, and wondered what life would have been like if she'd stayed with the Undersecretary. But then the image of his revolting hairs sticking to her body popped into her head and she gazed adoringly at her useless husband, who idled away the hours at the coffee house all day.

As for the Undersecretary, who finally came to accept that he'd lost Şehriban for ever when he received the decree absolute, he was desperate to return to the home he'd broken *for the sake of a despicable, notorious, worthless harlot,* and would have thrown himself at his first wife's feet with a contrite, *I'm so sorry!* but proud Naime would never take him back. She didn't care a twig for her ex-husband now. Whenever his name came up in the family, she'd curse him in a hail of spittle, *May he break his neck! May he be washed on the mortuary table!* She had already sorted out a new life with her four daughters, the youngest of whom had just started university whilst another was married with her own family. Relatively comfortable thanks to regular alimony payments (the Undersecretary was scared of his children's hostility) and the income from her own modest inheritance in – again – Tokat, she wasn't the least bit interested in the kind of shake-up that taking her ex-husband back would entail. She was in no state to think of anything other than her aching joints, at any rate. At his pleas for reconciliation, she sent word: *He should've appreciated me at the time. Tell him never to speak my name. Tell him I don't exist for him.* The girls backed their mother and sent him away when he fetched up at the door – and none too kindly at that.

Left high and dry, the Undersecretary took to drink. The hospital building that he'd fussed over was long forgotten. Construction was stopped. He was drinking in a sleazy bar in the Çınçın vineyards, whining, *Şehriban! Şehriban!* when he had a stroke; he lay in a coma for three months before dying.

Of all his daughters, **Çiçek, a philosophy undergraduate at the Faculty of Languages, History, and Geography** – one of his middle daughters, and two years younger than Şehriban – hated her father most, but even so she visited him in secret when she heard of his condition.

Cevdet was unconscious. As if she were viewing a total stranger, Çiçek stared at her father's miserable body, which looked like nothing more than gnarled bones and repulsive skin. This body with its wrinkled, shrivelled skin, this head with the sunken eyes and lips like burnt paper and the claw-like hands with the yellowed nails – they couldn't belong to her father. So alien was this pathetic scene that she felt sorry for this stranger – not for her father.

Death looked very close to this miserable wretch who was lying on his own in a crowded ward, but very far from the man she knew as father. It was as if this skeleton were not her father. Her father, who had deserted his family for some tart called Şehriban, must be somewhere else, roaring in his stentorian voice, face flushing with each tumbler of rakı he downed.

The only thing she could recognise as she stared at this pathetic body was the quarter-sovereign gold coin ring that her father never removed from the pinkie of his right hand. Amazed that no one had stolen it, she glanced around, reached out, removed the ring, which was on the verge of dropping off the scaly hand that resembled more the foot of a dead bird, and threw it into her handbag.

The Undersecretary died soon after this visit. On hearing about it, Çiçek withdrew into her room and cried for hours, not for the living corpse she'd visited, but for the image of the father who'd take her on his lap and played the game *Row, row, row your boat* way back when she was a child.

Many months later when her mother raised hell at discovering the signet ring – *What, you went to visit your dad?* – Çiçek replied in a dry, unemotional voice, *So what? Just as well I did, or it would've been swiped!* The *Row, row, row your boat* picture had long since faded. She was past caring about her father by then, neither the sick man in the hospital nor the cheerful dad of her childhood.

Staring at the appropriated ring, Naime shed a few tears for the man she'd married and their happy times. Then the pan boiled over and she darted off at the smell of burnt milk. As she cleaned the cooker, grumbling, she forgot about the husband she'd cried for. Nothing ever triggered such an emotional reminiscence again, barring the day she sold the ring after Çiçek had hassled her for a trip to Ilgaz, *I wanna go!* So Mr Undersecretary, the father of four, was completely forgotten soon after his death.

Fourteen years later, taking some friendly advice to try hot sands for her joint pains, Naime – having long since given up on doctors and tried all sorts of folk remedies to no avail – went to İnkum near Amasra with her four daughters, by now all married and with professional careers to boot. It was their second day there. Naime was sitting, her legs buried in the sand by her grandchildren, keeping sunstroke at bay with a flimsy parasol that had been tucked into her hands by the four girls, who had then retired to the fern-thatched tea garden to play 51.

Unpredictable as ever, the Black Sea weather turned abruptly and burst into thunder and lightning. The poor woman was trying to escape the rain and reach her children when she was struck and died instantly. The holidaymakers huddling in the tea garden were horrified at the sight of the bolt hitting the parasol as a flash of blue light pierced the air.

It was back around the time Cevdet Pektaş was still burning with desire for Şehriban that the hospital's foundation was dug and the ground floor was built. But chimney systems turned out to be missing from the plans drawn up by the **inept architect Halil Uyanık (endorsed by the Undersecretary himself)**. This, and other similar omissions initially overlooked in cursory inspections, was enough for the contractor to cop out.

Funding had been stopped, at any rate, and construction ground to a halt. The building was abandoned to its fate. All that remained was a set of iron bars shooting up from the first floor impotently.

As the recipient of barely a Pass from an unknown school of architecture, Halil Uyanık tried to point the finger at someone else and failed. Further failures in whatever paltry project he'd wangled eventually urged him to acknowledge his real talent lay not in architecture, but in sniffing out new land to grab, and he started property brokering in Ankara. Thanks to a superior talent in identifying building regulation amnesties, appropriation orders, Treasury land deals and development areas well before anyone else, he acquired vast tracts of land for pennies and made a pile in no time at all.

Many years after the festive foundation ceremony attended by the Minister of Health and Undersecretary Cevdet Pektaş – then still labouring under the delusion that his love for Şehriban made him the precious son-in-law of the city – construction was resumed. The country was preparing for the first general election after the coup. Halil Uyanık, who had given architecture up entirely in the interim, stood for the party headed by General Turgut Sunalp, he of the historic pronouncement that *Fascism was not as dangerous as Communism.*

Sadly, Halil Uyanık's nose was nowhere near as sharp in politics as it was in land to grab. The Nationalist Democracy Party firmly signposted as the only choice by the leader of the coup Kenan Evren – *You must vote for this party if you want peace* – had come a sorry third in the elections, and the bungling architect failed to get into Parliament. Flummoxed by the complicated relationships in the world of politics, Halil soon took a hint from his surname (meaning *Canny*) gave up on the idea of entering Parliament and instead nurtured friendships with politicians of all colours, thereby growing even richer.

Kenan Evren had absolutely no doubt at all that history would never judge him or his fellow generals, nay, that history would actually crown them. He wasn't far wrong: neither official historians, nor producers of all manner of spin-offs ever judged them. Moreover, for a very long time, the temporary articles inserted into the constitution and laws enacted at his insistence prohibited criticism, never mind bringing charges.

Decades down the line, unofficial historians would document – and in some detail – Evren's leading role in that coup, but the younger generation mostly knew him as the veteran who'd painted Sibel Can's bum; whilst said retired general was styling himself an artist at his easel in his Marmaris villa, the inept architect was battling with prostate cancer. With one foot in the grave, Halil was still locked in a tussle over a 240-*dönüm* plot in Rize. Kenan Canıtez, counsel for the other side, had turned out to be a tough nut; he wasn't going to let Halil Uyanık get away with the land.

On the day that Kenan Evren – he of the split personality vacillating between Pinochet and Picasso – announced that he'd surpassed the latter, the canny land-broker died. Upon hearing that he'd lost the case, he'd given his own solicitor a good tongue-lashing before he promptly had a relapse. His heirs subsequently plundered all the lands he'd been prevented from selling off by his lingering, painful illness.

Once abandoned, the new hospital building begun with such high hopes by the Undersecretary, became a shelter for herds of animals, the city's thugs and escaped prisoners. The animals fouled the interior and the fugitives lit fires that blackened the walls.

It was the first summer after the building had been left to rot. A gipsy tribe had hit the road, their wobbly tented horse carts trundling along to the clatter of the pots and pans hanging from the rear. **Chief Curly** had halted the tribe by the construction site the year before, when he saw it in the foundation stage; the women had dived into the site, pestering the young builders, *Gi'za few pennies, and I'll read your fortune*, spilling their dried beans on the ground in a scuffle, as the young kids pilfered whatever they could: a couple of broken beams, a bucketful of lime or a handful of nails. After fortunes were read, drums beaten and dances danced, Chief Curly had gathered his tribe again and set off for the skimpy stream on the outskirts of the city where they'd settled once the tents were up. The women washed the children's shitty clothes in the filthy waters and cooked in blackened pots by day, greeted the men drumming on their way back from the city by night; everyone sang and danced under the stars all night long, enjoying their freedom, fun and pennilessness.

The tribe was returning to the city now down the same road on their way to their usual campsite by the same measly stream. Surprised by the abandoned construction site, the chief halted the caravan, got down and nosed around: it was deserted. But the well sunk for the construction still had water: Good. There was no need to go all that way to the stream; the tribe spread out at once.

So quickly did they settle that the chief was still wondering *Should we stay, or move on?* By the time his wife had laid their mattress on the first floor in the open air and the girls lowered rusty tins into the well, any bits of timber lying around were collected at once, fires were lit, pots placed on those fires to boil the evening soup, and the kids who'd had evaded water all day long were caught and washed at the trough next to the well. The chief was poking into the columns, digging here and there, wondering *Could I get the iron out? And cut it if I did?*

The building site was well outside the city. The inhabitants of the few hovels nearby grew corn and grazed their herds on the unclaimed land, having sussed out that the construction was abandoned and set their sights on the building as a barn and store for hay and silage. They'd even built a trough next to the well for their livestock. Herding their sheep and goats baa-ing non-stop, they returned as the setting sun daubed the grey building in a coat of scarlet. They objected to the tribe's intrusion. When Chief Curly dug his heels in and tried to block the animals, a brawl broke out, sticks and stones and all. Passers-by informed the gendarmes. The chief stood his ground, advancing on the villagers holding a plank, oblivious to the gendarmes. When a fierce punch aimed at the leader of the villagers landed on the eye of **the gendarme trooper Flashy Salih** from Düzce (who was a day away from his discharge) things got out of hand.

How dare he punch our soldier! bellowed the villagers, attacking Curly with nail clubs. The gendarmes had to fire a few rounds into the air to stop the fight. The ringleaders were frogmarched to the station for a good hiding. The soles of his feet throbbing with pain, Chief Curly had gather his tribe and set off for the stream once again.

The year 1985, when the decision was taken to restart construction, was no less inauspicious than the previous few. The nation groaned under an increasingly oppressive martial law as the coup leaders put the screws on. That year, thousands were tried on charges of political crimes and over twenty convicts were executed without further ado. Hundreds of academicians were fired, countless writers, poets, publishers, painters, musicians and scientists were tried and hundreds of thousands were slapped with a foreign travel ban. That year, Kenan Evren – who wouldn't be tried in the future either – was awarded an honorary professorship by Istanbul University and an honorary doctorate in Law by the Law School in the same institution. Justice had become a joke.

So was life: a terrifying and tragic joke. Cüneyt Arkın, star of such Turkish epics as *Malkoçoğlu*, faced charges of communist propaganda for his part in *The Indestructible Man*, shot some six years earlier. Macit Akman, Director of the state-run broadcaster TRT, announced proudly he'd ordered the burning of the reels of *Tired Warrior* adapted from a Kemal Tahir novel. Years would pass, the internet age would dawn, and scenes of *The Indestructible Man* would make their way to YouTube – and several other sites – under the heading *Rollicking Scenes*; the thought of accusing Cüneyt Arkın of communist propaganda would be greeted with as much hilarity as the film itself; but the powers that be – who assumed the right to decide which facts the nation could be permitted access to – would silence the most entertaining phenomenon of the millennium age, whilst that very same nation would continue to bury their heads in the sand anyway, and even in this new age, nothing much would change in the country.

That year the number of the unemployed exceeded three million, price rises had reached 250 % in three years and the GNP per capita had dropped to $1,149. In Ereğli, a firedamp explosion killed one hundred and two coalminers. In Gebze, four of the forty children poisoned by tap water died. In Diyarbakır, the bodies of eighty-three victims were dug up from the ruins of a block of flats that had collapsed out of the blue. In Istanbul, printing presses fell silent due to a paper shortage.

The construction of the new building of the Mental Health Hospital was resumed in that horrible year.

The first task was to revise the plans. Times had changed; the urgent healthcare needs of the growing population had steamrolled over the love of science that had flashed oh so faintly, and the conference hall, once such a priority, had been omitted.

Newly qualified architect Çetin Kansız, a member of the revision team, had yet to do his national service. He was no more talented than

Halil Uyanık, the name behind the original plan, but determined to prove himself, and authorised by his superiors, he set about altering the plans entirely, practically designing from scratch.

The wide plot allocated to the new building was on the seafront. By placing the main entrance on the south, thereby positioning the building with its back to the sea, the young architect had created the peculiar aspect that confounded the viewer, and which was ascribed to his Black Sea origins – this being the region that bore the brunt of jokes for foolish wit. Except Çetin Kansız wasn't a Black Sea man at all; it was this project that had attracted him here for the first time.

The reason he turned the hospital's back to the sea was a brainwave that merited a bout of self-congratulation. He meant well; this building was far too small for the plot in his opinion, and an extension would soon have to follow. He wasn't entirely wrong either. Undersecretary Cevdet Pektaş had insisted that the building be completed as soon as possible; any plans that took into account projected population increases would have required the construction of a much larger facility. Yes, he was dying to grace his almond-eyed Şehriban's hometown with an elegant present, but surely a modest edifice would suffice.

That this small building would soon fall short of meeting the rapidly growing city's needs seemed obvious; after a cursory consultation with his superiors, Çetin had decided to blank the rear façade to facilitate coupling with a future block, and *that* block would face the sea whenever it would come to be erected. He could have done the opposite, positioned the main building much closer to the sea and blanked the southern elevation instead, but that would have necessitated additional footpaths for patients to walk all the way from the main road, landscaping, garden illuminations, you name it. And their limited budget might not even stretch to completing the original building.

The young architect was comfortable with his decision. He believed his ingenuity would be vindicated when the time for the second block came and couldn't wait for the need to arise. A few years later, however, the facility originally conceived as a general hospital was reassigned as an exclusively mental health institution, thereby obviating the need for an extension and consequently leaving this edifice as an aberration with its back to the sea. Not only did the genius fail to make his mark, but the architect anticipating accolades became instead a joke *in absentia*.

Unconvinced by a need for a conference hall, Çetin had begrudged it even a single window. That wasn't all. Having reduced the capacity to three hundred and fifty from the Undersecretary's grandiose dreams of a five hundred seater, Çetin plonked it in the finest spot on the north side of the top floor, in a corner that would have commanded a fabulous sea view if only it had windows. In actual fact, he'd failed to find space in the basement, and had approached his supervisors, *How about we give up on this dream of a conference hall?* In their customary apathy towards the hospital and its plans, they'd gone along with every single of his proposals up to now; but for some reason they baulked this time. Thinking, *We've given him an inch, and now he wants a mile!* they brushed him off, *There will be a conference hall in the building!* So Çetin drew a hall that could be divided up to serve other purposes in the fullness of time. But the need never arose.

Disconcertingly windowless and ridiculously wide, long corridors ran on the blind north side of the four-storey hospital. To be fair, there was a rational explanation. Çetin thought the future extension would be connected easily once the blind wall in these corridors was knocked through. Since there was no need to splurge on windows destined to be discarded, he'd decided it was cheaper to finish the ends with a brick wall. Not that every invention he used on the plan was based on logic. Other solutions he'd thought up to create harmony with the extension that wasn't even a prospect on the horizon had turned the plan into an inextricable mess.

The discovery of the unfeasibility of his plans necessitated a number of conversions: lots of walls were knocked down, new ones built, doors knocked through, and since all these modifications played havoc with the electrical systems and plumbing, new cables were laid, pipes attached to the exterior, and the brand new building ended up looking like a ramshackle affair.

This classic of *alla turca* construction finally opened after months of alterations. Just as it was settling into its new skin, a change of mind on the part of the powers that be, *Let's make it just a mental health hospital,* sparked off further alterations: staircases plonked here and there, and passages knocked through for additional access, not to mention the cancellation of outpatients clinics, laboratories, operating theatres and countless other sections superfluous to need, with the end result that Çetin's project was metamorphosed into an impenetrable labyrinth.

In actual fact, architecture had originally been the last thing on Çetin's mind, to be honest: he'd meant to sit the Air Force academy entrance exam to realise his childhood dreams of becoming a pilot. Neither construction nor architecture held any interest for him. It was a latent failing that he, like countless others, had never suspected, which altered the course of his life: he had a morbid fear of heights.

Çetin Kansız began reading architecture after his big brother Necmi's promise to meet all his costs throughout university with a *Just as long as you get a degree; I'm behind you all the way.* It was a totally random choice. Like all other university candidates taking the central exam, he'd put down medicine – the highest score required – as his first choice, and then listed the rest in decreasing order: mechanical engineering, electrical engineering, civil engineering and architecture. He hadn't reflected much upon that last one as he put it down, beyond an indistinct image of something resembling the Frauenkirche, that is.

He scraped through, but only just, sometimes cheating, sometimes begging for help from here and there, and occasionally even pleading with the lecturers. He ended up in the team commissioned with the alterations of the hospital before he even did his national service. Not that there was much of a team, since everyone seemed to be skiving off. Freshly qualified, bright-eyed and bushy-tailed, Çetin more or less shouldered the entire project. The end result was a perpetually troublesome building due to its unworkable plans.

He might have made a name for himself as an architect of high-profile projects, but architecture wasn't necessarily his calling. Once the hospital clumsily altered into a labyrinth was behind him, and thanks to the right moves he had made after much reflection, he was now a partner in a famous Istanbul architecture practice. A development that owed nothing to his non-existent talent. Fame hadn't come easy; it had required calculated steps, and taking them whilst still a student. He'd recognised he'd chosen the wrong career as early as the first semester; he really should have picked something like management or law instead. One day, during his summer holiday, he was stewing *Should I carry on in Year II, or should I drop out?* at the rakı table on the vast balcony of his brother Necmi's eyesore of a new build in Tavas. Necmi – who'd been paying for everything, from his socks through to his pens, coach tickets and student lodgings – boasted to his German guests by slapping Çetin in the back with a hearty *My strapping kid brother, eh? He'll become an architect, he will!* Instead of coming clean, *No, I'm no good at this, I'm gonna sit the exam again,* and wasting a whole year's expenses to boot, he carried on willy-nilly.

He was clever. It didn't take him long to suss out he'd get a degree of some sort, but didn't have enough talent to make a name for himself as an architect. The moment he admitted that what he'd need most in the future was a good partner, he set his sights on Vildan, the cleverest girl on the course. None of his mates chasing pretty girls could figure out why Çetin (who, let's face it, could have had his pick of their prettiest classmates) was fixated with this girl who wasn't much of a looker. Except Çetin had quite elaborate plans for the future. Yes, he could hang out with greater beauties, raise his street cred, have a great time, and enjoy a busy love life with all its ups and downs. But youth was transient, and you'd have to face the realities of life. What then? Would he spend the rest of life scraping by as an unsuccessful architect?

Praising her intelligence and talent, he won her over towards the middle of Year II. Not one to fret *How to look pretty,* she was quiet and unassuming. Çetin's opening line was, *Let's study together,* one thing followed another and soon they were going out.

Vildan's experience had been limited to a couple of unremarkable platonic romances; inculcated by the need to focus on her studies, she was a little disconcerted by this love. As they studied together in the university library or in one of the tea gardens nearby, she'd suddenly find her mind straying to thoughts of him. Her Year II marks dropped a little as a result. By the time they started Year III and the initial passion had settled, however, she'd gathered herself and soon regained her position as the brightest female student who topped the year.

Her eyes had opened in a while as she wondered *Why me, with all the pretty girls in the world?* But Çetin was determined to secure a cast-iron foundation for his life by marrying her. He reassured her, and they put on engagement rings in the summer before Year IV.

Just when they were busy with degree projects, this lukewarm couple fell out over a pointless fling of Çetin's. He'd suddenly had a bit of a funk. He knew he'd never get the opportunity for even the tiniest escapade once they were married and so, determined to sow some wild oats before marriage, he sneaked out with a girl from another college once or twice. But Vildan twigged straightaway and brought him to book, *What's going on?* He tried to squirm out of it, she didn't buy it, flung the engagement ring in his face, smashed their degree project model over his head and dumped him.

Çetin now knew for certain that he wouldn't dare dream of even the most commonplace carry-ons with anyone once he'd married Vildan. He'd be frittering away his freedom. He deliberated: the future looked agonisingly bleak. Regaining her heart was crucial, but this time flattering her intellect wasn't going to cut it. She knew she was intelligent, didn't need to hear it from him either. Çetin camped at her door for days, swearing time and again he'd never do anything like that again, and enlisting the help of the family who loved their future daughter-in-law. They finally made up and got married as soon as they'd qualified.

He might have missed big time in his choice of profession; but he had hit bull's eye in his choice of mate. Çetin relaxed as Vildan ran everything like clockwork. At first they worked in different places, including a stint as civil servants – which was when he drew up the hospital's plans. After discharge from his national service, he (together with his wife) made quite a killing with a clutch of summer houses erected on a piece of land Necmi had bought near Bodrum, and opened their own practice. Soon they had a critically acclaimed portfolio; or more accurately, Vildan designed and Çetin reaped the rewards.

Whilst the poor girl burned the midnight oil, eyes like saucers from lack of sleep, Çetin kept her stoked up with tea and coffee. He felt sad whenever Vildan's head dropped on the drawing table, let her doze for about ten minutes, then turned up with a strong cup of coffee and prodded her anxiously – yet with genuine affection – lest they missed their deadline. Reliable Vildan would immediately wake up, splash her face with icy water and resume drawing.

Round about the time when their still relatively new practice had shot to fame thanks to a high-profile project, an architectural magazine requested an interview. Çetin spent a good deal of effort to overcome the disappointment caused by Vildan's inability to utter anything of significance. She had always been tongue-tied at important occasions, mumbling a few disjointed phrases and was effectively incoherent. Hence her inability to sell her projects, no matter how good she was at what she did. Her presentations always confused her audiences. Çetin, in contrast, was a fantastically convincing speaker, able to adorn and thus sell even the most ordinary idea. Thus did a silver tongue and a golden pen join forces to become a terrific pair.

Çetin believed his vertigo was limited to flying; by refusing to fly or look down from heights at construction sites, he managed his condition reasonably well. Then one evening, when they were crossing the bridge on their way to a very important business dinner (since Vildan had no driving licence, Çetin was at the wheel as usual) an accident happened; one vehicle crashed into another from behind and traffic came to a halt. They were stuck in the tailback. Impatient to get a move on, Çetin made the mistake of getting out of the car to see what the hold-up was. The moment he stepped on the carriageway, he noticed the bridge shaking like a leaf. As an architect, he was hardly a stranger to the fact that suspension bridges vibrated, but a severe panic attack taught him that knowing it was one thing, experiencing it quite another.

Suddenly aware that he was standing some sixty metres plus above the sea, he blacked out and barfed on the bonnet of the car that was washed and polished inside and out twice a week. Furious with his gluttony (wrongfully assuming this was a self-inflicted upset stomach: he had polished off a doorstopper of a fried mussel sandwich in a half a loaf of bread in the afternoon) Vildan just sat in her seat, waiting for him to get better instead of helping. But Çetin wasn't getting better; now he was having an attack of shivers. In the meanwhile, the accident was cleared and traffic would have started flowing but for their car blocking the way. Horns were blaring behind them. The police arrived. When Vildan explained the situation, one of the constables took the wheel.

A groaning Çetin was stretched out on the rear seat. He sweated buckets until the traffic cleared and they were able to reach terra firma. Vildan asked the police constable to park somewhere convenient. They jumped into a taxi and went to the ferry station. Since Çetin would never be able to cross the bridge again, they took the ferry back to the other side. Thus did they miss the dinner and the commission they'd been angling for.

Their office was on the second floor and their flat on the third; they moved both to the ground floor.

Çetin had been under treatment for panic attacks since then. It wasn't just the Bosphorus bridges that he couldn't cross; viaducts were just as impossible. He no longer dared drive in case some viaduct popped up out of nowhere, and certainly never ventured out of town. He started going to the **Cypriot Psychiatrist Temuçin Birol** who bragged about sharing the same hometown – Nicosia – as the world famous Psychiatrist Vamık Volkan, recipient of countless accolades including the Sigmund Freud Award, and a Nobel Peace Prize nominee to boot.

Vamık Volkan was the genius responsible for Temuçin's choice of career. Many years earlier at coming across the great man on a beach in Kyrenia, Temuçin had grabbed and kissed his hands, trembling with thrilled awe before explaining that it was the professor's Bird Theory that had inspired him to choose psychiatry. Predictably flattered, Professor Vamık, however, graciously begged Mr Temuçin's indulgence: he was on holiday. What he wanted to do was swim in the sea, not chat about his Bird Theory. The Professor commended the young doctor, expressed his own delight, wished him all success for the future, and dropping his towel on the sand, walked into the sea.

A bird fancying craze had swept through Cyprus in the 1960s, with parakeets being the favourite in nearly every home and office. No fewer than two cages featured in every home. Birdsong invaded the island, a sad hum emanating from the depths that banished the silence of the night. Temuçin's grandfather fed more than fifty parakeets in over forty cages, some of wood, others made of metal. Every single bird had a name and assiduously recorded pedigree. The islanders raised birds in their suppressed gloom; whenever three people got together, they talked of birds, but no one was prepared to ask why.

It stemmed from a profound subconscious desire for freedom, suggested the Professor's theory: raising birds sustained an imprisoned nation's yearning for freedom.

What Temuçin had in fact meant by the Bird Theory was this psychoanalytical interpretation of the craze that had emerged out of the blue; he himself had fourteen parakeets, eleven at home and three in his surgery.

He was no lukewarm fan; over the years, he had made every effort to follow Vamık's work, devouring both the professor's papers and every article about him. To the extent that an item about an upcoming lecture by Vamık Volkan in a local paper called *The Black Sea Herald* had made this newly appointed registrar specialising in psychiatry at the Erzurum School of Medicine hop on a coach – just the opportunity he'd been hoping for!

It turned out to be a terrible journey. It was bitterly cold after a night when the mercury had dropped to minus thirty-two. Blizzards pounded snowbound roads as Temuçin was afraid that he wouldn't make it. At long last, the Highways Commission cleared the carriageways, and the young psychiatry registrar arrived at the city at the end of that gruelling trip.

He'd been more worried about missing the lecture than the troublesome prospect of being stuck. As an eminent clinical psychiatrist as well as social psychologist and memory sociologist, Professor Vamık Volkan worked at the University of Virginia; although a part of his summer holiday was spent in Cyprus, he rarely visited mainland Turkey. The opportunity to attend a lecture of his, therefore, was nothing less than a miracle.

Temuçin was chomping at the bit by the time he'd settled into the front row in the conference hall: soon he would see Vamık Volkan (the chance meeting in Kyrenia and the grasped hand being some years off in the future) whom he would thank profusely afterwards and mention his great admiration for.

The discovery that the guest speaker was not the world famous Vamık Volkan, but rather, **an ordinary psychiatrist called Namık Volkan with no academic title** was like a bucket of cold water. This diminutive doctor past middle age, who was sporting a ragged moustache, shuffling towards the stage (*sans* the vinyl covering at the time since the floorboards were still relatively serviceable) as though he were perpetually on the brink of stumbling, and clutching a few handwritten sheets, was in fact related to the hospital trustee, and was finally given the chance to lecture on *Nocturnal Enuresis in Boys*.

Throughout the speaker's preliminaries of wiping his nose, sneezing and spluttering, a bemused Temuçin tried to figure out where he'd gone wrong and fretted over the coach fare, the time he wasted time and the trouble he'd taken.

His strained finances – due to an obligation to send money regularly to his elderly parents in Nicosia – had forced him to share with two other registrars, one from the Black Sea and the other from Mersin, instead of renting a pad on his own in the centre of Erzurum. Their flat was in one of countless poorly constructed developments on the outskirts, whose roads were prone to closures at the first sign of snow. His wreck of a white Renault 12 thus rendered useless, Temuçin would have to walk to work.

At the time he was trudging in waist-deep snow to the city centre for that lecture, Temuçin had no doubt that it was the great man himself when he'd read about the scheduled appearance by Namık Volkan at the above-mentioned hospital, confident that it was a common misspelling since the world famous psychiatrist was relatively unknown in Turkey. The item had been in *The Black Sea Herald* that his flatmate had bought on his way back from his cousin's funeral (the flatmate also brought back a massive tin of salt fish, four loaves of corn bread, a sack of hazelnuts and two trays of *Laz böreği*, filo pastry filled with milk pudding).

When he arrived he had no difficulty finding the hospital, although he then had a devil's time of locating the conference hall. He finally sat down to wait, sighing repeatedly at the lack of appreciation as he attributed the emptiness of the hall to the professor's relative obscurity in the mainland, practically fell off the chair when he saw not Vamık, but Namık Volkan.

Blissfully unaware of Temuçin's outrage and suffering with a horrible cold, the doctor kept sneezing before starting the lecture he hoped would improve his dwindling patient numbers. The previous afternoon, he had discovered his home knee-deep in water: during a water cut, his absent-minded, clumsy wife gone out and left a tap open. The carpets were floating. His wife was nowhere to be seen. Grumbling non-stop, he swept the water down the stairwell and flung the dripping carpets on the balcony. He tried to wipe dry the floors. At long last, when they went to bed, they left the sitting room and lounge windows wide open to dry the flat, and in the middle of the winter too! So Namık had caught a cold.

The poor fellow had thought of cancelling, but hopeful of applying for a position should one become available, he hesitated lest he displease the Medical Director. Despite a raging fever of thirty-nine degrees, he mounted the lectern. When, during his irrational and slapdash speech that made no impression on his eight or ten listeners he sneezed right into the face of Temuçin who was sitting immediately opposite, the younger man who'd trundled all that way in the snow to listen to the great man couldn't take it any longer. He left the hall in a huff, as if it wasn't his own fault he'd come to the wrong lecture. He wanted to return to Erzurum straightaway, but there was no early coach.

He strolled along the seafront, beating himself up for having set off without doing his research first. That's when he noticed the bizarre architecture of the Mental Health Hospital. There wasn't a single window facing the sea; it made no sense.

As an islander, he knew from personal observation the depression that dogged seasiders when forced to live far from the sea. At first, at the start of his specialist training, Erzurum was in the clutches of such a terrible winter that he hadn't had the opportunity to notice it was the sea that he missed most. When summer came at long last, Temuçin wailed, *The sea! The sea!*

No one could miss the fact that the building had completely turned its back to the sea. As a matter of fact, schizoid Barış Bakış had obsessed about it for a while. One day, before he'd set his room on fire, sitting right by the window in the day room where patients played backgammon or cards (and some paced up and down, muttering to themselves), he was murmuring to himself *The sea's right at my back... The sea's right at my back...* Demir Demir, who'd just been talking to Veda Alkan, appeared and scanned the place to check that all was well; at catching BB's eye, he felt duty bound to sit down for a brief chat. He had no intention of conversing with Barış who blocked his way time and again, asking, *When am I gonna leave this place?* There was no way he could say, *Well son, it's like this: your mum's twisted my arm again, bent me to her will; you're here for a while yet.* Consequently he had taken to pretending he hadn't spotted Barış, and brushed off any persistent questions with *Ask Âlim; he knows best.*

The incident that had beckoned the Medical Director here, to this hall intended to be a place where patients could socialise and communicate with one another, was a natural outcome of the power vacuum caused by his obsession with the idea of writing a book.

He rarely dropped into the day room that had been kitted out thanks to the munificence of the city's second-rate businesses, from the carpets to the teacups and everything in between, down to the last curtain and pitcher – albeit in the cheapest possible materials – and which failed to approximate the sitting room of a private residence despite all this effort. To be honest, he could barely lift his head from paperwork long enough to see the patients. But when **the forty-one year old patient İsmail Çeliktaş suspected of a schizoaffective disorder** (originally hospitalised after creating havoc for no reason at all for the fifth time at the canteen in the cement factory where he worked and hitting someone over the head with a metal dinner tray) had suddenly up and smashed the backgammon board over the head of **the orderly Durali Yılmaz nicknamed Ofli Durali** and sent the fellow to hospital, it dawned upon the Medical Director that he needed to keep tighter reins on the staff.

Thank God Ofli Durali didn't die that day, but it was touch and go. Realising the risk of serious repercussions if he turned a blind eye to the orderlies arsing around, the Medical Director started doing the rounds often to check *Is everyone on duty?* instead of sitting in his office all day long to do research for his book.

Durali later accused İsmail of braining him for no reason at all; but in fact he'd been asking for it. His job was to supervise the patients and occupy them with pretend games, but he had a nasty habit of playing as if he was in the neighbourhood coffee house. He took it far too seriously, and as if it wasn't enough that he went all out to win, he stole checkers, loaded the dice, greeted every double with such vulgarities and loved to tuck the board under the loser's arm at the end of the game. But he paid dearly. İsmail banged the pointy corner of the board on his head, nearly piercing through to the brain.

İsmail Çeliktaş, who – unlike other similar patients – brushed his teeth regularly every morning and combed his hair before settling down to wait for visitors that never came (neither his mother, nor his sisters, wife or even lazy ne'er-do-well sons, the eldest of whom had just finished his national service) had attacked the orderly not because he was mentally ill, but simply because the man had got on his nerves. Durali had pissed him off so much that he'd have done exactly the same thing even if they'd been two sane men playing in a local coffee house.

Yet İsmail often heard voices that said his mum, wife or sons had come to visit, bringing a tray of potato pastry too; just as he'd got into his pyjamas and was about to turn in, he'd leap up saying, *Here they are!* and run to the door. The orderlies had a right time of it trying to explain there was no one there. He'd yell, *Give me my bloody pastry!* terrifying the whole ward before the orderlies calmed him down with a bit of cheese in a wedge of bread and forced him back down to bed. Tummy filled, he'd calm down and sleep like a baby thanks in no small part to the medication… but he'd write a complaint the following day, *The guards stole my pastry,* and drive the doctors round the bend as he tailed them all the time.

But İsmail received no visitors, not even a phone call, because there was another row at home: **his wife Beyaz**, who didn't give a fig how he was, and **his mother Hatun** were squabbling over money.

His employers had deposited his salary in the bank once the sick report was certified. Accompanied by her two hefty unmarried daughters (who'd turned their noses up at every infrequent humble suitor as if they could have found anyone better), Hatun Çeliktaş had then fetched up at his home, demanding half his salary from her daughter-in-law. Her excuse was ready. As her daughter-in-law knew, they had nothing; İsmail had been looking after his mum and sisters. And they'd been on their uppers since he was hospitalised. Now her daughter-in-law Beyaz had to do what her son had been doing, and hand over half the salary paid into the bank. There was no two ways about it.

A claim that wasn't anywhere near the truth. Yes, İsmail did give his mother some money, or more accurately, he was forced to hand over something just to get rid of her. Hatun waited at the factory gate every month to confront her son to ask for money, no matter how many hoops that son jumped to avoid her. He knew she pocketed the income from the fields left by his dad and never offered to share even a penny of the money the wholesaler paid for the corn and the beans; he'd fight and swear, but in the end would have to send her away with a quarter of his salary to spare himself any more shame in public. Their relationship had long since deteriorated into one of money and not love, to the extent that she'd only visited once when he was hospitalised, and all she brought was two packs of Anadolu cigarettes and half a tray of potato pastry. She'd never since looked up the son that she was now claiming had been treating his mother and sisters like queens.

The mother-in-law glowered throughout her speech, flanked by the two hulking sisters-in-law who stared at Beyaz rather menacingly. Except Beyaz was no less imposing in bulk. Hands akimbo, she squared up to the niggling mother-in-law and asked what the heck the family would be expected to live on if she gave her half the salary. The mother-in-law scowled, *Get your son to look after you,* as if it wasn't her own grandson she was talking about. And as if that wasn't enough, she ranted and raved about the slacker she'd raised and called a son, whilst her daughters nodded. The daughter-in-law who was by then old enough to become a mother-in-law herself, and who'd never got along with her mother-in-law all these years, made for the kitchen muttering, *God give me patience.* The senior sister-in-law blocked her way. She wasn't going to make do with just half the salary. Instead, she raised the nagging bar: *Hand over my brother's ATM card!*

What started out as a shouting match escalated. The daughter-in-law scratched the mother-in-law's face, the mother-in-law bit the daughter-in-law and the sisters-in-law hit the daughter-in-law on the head; her head split open, but ignoring the pouring blood that painted her clothes red and threatened to obscure her vision, she set upon her mother-in-law in retaliation. They went at it hammer and tongs. Finally, the neighbours called the police and all, and they were all run in, where they still screamed ultimatums at one another, *Never come to my funeral, and I'm never going to yours!*

They had no idea that they'd fought over nothing. In actual fact, the eldest son, **Rambo Fatih**, had already found the ATM card in İsmail's trouser pocket; it had only taken him two attempts to guess the PIN from the first four digits of the home phone number, before withdrawing the salary and spending it all.

No one else called him Rambo. One or two mates had used it at first, but later they only ribbed him. With four days to go to finish his national service as a commando in Şırnak, Fatih's name had come up amongst the wounded in a terrorist attack. That was where the nickname Rambo came from. But that's not what happened. Another squad had got into a skirmish on the mountain whilst he was picking over spinach in the garrison kitchens; although it was a Fatih Çeliktaş from Çorum's Dodurga who had been wounded, the records mistakenly stated it was Fatih Çeliktaş of Ordu's Aybastı, son of İsmail.

The error was quickly rectified, his family notified, Fatih was discharged and came home, but before the correction reached the neighbourhood. Unaware of this case of mistaken identity, Fatih was astonished at the hero's welcome that awaited him. Before he'd even had a chance to speak, Beyaz whispered into his ear, reluctant to relinquish *the status of being the proud mum of a war veteran*, and Fatih knew this was his chance for the prestige that had evaded. Instead of correcting the error, he adopted a swagger.

It was in the coffee house where local youngsters played okey – a kind of rummy game with tiles – and where he'd related an entirely fictitious account of the skirmish, substituting himself for the lad from Dodurga, and explaining that he'd been given the nickname Rambo. He kept referring to himself as Rambo Fatih throughout the account.

He might have guessed his father's PIN, but he was not bright. As he tried to tell his story, adorned with barely remembered scenes from *Rambo 2*, he failed to explain when asked how the heck he'd found a wild jungle on the arid hills of Şırnak in order to hide behind thick leaves to spy on the PKK. His mates, who had swallowed the war veteran tale for a few days, now had their doubts. Then another recently discharged lad discredited the story, *What veteran? That arsehole did his national service in the kitchen!* The boys felt reluctant to put Fatih on the spot and upset him, given he was newly returned, and his father in the mental hospital too. Until, that is, a week later, when Fatih was still telling the same story and claiming he'd been shot in the chest, they pestered him, *Show us the scar then!* Of course he couldn't show a non-existent scar; and the nickname that was never taken up was completely withdrawn.

Not only had his credibility lasted no more than a few days, but he was now the brunt of jokes too. After cracking his father's PIN, withdrawing all the money and taking his mates for a drink – or fifteen (perhaps they'd think better of him when they saw how he spent money like there was no tomorrow) Fatih had blown a month's salary in one night. So there was no money, and no one came to visit poor İsmail Çeliktaş.

Durali returned to work after recovering. But he'd developed a fear of the hospital where he used to swagger up and down, recklessly manhandling, taunting and even mocking the patients; now it felt like a horribly dangerous place. Yet he needed the work. Impressed with her soft face and gentle manner, he opened up to Psychologist Gülnazmiye Görgün, asking for help with his fears. But all that the lovesick psychologist could think about was rescuing her sweetheart Barış Bakış from his hellish prison. She did listen, yes, but just stared blankly in response. Doctor Âlim Kâhkeci wouldn't take him seriously either, other than offering the occasional bit of advice: follow the rules and there's nothing to be scared of. But Durali had taken to abruptly glancing behind him and suddenly resting his back against a wall for no reason whatsoever. It looked like he'd soon be a patient in the hospital where he was now an orderly.

When the Medical Director entered the day room just to make sure no one else got up to any mischief after this incident was hushed up, he caught BB's eye; there was nothing for it, he had to go over to this young man who stood apart from the other patients, with that angelic face under the black fringe and a book in his hand. Barış Bakış had already espied the Medical Director at any rate, got to his feet, and beckoned him over.

He had just received a call on his mobile from Veda Alkan, asking after her son in her clearly enunciated, sultry and alluring voice. The image of the faintly freckled, unforgettably bronzed décolleté conjured up by her dulcet tones had an instantly mellowing effect. They exchanged a few pleasantries. Before coming round to her son, she mentioned the relentless rains in

Europe, her mountain of work and this and that, all couched in terms that insinuated intimacy. He melted as he listened to the voice that sounded as delectable as the clinking of gold bracelets on a slender arm. Telling this darling of Ankara's élite society that Barış had taken enormous strides in his treatment, he took great pride in announcing, *How would we like to hear some good news today? We can discharge our son whenever we want; we could take him home whenever we wish.* She'd be equally delighted with this wonderful result, hoped the Medical Director, expecting undying gratitude.

Except that wasn't what Veda wanted to hear at all. She explained just how busy she was with endless meetings. But no mother could state she had no time for her son. Consequently, wielding her diplomatic skills, she interrupted the Medical Director in an even more seductive tone to express her profound appreciation. She simply couldn't thank the Medical Director enough. Massaged his ego no end by declaring in the sweetest and most complimentary terms *how delighted, how moved she was that her son was under the care and treatment of such a distinguished scientist,* and just how much she trusted in him, his hospital and his entire team. She was enormously happy at the news of her son's improvement, although she was committed to this foreign posting for another three months. She had no close family she could rely on to restrain Barış in case he were to be discharged, all that good work would go to waste, and her precious son could end up even worse than before. If the Medical Director were to insist, she would of course prefer to be with her son, *immediately resign her job of vital importance to the country* and dash over to his side. But was the *dear Medical Director* certain her son could be discharged? She had absolutely no doubt at all that he'd progress even further were he to stay another three months. She promised to come and fetch him the moment she returned to the country. Oh, by the way, she was truly grateful to him. She would be delighted at the opportunity to thank him personally were they to have a meal together once she was back.

At the end of this flirtatious conversation that took over half an hour, BB's treatment plan had been extended by another three months, and the Medical Director had started speculating about the suitability of potential venues for the meal promised by the plunging neckline. The Sultan Restaurant popular with the cream of the city's elite was out of the question.

Even if he were to have lunch with Mrs Veda Alkan – and he'd have preferred dinner, given half the choice – there was no way he could explain it to Sevim or anyone else for that matter. Assuming he did, there was no way he could prevent the rumours that would sweep through the city like wildfire if he were seen *tête-à-tête* with an attractive woman at the Sultan. Best to thank her with a *Let's take a rain check* when she eventually came to the hospital and invited him to dinner, and later find an excuse to go to Ankara. He could, for instance, contrive some business at the Ministry of Health. His Ankaran wife Sevim would obviously want to come along, that was absolutely fine. They'd travel together, he'd leave her with her relations, and then he'd go over to Veda and invite her out to dinner himself.

The Medical Director thus floated into the day room and sat down next to Barış. The kid was carrying the same book again: *Journals of a Non-Madman*. Never having picked up a book for years, it simply didn't occur to the Medical Director to look into what Barış was reading, and he felt no need to ask. What he wanted instead was to have a cup of tea with this handsome kid who bore a disconcerting likeness to his mother, and elicit a little information on that haunting, tanned, plunging neckline.

With no experience in fishing for information, he looked around and then asked, *Shall we have a cup of tea together?* by way of a preamble. Barış Bakış said neither yes, nor no, and just gave him a blank state. Taxi driver-cum-caretaker Cumali was standing in for Durali. The Medical Director asked for two teas; Cumali – molester of female patients whenever he had the chance – hated being asked to do anything, frequently swore out loud, but was scared shitless of Matron Servinaz Ceviz.

Today he was proper hacked off. The gas bottle had run out in the kitchen on that floor, so there was no tea. He'd worked his brother-in-law's taxi all night long and come straight to work, bug-eyed with sleep; loath to go down two floors to fetch the tea, he pretended not to have heard. As he flicked through the paper without paying a blind bit of notice, the Medical Director stared for a bit, and then repeated, *Cumali, I'm talking to you! Bring us tea!*

Cumali hated this hospital; knowing his contract would never be renewed, he was thinking, *Just a bit of aggro and I'll fuck off outta here!* At the Medical Director's voice, he thought, *That's my chance!* He was about to lash out, *The gas's off, there's no tea to be had!* when he remembered his brother-in-law had talked about selling the taxi. A heap of trouble flooded his mind: he was up to his eyes in debt and this was no time to be out of work, so he got up, grumbling under his breath, *Bugger your tea, and you, and your hospital.*

As if it wasn't him who'd just pretended not to have heard, he served them with an ingratiating grin and fussed over the Medical Director. His smarmy, *Anything else you require, Mr Medical Director?* was dismissed by a really annoying *Go away…* flick of the wrist. He was so steamed up that if he hadn't held back, he'd have laid into the grand Medical Director effing and blinding and never mind making a living.

Staring at BB's heartbreaking good looks, the Medical Director was musing upon the boy's mother – owner of the tanned embonpoint revealed by the neckline she'd been fanning with her air ticket – with a lust he rarely felt for other women, and fantasising about that hopefully *tête-à-tête* dinner (a highly remote possibility) when he recalled that he'd never cheated on his wife. Not because he loved her that much, or subscribed to a strict code of faithfulness, but because his obsession with cleanliness had grown throughout his marriage; nor could he be bothered with all that sex entailed. He did, as a matter of fact, enjoy staring at attractive women and imagining them naked, but he'd never met a woman clean and alluring enough tempt him into the trouble of cheating.

He'd once toyed with the idea of an affair with Nurse Zerrin, recently posted from Kâhta State Hospital. She wasn't much of a looker; quite the opposite with her bow legs and hunched gait, but she loved telling dirty jokes and had a filthy mouth, which made her incredibly attractive to the Medical Director. Needless to say, she would never presume to tell him such jokes. His repertoire of dirty jokes cultivated as a boarder at Galatasaray all but forgotten once he'd become a professional and entered polite company, he had cheered up at overhearing a few of hers, which had reminded him of his younger days. These obscene jokes and phrases were hugely arousing. He began following her everywhere like a shameless adolescent. But one day, when they were looking for a file in his office, they touched by accident, and noticing her skin smelled like feta left in the fridge for too long, he was sickened by her *and* the idea of sex.

That disgusting stink of sour cheese wouldn't leave his nostrils for quite a while. But what he'd found revolting wasn't Zerrin's skin at all, it was the guilt he would feel if he were to cheat on his wife. His subconscious had erected a barricade at the temptation and deceived his olfactory system into detecting a repulsive smell on the nurse's skin that in reality appealed to everyone else.

With a jolt, he came to his senses: Veda's fascinating body language began to niggle him out of the blue. That day, the Medical Director had tried to play it cool; except he had been cut down to size by Veda, who not only moved in high circles in Ankara, but also knew perfectly well how best to wield that terrific power called sex appeal. She'd steamrolled over him. Humiliated him, in effect. The interesting thing was that he hadn't been in the least bit bothered; he'd taken as much pleasure in that brief yet unforgettable conversation as if they'd gone to bed. But now he felt terribly ill at ease. His subconscious was working overtime to remind him of all that he'd suppressed.

The sudden and belated realisation – many months after the event! – that he'd been humiliated by the mother of this angelic kid proved to be quite upsetting. He was shaking. That *Chief expert* who'd been putting on airs all over the place had so dismissed the great Medical Director that she hadn't even bothered to use her sexual power. There was no way she could have missed how hard he tried to avoid staring, yet she hadn't hesitated for the tiniest bit or altered her behaviour.

Body language, however, was a topic that preoccupied the Medical Director. If Veda had wanted to say, *Don't make trouble or I'll twist you around my little finger with my sexual power,* she'd have revealed a little more, even if surreptitiously. If, on the other hand, she'd wanted to say, *All I'm asking is for you to do your job, so I don't need to flaunt it,* she'd have tugged at her collar and covered up quite naturally. She'd done neither. Instead, she'd indicated that he stood outside the area of masculinity as far as she was concerned, somewhere that meant nothing. No, not even that. That she felt no need to place him anywhere.

It was painful to admit. And that wasn't all. He thought of all the women who might have entered his life, but had not, and then thought of his wife. His pained mind was racing with headlines concerning sex and romance when Barış said something that made him sit up. The kid was staring at him with those deep green eyes as he asked that familiar yet unanswered question, *Demir Bey, why do you think Turks turn their backs to the sea?*

It completely threw him, what with his mind already in turmoil at recognition of Veda's contempt. He didn't know whether to feel bad, *This bastard's mum cut me right down to size,* or concur, *Oh, son, if only you knew how many times I've asked myself the same thing since I started working here!* They stared at each other blankly for a while. Just as the Medical Director was about to mumble, *No one actually knows quite why...* (since he felt himself duty bound to answer every question), Barış got up and left. He'd just seen Gülnazmiye at the door, the woman who, since that first chat on the scrapped four-seater, had regarded Barış Bakış as her boyfriend and adopted an almost maternal concern for him, worrying if he'd slept well, about his socks, his chocolates, and whether he might sweat and catch a chill. She also thought she'd given him all the right signs. Rather predictably, however, all Barış cared about was the fictitious wife whom he alleged was cheating on him with his left hand. He strongly suspected this young woman to have been engaged to observe him and report back to his mother – who, just then, was enjoying a prolonged lunch in a swanky restaurant near the principal EU building in Strasbourg.

The more Gülnazmiye showed an interest in him, the more suspicious he grew. As a result, scared witless at the prospect of dropping his guard and blurting out something about his imaginary wife, he responded instantly and passionately to her heart-wrenching lovesick attention. Which is why when he saw Gülnazmiye with the rosy pink lips at the door, no-longer-bashfully-hidden chest now proudly on display, he abandoned the perplexed Medical Director and went over, a move she interpreted as evidence of his great love.

As Barış and Gülnazmiye were murmuring to each other on the four-seater behind the hospital, their lips close enough for a kiss, the Medical Director had to invite the **anorexic social services specialist Buse Göçer** into his office. Buse was explaining that the condition of the retired literature teacher Zarife Gülercan was deteriorating. This was a case the Medical Director had to take a close interest in since Miss Zarife, this sweet lady, was a relation on his father's side, and a particular favourite of his at any rate. Following a second examination once she'd calmed down – *There's nothing wrong with me; why am I here?* – Dr Âlim Kâhkeci decided that those episodes must have been temporary, and discharged her. Her mental issues had to be rooted in grief, and however intriguing he found the case; it didn't merit further study in his view. And sure enough, Miss Zarife was indeed perfectly normal for a couple of days, before going off her head again, causing a huge scandal witnessed by Buse who was on a home visit as part of the treatment protocol. The anorexic girl was so agog over the incident that she had to tell him about at once.

Miss Zarife had insulted a neighbour who'd come over to wish her a speedy recovery, calling her a whore in full view of everyone present, and turning to the family frozen in shock, she'd added, *This slut shags anyone who comes her way… I saw her snogging the cable guy at the door with my own eyes…* She had then proceeded to name in increasingly vulgar terms the neighbour's paramours before breaking into a renewed laughter attack. The neighbour had raised merry hell, yelling, *Lies! All lies and slander!* Miss Zarife wasn't well, said her family, trying to soothe the neighbour, but these allegations instantly spread around the block and reached the neighbour's husband within half an hour.

Miss Zarife had indeed caught the neighbour kissing the cable guy at the door. She'd even taken a step back and hidden as he was about to look around, and seen him slip into the neighbour's flat. Her condition had played havoc with the scruples of the lady who'd normally have been horrified at the thought of meddling in other people's business. Yet this popular friend now freely rattled off an uninhibited series of profanities revealing whatever she thought about anyone.

The neighbour had locked herself in a room to sob uncontrollably as Miss Zarife's husband, **maths teacher Zeki Gülercan**, racked his brains for a way to calm down the neighbour's now apoplectic husband. Anorexic Buse had been asked to convey Zeki's request: would it be possible to perhaps give *Some official writing, report or something* to the effect that all of these lies were caused by Miss Zarife's illness? The enraged husband was insisting they prove Miss Zarife's *condition*, and the neighbour was threatening to kill herself unless that madness was proven.

Realising the gravity of his dear relative's condition, the Medical Director reached out to the telephone to ring Zeki and ask him to bring her here straightaway. His glance fell on the thick skin covering Buse's tibias in those atrophied calves. The wrinkled, sagging skin and crooked bones made him forget why he'd picked up the handset. He was murmuring to himself, *What the heck was I about to do?* when his secretary Nemişo entered to announce that the guest speaker due to deliver a lecture entitled *The Effects of Antidepressants on Patients' Sex Lives* had arrived and was being shown to the green room by the conference hall.

The professor of pharmacology was a middle-level manager in a pharmaceutical company that on occasion equipped the hospital quite generously, thereby alleviating the burden on the shoulders of the Medical Director weighed down by the twin pressures of inadequate funding and overcrowding. This was a guest who deserved to be looked after. In any case, the Medical Director truly enjoyed making a huge production of greeting his guests at the head of his army of junior doctors and nurses. Instructing Nemişo to convey the matter to Dr Âlim Kâhkeci, he gathered his colleagues and made his way to the conference hall.

By the time this welcoming committee – in identical snow white coats mirroring the Medical Director's – had entered the ridiculously large green room originally designed to allow for dividing up into offices, Âlim Kâhkeci was on the phone to Zeki Gülercan. The neo-devout psychiatrist felt guilty for having discharged the woman whose laughter attacks had returned with a vengeance. On the other hand, he'd found no psychiatric problem either. As he explained that it might make sense to examine her again, and even hospitalise her for a time, Nebahat, who'd stepped in carrying a platter of raisin cake right at the start of the telephone conversation, interrupted, *This is the work of a brain tumour, Âlim Bey. Best get a brain scan straightaway.* She was absolutely positive: tumours pressing on certain points in the brain triggered out-of-character acts. Nebahat might be strange in many ways, but she was good at her job, regularly followed medical literature and never missed a congress. Âlim wasn't swayed by her insistence, though, didn't necessarily trust her professional knowledge, and wouldn't take her seriously. He went over to the conference hall to speak to the Medical Director about this urgent matter.

The stumpy neuropsychiatrist followed her detractor all the way to the green room, still carrying the platter of cake. They began arguing in front of the guest the Medical Director had come to greet. The pharmacology professor was riveted by the whingeing woman in slippers carrying a mouth-wateringly golden cake. Then his attention strayed to the faint aromas of vanilla and cocoa, and he gulped. As the Medical Director was discussing the matter with the two doctors, the pharmacology professor was simply thinking *Hope I'll get a slice of that with the tea…*

Nebahat might have been unhinged, wandering around the hospital all day long with a plate glued to her hand, but she enjoyed the Medical Director's absolute confidence. He listened and cut the debate short: *Call her husband, tell him to take her for a brain scan.* Âlim Kâhkeci was surprised, tried to object, but ultimately had to concede. As Nebahat flip-flopped away triumphantly, the pharmacology professor was left gazing at the vanishing cake.

Debate done, chat over a cup of medium sweet coffee finished, the Medical Director led his guest to the conference hall. The moment they entered, BB's question popped into his still perplexed mind: what lay behind the gigantic wall with the white screen was the sea, and from one end to the other too. *What on earth was the architect thinking?*

It was this familiar – yet unanswered – question that actually stoked his interest in the hospital's history. All through the lecture on adverse effects antidepressants might have on the sex life, the Medical Director's attention strayed, fixated as he was on the idea of the sea stretching in all its immensity behind the white screen where one flashy drug prospectus was projected after another. As the guest (desperate to dash off to the Three Brothers Patisserie, still tempted by Nebahat's cake) was sent off with a ceremonial good-bye accompanied by the same army, the Medical Director set off for Âlim Kâhkeci's office. After discussing Miss Zarife's condition, they moved on to the building's blind façade: Should they perhaps knock out a couple of windows?

No one used to care one way or the other about the blind façade blocking that fabulous sea view. Whenever it popped up, someone would brush it off. It was only when Barış Bakış started niggling everyone he met, *Why do you think Turks turn their backs to the sea?* that the blind façade attracted attention. Self-styled experts emerged amongst patients and staff; some even dropped whatever they were doing to seek a solution.

In actual fact, knocking a window through the blind wall would have been child's play. But what good would windows in the corridors or storerooms do? Would the supplies feast their eyes on the sea? The conference hall wall was suitable, but windows would make it no longer fit for purpose. Or they'd need to find another site for the hall. Even if they did that, they certainly didn't have the budget for the move. There were so many other, much more urgent priorities.

Nearly every member of staff (with the exception of the Medical Director) found the tedious meetings that served no one, and the panels attended by official personages and ceremoniously recorded for posterity (yeah, right) by local TV stations – and therefore, by extension, the conference hall itself utterly useless. All the same, not a single voice dared to raise the suggestion *Mr Medical Director Sir, we don't need a conference hall. Let's knock this wall down and enjoy the sea view… and this place would be great for a cafeteria.*

He'd have raised merry hell if they did. It would have been out of the question to give up on the conference hall which, in his view, boosted the hospital's prestige. Moreover, he was keen on the guest speakers. He loved greeting them, swinging the hem of his snow-white coat adopted for its charismatic image, introducing himself as *Medical Director Demir Demir,* his hand held out as if to suggest *I'm the God of this place,* and personally giving guided tours to visitors from institutions he took seriously.

Except it really got on his nerves when some guests had the cheek to stare at his business card and ask, *Don't you have an e-mail address?* It wasn't printed on the card because he never used it. He just couldn't get his head round this thing called the Internet. The computer kid Emrah had explained it a hundred times if he'd explained it once, resorting to the most primitive metaphors imaginable: *It's like this Mr Medical Director Sir… think of a post box, and then the Post Office, right?* But he just couldn't get it into his head. When the Ministry of Health moved to online communications, he found himself tied up in knots at the computer. Eventually he threatened Nemişo with sacking *unless she learnt how to send that shite called e-mail,* and he didn't sound in the least bit like he was joking.

An affronted Nemişo sobbed for an hour and ultimately had to knuckle down. A few days later, when she'd finally succeeded in sending an e-mail without help from anyone else, she burst in with the good news. Her boss was astonished at the sight of the surprisingly cheerful girl he'd left in floods of tears not so long before.

But the Medical Director Demir Demir's trials by internet weren't limited to e-mails. What tested his patience to the limit next was the hospital's website. Thank God it didn't turn out to be as bad as he'd feared. The IT contractor's rep Emrah reassured him, *Website's a doddle Mr Medical Director Sir, just get me the information.* The idea of writing the hospital's history matured during the website preparation period to the extent that before the week was launched, he'd sat down at his desk and written the opening sentences. Showing some page printouts for the site that wasn't up and running as yet, Computer Emrah had said, *And when we click here, we'll read the hospital's history.* Totally unnecessary in the Medical Director's opinion; but once Emrah had shown the websites of other leading hospitals, he was convinced of the need for a few lines.

And write them he would, except he didn't know anything other than the fact that the hospital had been founded in 1898 by the dignitaries of the city. Luck then lent a hand: quite by chance, he gained a rough idea of the history of the place, and even found photographs of the founders. Studying these distinguished, far-sighted and patriotic men, each more handsome than the other, he decided that it was beholden upon him to write the book on the subject as soon as possible.

It was a mild, sunny winter Sunday, a scant flurry of snow a few days earlier having been followed by bright sunshine. Bored with sitting at home, he went to the Three Brothers Patisserie with his wife for some rose water pudding, where they met Turkey's oldest living woman judge Türkan Kaymakoğlu, who sat reading a book in her usual spot, cashmere shawl on her shoulders, teardrop diamond ring on her finger and gold-framed reading specs. This particular corner of the garden, enclosed by a glass wall (thereby sheltered from the blustery sea breezes) and equipped with patio heaters, was set aside for Türkan winter or summer. Whether she turned up or not, no one else was allowed to sit at that table.

Türkan was sipping her bitter coffee and savouring a double roasted pistachio Turkish delight when she noticed the dear Medical Director and his elegant wife, and invited them over with a wave. Saying they'd be honoured, they sat down and began chatting.

Just then, Psychiatrist Âlim Kâhkeci arrived with his **thirteen-year-old daughter Zehra who attended a private school**. Father and daughter had begun learning tennis that very day were carrying kit bags and racquets. Removing the expensive coat over her white tracksuit with the flared bottoms, Zehra glanced at the menu. She wanted to eat her fill of puddings; she'd sweated so much playing tennis, and now deserved every mouthful. But her dad only allowed her one portion; she was already overweight for her age and would no doubt become obese if she carried on. Zehra niggled and niggled, and finally they agreed to share two different types. Turning to the waiter to place his order, he was vexed at catching the Medical Director's eye.

It wasn't meeting the Medical Director Demir and his wife. It was the fact that the couple were sitting with Türkan, a lady he knew to be a staunch supporter of the strictest definition of the secular republic. Even though he didn't feel like it at all, it would have been incredibly discourteous not to greet the oldest living woman judge in the country. So he got up and went over. As he approached with a polite smile, he wondered whether to give the old woman as good as he got, since she was sure to put him down.

Exchanging a cool greeting, they enquired after each other's health. He then had a brief chat with the Medical Director. Sevim asked Âlim to say hello to his headscarfed gynaecologist wife, Tuğba. The neo-devout doctor's fears proved unfounded: The old woman hadn't irritated him by asking when he'd put his daughter into *tesettür*.

Just as he was about to return to his table, Türkan reproached him, *You never consider old people like me, Âlim Bey. I can't read your blog: the text is set in too small a point size, and the background is quite dark too.* a flabbergasted Âlim stammered, *My blog... too dark?* Türkan spoke of his blog and its visuals and background music, Âlim sat down, and they discussed the Internet for quite a while.

Watched by a stunned Medical Director, whose head swivelled between Türkan and Âlim as if at a tennis match, Türkan offered constructive criticism on improving the legibility of Âlim's blog. She also expressed appreciation for all the work he put into it, despite not necessarily always agreeing with the majority of his views. Stunned more by her tech-savviness than her friendliness, the doctor thanked her for the feedback he would certainly consider, and begging his leave, returned to his table.

Türkan asked the gobsmacked Medical Director why *he* didn't have a blog. She could be speaking Chinese for all he knew. Cringing, he admitted that he didn't know what that meant. *It means a web journal,* replied Türkan, *Short for weblog.* Prompted by the blank gaze reminiscent of a dim-witted pupil at an exam, she did what the resident nerd Emrah had failed to do all this time: illuminate the Medical Director on the world of the Internet. They moved from Âlim's blog to the hospital's website. Her obvious mastery of the topic was revealed in the first sentence, so the Medical Director was all ears.

The eldest granddaughter of the eminent Ottoman scientist **Şekip Sami Bey, lecturer on Internal Medicine at the Department of Medical Sciences of the Imperial University**, Türkan was a ninety-seven-year-old living history book. Thank God her memory was fine, however, and her mind was still razor sharp. Despite her advanced years, she was tremendously hale and hearty and young in spirit. She never slept for more than four hours and never started the day before reading all the papers from cover to cover. The old lady whose fundamental principle was to learn something new every day might have shrunk to a tiny size, but was perfectly healthy other than needing a walking stick.

She used to have a much more active social life, but she had pretty much stayed out of local affairs after reaching eighty. All the same, the city's officials and elite frequently visited her. If these visits tapered off, she would hold a party at her mansion instead, mention local problems and help the authorities to find solutions. The Medical Director had also attended these exceptional parties flowing with milk and honey.

Türkan had been living with her staff in the Grade II-listed Kaymakoğlu Mansion opposite the Ethnographic Museum since her retirement on age grounds. This three-and-a-half-storey, eighteen-room stone mansion had a double-staircase front entrance, a sixty-metre-square marble Turkish bath of four washstands, crystal newel post finials,

Florentine porcelain door handles and enamelled wardrobe handles; it was worth tens of millions in new money.

Having dedicated her life to dispensing justice across the country for years, Türkan had never got round to marrying and consequently had no children of her own. Her six heirs – children of her nephew and niece – counted on inheriting this mansion, along with the office blocks bang in the city centre, flats, hundreds of acres of land and several other properties in Istanbul and Ankara once she died – and didn't she have one foot in the grave anyway?

Türkan, who was a graduate of the Ankara Law School at a time when girls were lucky to be taught to read and write, had only one brother: **İmdat Hızır, a keen fisherman**. The black sheep of a family renowned for great education for generations, İmdat hadn't even managed to finish lycée. Instead, he'd been the bane of his father's existence, messing around and getting into scrapes, small and large.

Their father **Tobacco Baron Emrullah Kaymakoğlu** had finished the Ankara College of Agriculture with top marks and chosen to dedicate himself to the development of his hometown instead of following in his scientist father Şekip Sami Bey's footsteps. Tobacco farming and trade might have been his chosen path, but he'd always kept up with the science of agriculture. His triumph in the fight against the tobacco moth, which had been laying waste to all that toil and leaving hundreds of families destitute, had put a smile on the tobacco grower's face.

His public services hadn't been limited to that particular fight either: he had built many schools, one of which he had named after his wife who'd died too young, led the way for – and mostly funded – a variety of vocational courses at the Public Education Centre and taking Atatürk's pronouncement *Oh the new generation on the rise, you are the future!* as his motto, he had financed the educations of countless young people regardless of sex.

But like many pioneers who dedicated themselves to their country, his memory was subjected to a shameless campaign of calumny for a variety of reasons after his death. Some politicos who wanted to mould public opinion to serve their interests were disconcerted at the prospect of a progressive personality setting a solid example, whilst other denigrators were simply envious of the profound marks this humble patriot had left on the history of the city. As a result, spurious accusations arose, from attributing the fight against the tobacco moth to someone else, to alleging that he'd reclaimed the cost of the schools he'd built. There was a deliberate and concerted effort to erase his services from collective memory.

So rife was this ingratitude that it was even joined by a recipient of Emrullah's generosity, someone who'd owned nothing, not even a pair of underpants. It was only after this fellow joined the handful of the city's rich thanks to his biscuit factory, entered politics, and then had the nerve to raise the bar, *Seems he even reclaimed the chickenfeed of a scholarship he'd given me!* that this degree of ingratitude prompted a few holders of common sense to take the situation in hand with a *That will do!* and the rumours calmed down somewhat.

Türkan's return to her hometown whe she had retired further changed the situation. The Lady Judge with close friends in the highest echelons of the state would obviously leave no stone unturned to protect her father's memory. Former ingrates now desperate to ingratiate themselves with this lady who gave every indication of having a say in the city's life, and benefit from her social circles, feigned shame and backpedalled.

Now Emrullah was praised to high skies with equal alacrity. The road where the Kaymakoğlu Mansion stood was renamed Tobacco Baron Emrullah Bey Road and local papers commemorated every anniversary of his death with panegyrics to his services. The one thing they emphasised, however, was the fight against the tobacco moth – a topic that had become old hat – and the contribution to the city's economy, rather than his sensitivity to educating girls. Türkan carried on where her father had left off: she offered scholarships and regularly stocked schools with basics that the Ministry of Education failed to provide. Wise to the hypocrisy of potential exploiters, and happy to ignore these parasites practically queuing at her door, she took the wind out of their sails.

Emrullah had changed the future of dozens of youngsters, helping them all grow up into well-educated professionals, but his own son had turned out to be a disappointment. Nothing worked: neither kindness, nor reprimands, nor indeed the rod. İmdat Hızır repeated every single school year; Emrullah held no hope that his son might one day get a diploma. *Perhaps marriage and a family will help him settle down,* he thought, and married his son off to the daughter of **Celal Öztaş of Yalvaç, headmaster of the primary school** whose construction he had personally supervised.

Bad-tempered and quarrelsome Nihan, whom İmdat Hızır had married in a splendid ceremony once he was back from his national service, wasn't in the least minded to have a family, or run the mansion; that she was in fact only interested in finery, parties and spending money became clear on the very first day. In spite of his conviction in prudence as a virtue, Emrullah would never deny his daughter-in-law. He loosened the purse strings (that were never too tight in the first place) just for a bit of peace and quiet at home. He turned a blind eye to her buying whatever she wanted, from 22-carat gold cuff bracelets through to pearl brooches, from silk dresses through to a fur coat. He even increased the number of domestic staff (quite unnecessarily) so she would never have to do a stroke of work around the place.

But his boundless tolerance and indulgence didn't work. Nihan just went from bad to worse. The first thing she did upon her arrival was to bring to heel **the housekeeper Rukiye who'd been running the mansion like clockwork**: Rukiye, whose Sudanese ancestry stopped everyone dead at first sight, had been a mainstay of the family since childhood. Trusted and respected by Emrullah for her common sense she might have been, but Rukiye was now effectively sidelined. In her total devotion to the Kaymakoğlu family, she never once complained despite spitting blood at Nihan's hands, never once opened her mouth to say in her adorable Black Sea accent (startlingly incongruous with her dark skin), *Eh, better teach that daughter-in-law of yours some manners!* Whenever their paths crossed, Rukiye simply pursed her large lips, bowed her head and passed by, advising patience to the other members of staff, telling them this would not carry on for ever, that sooner or later, things would sort themselves out. Any of the cleaners who tried to object were rebuked for failing to show respect to the daughter-in-law of the family. Whenever Emrullah tried to complain to his loyal housekeeper, no matter how hesitantly, she requested in the gentlest terms possible that he put up with it for the sake of her İmdat Hızır, the orphaned boy she'd raised.

The shameless daughter-in-law who wanted to be sole ruler of the household and even bring her father-in-law to heel just to get her own way, no matter how trivial, carried on picking quarrels and slamming doors hard enough to smash the glass. It was as if she had a bottomless pit of rancour.

It wasn't like Emrullah had deliberately thrown his own son into the fire. Quite the opposite; he had believed this would be a great match. He had known the family and their daughter, whom he'd mistaken for a homely, modest girl, for years. Whenever he went to visit them, she would pitter patter to his side, prop up cushions behind him, *Better make Uncle Emrullah comfy,* make his coffee with her own hands, dance attendance around him and in general make a credible show of respect and love.

Despite being an advocate of women's obligation to work, and proud of his daughter who was serving as a judge in remote districts of Anatolia, Emrullah contradicted his own progressive convictions when he wanted a decent housewife for his son, a girl who would look after her family and keep the home fires burning. Placing his trust in the proverb, *Look at the edge and buy the cloth, look at the mother and take the daughter,* and impressed by the perfect wife and mother **gentle and capable Lütfiye Öztaş**, he had mistaken her daughter Nihan for just the person to change his son.

Change her husband she did too; just not in the way that Emrullah had been hoping. Yes, İmdat Hızır did distance himself from his ne'er-do-well mates, but he also lost his the will to live due to his bad-tempered and quarrelsome wife. He became a total introvert, spending the entire day sitting on a chair placed outside his father's tobacco warehouse, staring into the distance. In time, his former rabble-rousing mates with whom he used to drink all night long gave way to fishermen who steamed into the ferocious waves of the Black Sea in their rickety *taka* boats, and the sleaziest taverns of the city were replaced with unassuming rakı tables set on the decks of the said vessels. İmdat Hızır was so unhappy that he stayed away from home for as long as possible, sometimes setting off on week-long fishing trips, and handing out turbots the size of a sail and bucketfuls of anchovies to friends and neighbours as they could never eat it all. The more the once wild İmdat Hızır withdrew into himself and the darker his face grew, the more Emrullah tormented himself.

The primary school headmaster, who gave himself all sorts of airs and graces for having married his daughter off to the son (never mind that the boy was a layabout) of the city's leading personage, and complained about İmdat to Emrullah instead of trying to talk sense into his daughter after every quarrel, had been hospitalised soon after the birth of his second grandchild. Thrombophlebitis had led to gangrene; his right leg had to be amputated. The consumer of sixty Birinci cigarettes a day survived the operation, but not the hospital. He died of an infection twelve days later.

Shameless bitch that she was, Nihan went as far as holding her father-in-law responsible for her father's death. When she openly accused Emrullah of failing to put her father in a private hospital or hire the best doctors, those strained relations finally snapped altogether. Yet Emrullah had been devastated by Nihan's father's illness and had mobilised the entire medical contingent of the State Hospital. Daughter-in-law and father-in-law no longer ate together, and rarely left their rooms to avoid coming face to face.

Mistaking this for gained territory, Nihan went further. When she tried to forbid her children from seeing their grandfather (and they all lived in the same house) Emrullah's patience finally ran out; he sent his daughter-in-law packing and kept the grandchildren. No match for his roaring fury, Nihan's tears and pleas fell on deaf ears and she was forced to live with her mother in Yalvaç. Lütfiye, whose mind had been on her hometown throughout her marriage despite the modern lifestyle they'd enjoyed in a variety of cities, and who'd always detested giving dinner parties, had moved back to the house left by her father after her husband's death, stuck her feet into the cheap Gislaved rubber shoes so popular in the countryside, and got stuck into cultivating her garden and rearing chickens in the coop.

Nihan was sure Emrullah's fury would eventually abate and he'd call her back, and that İmdat Hızır would come over and throw himself at her feet. That's why, instead of digging her heels in, *Not without my children!* she'd just kissed and cuddled them both when she left, promising to return soon. But her father-in-law didn't back down, and instead of throwing himself at her feet, her husband filed for divorce straightaway. Her initial attempts to contest it soon floundered when she realised she'd bitten off more than she could chew; she agreed to the divorce and gave up custody of the children in exchange for a huge amount of money and property that would last her for years.

Strictly speaking she was determined to make Emrullah wish he'd never been born; one day, though, strolling in her Yalvaç neighbour's rose garden and mouthing off about her father-in-law, she fell for **the swarthy Alişan** at first sight. Smitten by this handsome young Kurd with eyes sparkling like amber on that dark face, she had eyes for nothing else from that moment onwards.

Alişan came from Mardin, but lived in Istanbul where he worked as a buyer for a cosmetics manufacturer; regular rose petal buying trips took him to Isparta and its environs. The frequency of his visits to Yalvaç suddenly rocketed as he, too, was similarly struck. Nihan's marriage to İmdat Hızır had given her not love, but money; the divorce case had yet to conclude when, sneaking to the rose gardens again and again with Alişan, she fell pregnant. Her four-month bump concealed under a tightly wrapped sash, she wept softly throughout the final hearing lest her father-in-law smelled a rat and changed his mind about the settlement.

Those crocodile tears would soon be replaced by real ones. The amber-eyed sweetheart she was head over heels in love with, the man she'd been dreaming of marrying soon as she was rid of İmdat Hızır, turned out to have a wife back in Mardin. Alişan had been married off at seventeen and had no intention of divorcing the officially wedded mother of his two sons. Having finally found love, Nihan not only had to content herself with a religious ceremony instead of an official wedding, but also put herself at his beck and call so the man she was mad about wouldn't leave her. And she handed over all the money she'd extracted out of her father-in-law.

They moved to Istanbul. Alişan lived like a lord between Mardin with his official family and Istanbul with Nihan and his daughter. This was the life; he had no complaints, neither of his life, nor of Nihan, whose divorce settlement he was spending to his heart's content.

But life was no longer a bed of roses for Nihan. If her husband and father-in-law had cursed her, it had certainly worked; she was now paying several times over for having tormented them. Having borne two sons after the daughter with amber eyes like her father, she was now left to look after three kids in the house where her man dropped in whenever he felt like it. Alişan's passion had quickly waned, although he neither killed her, nor cherished her. Just gave her a good hiding whenever he lost his temper. He married a third woman (a strapping Azeri with dark eyes and even darker eyebrows), again, a religious wedding, and set up a new home with her too. Not content with three wives – one official – either, he'd have flings lasting a few months and since he felt no need to hide them, put Nihan, who would love him until her dying day, through hell. So wrapped up in Alişan was she that she barely recalled the son and daughter (who'd been five and two, respectively) left behind in the mansion, to be cared by a clutch of female servants supervised by Rukiye Kalfa.

As for İmdat Hızır who'd devoted himself totally to fishing after the split-up: he rarely saw his children now, since he spent all his time in a second hand vessel bought over his father's objections. Emrullah's heart broke every time he looked at his grandchildren seeking maternal love in their nanny. But there was even more trouble in store for the poor man. İmdat Hızır passed away when his boat sank in a violent storm. At the time his lifeless body vanished in the depths of the Black Sea, his son was seven, and daughter four.

Blaming himself for the tragedies that had plagued his family and heartbroken at being denied the solace of giving his only son a decent burial with a cypress to watch over the grave, Emrullah doted upon his grandchildren; unfortunately, he failed to prevent them from turning into spendthrift heirs.

Grandson Şekip Sami Kaymakoğlu, who became a chemist, following in his ancestors' footsteps in the sciences, confronted his aunt as soon as Emrullah had joined his Maker. He was demanding his share of the funds and property at one go; his aunt – who claimed that he'd waste it all – was the only obstacle to his fantastic projects. To be fair, they both meant well, and they both had a point. Şekip Sami wanted to prove his chemical genius to the whole world, and Türkan worried that the grand projects occupying her nephew's mind for years were nothing more than castles in the air that would only bleed his inheritance dry.

Not that aunt and nephew knew each other that well. Except for the brief summer holidays in the mansion, they'd hardly spent much time together, or had the chance to get close. All the time Türkan served as a judge in Anatolia, Şekip Sami had been raised under his grandfather's watchful eye, cosseted and sent to Istanbul for his education, money being no object. Racked with guilt, Emrullah had bought a fantastic flat in Maçka Sports Road and furnished it completely just so his grandson would lack no comfort.

Şekip Sami was still university student living in the lap of luxury when he fell for **Maçka's most beautiful girl Füruzan**, and married her the moment he graduated. Spoiled rotten and showered with money by Emrullah, everything seemed all right as far as the young couple were concerned. Şekip Sami's inability to hold down a job failed to attract much attention. But after Emrullah's death, when Türkan insisted on putting her nephew and niece on an annuity, Şekip kicked off.

By now a great judge of character, Türkan's instinct was rarely misplaced. Even in the brief time they'd spent together, she'd sussed her nephew out as a perpetual dreamer looking for yet another new-fangled idea. That predisposition to squander his life on some reverie was worrying indeed.

If only Şekip Sami had married someone with a modicum of common sense; then this bastion of justice would never have made a fuss over divvying up the inheritance between the rightful heirs. Unfortunately, Füruzan appeared far from capable of managing her husband, and Türkan's fears had only been compounded by the eyes of **Füruzan's widowed mother Fatoş**, which sparkled with fiendish intelligence. The mother-in-law, whose looks defied her advancing age and outshone her daughter, insisted on a magnificent wedding at Istanbul's Hilton Hotel, attended by the entire contingent of the merry divorcées of Maçka and Nişantaşı. As drinks flowed liberally, Fatoş flaunted her beauty and femininity to all present, but especially to Şekip Sami in an overt show of familiarity as if to say, *Don't marry her, marry me* – conduct too inappropriate in Türkan's view. Even more outrageous was the mother-in-law's eyes, locked onto the family heirlooms on Türkan's neck and fingers, further evidence of the low class family Şekip Sami had married into.

Deeming even the slightest remark to be beneath her, however, Türkan kept her own counsel.

The marriage was trouble-free for a time. Fatoş moved in with the young family upon the birth of their first child, and since she made no attempt to seduce her son-in-law, Türkan's mind was finally at ease: frivolity must be in this woman's nature. Femininity was the only thing she knew, which she ultimately proved when the flirtatious airs were abandoned in favour of the domineering mother-in-law, a role that clearly had been rehearsed to perfection.

The self-styled chemistry genius, on the other hand, had his head in the clouds; no amount of mother-in-law's nagging made any impression. He spent all his time looking for opportunities. He applied to holding companies and universities and even looked for funding abroad. He had tons of projects he'd love to put into practice all at the same time if he could. Upon the death of his grandfather, he was terrifically excited at the prospect of finally realising his dreams.

Holding no great hopes for her niece, Türkan was ready to hand over Zeynep İkbal's share of the inheritance at once. That being said, a few rumours she'd heard around the city drove her to be a little more prudent. She wrote to her nephew and niece to explain that their inheritance was safe; since she was concerned about the prospect of it being frittered away, she was proposing to manage the funds and the property, and she would regularly deposit a sizeable sum mutually agreeable into their bank accounts every month. Unconcerned by the fact that she'd lost her grandfather's love, Zeynep had been living it up on the French Riviera; and took her time before replying with a *No!* Whereas Şekip Sami had grabbed the phone straightaway: this was out of the question.

Türkan was staying at Pera Palas to renew two rental contracts for a couple of office blocks in Istanbul: one in Banks Road in Karaköy, and the other in Six Roads in Kadıköy. She visited her nephew in order to discuss this matter at length.

They argued all evening. The merry widow mother-in-law's attitude made Türkan reassess her earlier view; she had to hand it to Fatoş, who sided with the aunt openly and earnestly: *I beg of you Madam, please don't hand it all over. His heart's set on foolish pipe dreams; he'll sink that huge fortune, I swear, and ruin us all!* So she was no gold-digger after all. Her ill-mannered interest in the jewellery was evidently not appraising, but a simple feminine instinct; Türkan suddenly warmed to her.

But not even Fatoş was able to help, and the aunt departed, having come to no agreement with her nephew. Şekip Sami would eventually come to his senses, thought Türkan, deciding to avoid making a big thing of it and returning to her hotel after saying, *Think about it for a bit, we can talk again.* That **upstart of a lawyer Abbas Koşar** who dropped in on her at the hotel the following day, however, made her blood boil. Teeth thick with sesame seeds from the *simit* bread ring he'd consumed on the way, this man who announced himself as Şekip Sami's solicitor delivered an unequivocal demand: the immediate release of his client's share of the inheritance in full; failure to do so would lead to court action.

Türkan felt just then that she never wanted to see her nephew again. *All right,* she interrupted and instructed her own solicitor to proceed at great speed. Handing over whatever fell to Şekip Sami's share (including furniture and objects large and small from the mansion and family heirloom jewellery) she cut off relations with her nephew.

Finally in possession of the inheritance he'd been expecting, Şekip Sami dedicated himself body and soul to what his imagination had been concocting day after day: he would prove himself a chemistry genius and these fantastic projects would make him a fortune – as if he needed it. The new project entrepreneur thus rolled up his sleeves.

He set up his first venture in Istanbul's Mecidiyeköy, then consisting of fields and orchards: a modern factory that would revolutionise furniture polish. This invention really did give wooden furniture a sparkling finish, made it all look amazing, but it had a cloying smell that lingered. Almost as soon as the first batch had been delivered, complaints about the polish he'd marketed with such high hopes, and had spent a fortune advertising, hit the roof. Tiny workshops through to big factories all returned the stock with demands for compensation. Şekip Sami was on the verge of inventing a new formula that would reduce the smell; he'd have succeeded if only he had a little bit of time, but he failed to convince his customers. It wasn't long before the factory thundered into bankruptcy.

This first setback plagued him for a long time. He stopped eating for days; it took ages to pull himself together. In due course, having given up on proving his genius in chemistry to the whole world, he attempted to prove to his nagging mother-in-law that he was a great businessman. With no office to go to, he spent entire days in the vast five-bedroom flat, patting his two daughters in the cradle; the worse things got, the more Fatoş piled on the scorn as her fondness took a dive.

So fed up was he (and so eager to embrace any invitation to a partnership) that he swallowed *a cure for alopaecia* and invested a fortune in a joker's factory, which would become the world's top state-of-the-art cosmetic laboratory. He never got a chance to test the efficacy of that shampoo, though. The man with no business sense was swindled by the partner, who then did a runner.

No longer prepared to trust others, therefore, Şekip Sami resolved to abandon grand schemes. In an effort to recover his earlier losses, and hoping for a quick return, he founded a small company to import milk powder from England. Not the most sought-after product, it went mouldy in insalubrious warehouses.

He invented a new food preserving method, and was about to put it into practice when someone else came up with a better one; so it blew up in his face.

He tried to import water pumps from Italy; there was a devaluation.

He went into wholesale biscuits; his warehouse was flooded.

He founded a paper mill; a fire broke out.

As every single venture came apart in his hands, he sought solace in tumblers of whisky that he downed one after another.

If he had only taken his mother-in-law's advice to take it easy, living on the income – instead of investing in his projects – that astronomic fortune would have doubled of its own accord in any one of the banks which had been pursuing it. But fate would persistently, and quite unfairly, harass Şekip Sami as he continued to refuse to wise up.

In time, he had two more daughters; his home turned into an infernal racket of non-stop chatter thanks to a mother-in-law and four little ones. Blessed with beauty but denied a scrap of intelligence, common sense or prudence, Füruzan gazed in the mirror all day long, or was at the dressmaker's or hairdresser's; instead of a rebuke, she waited on her mother's words, harping on about poor Şekip's lack of business sense and generally making life hell for him. Cursing fate, the thwarted genius was on the verge of committing suicide, when, after four hours spent in the sun – in her obsession with a tan despite her advanced years – at the Hilton Hotel pool, his mother-in-law had a stroke, lingered in hospital and died.

Her death brought the husband and wife closer together. Şekip Sami enjoyed a little bit of peace now that the mother-in-law nagging had come to an end. Sadly it wasn't to last long. This time it was the girls, who'd been trained by their grandmother to nurse a grudge against their feckless father: they turned their mother against their father.

Despite all his commercial misfortunes, Şekip Sami had spared no expense on his daughters's education; he'd bent over backwards to send them to the best schools. But they had little inclination to set solid objectives for their futures.

His eldest Elif who'd read communications at a mediocre US university (having failed to get into a decent undergraduate programme) had settled in Los Angeles after marrying an African American. The next two followed in her footsteps, scraping through equally unexceptional universities, switching courses throughout. An Arts Major from America was the new trend amongst the bohemian circles the girls frequented; they most certainly had no intention of missing out. All they cared about was becoming actresses; failing that, directors; failing that again, art directors, or at the very least, be something in advertising. In short, somehow joining the ranks of major figures in some creative profession. Thanks to the money their father sent like clockwork every month, they flitted between courses like acting, dance and creative writing, dipped in and out of jobs, and lived without making a go of anything.

His youngest Esra was a little smarter. Making it there was no easy feat, she'd realised on her brief visits to the States. She chose to live in Istanbul. Not that she had much professional success to speak of. Ostensibly a manager at an art gallery, her role in those circles was – could never be – little more than that of a bit player. Riled by her own failure to amount to anything much in this rarefied environment, she took it out on her father, and took her mother under her wing just to hack him off. Quite out of the blue, convinced of her youngest daughter's intelligence, Füruzan rose to Esra's bait and up and left her husband. This was a totally unexpected blow that was the beginning of the end for Şekip Sami and his family.

The series of events that led to the dissolution of the family started with a decision to renovate. Now that the fabulous Maçka flat was beginning to show its age, a thorough overhaul was unavoidable: the windows were falling to pieces, the taps were leaking, and the kitchen cupboards were coming apart in their hands. Once they finally decided to go ahead, the self-styled aesthete Esra picked every single item of building material personally, decided which walls would be knocked down and what would be built where; then, having hectored the tradesmen engaged by her father, went on holiday with her mother, leaving her father in charge.

Füruzan had been unwilling to stick around during the works, and so accompanied her daughter to **the gallery owner Besim Varlık's** summerhouse in Assos.

Whilst mother and daughter enjoyed their holiday, dining on sea bass, jumbo prawns and stuffed courgette flowers, sipping good wines, and skimming over the waves in Besim's speedboat before a dip in the open sea, Şekip Sami was supervising the builders, dripping with sweat in thirty degrees, working his guts out to finish the renovations before his wife's return.

Except he'd made a grave mistake. What remained of that colossal fortune being on the verge of running dry, he'd ignored his daughter's instructions and cut corners – and quite badly at that. Upon her return, Esra was thunderstruck at the tacky transformation of what had been a magnificent flat in the spectacular block in Maçka, the district of choice for Istanbul's crème de la crème. It looked like something erected by the shoddiest two-bit contractor. Without a trace of the exquisite materials she'd chosen: the parquet was not solid wood, the taps were not German, the ceramics were not Spanish, and nothing bore any trace of Esra's refined taste. She launched into an uninterrupted stream of abuse at her father. Let fly without even pausing for breath as she rattled off the gravest of insults. But when Şekip Sami – who'd had it up to here by then – opened his mouth, no longer prepared to grin and bear it, that violent argument ended with Esra taking her mother and leaving.

It would turn out to be much sadder for the poor fellow. The girls colluded to force their father to sell whatever few properties remained along with that gorgeous flat, where he was living on his own, and divvied it all up. Şekip Sami was shafted time and again throughout his life, but the worst came from his own children.

But God moved in mysterious ways. Soon after that bust-up with her father, Esra was dumped by the gallery owner. Her world turned upside down; she was seriously in love with him, a man old enough to be her father. But she wasn't going to give up. She soon pulled herself together, shook off the blues and made her mind up to fight for her lover. Assuming a non-existent entitlement, she tried to bust his home by telling his wife, *Let 'im go; haven't you sucked his blood enough?* Her reward was a good hiding from the elder son who happened to be home; scandal followed scandal, rumours hit the roof and she was gutted.

Being snubbed by bohemia hurt her worst. The prestige she'd enjoyed as the art market luminary Besim Varlık's mistress had vanished overnight. No one acknowledged her in the cafés and galleries she used to frequent daily or greeted her back in her former strutting spots. She was ignored by the members of the arts world; her cosy chat companions until very recently.

Hoping to get away from it all, she decided to take her mother and visit her sisters in America. There she met **her African American brother-in-law's cousin Edward** and married him on the rebound – the gallery owner never replied to her letters, refused to take her calls and just wouldn't say, *Come back, we'll take up where we'd left off,* no matter how hard she tried. She settled in Chicago with this kindly fellow. They could have been happy together if only she'd stop simmering with rage; Eddie was gentle, affectionate and sensitive. But no; no matter what she did, she couldn't forget Besim Varlık, or more to the point, the hurt caused by that heavy loss in what was little more than an unremarkable affair.

Füruzan lived to regret leaving her husband as she shuttled between the four daughters for the rest of her life. She stayed with each for a few months, during which time she never even got to step outside as she worked her fingers to the bone, cooking, sweeping, scrubbing, and looking after her grandchildren. Scrapping over their now unpaid maid-servant, the sisters blatantly went at one another in front of the poor woman, *Well, she stayed with you for a fortnight longer! And you'd sent her ten days late last time!* Now in a depression, Füruzan would have returned to Turkey and thrown herself at Şekip Sami's feet, but her daughters wouldn't even hear his name; they never let their mother go.

Whilst Füruzan spent her days serving her daughters, Şekip Sami had taken shelter in an unlicensed attic conversion in the Refet Bey Block in Topağacı, Nişantaşı with what little he'd managed to save from his children's grasp. He lived from hand to mouth, eking out what remained of his former money.

Invisible from the outside, the flat tucked under the roof had no external windows. But thank God there was a huge light shaft bang in the middle of the sixty-four square metres, and two big windows filled the interior with daylight. This attic comprising two small rooms, an alcove kitchen and a tiny bathroom served Şekip Sami as home for quite a while. When he died of pancreatic cancer, all alone, lingering in hospital, he left his children nothing more than an enormous unpaid rent bill and the draft formula for a brand new exterior coating that, unbeknownst to all, would have revolutionised the construction sector.

His landlady Sevinç Okutan, owner of the sixty-four square metres, became his last and only true friend. Never asking for the overdue rent, she'd taken it upon herself to help sort out this gentleman she regarded as nothing less than nobility. Şekip Sami thought he had an ulcer; but Sevinç knew it was cancer. As his closest friend, she talked to the doctors, secretly paid for treatment, and even accompanied him to hospital, the man on his deathbed who, in her view, had been treated so badly by fate.

Şekip Sami died without understanding where he'd gone wrong. He'd waited hand and foot on his wife and daughters, spoiled them rotten, and it had all been in vain. His aunt Türkan, whose foresight he never admitted, had written him off and turned him away without a glance, no matter how many times he'd gone to her door. Just when he was on the verge of getting closer to his only sister, hoping to get over his children's betrayal, Zeynep died in an unfortunate accident – yet another fragile branch that snapped in his hand.

His only remaining wish was to die as soon as possible, a lonely man in a hospital ward where six patients groaned at the same time, a forlorn victim of his exuberant desires and brilliant, yet uncontrollable, intelligence, a man who'd failed at everything in life and for whom everything he'd touched had turned to dust.

God took mercy on his suffering servant. When Şekip Sami, who'd been drinking like a fish after every failure succumbed to pancreatic cancer, Sevinç was away. The old lady had gone out to get some milky pudding in the hope that he might have a spoonful (although he was even beyond asking for water by then) when he quietly breathed his last.

Generous of purse and heart, Sevinç had brought puddings for everyone in the ward. She was murmuring softly, trying to feed the motionless man with the open eyes when she realised he'd already given up the ghost. No one had noticed. Gently, she closed the still warm eyelids and waited by the unfortunate body until he was stretchered away to the morgue.

She had lost her last friend. Neither **her daughter Sevda Okutan who sold designer objects** in her shop three streets away, nor her son who lived in Beykoz, could be bothered to even think about visiting their poor mother. They did, give them their due, ring her frequently though. Having also lost her children, in a manner of speaking, Sevinç had neither the time nor the inclination to cultivate a new friend to dispel her loneliness. She'd had enough of life.

She went up to the attic and riffled through her last friend's documents. Discovering an old business card, she rang the solicitor with the news. The once upstart lawyer Abbas Koşar struggled to figure out whom the old woman was talking about, until it dawned upon him that this was the Şekip Sami whose fortune he'd exploited for years, a realisation that prompted a silent *We-eel… Şekip Sami Bey was my client in the dim and distant past; can't be arsed about him now!* As he listened to Sevinç however, that jolly face popped up in his mind and made him feel terribly sorry about the man's tragic end. He wasn't that heartless after all. He flicked through his old diaries, found Türkan's and the youngest daughter Esra's telephone numbers, and rang them both to announce, *Şekip Sami Bey has sadly passed away.* He sounded genuinely sad.

By this time, Esra – who neither found what she wanted in life, nor even knew what she wanted in the first place, and was perpetually unhappy as a result – was in the midst of translating *Twentieth century mourners grieve for one year, no longer,* a line from Nâzım Hikmet's *Letter to my Wife* for the bilingual *Turkamerican* published in Chicago. Having turned her back on painting, she had dedicated herself to translating poetry. She was really cut up about her father's death. Cried for hours. Eddie came home to find her face red and swollen.

This brought together the sisters who'd fallen out a while back. They mourned for a few days, remembering the father they blamed for their present circumstances for having frittered away an enormous fortune on pipe dreams. But the sisters were millennial in mindset. Their grief blew past like a gust of wind instead of lasting a year. Before the week was out, his memory had vanished into the distance. They carried on, miserable in their usual helter-skelter. Their father's death had been a sudden shock, but not enough for even the prospect of going to Turkey and burying him to flit through their minds.

As for Türkan, who had recalled the upstart lawyer Abbas, sesame seeds on teeth and all, the moment she'd heard his voice on the phone: something gave way inside. Devastated, she felt an unfamiliar sense of guilt. At the same time, she was a realist who believed that people made their own fate.

Şekip Sami's tragic death affected his landlady most deeply. Sevinç Okutan had spent so many hours, nay, days, with this sad gentleman; they'd enjoyed the calm – and no longer sexual – companionship of a very old and very loving couple who slept in separate bedrooms to avoid disturbing each other. She would add tahini and molasses to her shopping list because he liked them, and he knew where she'd put her reading specs. They never called it love, but they both knew this was nothing less. The old lady grieved far more than she'd done at her husband's death; it was impossible to get used to the void Şekip Sami had left behind. Six months later, she hanged herself from the wardrobe rail using the sash of her bathrobe. It was her seventy-second birthday; she knew her children were sure to have far more important things to do than come over to celebrate, but they would ring. She'd thought they would worry when she didn't answer the phone and find her body before it started to smell, and she was proven right.

The attic housing Şekip Sami's goods and drafts of endless projects remained untouched for a long time. Türkan had contented herself with having his body brought over in a private ambulance for burial in the family plot but hadn't gone to Istanbul afterwards to clear out. A black coating of dust settled on Şekip Sami's dilapidated effects over the years.

Five years after the suicide of the lonely Sevinç, **her young painter grandson Yalın Tağmaç** returned to Turkey, having finished his education in the Accademia di Belle Arti di Firenze. Yalın, who eschewed chemical paints, preferring to paint with organic ingredients like tea, coffee, wine, soy sauce and vegetable juices as well as natural root dyes, which he combined with a bizarre choice of materials, decided to convert this space inherited from his grandmother into a studio. What he had in mind was the total removal of the roof, to be replaced by glazing that would give him all the daylight he needed. He drew up a plan straightaway, contracted an architect and got down to it.

His mother Sevda Okutan (whose superb degree of self-confidence had turned the speech defect stemming from a prognathous jaw into a distinctive accent) had asked her office boy to clear the attic flat in the block she'd rarely bothered to set foot in when her mother was alive. The boy, who already moonlighted at a supermarket, took his relatives along to loot the flat and grab whatever they took a fancy to; they left the place in a mess. Palming the thousand dollars he found in the safe, he buzzed off, never to be seen again.

So Yalın had to go through the flat that had been cleared of anything sellable, and where Şekip Sami's memory was gathering dust. What he found was as follows: tons of empty bottles, a Facit calculating machine dating back to the polish factory, an old-fashioned black telephone, a table lamp, threadbare garments, chemistry magazines in English, heaps of incorporation documents, commercial record gazettes and photographs in countless boxes as well as the drafts of the exterior coating formula that was Şekip Sami's final project. It would have all gone in the bin, but Yalın's fancy was caught by the complicated chemical formulae beautifully written in sepia ink and the texture of the stencil paper long since unavailable. He separated the formula sheets and handed over the rest to the **concierge Mevlüt** to throw away, documents and photographs and all.

Mevlüt, the bane of the **block's recently elected manager Tijen** for persistently parking his tinny Suzuki Maruti outside the block where premium wheels such as BMWs, Mercedeses and Hondas normally lined up, was cross at riffling in vain in Şekip Sami's goods for something worth his while. Knowing full well they'd fetch nothing, he still set aside the calculating machine, the telephone, the books, magazines and photos, and a serviceable fur-lined car coat, and threw the rest out. He'd wear the coat himself, and sell the calculating machine and the telephone to the junk shop and the rest to secondhand book dealers. Just when he was placing it all in the boot, he came face to face with Tijen. Since her own street was full, she'd had to tour all of Nişantaşı for about twenty minutes, ultimately had to leave her car at a greatly inconvenient spot behind the American Hospital and walk back in a hot sweat. Spotting the Suzuki Maruti outside the door, she tore him off a strip, and quite loudly at that.

But the concierge gave as good as he got. He let rip without allowing her a word in edgeways, accusing Tijen, who boasted of her membership of an egalitarian social democratic party, of snobbery and discrimination. Her suggestion that he find somewhere else to park elicited *So I should burn my car in Taksim Square just because I'm a concierge?* His arguments solid enough to leave her gaping, he pressed his advantage with *Don't I have a right to park outside the door?* The primary school dropout from Kastamonu had spoken like a machine gun as he gave the grand electrical-electronic engineer a good lesson in equality.

Rendered speechless by the caretaker's protracted eloquence the block manager might have been, but she did take advantage of his absence when he drove off for Çukurcuma. Blocking the spot with an old chair that stood at the entrance, she traipsed all the way back, collected her Volkswagen Golf and parked it in the spot Mevlüt had vacated. As she locked her car with the remote, she savoured a pointless sense of triumph at having thwarted the insolent caretaker.

Mevlüt went to a junk shop he knew, owned by the earringed Ömer Çakır who happened to be related to earless Ziya, the lazy caretaker of the Mental Health Hospital – unbeknownst to both.

But the failed antiques dealer (having long since lost hope) was out, trying to flog a full set of the *Encyclopaedia of Istanbul* he'd discovered in a house clearance. His target was his friend **Numan, a secondhand book dealer known as the Fountaineer** in a tribute to his mind-boggling depth of knowledge about Istanbul's fountains, and he was busy tidying up the Aslıhan Arcade shop he had opened with his partner Haymon Yener, the antique dealer.

Knowing the idea of employing someone was anathema to his grumpy partner whose expertise in secondhand books was second to none, Haymon had come to help in an uncharacteristically casual pair of jeans and a t-shirt. They'd opened their shop a week earlier, but it was still nowhere near ready. Haymon, who normally wouldn't even so much as move a teacup in his gently air-conditioned elegant gallery, and who never gave his employees a moment's peace, was opening boxes, patting and dusting the books, and wiping his sweat on his elbow, oblivious to the dust and filth. The antiques dealer, as keen on historic postcards as he was on Orthodox icons, was all eyes as he opened boxes stuffed with commonplace ephemera, *What if by some miracle a Fruchtermann, an Ottmar or a Rosenberg postcard were to emerge?* Which is why he missed the question posed by Aydemir Güzeldere, the psychiatrist whose star had risen at an astronomical rate since moving to Istanbul after abandoning his earlier research into substance addiction in favour of psychotherapy.

Only a few days earlier when the famous psychiatrist was chatting to the Medical Director on the phone, his uncle had mentioned the book he was trying to write, but complained that he didn't know how to go about it. If only he had an example! It would help, but he had no idea how to get hold of one. Vaguely recalling a book on the pioneering Bakırköy Mental Hospital, Aydemir had said he'd look into it and had therefore come here to keep his word, to the arcade thick with secondhand bookshops were located.

Numan was stacking police thrillers on a shelf when he heard the psychiatrist, and replied, *Not Bakırköy, but someone's writing Mazhar Osman's biography…* He was sure, because a doctor who was writing a biography had enquired for documents related to, and photographs of this luminary; the founder of the first modern mental health institution in the land, Mazhar Osman. As far as he knew it wasn't yet published; the authors were looking for a sponsor. As Aydemir was telling his uncle on the mobile, *It's not finished yet, and it was about Mazhar Osman anyway,* he crashed into Ömer Çakır who'd walked in carrying the encyclopaedias. They exchanged apologies.

Ömer stepped in. Although not especially rare, this encyclopaedia did have its fans, and this particular set looked in pristine condition that invited an eager flick through its pages. In the meanwhile, Mevlüt had already dropped off his haul at Ömer's shop over the whining objections of the apprentice, *Abi, please don't drop em off here! Give em to Ömer Abi when he comes back!* and had returned to Refet Bey Block in Nişantaşı.

He wasn't in the least bit surprised at finding his spot nabbed by Tijen; she'd have been waiting for the opportunity anyway. Unfazed, he was about to turn into the street at the rear when he saw Yalın and **his freckled girlfriend Ebru Başusta** leave.

Sick and tired of the meaningless requests and whinges of the old and capricious residents, Mevlüt had taken to this young couple he'd recently met. The day they'd come to see *What do we need to do to make this flat work?* Yalın had ordered a takeaway not only for themselves, but also Mevlüt and his daughter, an act that had instantly put him in the concierge's good books. And Ebru, a photography undergraduate at Mimar Sinan, had set about shooting photos of Mevlüt's five-year-old daughter (cuteness personified with curls falling on her forehead and a string of blue beads on her neck), promptly conquering the man's heart.

Mevlüt pulled over and descended from the Suzuki, making sure he wasn't blocking the way, and said, *At your service!* Yalın patted him on the shoulder, *No worries, dude, keep it cool,* and entered his car, chatting to Ebru. Freckles sparkling in the sun like golden dots, Ebru suddenly remembered she had to ring her dad, and keyed the number grumbling, *I bet he's gonna say it's too expensive…*

That was just what Metropolitan Mayor Tacettin Başusta needed. His unexpectedly warm greeting was because he'd had it up to the back teeth with the Medical Director, who had dropped in. It would have been too rude to interrupt the bombastic soliloquy about the history of the hospital the Medical Director would write, and what a momentous cultural service it would be, as he hinted at sponsorship from the metropolitan authority. A downright tedious speech, in the mayor's view, one he hoped to cut short by saying to the phone, *Urgent, you say sweetie? Fine… Ring you back in five minutes…* He stood up and gave the Medical Director an apologetic look that was a wordless dismissal.

A disgruntled Medical Director Demir Demir plodded down the city council hallways whilst Tacettin Başusta's affectionate tone grew distinctly cooler as he dashed his daughter's hopes to the ground: the flat she wanted to buy was far too expensive, it was out of the question to shell out that much.

As Ebru whinged in the car, *What do you mean dad? This is Istanbul, you can't even buy a chicken coop for that here!* Mevlüt entered the block, laughing up his sleeve at Tijen who had to be watching. He was about to descend the concierge's quarters in the basement when he had to run upstairs instead at hearing a bloodcurdling scream from number seven, his mind on the **Filipina Rufa Mañez**, who must have screamed, she of the flat nose and sunken eyes he'd never fancy, yet had a pair of column-like legs he just couldn't get out of his mind.

The half-Spanish, half-native Rufa – who'd failed to learn even a simple *Yes* or *No* despite living in Istanbul for the past eighteen months – was employed as carer to **the once illustrious brain surgeon Yaşar Mustaki**, now bed-ridden as a result of a stroke five years previously. She'd been recruited as nanny to a famous industrialist's child in Istanbul, but her luck hadn't held out. The industrialist divorced his wife because he'd caught making love to his driver in his favourite vintage car, and the unemployed Rufa had tried several new jobs before ultimately accepting the position of live-in carer for Yaşar Mustaki despite knowing nothing of patient care. Still only twenty-one, Rufa had a chronically ill five-year-old son born with a single kidney. She had no choice but to care for a patient thousands of miles from her home to cover the medical costs of the boy who lived with his grandmother.

Not that Rufa was expected to do very much for the man lying with his eyes fixed on the ceiling in the room equipped like a state-of-the-art intensive care unit. Yaşar's wife had died twelve years previously, and both his children lived in the States; a professional nurse who came every day took care of everything, including hygiene, and all that Rufa had to do was to play solitaire, watch the English channels on TV and talk to her mother on the phone.

Yaşar – whose name had been changed to *Yeshua* by his father when they'd migrated to Haifa – had no intention of settling in Turkey until a neurosurgery congress in Michigan introduced him to **the famous brain surgeon Gazi Yaşargil**. This meeting would alter the course of his life.

Yaşar had been impatient to meet Gazi, whom he only knew by reputation, and whose work he'd been following closely; never having seen his face, though, he was reduced to peering at everyone's name badge. By sheer fluke they were seated together at dinner the first night. One glance at the name badge, and Yaşar addressed his hero with an *Afiyet olsun efendim...* Coming at an unexpected moment, this courteous *Bon appétit, sir,* in Turkish sparked up a professional conversation between the two surgeons.

During that dinner, Yaşar talked to his fellow surgeons of not only the milestones in his professional career, but also how his father Rıfat Mustaki – who had turned his back on his homeland after having been swindled during the time of the Wealth Tax – spoke Turkish until his dying day, listened to Turkish music, and occasionally overcome with homesickness travelled to Beirut just to eat kebab with yogurt in a Turkish restaurant, throwing piety to the winds – kosher-schmosher! Overwhelmed by the recollection of the Bijou Yalı they'd had to leave behind, shafted by that unscrupulous Dairy Magnate Hulki, Yaşar suddenly longed for the Bosphorus shore where he'd grown up.

Gazi introduced him to **the Istanbul neurologist Ali Mukbil Özüpek**, who in turn made the offer which prompted Yeshua Mustaki to reclaim his birth name of Yaşar and move back. Ali Mukbil might not have been the most resourceful instigator of ingenious treatment methods, but he was a superb administrator; at the time he was busy setting up a private hospital that Istanbul sorely needed. A team of distinguished doctors was high on his agenda.

Except that wasn't the first topic of the evening. Ali Mukbil was a devoted fan of Sadegh Hedayat, the celebrated Iranian writer who had gassed himself in a Paris hotel room. The study of foreign hospitals' organisation charts took up so much of his time, but whenever he had the opportunity, he worked on the translation of this great writer's *Zinde Be-gūr*. The surgeon's mother came from a leading Teheran family, so he'd grown up speaking Farsi with her and his grandmother, and had learnt the script at secondary school. Any possible regrets of having studied medicine like his uncles, aunts and cousins instead of linguistics notwith-standing, he knew it was too late to change course now. So, he'd taken up the translation with an amateur's enthusiasm. Once he had started, however, he realised that this wasn't quite as easy as he had thought.

Ali Mukbil had translated the subtitle 'From a Madman's Notes' and the first page, but the right phrase for the title of the story itself seemed to be eluding him. *Fit Burial* didn't cut it; *Buried Healthy* most certainly didn't work. He was neither an adherent of passé Ottoman, nor a particular fan of the *PureTurkish* that was such a fad at the time. What he aspired to was something that would elicit praise from both the critics of Pure-Turkists, who frothed at the mouth on the pages of the *Tercüman*, and the denigrators of *archaic* language on those of the *Cumhuriyet*. Language that would enchant whoever read this splendid tale. He had no problems with the text itself; the translation would clearly go reasonably well. But it was the adjective *zinde*, so ubiquitous in everyday contexts, that flummoxed him. *Fit? Hearty? Vigorous?* It was during that chat in Turkish with the brain surgeon that the words he'd been looking for suddenly came to him.

Choosing his phrasing with extraordinary caution, this being a sensitive subject, Yeshua Mustaki was relating how his father Rıfat had pined away for his beloved Bosphorus after leaving Istanbul for Haifa. His voice betrayed the hurt both of the bad treatment his father had suffered and of that unjust exile. As Yeshua repeated his elderly father's *When I look out and can't see Arnavutköy or the hills of Bebek… you might as well bury me alive!* Pointing at the barren view outside his window, the translation of *Zinde Be-gūr* flashed in Mukbil's mind: *Buried Alive!*

He wouldn't live long enough to see the short story translated and published thirty years later with the exact same title; filled with a sudden liking for Yeshua who'd inadvertently done him a huge favour, however, he made the aforementioned offer. The two men discussed it in some detail over the next few days. The surgeon's bright future was obvious from the attention he'd drawn at the congress; Mukbil gave him *carte blanche* on the job description and cited an astronomical salary.

Yeshua's passive and depressive wife Ida, who never queried a single decision he made concerning their lives together (nor did she express assent or dissent) was surprisingly thrilled on this occasion, and very enthusiastic about moving to Istanbul. She'd felt lonely and neglected all this time due to the intense demands of the successful surgeon's career, but all her relations lived in Istanbul and she'd secretly been longing to move there. It had been her father-in-law's bitterness at this city that had prevented her from ever voicing what she thought was an impossible dream to enjoy the company of family and friends.

Her delight made it easier for Yeshua to make his mind up. They packed in no time and left for Istanbul, where they moved into a rented garden flat in Bebek. Ida soon turned into a woman full of life. Her depressive moods and crying attacks were gone, and she had wonderful time visiting with her relations, laughing and chatting all day long.

The first thing Yaşar Mustaki did in Istanbul was to visit the Bijou Yalı of his birth. The dilapidated state of the house he'd thought he would find as he'd left it cut him to the quick, but the *For Sale* sign was exciting. He pushed open the broken wooden gate, crossed over to the seafront and stared at the flagstones of the quay his father used to wash with bucketfuls of water hauled from the sea; the memory of night-time swims in the phosphorescence of the Bosphorus filled him with a terrific longing for days that would never return. He wasn't quite that prosperous as yet, but he still wanted to buy the yalı somehow, even if it meant borrowing from his wife's family.

Ali Mukbil Özüpek came to the rescue. Buoyed up by that promise to help out, the surgeon who had reverted to his childhood name went to the estate agent's office to meet the proprietor. He expected a distasteful negotiation with some boor oblivious to the value of the past; the dairyman who'd tricked his father must have long since have sold the yalı. The proprietor, however, turned out to be the dairyman's daughter Bedia, the love of his six-year-old self. Yaşar recognised her at once, the intervening years notwithstanding; those huge brown eyes were as alluring as ever.

But Bedia genuinely didn't remember him. Not for her to be ashamed of the past as the daughter of a dairyman; self-confident enough to never stoop to re-writing her past, or feel self-conscious about her humble origins, even if she didn't necessarily need to bang on about it. She certainly would have chatted about those days if she had remembered. But her own life was shambolic, having fallen for her stepson Erdem

Bakırcıoğlu; all she wanted was to sell the yalı as soon as possible, share the proceeds with her sisters, and sort her own life out.

Starting at the ground and making excuses for the yalı's run-down state, she gave him a tour. They'd finished the first floor when she pointed to the narrow staircase leading to the attic, said, *There's another room upstairs. A bit small, but you feel like you're on the deck of a ship when you look out the window,* and something broke inside Yaşar. That was where he used to play ships as a child. Whenever he went up there to stare at the sea, he'd imagine himself as the captain of an enormous transatlantic liner he'd seen in the papers, talking to himself and raining commands at a non-existent crew.

They mounted the stairs together. As he watched the eddying waters of the Bosphorus, Yeshua Mustaki felt his heart bleed. He no longer wanted the yalı; it was time to let go of the past. Turning a deaf ear to intimations that the sellers would be open to offers, he said, *It's not quite what I had in mind.* He wasn't lying; the past was nothing like what he'd had in mind.

So he lived in the rented Bebek flat with his suddenly happy wife and two children until he bought four flats off plan in the Refet Block in Nişantaşı when his daughter started school. They moved into number seven as soon as construction was finished.

Later, he lost his wife quite unexpectedly in number seven where he lived throughout the brightest years of his professional career. With a new lease of life since their move to Istanbul, Ida went visiting seven days of the week, put on a huge amount of weight and developed diabetes, but refused to moderate her food intake. She was especially fond of sweets. Whenever she saw gipsies with baskets full of pink rose petals or peeling jam figs at the Peony Street crossroads, she'd ignore her own *Not buying any!* And buy them she did, to hand over to a gifted housekeeper who made jams out of not only rose petal and fig, but also sour cherry, strawberry and apricot, and orange marmalade too; Ida then hid the jars from her husband in her cousin's flat upstairs so he wouldn't object. Yaşar thought she had reduced her breakfast to a frugal meal since her diagnosis. The moment he left for work, though, and ignoring her high blood sugar, Ida would sit down to a second and very rich breakfast together with her neighbours, a table she would only rise from once she'd put away an entire jar of jam before nibbling on sweets and cakes the rest of the day.

One day when Yaşar was abroad, she ate so many desserts and chocolate that she went into a hyperglycaemic coma. She didn't survive. This was before the invention of mobile phones; Yaşar couldn't be reached in Milan where he was attending a neurosurgery congress. He and a few friends had skived off from that day's session, hired a car and gone to Siena where they wandered in a daze, giddy with the beauty of the city. Devastated by the news of his wife's death that awaited him at the hotel, he struggled with a sense of guilt for a long time. Just as he'd finally pulled himself together, and managed to get over her death, he had a stroke that paralysed him. The flat that had been the background to so many happy years of his life both professionally and personally was where he died in silence, all alone, as Rufa was playing solitaire on the dining table.

Ali Mukbil Özüpek had been instrumental in bringing Yaşar to Istanbul and thereby enriching Turkey's medical community; he died long before his colleague, well before his dreams were vindicated by the high standards of the hospital, and without having finished the translation of *Buried Alive*: he died of a sudden heart attack in the most productive period of his life. It might have appeared enviable, but he had never found happiness.

Soon after his death, his wife sold that extensive library to the extreme leftie **secondhand book dealer Dev-Yol Oğuz**. Without the slightest idea of the value of this treasure lovingly accumulated shelf by shelf over the years, she asked for a ridiculously low figure. The books were boxed and taken away within the hour, and she had that lovely bookcase taken apart and burnt in the boiler room.

Unable to decide whether Ali Mukbil had been a petty bourgeois or a big one, Oğuz had entered the deceased's home in his usual, profound class enmity; but spotting *Das Kapital* by Karl Marx – and an original gothic-type German edition at that – on the first shelf he'd reached out to, he bought the lot without an attempt at haggling, loaded it all into the car, and took it over to the former coal depot he'd recently rented as warehouse.

Oğuz kept his dangerous leftist literature at home. He was looking forward to sorting through Ali Mukbil's books when the police raided and found all his hidden banned books. He was sent to Metris where he would languish for many years, charged under the notorious Articles

141–142 to the tune of *Membership of an illegal association… Overthrowing the constitutional order by means of violence…* every word of which struck fear in the hearts of the public at the time. Many years later, kidneys wrecked as a consequence of a hunger strike, and a leg useless as a result of torture, he hobbled out of prison with a walking stick to find nothing in the place of the shop he'd left fully stocked.

Ironmonger Kadri, the owner of the warehouse, got into a proper flap at news of the arrest of Oğuz as a communist. He'd had no idea Oğuz was a commie, and he didn't know what the warehouse contained. He ran over straightaway, and nearly jumped out of his skin when he saw the books; they'd cause him no end of trouble if they were found. He had to destroy them at once. There was no time to carry it all home or the office to burn them in the stove. He was deadly scared that the police would make Oğuz talk, learn about the warehouse and raid it, and he'd get into trouble. Heart thumping in his chest and pretending he was having a clear out, he scuttled to fill a large kerosene barrel with loads of battered furniture along with Mukbil's exquisite first editions and signed copies mostly in Turkish but some in English, German and Farsi.

Except that surprising last batch made him stop. Ignorant of the existence of a language called Farsi, Kadri thought they were Islamic texts in Arabic, his knowledge of such matters being even less than rudimentary. Well, if they were in Arabic, they couldn't have anything to do with communism. He set aside a few picked at random, considering them not to be dangerous. He'd have saved them all, but was scared of attracting attention if he was to carry a whole heap of books. After dithering for quite a while he finally chucked into the barrel those splendid books in Farsi, including a translation of Nâzım Hikmet's *Human Landscapes from my Homeland*, thereby burning to a cinder the greatest masterpiece of that luminary who'd served his nation for years.

Those were the dark years, marked by political violence raging through the streets and oppressive martial law. Hands shaking, terrified that the smoke rising in a silent elegy would attract attention, Kadri poured in the kerosene and struck a match with a *besmele*. Thank God it was winter; no one would notice burning books in the impenetrable smoke of the cheapest coal that the poor could afford.

He brought only five books in Farsi back to his ironmongery: two Sadegh Hedayats, one Omar Khayyam, and a couple of nondescript volumes. They were small and thin, easily put into a pocket. Even if the police was to stop him and find them, he could easily explain they had nothing to do with communism, being written in Arabic.

The books did the rounds and ended up with **the unlicensed second-hand dealer Gürbüz** who had a book stall behind Rize's Central Mosque. There did *Zinde Be-gūr* languish until espied on a day trip by literature teacher Zarife Gülercan.

At one end, the stall was stocked with light romances, old police thrillers, dated magazines on architecture, art, travel and women's fashions, chick lit, old photo plays, graphic novels and similar publications, then continued with once popular world classics such as *The Charterhouse of Parma*, *Wuthering Heights* and *Jane Eyre*, old editions of novels by Hüseyin Rahmi and Reşat Nuri for instance, literary magazines, bog standard stories published a few years earlier to no great acclaim, pointless books by small publishers who'd started out with huge aspirations and gone bust within a few months, long sellers by such popular poets as Nâzım Hikmet and Orhan Veli, and books on politics, history, research and biography; the array ended with religious books bearing the obligatory gilt lettering on the covers.

After a lengthy inspection, Miss Zarife picked up *Three Istanbuls* by Mithat Cemal Kuntay, *The Master and Margarita* by Mikhail Bulgakov, *Murder in Yolpalas* by Halide Edip Adıvar and *A Portrait of the Artist as a Young Man* by James Joyce, and eventually reached the stack of religious books. She was about to pass on when she espied *Zinde Be-gūr* that stood out by being so plain, unadorned with any gilding. She made out the word *Zinde*. With a bit more effort, she deciphered the rest and read Sadegh Hedayat's name. It was an Iranian writer she had heard of, and she wanted to read the whole book once she'd flicked through it. She had been such a fan of the Dawn of the Future movement at university! Her old passion for learning Farsi resurfaced, she pillaged through the bookcase and found her Farsi-English dictionary the moment she got back.

Unable to find a good Farsi-Turkish dictionary when she'd first taken up the language, Miss Zarife had bitten the bullet and ordered an English one instead from abroad at great expense, a volume that weighed a ton and ended up helping more with her English than her Farsi. Now she took down the hefty dictionary from the shelf where it had been gathering dust, opened the Sadegh Hedayat, and started studying again. She carried on for a few months before slacking, and ultimately abandoning it altogether. Just when she was about to resume, she heard of her son's death. Miss Zarife's scary attacks of laughter and inappropriate language emerged soon after, and eventually sent her to the Mental Health Hospital several times, when at long last, she was sent for a brain scan over the objections of her doctor Âlim Kâhkeci. That same doctor now stood baffled, holding the tomography report: here he was, ready to recommend disqualifying stumpy Neuropsychiatrist Nebahat, and she had been right all along. He reached for the phone.

The Medical Director was stomping towards his car, disgruntled at the Mayor's reluctance to offer support for his book when his mobile rang. It was Dr Âlim Kâhkeci: Miss Zarife's scan had arrived just now, and Nebahat and he had studied it. There was a brain tumour. It was in an extremely critical place, pressing on a group of nerves, thereby causing unpredictable fluctuations in the patient's mental state, and since her brain was incapable of suppressing her words, Miss Zarife was kicking up an almighty storm, brandishing insults like *Whore* and *Pervert* to all and sundry, and effing and blinding at the maid when she was five minutes late with the tea.

The news sent the Medical Director straight to his Zarife Abla's home where he found her reading *Zinde Be-gūr* at the top of her voice, her love of Farsi having recurred with a vengeance. He was joined soon after by Âlim Kâhkeci and Nebahat, who was on cloud nine since her instant diagnosis *This is the work of a brain tumour, Âlim Bey. Best get a brain scan straightaway,* had been vindicated. The three doctors held a consultation then and there, concurred on the need for surgery and recommended that her husband take her to a neurosurgeon.

Zeki would happily sacrifice what few properties they owned for his wife's health, and no longer needed since the death of their son. He wanted the very best brain surgeon, and would have taken her abroad if need be. He'd lost half of his heart with the death of his son; he couldn't live if he were to lose the other half. He asked Medical Director for the best name in the field.

The Medical Director rang long-lost colleagues for recommendations. The answer was nearly unanimous: **the bright and young Brain Surgeon Kerem Savul**. Not content with what he'd heard, Zeki conducted his own search, found Kerem Savul's website and studied it. The Hacettepe-qualified doctor's biography was convincing; he'd even won several awards and the list of his papers ran to several pages. Except he still looked a little too young to be convincing. The Medical Director explained that youth was an advantage in surgery. Younger doctors were far more energetic than their older colleagues, and pursued further professional development abroad. At any rate, technology had developed to such an extent that it was equipment and not experience that mattered in the operating theatre; the hands just took the credit. Zeki was finally convinced, and took his wife (still clutching her *Zinde Be-gür*) to Istanbul, to the hospital where Kerem Savul worked.

Noticing the proximity of the tumour to the right eye socket, the young professor sought a second opinion from Ophthalmologist Berkay Özberk. They were studying the scans together when the woman – who'd been quite compos mentis for a while – was racked with a new laughter attack. Doubled up, guffawing and uttering vulgarities along the lines of *Why'dya got your bonces shaved? Can't pull sluts with your bald heads?* she slapped the two doctors on their glistening pates. Berkay promptly stormed out with a brusque *I can't help you here. You carry on, we'll talk later.*

Kerem took Zeki into another room to explain that the only person who'd have dared to open Miss Zarife's brain in Turkey was Yaşar Mustaki; sadly this renowned surgeon was no longer alive. In a bizzare twist of fate, he'd succumbed to high blood pressure and been paralysed following a stroke. Worried when the famous doctor's door stayed shut during his morning round, and spotting the car still hadn't moved by noon, concierge Mevlüt had informed the surgeon's friend Sevinç. They opened the door using her spare key; found him in the bedroom, face down, one side paralysed, and had him taken to hospital.

Yaşar's two children came over from America straightaway. His condition was serious and it was too late for an operation. The celebrated surgeon stayed in reanimation at the American Hospital for three months. Despite several private health care plans, treatment was enormously expensive; at any rate, there was little point in keeping him in hospital since recovery seemed improbable.

The son had to get back to work in New York, so he only stayed for a fortnight. It fell on **Yaşar's daughter Sarah Steinberg**, who lived in Chicago, to manage her father's care. She converted one room into an intensive care unit, engaged a professional nurse and a carer, and stayed long enough to make sure that he was being looked after well. She would have stayed longer. She'd been missing Istanbul; she'd looked up school friends from Şişli Terakki, and they had a great time catching up and going out. But then her husband – a German Jew, as it happens – broke a leg in a traffic accident, and she had to go back.

Sarah had been planning on returning to stay with her father as soon as she'd sorted things out in Chicago; it would've been nice to open up a second window on life in Istanbul. But something always came up. First they bought a new house; it needed so many bits and bobs that it took ages before they could move in. Just as she was about to come, her elder daughter went into a depression following a miscarriage, so Sarah had to stay with her. The daughter got better; but fed up with all this unforeseen expense, Sarah thought she'd wait for a cheap ticket… and then was devastated to learn that **her younger daughter Daisy** (a Turkology undergraduate who translated short stories for bilingual magazines and *Turkamerican*) was on drugs. Daisy went into a clinic in Fresno, where Sarah stayed throughout her daughter's rehab. *I'll go once I've sorted this*, she thought, or *I'll go once I've sorted that…* And a long time went by. For four years, she just couldn't travel to Istanbul; all she could do was to monitor her father's progress by phone.

When Mevlüt ran up to the flat at Rufa's scream, he knew Yaşar Mustaki was dead. It had been expected for quite a while, so he didn't panic. First he rang Yaşar's doctor in the American Hospital, and then Miss Sarah.

As queen of drama Rufa rang the employment agency to inform them in floods of tears, Mevlüt was casing the joint. Yaşar's flat was dripping with valuable paintings and antiques, and the concierge was trying to reckon what he could get from Ömer Çakır for all this stuff. He was sure that Miss Sarah would give him most of the furniture when she came to bury her father, like many of the Refet Bey Block children before her.

They would usually pick a few valuable items and leave the rest for Mevlüt to dispose of, being uninterested in the effects of their dead parents. And he'd got used to lining his pockets by flogging the lot to Ömer.

He was tempted to carry off the silver menorah or, say, the carriage clock with the Hebrew numerals as he watched Rufa pack, swearing at her shitty fate in English all the while; did he really need to wait for Miss Sarah? But he'd done well to resist the devil's temptation. Because Sarah Steinberg (who had placed a quarter page obituary in the *Hürriyet*, thereby ensuring the attendance of all friends and family in the country and abroad, as well as her father's students and even some of his patients) knew everything in the flat, down to the last salt shaker and shoe horn. Having planned it all as soon as she'd arrived four years ago, she had agreed on a sum with **Mesut Hürel, the antique dealer who had moved his shop from Horhor to Nişantaşı a few months earlier and thus become a rival to Haymon Yener.** And for a sum that would have blown Mevlüt's mind.

Mevlüt was on his way back from the bank where he'd paid an elderly resident's telephone bill when he saw Miss Sarah and a man stood next to a brand new lorry at the door, gesticulating at the porters as she supervised the removal of her father's furniture. It hit him like a bucket of cold water. She'd sold the lot without leaving a single pin.

His intended accomplice Ömer Çakır turned up just then. Mevlüt had counted his chickens before they'd hatched; and now the junk dealer's innards melted when he saw the furniture being loaded into the lorry. Dying to ask how much she'd sold it for, and even perhaps find a suitable opportunity to make an offer, he wanted a word with Sarah.

He didn't get the chance. An altercation flared up when the block manager Tijen tried to scold the antiques dealer for parking his Mercedes, *As if the lorry wasn't bad enough!* Denied a parking spot outside the door once again, she was piping up in a nerve-janglingly reedy voice quite unexpected from one her size *You will move your car, Sir, I live in this block, it's my right to park in this spot. Go park your car somewhere else!* pointing to the pavement. Biting his tongue out of courtesy to his customer, Mesut Hürel said he'd be gone in half an hour; but at Tijen's grumbled *Well! And now we have to bow and scrape to a junk dealer!* he went puce, strode up and roared, *Who the fuck are you calling a junk dealer? I'll show you and your army who's who!* the arteries in his neck pulsing and lips frothing. Bottling out at this sudden fury, Tijen didn't dare answer back; instead, she carried on whingeing almost inaudibly as she got into her car to look for somewhere else to park. Mevlüt revelled at the sight of the parking spot monitor cut down to size when Ömer, daunted by the prospect of approaching Sarah, took it out on him instead with *Fucked up my day, haven't you! Why bite more than you bloody well can chew, eh?*

Untroubled by the concierge's disappointment, Sarah said she'd engaged an estate agent to rent the flat and asked for return of the key Mevlüt had acquired after the death of Sevinç. Now really pissed off (he wasn't even going to benefit from renting the flat) he flung it in her face. He was cross, he was angry. He'd been at their beck and call all these years, and even stood watch by the paralysed man. And this was his reward, was it?

On the day she was to leave her father's home for the last time, Sarah asked him to hail a taxi, as if she hadn't even noticed his grudge. Sticking his head out of the door he barely opened a crack, Mevlüt yelled, *I'm busy, can't get you no taxi or nothing!* and shut the door without so much as a goodbye for the woman who had the cheek to still expect service.

As Sarah shut the door behind her, hailed a cab, loaded the menorah, a few paintings as mementoes of her father and a few other valuable bits and bobs, and set off for the airport, the young painter Yalın Tağmaç was studying the stencil papers with Şekip Sami's exterior coating formulae, placing them next to a fox cuff – a relic from his grandmother – and planning his new piece of work.

This would turn out to be his girlfriend Ebru's favourite piece, created in the fabulous studio with the glazed roof in the attic: a collage of scraps of fur snipped from the cuff and Şekip Sami's sheets. Yalın's ostensible objective might have been the *Debatable relationship between the whole and the part*, but the only really debatable thing was the relationship between the work and the sentence. Its point remained elusive although viewers examined it as if they actually got the point, or even found it ingenious; in contrast, his drawings in natural dyes were really beautiful. This piece unimaginatively entitled *Relativity* was placed at the centre of the young artist's first exhibition along with Şekip Sami's coating formulae.

He knew nothing about the fine arts scene in his homeland. He had no idea that whilst his fellow artists might not have attained the level of proficiency to compete with their European counterparts, they were certainly on par with anyone on the planet when it came to pontificating, which meant that his titles – *Relativity* being top of the list that included *Ying-Yang* [*sic*] or *Quantums End* [again, *sic*] – were met with universal derision. Not that he would care if he knew, such was the measure of his arrogance.

 Green with envy, however, younger fellow artists soon backpedalled, and bent over backwards to make friends. The doyens of the art world recognised Yalın's dual distinction: belonging to a well-known, good family and being nominated as a *Promising Young Talent* in a major event in Italy. He was therefore welcomed with open arms as this unanimous blessing by the arts canon sparked several articles and interviews in the press, and all before much of his work had been seen by anyone.

This fascination owed as much to the splendid family tree of the young man of superior taste as it did to his highly photogenic, handsome features. Strictly speaking, he wasn't a total piss artist; he did possess an original style and a noteworthy concept of art. That being said, he appreciated that neither illustrious forebears nor artistic accomplishments (a living member of the Ottoman dynasty? A postmodern Leonardo?) would have secured magazine covers if he'd been a grotesque horror, so he took great pains to look after that main asset: his face.

No more than a handful of the old crowd were around when he had returned from Florence; a crestfallen Yalın had drifted idly for some time. Then he was invited to a barbecue party at a mate's terrace that commanded a breathtaking view of the Bosphorus spread under their feet and met Ebru; they hooked up straightaway and she dragged him out of his despondency. That wasn't all. She lost no time in introducing her boyfriend into the arts environment into which she herself had charmed her way whilst still a student. It was she who took those stunning portraits that would launch his face into the focus of attention. Whoever saw a Yalın Tağmaç portrait *by Ebru Başusta* (signed in English) wanted to know *Who's the kid?* All Ebru had to do was to polish his God-given sex appeal, his innate capacity to invite deep feminine adoration.

His reputation confounded envious fellow artists in view of the lack of any significant work to speak of, and predated his first exhibition at Besim Varlık's gallery that turned out to be such a grand affair. An elite throng of curators, critics, art correspondents, gallery owners, collectors and journalists filled the hall. Judging by the way they pranced around holding red wine balloons, bursting with pride, his divorced parents Sevda and **Erel Tağmaç** (who'd never fail in their duty to their son on such occasions) could have easily been mistaken for the parents of Andy Warhol – and not a young artist who'd opened his first exhibition. They were both accompanied by their present co-habiting partners: mother, father, mother's boyfriend and father's girlfriend flaunted this civilised foursome, peals of laughter punctuating that merry chatter as they fell over one another to compliment Yalın's freckled girlfriend Ebru.

A diplomat was amongst the sizeable foreign contingent of art lovers there: Emil Pavulescu, Romanian Chargé d'Affairs and occasional (whenever she found the opportunity, that is) lover of Veda Alkan – political expert and mother to Barış Bakış, the angelic-looking inmate at the Mental Health Hospital. The Chargé d'Affairs was scheduled to return to Ankara the next day, having attended a meeting at the Istanbul Romanian Culture Centre named after the Ottoman historian Moldovan Prince Dimitrie Cantemir. The topic being a joint exhibition project intended to engender a bilateral cultural exchange, several gallery owners had also been invited, which is how Besim and Pavulescu had come to be introduced. Besim had then mentioned the young talent Yalın Tağmaç, whose inaugural exhibition he was honoured to host, and invited the Romanian to the opening.

Pavulescu had actually made other plans of a more romantic nature as was his habit each time he visited Istanbul, involving dinner at the Yutaka Japanese restaurant before proceeding up to his room in the Divan Hotel, accompanied by an attractive female companion whose identity had so far eluded Foreign Affairs. He would catch the early morning flight after a long night of passion. But his hopes had been dashed to the ground. The attractive lady had been forced to make her apologies on the phone and postpone their rendezvous to some indeterminate time in the future as her husband had quite unexpectedly cut short his trip abroad.

Ankara was rife with rumours concerning this attractive lady, rumours that Pavulescu knew how to leverage. The diplomatic community speculated on the her identity whenever the two of them appeared at unofficial occasions hosted by Istanbul's glitterati. If anything, there was a split. Some, who'd failed to spot this legendary beauty in Istanbul, claimed no such lady existed, adding that it begged the question why the most indisputably charismatic and handsome diplomat in Ankara's ambassadorial universe saw the need to invent such an imaginary figure. Others had seen Emil Pavulescu dining with an attractive lady at the Yutaka, and even stepping into the Divan Hotel lift together. They were sure she was real, and were dying to know who on earth she might be.

Although the charismatic and handsome diplomat did all he could to stoke this *legend of the mysterious lady*, the reality was far less intriguing. The lady in question was none other than **the former beauty queen Harika, who'd landed a rich husband** and retired from modelling and public life upon reaching a certain age. She was a truly stunning woman aptly named *Wonderful*; but since she came from a lower class family, and hadn't been that successful at modelling either, she'd failed to bag a top-level industrialist to ensure entry into Istanbul society. Instead, she'd married **the coarse mafioso Arslan Özyılmazel** whose line of business involved dark deeds in his casinos in Romania and Cyprus, and who was vulgar enough to scatter handfuls of dollars over the singers at his own wedding.

Diplomatic immunity protected Emil Pavulescu from all manner of peril, including the husband who never went anywhere without his Smith & Wesson and a double magazine at his belt; but the reason Harika cancelled their date was not her husband's untimely return. The former beauty queen just didn't want to see him. Hubby was still in Kiev, busy spilling the brains of some arsehole who'd tried to double-cross him; what his wife was doing with anyone was the last thing on his mind.

Harika knew her husband would stay in Kiev for a little longer; she just wanted to do dump Emil. She'd had enough of him anyway, what with all this struggling to communicate in her scant English, and they'd been playing stoppages for a while now. The diplomat had served his purpose, opened doors and introduced Arslan to many Romanians in critical positions of authority. Any more, and it was just a chore for her.

When Emil Pavulescu had rung to say he was in Istanbul and wanted to meet, Harika (who'd learnt at a very young age that you never said *No* to a man straight off and that feminine wiles meant you waited for the opportunity to bend men to your will) had accepted knowing full well she wasn't going. When she rang him the next day to apologise, she was picking some silk pyjamas for a jolly pyjama party thrown by one of her former model friends who'd founded a casting agency targeting TV soaps and adverts.

Caught on the hop, Pavulescu had decided to go to the opening instead of idling the night away. As he idly chatted up the artist's over-the-hill mother Sevda Okutan, he inspected the works on display, which he liked a great deal. He purchased three pieces, including *Relativity*, which he shipped to **his daughter Steliana Pavulescu, a fine arts student in Bucharest**, who would turn nineteen the following week. He took the other two pieces to Ankara.

Veda Alkan, who was in the capital for a fortnight just then, intended to make use of this opportunity to visit her son in hospital. It had been a long time since she'd last seen him, and she'd been missing him very much indeed. This visit would serve them both for a couple of months. In fact, she might even butter up the Medical Director, bend him to her will and keep Barış in hospital for another three months at least.

She'd take him the pyjamas dotted with ladybirds, and flannel-lined slippers purchased in an exquisitely chic and very expensive boutique in Brussels at one of those moments when the maternal instinct mingled with a guilty conscience and gave her a faint heartache; she'd sit close to Barış in the Medical Director's office, kiss his silky cheeks, and even – if his doctor allowed it – take him out for a fish meal in the Sultan Restaurant at the Diamond Hotel. She'd planned to set aside a whole afternoon to her only son. This would constitute a serious sacrifice for a terrifically busy political expert like Veda Alkan, so she had to use her time well. Just as she was about to make a booking to fly Saturday morning, returning in the evening, her mobile phone trilled with a few bars of *La Traviata* sung by the acclaimed Romanian soprano Leontina Vaduva; the caller had to be her sweetheart Emil. She answered eagerly. At his syrupy voice, all thoughts of the son who'd been in hospital for months flew from her mind.

She'd just come out of the shower; wearing nothing but a bathrobe, and she stretched out on the sofa and chatted, reproaching her sweetheart: he hadn't called for a whole month…

As Emil explained how much he'd been missing her, an account liberally sprinkled with subtle double entendres, Veda (who recognised this talk of emotion-cum-lust as nothing but a pack of lies) was applying body moisturiser, painfully aware that although she was still as attractive as ever, she wasn't getting any younger, and spur-of-the-moment nights of sex were getting few and far between. Of course she'd heard the legend of the mysterious beauty. But she had no intention of creating a scene and so lose one of the few lovers she had left. She put the phone down, the planned visit to her son postponed to her next trip home.

Sweetheart Emil rang the doorbell with a Yalın Tağmaç under his arm, by which time an impatient Veda had changed into a silk blouse in old rose revealing more of that bronzed décolleté than warranted, opened a vintage chianti and lit candles in anticipation.

She looked wonderfully attractive in the soft candlelight that blurred her age. Nibbling on Roquefort and sipping wine, they chatted for a while. Emil Pavulescu mentioned the slivers of fox fur and sheets covered with chemical formulae on the piece he'd sent his daughter; Steliana had rung up to say how much she'd loved her present. He was hoping Veda would also like this piece entitled *Quantums End*. They moved into the bedroom, lightly sozzled, as Veda seethed at the thought of having to hang up this moronic hodgepodge of an eyesore.

Thanks to a young artist, the drafts of Şekip Sami's final project survived in the room of a young woman in Bucharest, albeit in a form light years away from their original purpose. At least the undiscovered chemistry genius had left behind some trace of his existence, which was more than can be said for his sister Zeynep İkbal, who was killed in an accident on the way to Yalova.

Emrullah wanted his youngest grandchild to become a doctor, visualising his favourite with a stethoscope on her neck, hair falling down in long waves onto the shoulders of her white coat. Not that he failed to recognise this as anything other than an impossible dream. Zeynep had absolutely no intention of taking up such an arduous field of study or seeking approbation for her accomplishments. A habitual truant gadding about here and there, she got it on with with **Suphi Karakurt**, who was eight years her senior.

Determined to drop out and get married, she'd tried to see how the wind blew, but never got beyond *Medical school's s'posed to be really hard…* before her grandfather let rip. Stern of disposition he might have been, yet the old man rarely lost his temper. On this occasion, he gave her a serious talking to. He had long since suspected her of being a frivolous airhead, at any rate.

He wouldn't budge, she realised, and avoided the topic again. She just didn't come home one day. Rukiye, the capable housekeeper Emrullah trusted more than even himself, knew how to handle the grumpy old man. She also loved (and pitied) the poor girl abandoned at two by that bitch Nihan, and took it upon herself to cover up for Zeynep's misdemeanours. She knew Emrullah had problems with his granddaughter (whose course wasn't that promising if truth be told); but terrified at the prospect of his rage, she bottled out of telling him Zeynep hadn't come back yet.

Emrullah sat down to dinner, noticed the granddaughter's absence and immediately asked where she was. As if she hadn't heard, Rukiye started explaining how she'd just cooked the kale wraps and how delicious the buffalo yogurt she'd bought at the market was, hoping to string him along in the hope that the servants would soon locate and fetch the girl.

But Emrullah knew his housekeeper of many years very well; realising she was trying to duck the issue, he roared, *Rukiye, answer my question: where is Zeynep?* furiously enough to nearly crack the fine cut glass on the table. Rukiye froze, stumped before this violent rage. Just then the doorbell rang. Emboldened by years of service in the mansion, her consequent authority and her self-appointed right to stand up to her boss she'd give her life for, she grumbled on her way to the door, *Will'ya stop your shouting, eh, here she is!* But it wasn't. It was a well-dressed gentleman in his forties.

İbrahim, an uncle to the Karakurt family by marriage, had been sent as an envoy to announce that Zeynep had run away to **Suphi Karakurt**. The family were ready to embrace Zeynep as their daughter-in-law, he added extremely politely in well-rehearsed stock phrases applicable in such circumstances. Of course the Karakurt family would have preferred to ask for

Zeynep's hand by the command of Allah and the consent of the Prophet. But the young couple had fallen in love and thought Emrullah *might have withheld his blessings to this marriage out of some inadequately explicit concerns*; so instead of going through the customary channels, had taken such an ill-considered course. But since the damage was done, it now fell upon the families to keep it secret from all and sundry, forgive the young couple for their ill-considered action and allow them to marry in accordance with custom. The Karakurt family were ready to bring Zeynep back to her grandfather's home in preparation for a grand wedding, bla bla bla.

Envoy İbrahim (a columnist in the local *Coast* newspaper published at the time) concluded his speech and offered a small present. **Suphi's father MP Mustafa Nadir Karakurt** had sent the tobacco merchant a bespoke shisha from Aleppo; it was his humbling honour to present this gift in the hope that it might be acceptable. But before the Karakurt family spokesman had a chance to present the gift, Emrullah had a stroke. His right hand turned into an empty sack and he tumbled down from his chair.

Her suspicions raised by the silence of the old man, Rukiye was already waiting on tenterhooks: the Emrullah she knew would never have let this vapid speech carry on. He'd have flung something at the head of the envoy and told him to fuck off. She dashed forward and prevented him from banging his head, but the poor man's right hand side was paralysed. At recognising the name of Zeynep's intended as the good-for-nothing son of an MP from a conservative party whose politics he detested, a vein had split in Emrullah's brain and left him at death's door. The pricipled tobacco magnate was hospitalised in a hurry.

The story did the rounds at once. The paralysis announced to the entire city that the precious granddaughter of the tobacco merchant had eloped with the MP's son. The Karakurt servants had blabbed before Zeynep had a chance to return to her grandfather's home.

Türkan gathered Ankara's leading professors, rushed over to her father's side and took his care into her own hands. She also sent word of her reproach to her niece. As if having caused Emrullah's paralysis weren't bad enough, Zeynep was continuing to live, still unmarried, at the parvenu mansion of the Karakurt family. The only effect that this rebuke had on Zeynep, however, was a couple of days of enraged bawling.

She hated her grandfather she blamed for causing her mother to run away, and she was madly in love with Suphi besides. Thank God the old man recovered soon. He had a strong constitution and was nothing if not strongminded; he came round within a month, although his right arm was left permanently paralysed.

İmdat Hızır might have made the wrong sort of friends, never finished his education and ruined his own life with that unfortunate marriage; but at least he'd never disgraced his father. His charge Zeynep, on the other hand, broke the tobacco merchant's heart. That his precious grand-daughter might elope had never even crossed his mind. He was forced to consent to the marriage to save face.

Suphi's parents waited for Emrullah to get back to his feet and organ-ised a wedding sufficiently grand to restore the reputations of both parties. Despite the MP's conservative credentials, the alcohol flowed like water in the open-air wedding where Türkan put up a brave face and a silently stewing Emrullah reluctantly tried to make friends with the hypocritical MP now that they were related. He presented the loathsome groom with a valuable watch and Zeynep with a family heirloom: an antique necklace of teardrop emeralds sparkling on the fair skin dewy with the freshness of her seventeen years dazzled even from a distance. Still a chemistry undergraduate in Istanbul at the time, her brother Şekip Sami had refused to attend, being violently opposed to this match (his sister *should have gone through the proper channels instead of eloping*) and worse: he was outraged that Zeynep wasn't being disowned.

But an unfortunate event occurred at the wedding attended by the entire contingent of the city's dignitaries and even the father-in-law's fellow MPs who'd come all the way from Ankara. The MP and his rela-tions all loosed off an entire magazine of bullets one at a time, and feeling he had to match them as a Black Sea lad himself, Emrullah drew out his handgun too. His right arm being out of action, however, he tried to shoot into the air with his left, and hit **Saadet, the spinster maid** (who was offering ice-cold cherry juice) in the shoulder, thereby bringing the wedding party to an early close.

What really devastated Emrullah wasn't the fact that Zeynep had eloped. He was prepared to grin and bear it and put up with that disgace,

She's young… and a double orphan too… a foolish mistake, after all. But she accused him of ruining her wedding. Without even a glance at Saadet – who'd flipped at the sight of blood and was busy convulsing on the groung with screams of, *I'm deaaad! I'm deaaad!* – Zeynep had rounded on her grandfather and yelled, *Like you'd die if you didn't come to the wedding! Senile bugger!* in front of all the VIPs present. Emrullah cursed Allah for not taking his life then and there.

Grandfather and granddaughter never spoke after the wedding. No matter how much Türkan agreed with her father, she wanted him to forgive Zeynep lest the family would scatter altogether: they were down to four now, at any rate. But it was in vain. The tobacco merchant stood his ground. He didn't cut Zeynep off his will, but he never wanted to see her again. He withdrew from life. Handing over the management of his endless tobacco plantations and countless other properties to his stewards, and the auditing of the accounts to his daughter Türkan, he locked himself up in the Kaymakoğlu Mansion. There he would live for many years, frustrating Zeynep's curses and groaning under the burden of the arm which rose of its own accord whenever he yawned.

The old man was tearing his heart out. He wanted to see the baby who might really have been premature as was announced (had Zeynep fallen pregnant before the wedding?) Türkan swallowed her pride and contacted the niece who'd made no effort to be forgiven. Zeynep had moved to Ankara by then; Türkan sent word through Zeynep's in-laws: they expected her to visit her grandfather and bring the baby too. *I want nothing to do with the Kaymakoğlu family!* came the unbelievable response. Türkan didn't have the heart to repeat it to her father. Instead, she gently steered him away, *Why would you want to see the child of the granddaughter who doesn't even see you as her grandfather now?*

The groom's father Mustafa Nadir Karakurt was serving his third term as MP, and had even briefly held a Cabinet post. Casual as he was about his parliamentary commitments, he still lived mostly in Ankara, visiting his hometown occasionally just to keep his constituents sweet. Since he wanted his son and daughter-in-law to live nearby, he bought the top floor of a block of flats built by the Niğde-born contractor Abdülkadir Çemiş, furnished it and moved the newlyweds there. That's how Zeynep became an Ankaran and erased her family from memory. Instead of introducing herself as ... *granddaughter of the tobacco merchant Emrullah Kaymakoğlu,* she boasted of a Cabinet post now well in the past with ... *daughter-in-law of the former Minister of State Mustafa Nadir Karakurt.*

Handsome groom Suphi, the minister's only son, had finished the Faculty of Political Sciences, but never mended his ways. The perks of a cushy job at the Ministry of Culture and Tourism (that his dad had got him) included countless information gathering trips abroad where he set anchor at the gaming table. To be fair, though, he took a break from these exciting trips so he could be with his pregnant wife, the girl he'd met on an annual holiday in his hometown and married in haste.

Whilst still in their honeymoon glow, he promised to get her anyone she wanted as a maid, so Zeynep asked for Saadet in order to spite her grandfather, who, in his lasting regret for having accidentally wounding the spinster, had showered her with money.

So Saadet settled in a few months before the birth of **Nadir, the son Zeynep would name after her father-in-law** who clearly wasn't gonna die any time soon (and not her dead father İmdat Hızır). The poor old maid of a maid with marriage on the brain proved to be all right, except she refused outright to wash the floor-to-ceiling windows on the outside for fear of heights. When Zeynep was closer to her time, Suphi gave Saadet strict instructions to ring him the moment contractions started and stuck a piece of paper with his office number onto the telephone.

Idling on her bed one day, Zeynep fancied some bananas. She called out to Saadet (who was elbow deep in suds as she did the dishes, 24-hour running hot water being one of the perks of the flat) *Tell that greengrocer opposite to bring us bananas.*

Saadet was badly smitten by the **sweet-talking greengrocer Bahattin with the black moustache**; he always carried their bags all the way to the lift, and had said (when they had a brief chat) his wife had died last year of TB. He was actually ugly and spoke in a whistle through a missing front tooth. But he was cheerful, had a ready smile, was tall, had his own house, and more importantly, had no children. Saadet knew she was an old maid, and as none of the nice friends of Suphi Bey were likely to become her *kismet,* she was keeping an open mind; no prospect was too lowly for her

So far there'd been no chance of a date with the greengrocer, thanks to Zeynep Hanım's caprices, but he did respond to every flirty gesture with a roguish smile, which gave Saadet hope that she might pull him in a few months; she was already dreaming of their wedding day.

So she went out onto the balcony. She'd have shouted out *Bahattin! Bring us a bunch'o bananas if it's no trouble!* but her darling black moustaches was chatting with **Müjgân, the brazen daughter of the concierge**. Pockmarked Müjgân's only claim to beauty was her gloriously thick, long hair swishing against her hips. Whenever their paths crossed in the greengrocery, she'd make Saadet feel they were rivals, simpering as if to say *Bahattin's mine, don't you dare!* The way she touched his arm and giggled all the time got Saadet's back up; but the way she hoicked down her shirt collar to display the crack between her boobs as if by accident was really maddening. Saadet would've cheerfully killed Müjgân for trying to steal her kismet away.

Bahattin and Müjgân crossed over, still chatting, and stopped outside the block. They kept moving in and out of her sight. To see what the hell this pair were up to, Saadet had to hang over the rails; her soapy hands slipped all of a sudden, she lost her balance – the poor girl who wouldn't wash the windows on the pretext that people would say Saadet threw herself off the sixth floor when she couldn't find a husband – plummeted down, right on top of the flaxen-haired Müjgân.

She died on the spot and Müjgân was crippled for life with a broken spine. Bahattin saw the whole thing, went nuts and had to stay off work for a while. In time, though, he forgot this incident that had occurred right before his very eyes, and expanded the stall outside his shop all the way to where Saadet's brains had spilled.

As Saadet's corpse and Müjgân's gravely injured body lay on the ground, someone in the crowd sat Bahattin down and forced a drink of water into his jaw locked in shock. No one crowding around Müjgân dared touch her as they waited for the police and the ambulance.

That's when Zeynep felt her first contractions. She yelled, *Saadet cooome!* but no one came to her rescue. She had no idea the poor girl had fallen from the sixth floor, so she yelled and yelled, and when it finally dawned on her that Saadet had vanished, she went to the door to ask for help. But everyone in the block was downstairs, busy commenting upon this horrific incident that would be altered beyond recognition by the time it reached ears in the next neighbourhood.

No one heard Zeynep. It took her a while to think of ringing Suphi up. He arrived, face white as a sheet. As she left the block on his arm, she spotted the ambulance, thought it had come for her and gave her husband an adoring smile, labour pains or not. She nearly passed out at hearing of Saadet's fall to her death.

The hospital thronged with the MP's nearest and dearest in Ankara. Zeynep had a very difficult birth after a sixteen-hour-long labour, and this horrifying event changed her life. *That's the spot where Saadet's brains splashed out… butcher Hilmi had a bugger of a time scraping off bits of brain stuck to his shop window,* blurted out by a neighbour, who – to add insult to injury – pointed to that very place, thereby triggering a terror which, combined with a serious case of post-partum depression, proved to be devastating to the new mother freshly back from hospital, baby in arms. When she began threatening to commit suicide, Suphi wangled some mission abroad. Leaving the three-month-old baby with his mother, he took his wife on a fortnight's totally unnecessary official trip to France.

Suphi had never admitted his addiction to gambling, no matter how many times he was grilled by his father. More importantly, he had avoided even touching playing cards for a whole year after the wedding. And would have carried on. But they were in Nice, Monte Carlo beckoned right under their noses, and Zeynep was still in a depression. Trumping up what he thought was a good excuse *I'd better help her lighten up,* Suphi took her to Monte Carlo. That first gaming table where they sat would be the beginning of a very long end, not only for Zeynep, but for the whole family.

Thus aroused, her hitherto latent gambling gene kept the young couple in its thrall for a fortnight. They made friends with another Turk named Tarık Bakırcıoğlu and blew a serious amount of money at both types of tables, gaming as well as dining, laden with caviar and champagne in the case of the latter. If the young parents were looking for validation for the blessings of marriage, Tarık was the wrong role model: his tears at the and of his extended and colourful tale of his second wife Bedia – whom he referred to as *Cursia* – who had seduced his son –were heartbreaking.

Upon their return, they engaged a live-in nanny for Nadir so they could spend a few nights a week in Ankara's secret gambling dens. The flat Mustafa Nadir Karakurt had registered in Suphi's name as a wedding present was sold on the pretext of being unlucky, and concealing their intention to spend the proceeds at the gaming table they told the MP they'd bought the flat they were actually renting. Zeynep turned out to be a worse gambler than Suphi. When she was pregnant with **her second son Tarkan** she went into labour at the gaming table. But she'd taken things to a new extreme. *I'm on a lucky streak for once in a blue moon!* she said, and wouldn't get up until her waters broke and drenched everything in sight.

It got worse. Mustafa Nadir Karakurt died soon after a massive row caused by the discovery that they lived in a rented flat. Feeling a weight lift now that the MP's shadow had dissappeared, and thanks to a sizeable inheritance, they decided Ankara's sleazy, sneaky dens weren't good enough; hopping on a flight, they whizzed off to the French Riviera. His life of ease at the Ministry less secure after his father's death, Suphi would have returned once his leave was over; but Zeynep was too busy eyeing up the poolside gigolos all day long, and running off to the casino the moment she'd put the boys to sleep. Nadir and Tarkan were school age by then, so she said, *Take the kids and go, I wanna stay for a few more days.* Which prompted Suphi to concoct some excuse to extend his leave, which in turn undermined his position in the Ministry all the more.

The MP's legacy was running dry when Emrullah died. Her brother's upstart solicitor Abbas Koşar contacted Zeynep too, offering his services should she wish to sue her aunt for a share of the inheritance. It fell on deaf ears. Immediately after her refusal of her aunt's polite letter proposing to manage the inheritance, Zeynep's share had been transferred, which meant she didn't need a solicitor.

His head turned by his wife's enormous legacy, Suphi saw no reason to carry on as a civil servant in that job which had become such a bind. He resigned. And with no need to stay in Ankara any longer, they moved to Istanbul, whose gambling houses were ready for conquest. They gambled for many years in Istanbul. At times, seeing that colossal fortune melt away, they got worried enough to say, *Let's pack it in!* behave themselves for a few months … and gave in again as one or the other was tempted by the devil.

They spent the last few crumbs at the poker table in a fuggy basement in a three-storey Yalova house where a poor family were housed free just in case of a police raid. When they were up to their eyeballs in debt, Suphi took on a job as general manager of a shipping company with shady dealings.

The fortune was gone. The circle was tightening, usurers' loans mounted up. Whenever Suphi gave into despair, Zeynep consoled him with the thought of the aunt with one foot in the grave. Zeynep and her big brother would get an even more enormous fortune than İmdat Hızır's legacy at her aunt's death, given Türkan had no family of her own. *Curse the old bitch who just wouldn't die!*

The addiction that would ultimately cause their end had triggered a deep hatred in their children. The two boys who grew up unloved were still at university when they severed ties with their pathetic parents. The sociable Nadir, who was blessed with his MP grandfather's gift of the gab, committed a crime he convinced himself he was forced into just to save himself: he stole his father's Rolex watch, his mother's teardrop emerald necklace and a few other pieces of jewellery, and went abroad with the money. Suphi and Zeynep were beside themselves with fury at discovering their son had stolen the fortune they'd secreted away. They were enraged not so much at that their son had stolen from his own parents, but at the loss of their rainy day fund for the gaming table.

Nadir hoarded and scraped by. First he toured Europe for a bit. He then met a Canadian in Paris and followed her to Montreal. They were together for a while, but when she dumped him, he had no job, no money or anything. As he had only worked in petrol stations and McDonald's and the like, fortune showed her fickle face once again. He found a job in a casino. His parents' circumstances might have sworn him off gambling himself, but he had no problem with letting others gamble, and started work as a croupier. He was bright, caught on quickly, and once he'd learnt all the ins and outs, he dashed off to the capital of gambling: Las Vegas.

As for Tarkan who'd come this close to being born at the gaming table: having recognised his preference for men whilst still at secondary school, he'd grown up resentful and tense, an introvert barely noticeable at home. Whenever he came back from school, he'd grab a bite of whatever he could find in the fridge since there was no decent food around anyway, shut himself in his room and try to cheer up by practising mime before the mirror. He had a real talent for acting. It was this childhood companion, his skill in mime, that got him into the Conservatory with top marks.

One day in his second year, Zeynep and Suphi had gone to their most recent haunt, a casino done up like a club in a timber mansion in Suadiye. Certain that his parents wouldn't return for at least forty-eight hours, Tarkan invited Esat round, a fella who'd got into the Conservatory thanks to a baby face and magnificent body, and not through any gift in the way of acting, said deficiency having earned him the rather aptly rhyming moniker **Esat-but-Vasat**, *Second Best Esat*. They weren't lovers as yet. That mutual attraction permeated both down to their last cell, but they had not opened up. That night they not only consummated their love, but also survived the most horrendous moments in their lives after being caught in the shower by Tarkan's father. It was a horrible night of blood.

Perfectly aware of, and totally unbothered by his lack of talent, Esat-but-Vasat trusted his magnificent physique to open every door. Which it already had; since he'd been picked amongst dozens of actors for a fridge advert. All the same, he asked for Tarkan's help: Esat didn't want to fall flat on his face on this, his first break, and Tarkan's talent was unanimously hailed by the lecturers. According to the script, Esat was the young fiancé of a real beauty, whose cheek he'd kiss by the fridge and rattle off standard advertising sentences along the lines of how he was burning with her love. Madly in love with this living statue of David, Tarkan invited him home on the pretext of rehearsing undisturbed. He hadn't cottoned on to the boy's real intention (the part was just an excuse). They'd put their hearts into rehearsing by the all-but-empty fridge when the anticipated thunderbolt finally struck … and they started kissing.

In the meanwhile Zeynep, unable to join the table she'd wanted (it was full), had just gone downstairs in the casino that operated under the name *Gentle Approaches to Nature Club*. She was going to grab a bite at the lavish buffet table in the hall decorated with tacky posters and cheaply printed brochures to prop up the pretence of a real club. Casting a chance glance out of the window as she bit into her smoked tongue sandwich, all her senses suddenly went on the alert: the street was awash with an inordinate swarm of headlights.

Police cars. A tip-off had sent a squad who were, even at that moment, surrounding the mansion. Seeing those headlights doused one by one, a trembling Zeynep warned Suphi – who'd just taken a loo break – *The police are here for a raid!* Panicked, they sneaked away through the back door opening to the garden. They'd made a habit of parking a couple of streets away as a precaution; driving past the mansion on their way to Baghdad Road, they saw the police leading out, one by one, the hardened gamblers who'd been caught red-handed.

When they got home, Tarkan and Esat were still in the shower. Zeynep and Suphi – hearts still in their mouths – were happy to have got off so lightly. Desperate for a pee, Suphi, who'd been holding it all this time, dashed to the bathroom, but the door was locked. Hearing the sound of running water, he thought his son was having a wash, and shouted, *Open the bloody door, I'm gonna piss myself!* The lovers blanched and nearly died of fright. When there was no response from the other side of the door, Suphi thought his son was overcome by the LPG heater's fumes and smashed the door in with a shoulder. His bladder emptied when he saw his naked son with a male lover. He darted off to the kitchen to grab a knife to slash them both, beside himself, urine dripping from his trouser legs.

Bellowing he would kill them both, pierce them into sieves, he waved the knife about. Esat was shielding Tarkan when his lovely, muscular chest was slashed from one end to the other. Zeynep had been trying to hold her husband back, but fainted when she saw the white bath towel turn blood red. After many minutes of a life-and-death struggle, homophobe Suphi chickened out at the prospect of murder and let the boys go.

They wept as they dressed Esat's chest back in his humble student bedsit. Tarkan's non-stop pleas of *Let's go to the hospital* throughout the journey had been rejected; Esat said the police would get involved, they'd have to explain the situation, Suphi would get into trouble and threaten Tarkan's life in his rage. Esat's wound wasn't fatal; the bleeding stopped, but Tarkan's tears didn't. In the morning, they hopped on a coach bound for Antalya; Tarkan's dreams of finishing the conservatory and becoming a great actor lay in tatters and Esat's chest – fabulous until yesterday – now bore an indelible trace of that night.

It was a dog's life in Antalya for the penniless pair. Summer was still a long way off, so hotel jobs were very hard to come by. Tarkan had been ringing his big brother on and off since the other had run away to America; he called again to ask for money. Nadir snapped, *I've managed on my own, see? You do the same!* So Tarkan knew he had no one else in the world besides Esat-but-Vasat who'd shielded him from his dad's knife with his own broad chest.

They found work when holiday villages woke up in the summer. Tarkan was a mime artist. At first he only did simple shows for children, like a man who spills food at the table and a man who falls off the pier whilst flying a kite. Later, he added a sad romance for the benefit of the adults: he was dancing and making love with a non-existent sweetheart, he was abandoned, and ended up crying pitifully. It was so impressive that his audience could have sworn he was crying even though his eyes were still dry at the end of the show. Esat, in the meanwhile, had tried his hand at entertaining a couple of times, but no matter how hard he tried to conceal it, the scar attracted attention; so he chose to work as a waiter instead. He didn't have to undress to serve vulgar holidaymakers who thought they'd only get value for their money if they ate as much as possible in those all-inclusive holiday villages; and since he avoided swimming on his days off, no one saw the scar.

Tarkan wasn't talented enough to become a great actor. But his fame grew and grew with his shows lighting those inner fires. He expanded his repertoire and was offered new jobs. Eventually they opened their own nightclub, prospered, and lived life as they wanted. Tarkan never looked at another man. Esat-but-Vasat loved him right back, although perhaps less loyally, but Tarkan's love and sense of gratitude always won out, he forgave his lover, lay on Esat's chest after their dramatic blow ups, rested his lips against the scar and wept.

It was as if Tarkan had fallen to earth. He never used his surname unless required by some official document. When his great aunt had discovered his number and rung him with news of his mother's death and impending funeral, he told the lady he'd never seen, *I'm not coming; I have no parents, never did have.* That was the last thing he ever said about his past.

Zeynep and Suphi carried on losing everything they had, right down to their dignity; forced to move from that palatial two-hundred-square-metre Etiler flat to a nondescript block in Pendik, they were now regulars at a sleazy gambling den in Yalova. One horribly hot July day, when Suphi's company car (the transport firm of shady deals) had broken down and was in the garage for repairs, all Zeynep and Suphi they could think about was how they were going to get to Yalova. Swallowing what was left of their pride, they asked Turgut and Berat, their neighbours across the hall, to borrow their Renault Broadway, citing an invented funeral.

Engrossed in the *Cumhuriyet's* Sunday crossword, Turgut was taken aback, but couldn't refuse the charming neighbour, and Berat handed Zeynep the key. Their son Tümay objected after Zeynep and Suphi had got in the car and left, *Dad, why d'ya do that, eh? Who'll pay if they have an accident?* Neighbourly relations being one of her strong points, Berat would hear no more of it, *Neighbours need one another son… and Yalova's not that far, is it?* Except this didn't make her feel any better; she might not know the man all that well (she saw him so seldom) but she didn't think much of the wife at all.

Tümay was proven right. Speeding to get to the gaming table, Suphi blinked, dazzled by the setting sun, and ended up under a lorry coming in the opposite direction. Zeynep died on the spot and a seriously injured Suphi was hospitalised.

At exactly the same time, someone else lost her life five hundred kilometres away. Emrullah's bitchy daughter-in-law Nihan, the mother Zeynep was convinced had been banished by her grandfather, the woman who was still madly in love with the now ageing Alişan was carried away by an awful, murderous mudslide that swamped the town centre in Isparta's Senirkent district, where she'd been living a wretched life. Mother and daughter expired at the same time. Neither Şekip Sami knew it, nor Türkan. By the time they'd heard of Zeynep's death, they'd already read the horrifying news of the seventy-four souls lost in the mudslide after the torrential rains lashing Kapıdağ, an extraordinary environmental disaster.

Burying Zeynep fell upon Türkan, who turned out to have outlived both her nephew and niece. She carried out her final duty without protesting. She'd never leave them unclaimed; both her nephew and niece who'd died at different times were interred at the Kaymakoğlu family plot.

Zeynep died before her big brother Şekip Sami. When the police informed Türkan of her niece's death, she instructed her solicitors, and asked them to discover Nadir's phone in Las Vegas, and Tarkan's too, never mind that his whereabouts had been a mystery up to then. She told them both that their mother had died in an unfortunate accident, and informed them of the time and the place of the funeral. Nadir said, *I'll come,* but didn't. Türkan kept looking out for him all through the funeral. She'd let the Karakurts deal with Suphi's fate, but she'd had the Koran read for Zeynep and even paid Turgut and Berat for the Renault that was a write-off.

That death didn't particularly affect her great aunt. Zeynep had been crass enough to insult her grandfather (whose paralysis she'd caused in the first place); that girl had always had a nasty streak, a cold heart. But Türkan trembled at news of Şekip Sami's lonely death at the Şişli Etfal Hospital, even if they'd been totally estranged over the inheritance. It was impossible to stop thinking about that superb intellect, the intellect that had been channelled hither and thither by his uncontrollable passions, thwarting the promise of his childhood; her poor nephew had never quite matured beyond an adolescent. Unable to succeed at being an adult, he'd frittered away his brains and his life too.

She arranged a funeral ceremony suitable to the Kaymakoğlu family for Şekip Sami too, hoping at least one of the four daughters would come. Thinking *It's their father after all, they have every right to know… they'll want to come,* she rang Esra; but the upstart solicitor Abbas had pre-empted her, and Esra said they weren't coming. Türkan's heart sank on behalf of her nephew. What was the point of children if they wouldn't even take responsibility for your funeral? All right, neither Zeynep, nor Şekip Sami would win prizes as good parents; they'd frittered away an enormous inheritance, and left not even a penny to their own children. But this couldn't have been a good enough reason to shun their funerals.

Türkan put her thinking cap on. She had to decide what to do with the fortune left by her father Emrullah and grown to mind-blowing proportions under her prudent management. Loath to leave it to this delinquent six, these great nephews and great nieces she'd never met, she called her solicitors and before a public notary bequeathed her assets to several institutions from the Turkish Foundation for Reforestation, Protection of Natural Habitats and Combating Soil Erosion through to the Red Crescent, the Darüşşafaka Equality in Education Foundation, and the Turkish Education Foundation.

During a chat with a lawyer, one of many Nadir had met in Las Vegas, he twigged that they might declare the great aunt mentally incompetent to get their hands on the assets – him and his cousins.

Nadir had been in contact with his cousin Esra for some time. One day, somehow having got hold of an issue of *Turkamerican*, he'd spotted the translator's name under a Nâzım Hikmet poem, put two and two together and sent an e-mail to Esra Kaymakoğlu he believed might be the daughter of his uncle Şekip Sami he'd seen once when still a child. That name had suddenly awakened something inside, some joy at finding family just when he'd been feeling totally alone, without a future in this country. It would be great to have a relative no matter how far away she was.

He got a reply right away. Esra was happy to hear from her cousin even if she'd never met his mother (and therefore her aunt) before. They began corresponding in English. Nadir invited her to Las Vegas. Who'd say no to a free holiday? Not she! The fares were high, but she saved up, and she and her husband Eddie stayed with her cousin for a week. They scoured Las Vegas from top to bottom, had a flutter in the casino where Nadir had a low paid job, and got soppy over their evening drinks. Blamed their parents for never introducing them.

Then talk turned to the fortune they'd get their hands on if the great aunt was placed under guardianship. Nadir was breaking his back to make a buck. With no idea that those assets had already been earmarked, he said it would make sense to get together, find a lawyer and grab the fortune from the aunt who was now over ninety and still wouldn't die. Esra readily agreed. Her sisters were all having a hard time making ends meet; and they all got excited at the idea. They did an internet search, found **Mithat Gürtunca**, had no idea what a jerk he was, gave him a power of attorney through the consulate and instructed him on their wishes.

But Türkan had taken precautions long ago. With a rock solid mental capacity report, she had guaranteed that her fortune would go to the right places after her death. Not to mention the fact that the designated beneficiaries were no weaklings that would buckle under the pressure of those desperate great nephews and -nieces.

By the time Mithat Gürtunca – now instructed by five cousins – had driven into the city, it was noon and he was ravenous. Fancying a spicy sausage Black Sea flatbread before getting down to research, he entered the first likely spot. As he waited for his egg-and-cheese pide, he'd enquired about Türkan Kaymakoğlu of the surly bloke he'd mistaken for the proprietor. It was the owner's cousin from Gümüşhane, though; he'd never heard of her. One of the patrons wanted to help the lawyer, but confusing her with someone else, piped up, *She's pegged it, she has. And it's been years now!* There being nothing more natural than someone in her nineties dying, Mithat swallowed it whole. With no need to worry now about a mental capacity report or a court case, he'd conclude the matter of the inheritance just like that – an extraordinary fortune it was too according to his clients – and he himself would pocket a tidy fee.

He went over to the Register Office to look into probate, yawning non-stop after the bloating lunch. Unlike the Gümüşhane man though, the official was a local, and he was no stranger to the renowned Türkan Hanım. *Says who! She'll bury you and me yet!* he said. And even if she did die, her relatives could go whistle for it. He then proceeded to wax lyrical about this superannuated lady's power in the city, her intellect and all her accomplishments. Having thus been informed that Türkan was no lightweight, and what solid charities she'd picked, the lawyer gave up. Except he never told his clients. Fabricating one excuse after another (stamp duty, notary fees, mental reports, etc., etc.) he set about bleeding the greedy relatives ignorant of the ways of the law.

Back at the Three Brothers Patisserie, the astute testator talked on about the Internet, Âlim's blog and interesting websites, whilst the Medical Director listened in wonder, unable to find the words to express his admiration for the old lady's vast knowledge of the virtual world.

In the meanwhile his wife Sevim ate her pudding *Without rosewater please,* using the spoon she'd brought along in a tiny bag, careful to avoid touching the table top she'd wiped twice.

At his table nearby where he sat with his daughter Zehra, Âlim Kâhkeci was no less amazed: the eldery lady's feedback on his blog was spot on. Father and daughter had finished the two types of puddings they'd ordered. Zehra's hungry whingeing was ignored, and they collected their racquets and kit bags. Âlim approached to say good-bye as Türkan was telling the Medical Director about her archive containing photographs of **founder Governor Hüsnü Simavi Bey** and members of the hospital's board, *It behoves you to upload their portraits onto your website.*

That archive held not only the photos of the hospital board members, but also pretty much anyone who had been anyone in the city and posed for Karnik Sabuncuyan, the Armenian photographer who'd been born in the nineteenth century and died in the twentieth. After moving back to the Kaymakoğlu Mansion, the old lady had set about collecting documents on the history of her city where her family had lived for five generations, and gradually gathered a number of valuable items. Some of Sabuncuyan's work she had was still in the form of glass negatives; others had been lost through the years as they passed from hand to hand.

The photographer was originally from Meram in Konya; but his contribution to this Black Sea city's visual history was undeniable. One could say he was the author of its illustrated history. It seemed to Türkan, as she looked at his sepia prints (each one a superb image), that if Master Karnik hadn't passed this way at the end of the nineteenth century, the city would have been denied its history, no, it might not even have become a city.

She had been sponsoring prayers at the historic Grand Mosque for the dead on the fourth day of every Feast of Sacrifice for years, prayers for all her family and anyone who had ever contributed to the city. She always insisted these prayers include the Armenians and Greeks who'd served the city, such as Karnik Sabuncuyan, Ardıçoğlu Totodaki Bey and Kalustyan Ara Bey. There had been (and continued to be) several objections from the VIPs as well as the public, *Why would we pray for those infidels?* But they were stilled either before her intellect and eloquence, or barely whispered since no one dared to antagonise this still powerful lady, regardless of her age.

More and more of those nasty voices had been buzzing around the city of late. There had been a number of attempts to discourage the public from attending the prayers, as if they exclusively paid tribute to these non-Muslims (whom they badmouthed quite openly). But the poor still filled the long portable tables set out in the mosque courtyard for the lavish feast that followed the recitation. To be honest, some were scared off, *What if Türkan Hanım's enemies got our names, and stopped their Ramadan handouts?* And then there were quite a few who, unable to resist the mouth-watering aroma, perched at the table and bolted their food down so they could leave as quickly as possible.

The photographer behind the legendary panorama called *The Clock Tower and the Town on a Snowy Day* was Karnik Sabuncuyan, son of **stonemason Mıgırdiç**, the famed womaniser of Meram. Few knew about the stonemason's childhood aspirations: Mıgırdiç would have become a great man if only life had let him go to school, but it didn't. After the death of **his father soapmaker Agop** (scalded by a boiling cauldron of the tar soap he made at home) his mother had grabbed the arm of the boy who just wanted to go to school and turned him over to her relative **stonemason Puzant** with the customary phrase, *His flesh is yours, his bones are mine; teach him a trade so he can earn his bread.* Puzant had a well-deserved reputation in the area as a great bas-relief craftsman; he wasn't nasty, but he did enjoy being cruel to be kind. He gave the tender lambkin no quarter; he forced Mıgırdiç to work until the boy's fingers bled and beat him for running away to idle in Meram's vineyards at harvest time. But Mıgırdiç was as famous as his master before he'd turned seventeen; people referred to the proverb when they mentioned him, *The horns pass the ears they say… his apprentice has passed Puzant now.*

Mıgırdiç complained of the work though; his fingers could barely move after all that work with stone. Yet he was a great craftsman: every single stone he carved, everything he turned out was met with astonished wonder. He stayed for quite a while in Ürgüp, where his work on the façade of a mansion had made quite an impression, so much so that local dignitaries (Greek and Turk alike) queued up with promises of mindboggling fees so he'd adorn their mansions too. But this adoration came to an abrupt end when, unable to keep it in, he'd seduced a Greek lady.

The much-admired stonemason had to run away dressed as a woman to save his skin.

Blessed with a poetic streak, and the gift of the gab too, two skills crucial to a seducer, Mıgırdiç also read whatever he could lay his hands on. He wanted his son to go to school and become a great man instead of *squeezing his bread out of stone*, as the saying goes. So, he sent Karnik to the Mıhitaryan Armenian Lycée in Istanbul.

His father wanted Karnik to be a clerk, with visions of the boy as a gentleman of letters seated at a large desk, black cuffs over sleeves, dipping a pen into the inkpot to write something. But before Karnik had even settled into boarding school – or got used to its strict discipline – when *He who lived by the sword*, as the saying goes (again), *died by the sword*: Mıgırdiç was knifed to death in a quarrel over a woman at an orgy in a Meram vineyard. That was in an age when the post took months to get anywhere. By the time the sad news reached Karnik, his father had been buried months before.

His mother, **black-haired Zabel**, was one of those women who couldn't survive without a man by their side. With no idea how to claim her rights, poor and meek to boot, she accepted her lot in silence. It had never occurred to her to bring Mıgırdiç to book on the rumours of his womanising that raged through the town. Then he died and she was left high and dry. It was the support of her neighbours that kept her going, the Turks, Armenians and Greeks. She thought her relatives *might take us under their wing*, and yes, they did share her grief for a while, and offered a helping hand, but eventually they all sank back into their own concerns. Soon no one asked after Zabel or her daughter.

Now in her black weeds since the start of the forty-day mourning period, black-haired Zabel and her black-eyed nine-year-old daughter Maral lived in their single storey house whose humble façade Mıgırdiç had adorned with bas-reliefs; mother and daughter lit incense, prayed and wept as they huddled close at night. So miserable were they some nights that Zabel sang hymns and told stories until daylight to divert her daughter from crying with hunger.

In the meanwhile **Headmaster Serop Efendi** was fretting over scrawny Karnik. Since his father's death, no one had asked after the boy dying to see his mother and sister, alone and helpless like a paper boat on the ocean of life. With a dolefule stare like a consumptive, he begged Serop Efendi every morning in floods of tears, *Please send me to Meram!* Surely it was impossible to send Karnik all that way on his own? The poor chap finally relented and promised to take the boy to Meram before the end of Lent, so mother and son could be reunited at Easter. Karnik began counting the days.

Sadly they never made it. The middle-aged headmaster – a devout bachelor known as a wingless angel – was forced to resign before he could keep his word. Serop was a gentleman, trusted by the congregation, a good teacher who took a close interest in the pupils. On the thirty-second day of Lent, however, in a shocking attack of insanity, he attempted to rape **Music Teacher Lerna**, and in full view of everyone too.

The eyewitnesses couldn't believe their eyes: Serop Efendi, who'd never put a single foot wrong all these years? He'd been perfectly normal, his usual self in the morning, but an hour after lunch he'd burst into song at the top of his voice before intercepting and assaulting the happily married young woman.

The teachers panicked. They had the devil of a time lifting him off Lerna as he was on the brink of taking his member out of his trousers. It took a while, but at long last the poor woman was sent home. But the solemn headmaster wasn't done yet. This time he thrust Lerna's violin into another female teacher's hand, insisting *Play!* Clapping his hands, dancing, attempting to drop his trousers and insulting the girls all the while. The school was in uproar. Female teachers fainted right and left, male teachers ran hither and thither and the pupils piling in doorways screamed. Serop Efendi sank deeper into insanity, talking to himself and cursing; no matter what they did, the caretakers and male teachers just couldn't keep him under control as his legs trembled and face twitched until he fell in an exhausted faint five hours later. The next morning, upon realising the extent of his actions, he immediately presented the governors with a letter of resignation.

No one remembered Karnik's pain or hopes either during, or in the aftermath of this enormous scandal. Except he had been expecting to set off the following day so he could be reunited with his mum, and in his excitement thinking *You never know, what if he said Let's get going now?*

had washed with icy cold water before daylight, waiting for Serop Efendi to say, *Be ready tomorrow; we're going to Meram to find your mother.*

None of the eyewitnesses to the scandal could comprehend what had happened. Neither could Serop Efendi. It was actually very simple: The previous night, the headmaster who'd eschewed alcohol and animal produce throughout Lent had cooked the fresh mushrooms he'd bought from a street vendor. Later, spotting the plain pasta sprinkled with walnuts in the wire mesh cupboard, Serop had decided not to waste the leftovers. The stew taken to school in the mess tin and enjoyed on dark bread with a sprinkling of salt was in actual fact not of Ceasar's mushroom, but fly agaric, a highly toxic psychotropic fungus that rarely killed, but did cause a temporary state of psychosis.

The governors and faculty might have been prepared to overlook this one extraordinarily incomprehensible event, but the devout parishioner of the Church of Vosgeperan wouldn't change his mind on the basis that he could never face anyone at school again, certainly not Lerna Hanım. So mortified was he that he could no longer stay in his ground floor flat in Beyoğlu's Mastic Tree Street either, since everyone there had heard of his scandalous behaviour. He moved to Kınalıada, where he saw very few people, did odd jobs here and there, ate from hand to mouth, and spent most of his time praying at the Church of Surp Krikor Lusaroviç.

Serop Efendi's resignation quashed Karnik's dreams of going back home. The new headmaster did carry out a perfunctory investigation through the church; but what he heard about the mother of the destitute, sad boy wasn't particularly encouraging. Zabel of the famous black hair was said to have married **a tall, strapping brigand known as Laz Hüseyin** and, taking her daughter Maral, settled in some Black Sea city. Rumours varied about where. Everyone talked at once as the list of possibilities started with Hopa in the far east and ended with Amasra in the far west. Heartbroken at the thought of being abandoned and forgotten by his mother, Karnik couldn't bring himself to accept her marriage before his father's bones hadn't even rotted.

If Serop Efendi hadn't eaten that hallucinogenic mushroom, they would have set off the following day, reached Meram after a week-long, arduous journey, and found Zabel and Maral weeping. Laz Hüseyin would just have proposed, Zabel would have bottled out when she saw her son, and Karnik would have been destined to look after the family at that tender age just as *his* father had been forced to at his father's death. He would have dropped out of school, apprenticed himself to the Turkish blacksmith next door, or at best, the Greek pharmacist, growing old as he pounded medicines in a china pestle in the windowless backroom. The headmaster's misfortune not only changed the course of Karnik's life, but also ultimately called forth the skill that would leave such an indelible mark on the history of this Black Sea city.

Laz Hüseyin and black-haired Zabel married before God. There was no official ceremony. A while back, when Mıgırdiç was still alive, Laz Hüseyin had happened to be passing through Meram, seen Zabel brushing her long black hair early one morning in the sunny garden, fallen in love at once, but restrained himself and never even cast an untoward glance at the married woman. One evening, once she had been widowed, he crossed her path in the gloaming and asked for her hand, *Be my wife by Allah's will and I'll cherish you until my dying day.*

Zabel accepted this hasty proposal in a heartbeat. It had been months since the forty days of mourning had come to an end, and the food with it; wrapped up in their own concerns, their kith and kin had all but run out of charity. Winter would come by and by, and they didn't even have a single twig to burn or a handful of bulgur to cook. Her Maral was growing thinner by the day as the pasty hollows under those lovely black eyes sank deeper. Laz Hüseyin wouldn't dream of disgracing his lover, but couldn't stay away either. That night he came in secret after dark, after everyone had gone to bed, encircled Zabel's waist with a gold belt and swore he'd never even glance at another woman until his dying day.

Zabel had never had to take a single decision all her life until that day; she packed up within the week over the congregation's violent objections that she was offending her husband's memory and followed Laz Hüseyin, Maral in tow. Somewhat embarrassed at having taken a shine to the tall, strapping, handsome brigand with the childish, kindly eyes, she still couldn't forget that her husband was killed in an orgy.

The guileless brigand took his beloved Zabel (tiny enough to be lost in his lap) and Maral, whom he had sworn to look after like she was his own daughter, and took them to a mountain village in Rize. He made them profess the faith before his mother and went to the village imam for the ceremony. When Zabel kissed her hand, Hüseyin's **old mother Guri who spoke nothing but Laz** removed a gold bangle from her own arm and placed it on Zabel's to demonstrate approval of her new daughter-in-law. Laz Hüseyin had told her mother that Zabel was an Armenian virgin who'd been left all alone when her parents had died in Meram, and said Maral was her sister.

Old Guri adored her precious Zabel's glossy black hair, and whole-heartedly embraced her *ucha mskva* – dark beauty. They were poor, yes, but made up for it with affection. Maral had been born on an endless plain where fields stretched as far as they eye could see; now she'd come to love wandering on steep hillsides thick with wild forests, washing in the stream and eating corn bread. Neither Zabel, nor Maral missed their homeland before this magnificent bounty of nature.

Karnik was wrong, however: all Zabel could think about was her son. No matter how tender Laz Hüseyin was, how well the blue-eyed Guri fed her *ucha mskva* daughter-in-law with her own hands, Zabel's heart wouldn't stop burning. Hot tears flowed every night at the memory of her Karnik. They'd only been married three months. His wife's sorrow was his own, Laz Hüseyin decided; he'd go to Istanbul as soon as possible and bring Karnik back. He had dreams. First he'd reunite his darling wife with her son, then he'd extend the derelict hut in the forest, cut down eight or ten trees to make a shortcut to the stream for Zabel, and enlarge the hearth in the room with the wide sofa where his mother sang Laz songs in her stirring voice. After all this was done, Zabel would bear him a son, and then another, so they'd be a big, happy family. Perhaps then he could even give up on this brigandage business, and take up another trade. But he couldn't make his dreams come true. True to his reputation as a highwayman, he was killed in a skirmish on the road to Trabzon. Zabel lost her new husband, and all hopes of finding her son.

In her despair, she lay aside her worries about Karnik; all she could do was hope he was taken under the wing of some charitable souls at school. She wanted to return to Meram and seek shelter with her relations. Guri cottoned on; blue eyes sparkling like gemstones on her pure white skin, she held her son's pistol by the barrel and said, *Take this for protection on the roads.*

Zabel understood, even if they shared not a single word. She took the pistol with the carved butt, the only thing left by her darling Laz Hüseyin taken far too soon, and tucked it into the waistband of her baggy trousers under the black cloak. Mother and daughter-in-law exchanged farewells in tears. Zabel sold the gold bangle so she could set up a new life in Meram, but concealed Laz Hüseyin's gold belt on her bare skin.

No amount of huddling in black cloaks would have made it possible for a woman and a girl to travel unaccompanied by a man, however. She, who had never stepped outside Meram until Laz Hüseyin had turned up, whose concept of life had been confined to the church and the home, was now suffering as she trudged this unfamiliar road, carrying a daughter with feet too sore to walk and catching a ride in buffalo carts whenever she could. On occasion, the pistol that she'd regarded only as Guri's memento was called into action: it defended her honour and that of her daughter's too, and saved their lives. It didn't save her from being swindled by some unscrupulous rascals, however; Zabel was robbed of the gold belt on her waist, and mother and daughter eventually fetched up in Bingöl instead of Meram, wretched and miserable. They were exhausted; they hadn't eaten a bite of hot food for days. They would have died if the sun had set on them one more time. Zabel had no hope left; all she could do was beg God to spare her daughter.

In the glow of sunset, **Kurd Fariz Ağa, chieftain of a leading Bingöl clan**, was returning to his mansion and saw Zabel stretched out at his gate, filthy, in a faded black cloak, one hand out as if begging, and Maral huddled up like a kitten next to her mother; he beckoned his men and ordered them in. The female servants recognised the mother and daughter as Armenians at once, fed them, bathed them, and discarding the filthy rags, dressed them up in lovely Kurdish embroideries. Rubbing their backs, they soothed Maral whose tears wouldn't stop and Zabel who sobbed at every mouthful.

A generous heart was concealed behind Fariz Ağa's harsh façade. Whenever he roared to call one of his tenant farmers, everyone in the mansion leapt up; he did, after all, call the shots in the region – and not just in Bingöl. It was only when he was talking to **his favourite son Blind Reşo** that his voice softened into a honeyed tone. One week after taking pity on Zabel and Maral and offering his hospitality, Fariz Ağa, who stared into the distance when he talked to women instead of looking them in the face, called them and told them that they now belonged to the contingent of female servants in the mansion. Zabel spoke no Kurdish, but she did pick up the sprinkling of Turkish he had uttered, figured out that she'd be working in the kitchen and that Maral would now serve Reşo; she nodded her assent.

Reşo had lost his sight as a result of childhood trachoma, not that anyone could tell by looking at him. So fast did he ride when he leapt on his horse that the dust clouds in his wake blinded all.

The three months it had taken them to reach Bingöl had turned Zabel into a bag of bones; her once glowing skin had hardened and her face had sagged. She cursed her fate. She would have plunged a knife into her own heart but for Maral. She gritted her teeth and started working in the mansion for her daughter's sake. The sumptuous meals served every hour in the three rooms of Kurd Fariz Ağa's mansion were famed across the region, all the way from Muş to Diyarbakır; there were days when they fed fifty. Zabel was so worn out by evening that she had no energy to reach out to the bread on the lavish tables set for the staff. All she could manage was fall into bed with the household and sleep until daybreak. Three years of chopping meat, shaking ayran and doing the dishes bent her back. She no longer had any strength to expect anything out of life. She breathed her last in her sleep after Maral and Reşo's wedding, a magnificent celebration that would be spoken of for years and years. Reşo cherished Maral; Zabel saw with her own eyes how he stroked her as if he was holding a china doll, and Maral blew a dewy breath on his lips so he could feel her presence. Her daughter loved and was loved in return. Zabel gave up her soul in peace.

Kurd Fariz Ağa's favourite daughter-in-law Maral bore Reşo five children, all with huge green eyes, and all in robust health. He saw no need for her to change her name; it was enough that she had already become a Muslim. Maral was still Maral. But in time she forgot her Armenian. Except for the word *mayrik* – mother. By the time her big brother Karnik's memory was nothing more than a fuzzy dream, her mother tongue had dissolved into a pitted board. In time, no one was left who knew the Kurdish bride Maral was actually Armenian. She spoke fluent Kurdish, spoiled her children in Kurdish and gently chided her husband in Kurdish. When local Armenians were banished from their homeland and forced onto the roads, she never knew that her childhood friends back in Meram were spared by the intercession of the Governor of Konya Celal Bey.[3] Neither was she ever destined to know just how desperately her big brother Karnik had once looked for her.

Years passed. Karnik, who never forgave the mother, whom he believed to have wiped him from her mind, was taught photography by **the Bulgarian émigré Nikolai that canto singers called 'one-dimple-Niko'**. He was still at school when he'd started working for pocket money at Nikolai's Pera Road studio, a particular favourite of Istanbul's *artistes*. Ladies' Man Niko had a dimple on his left cheek, wore his fez at a rakish angle, and stole a new heart every day; once he'd noticed how well the sad-eyed lad did, he took to chasing women with ever more alacrity, thereby allowing Karnik to develop his skill in his occupation of choice.

Nikolai made himself scarce upon the discovery of his under-the-counter trade in obscene photographs of Armenian and Greek singers; by the time he'd resurfaced as Bulgarian Dimov, proprietor of a new studio in Kadıköy on the Asian side, his dimple now surmounted by a scar, one of Istanbul's famous photographers Pascal Sébah had died after three years of paralysis, and fate was getting ready to sweep Karnik Sabuncuyan over to cities along the Black Sea coast.

After One-Dimple Niko vanished, Karnik joined the celebrated photographer Pascal's brother Cosmi Sébah. But life was getting tougher, Istanbul was getting to be a little too crowded: Cosmi had taken over his big brother's studio after Pascal's death in 1886, and soon, Pascal's young son Jean Sébah joined the firm two years later; even at sixteen, he looked certain to follow in his father's footsteps. Supported by his uncle, he went into a partnership with Polycarpe Joaillier, another famed Istanbul photographer. Since Cosmi already had a full contingent of staff, he sent Karnik to the new studio.

Put out as he was, Karnik was still tempted by Jean's superior equipment, not to mention the clientele that was the crème de la crème. He worked patiently in what was the most advanced studio of the time. His job wasn't limited to taking photos of ordinary clients or working elbow deep in acid baths in the darkroom; he also served Jean in the studio and entertained elite clients, from lighting their cigarettes through to making their coffee. But Jean Sébah, far too young to appreciate this fortitude, denied Karnik the opportunity to develop. Unable to see a future for himself here, struggling to get along with Jean, Karnik increasingly grew more tense and more impatient, and Jean eventually sacked him.

A forlorn Karnik decided to look for his mother and sister instead of getting another job with a view towards his future. He'd always known he'd have to make this decision one day, always known he'd have to hit the road. He'd been going to bed on an empty stomach, wandering in shoes with holes in the soles and saving every penny so he'd be ready when the time came to embark into the unknown. Purchasing a secondhand camera, he set off and wandered from town to town with his camera on his back. He made a living as a wandering photographer as he continued to look for Zabel, but to no avail. His heart leapt at the sight of every woman he mistook for his mother and he stared at every girl he saw on the street, the mental image of his sister being still a little girl with double plaits, despite all the years that had passed. After scouring nine towns and cities large and small, he ended up in the Black Sea city where he was destined to meet Kalustyan Ara Bey.

Karnik was busy setting up his camera at the coffee house on the seafront just as Governor Hüsnü Simavi Bey was addressing the city's notables gathered in his mansion, *Gentlemen! Let us levy forty para on each bale of tobacco and thirty on each merchant's despatch note to enable us to erect a hospital in our fine city!*

This was the sentence that would set in motion the history of the Mental Health Hospital positioned with its back to the sea. Kalustyan Ara Bey took the minutes, signed at the bottom of the page along with the other members that now formed the hospital board, and once they'd agreed on the next meeting's date, they dispersed.

Ara Bey was on his way back to his shop in the market when he noticed Karnik taking photographs. He went over, asked a few questions to determine who this chap was, and once he'd ascertained this was a poor

Armenian trained by a famous photographer, he summoned Karnik to his mansion; Ara wanted his portrait as well as one of his daughter.

That evening, in the mansion practically lapped by the wild waves of the Black Sea, Karnik met **Ara Bey's churlish daughter Nıvart**: a sombre and stern-gazed girl, chest tense as if ready to rebel any minute, and lips pressed into a thin line. Her thick, brown hair was parted in the middle, plaited and wound around her crown. Her purple satin dress with a full skirt that swept the floor looked incongruously muted in the splendour of her father's mansion. Noticing her unadorned neck and ears just as the photograph was about to be shot, Ara Bey asked her to put her jewellery on. When she returned wearing a necklace, earrings and a ring of hazelnut-sized rubies encircled by countless diamonds, her thick, scowling eyebrows attested to her displeasure.

Karnik took many shots of the father and daughter that day. Afterwards they sat down to a lavish table set in the garden. Ara Bey listened to the details of the story that had brought this sad-faced young man all the way from Istanbul. As Karnik spoke with no trace of self-consciousness about the yearning, pain and bitterness that filled him, Nıvart kept interrupting with questions on photography. That night, neither Nıvart fell in love with Karnik, nor Karnik with Nıvart. But Ara Bey had a flash of inspiration.

Once the wealthy and esteemed draper had verified the tragic story of the young man who looked like some crazed consumptive, he was convinced that it was grief that caused the pallor of his countenance. Ara Bey genuinely did feel sorry for the young man, at least in the one corner of his heart that sank at the sight of this childish face. On the other hand, his affection and interest did have an ulterior motive, not a malicious one, but not entirely innocent either. He proposed opening a studio for Karnik if the photographer were to settle in the city. The lad was still determined to look for his mother and sister, hopeless or not; so Ara Bey explained just how vast this region called the Black Sea was. Who could be sure that he'd find his mother if he were to scour nine more cities, when he hadn't found them in the first nine? Was he going to wander all his life? He'd come to a lovely place; if he were to settle down here, there could be a good future in store for him.

Tired of looking for his mother, his last crumbs of hope now gone, Karnik was impressed enough to accept. And he not only accepted. He also married Nıvart (who'd had a miscarriage when her fiancé had fallen from his horse and died) in a magnificent wedding. Thus did Ara Bey attain his ulterior motive and open the Sabuncuyan Photographic Studio that would leave such a mark on the history of the city.

Ara Bey had told Karnik a little about Nıvart's troubled past, or more accurately, that her fiancé had died, but had concealed the miscarriage arising from the intimacy that had flown in the face of the morals of the time and the place. He knew it would emerge sooner or later, but perhaps by then, he might be pulling the strings, might have got the lad fully under his thumb with the promise of a bright future. Ara Bey's earlier reluctance to appear in public – to avoid gossip – wasn't dispelled entirely after Karnik's consent to the marriage. It took weeks for the older man to stop worrying after the wedding, *What if the bridegroom were to pack up and walk out when he learns?*

By the time the rumours about Nıvart reached Karnik, Ara Bey had splashed out – in total contrast to his moniker of *tightwad* – and opened the exclusive Photo Saboundjian in the best spot in town, thereby offering the young photographer the opportunity to conduct his calling in the best possible circumstances. At first the bridegroom didn't pay much attention; but once he was convinced the gossip was true, he was shaken up, and very nearly went out of his mind.

All day long he considered kicking this opportunity in the teeth and going away just as easily as he had come. That night, he and Nıvart had an awful argument in the bedroom warmed by a colossal Russian stove, the bedroom Ara Bey had spared no cost to furnish with velvet curtains and satin covers. Or more accurately, Karnik yelled uninterrupted, and Nıvart wept uninterrupted. So much so that Karnik had no heart to abandon her.

He wasn't kindly enough to be taken in by this churlish girl's tears. But Nıvart turned out to be more outspoken than her father. Through her sobs, she admitted quite openly that she had loved her fiancé, which was why she'd not shied away from consummating their love, something she didn't regret in the least. The poor girl genuinely thought Karnik knew, and was grateful to him for marrying her despite her disgrace.

It was in the small hours, when Nıvart had no more tears left to shed and Karnik was brooding over how happy he was in his studio, but just couldn't stomach his father-in-law's deception. Pride prevailed. He would leave. It was a very tense and tragic moment. Just when he made for the door, Nıvart darted up and shielded the door with her taut body. *I'd have preferred to come to you as an unblemished maid if I'd known I'd come to love you one day,* she exclaimed.

Karnik realised Nıvart was an extraordinarily strong character. Her honesty and candour filled him with admiration, as did her mature face – not, perhaps, conforming to the generally accepted standards of beauty, but illuminated by a pair of thoughtful and sensitive eyes all the same. He also realised that Ara Bey had tricked his own daughter too. Suddenly filled with warmth towards his wife, and feeling strong enough to withstand rumours, he was certain that Nıvart's past shame would be forgotten in the fullness of time. Then there was the almost unbearable thought of leaving behind a studio advanced enough to compete with any in Istanbul.

That early crisis would never be repeated as they settled into a lifelong happy marriage. Nıvart had asked Karnik to stay because she loved the young man who had a passion. It had nothing to do with fearing that were he to pack up and go, the rumours would grow, and she'd never be free of her stained past. They hadn't married for love, but love did come and grow as they bonded closer and had two daughters.

In time, also, the fame of his photographs spread near and far. Dignitaries of nearby counties all the way from Trabzon to Amasya were queuing up at the door. The rumours that Karnik had found so harrowing at first soon melted away by this success. An unexpected outcome was Nıvart's discovery of a hitherto unsuspected propensity for this career as she set out to assist in the studio; she turned out to be as skilled a photographer as her husband. Muslim women, in particular, came to her so they could pose uncovered, and she charmed them all, her former grumpiness softened by her love for Karnik.

In time, again, art triumphed over life: Nıvart came to be known for her art and not her past indiscretion. Except history was never just. Nıvart Sabuncuyan's art might have won hearts, but it was only *Karnik* Sabuncuyan whom history noted as a photographer.

Handing over to his wife portraits, women's in particular, Karnik went outdoors to shoot not only grand edifices, but also countless landscapes and panoramic cityscapes. His bird's eye *The Clock Tower and the Town on a Snowy Day*, in fact, was the greatest photograph of the city of all time. For many years, it would adorn the stone mansion of **Ardıçoğlu Totodaki Bey**, another hospital foundation board member.

Totodaki Bey would die before the tenth anniversary of the proclamation of the Republic in 1933; his children moved to Istanbul one by one after his death, and to Greece after the Events of 6–7 September.[4] **His youngest son Stavro Ardıçoğlu, the last to leave home**, took a few family heirlooms but not a pin more from the splendid mansion that was sold to a Turkish family. By the time he'd noticed he'd forgotten *The Clock Tower and the Town on a Snowy Day* on the wall, it was too late.

Stavro became one of the trustees of the Aya Dimitri Church at Istanbul's Kurtuluş Final Stop and was the only member of the family not to emigrate to Greece. Then still a single young merchant, he was actually away on a long trip from Beirut through to Teheran to explore the potential for trade in the Middle East. That is why he only heard of the riots much later, when he finally returned to Istanbul, by which time things had calmed down. Saddened as he was by the departure of several fellow Turkish Greeks – they'd certainly be missed in his own district of Kurtuluş – since he had been spared that awful violence, it never occurred to him to emigrate to Athens.

Stavro was the godfather of Haymon Yener, proprietor of the Nişantaşı antique gallery. Older by this time, Stavro loved the godson like his own flesh and blood; *Aymon* as Stavro called him, in turn, never failed to show his godfather the respect he was due. Whenever Stavro dropped in, and did so frequently, he ignored the antiques in the vast shop and made directly for the small back room opening out to the limestone-paved courtyard. At such times Haymon would have the shisha lit (kept specially for the old man), order him a bitter coffee, and then stack before him photo albums, photographs, notebooks filled with the old script and other items of a similar nature. Stavro Ardıçoğlu would spend a long time flicking through hundreds of photographs and dozens of pages, indoors in the winter, and in the courtyard in the summer.

Haymon's old shop in the Tunnel Arcade was renowned amongst ephemera collectors as *the* address for Istanbul postcards, particularly famous for Max Fruchtermann's Ottoman series published in Breslau. After nearly ten years of selling Fruchtermann as well as Rosenberg, Ottmar and Ebüzziya Tevfik postcards, Yener's new interest in antiques caused him to neglect this first shop, then to ultimately close it after falling out with his landlord over the rent. His ephemera collection moved to the warehouse.

Fountaineer Numan had the same problem. He had resigned his job at the Ragıp Paşa Library in the wake of the 1999 Marmara Earthquake and gone into secondhand goods; a fall-out with his Fortune Street landlord had forced him to move to a basement in Pirate Cul-de-Sac. But the damp was terrible for delicate ephemera.

And ephemera it was, along with secondhand books that were auctioned by the Aslıhan Arcade shopkeepers, when Numan found himself sitting next to Haymon. The two acquantainces were bidding for the same items. Haymon bought some and Numan the rest. Afterwards, chatting of this and that, they ended up exchanging woes over their shops. No one could touch Numan when it came to secondhand curios, but he was terrible when it came to money. A light bulb flashed in Haymon's head: he'd clocked a good shop in Aslıhan, but had no one to manage it; his proposal of partnership was accepted.

The curios and ephemera that found their way to Haymon's antique gallery on Bronze Street first underwent inspection under his expert gaze. He would then set aside rare items for his select customers, send the rest to Aslıhan and entrust the first group to his godfather. Stavro was as keen on social life as much as he was on history; he was also very good at reading the Ottoman script. Two qualities that made him the ideal expert for Haymon's latest set of acquisitions: would he please skim through these journals and photographs and perhaps identify a few?

Blessed with a terrific memory, the first thing this genuine enthusiast did was to stare at the pictures with the naked eye. And duly remarked on any face he recognised from his years as a young man, and later, a mature man-about-town in the most exclusive nightspots and the society magazines of bygone times, *This is doctor So-and-So, that is merchant So-and-So…*

He might even relate their fate in a sentence or two: *That's Stationer Tarık Bey,* for instance, *His wife Aydanur lost her mind when her sister Yurdanur committed suicide; she was locked up at La Paix for years.* Of course there were faces he didn't recognise. Even a single one in a crowd was good enough for Haymon, though. Ignoring the photos on occasion, the godfather would pick up his magnifying glass with a silver handle and immerse himself in the texts, chuckling or frowning as he offered a snippet here or there, *That's the diary of a young man. A fickle blighter he was too… falling for a new girl every week…* or *This is the cash book of the profligate geography master at the Imperial School. The whoremonger owed to all and sundry…*

Uncommonly animated by a faint inscription in pencil on the reverse of the photo Haymon had shown him with a *Who d'you think this could be?* Stavro had grabbed it, left without another word, returned the next day and announced, *This is a portrait of Kalemkâri Beardless Kasım Pasha, a favourite official of Sultan Abdülaziz. Hailed as a statesman with a future. Shot himself with his service pistol in a spa hotel in Budapest over some woman.*

The old man's face was glowing with the thrill of what he considered as a major discovery. Since the name Kalemkâri Beardless Kasım Pasha meant nothing to Haymon, however, the godson shared none of that thrill. The portrait with the moustache darkened under the photographer's hand was turned over to Numan with the suggestion *That doctor of yours who collects portraits? Might be interested. And if he isn't, don't worry; we'll auction it.* That last course of action wasn't necessary. Numan flogged the Pasha's portrait to the brain surgeon for a tidy sum.

The photo greedy Hürmüz had pocketed upon being shown the door at Kalemkâri Beardless Kasım Pasha's Çengelköy yalı had landed in Haymon's warehouse without changing hands too many times (unlike the ruby ring she'd also pinched, but more on that later). Yes, she had moved from place to place; thankfully, the photo tucked into the illuminated hand-written Koran stayed as fresh as the first day it had been taken, over a century ago.

Widowed at nineteen, then tender Hürmüz was handed from lap to lap – as it were – always a mistress, never a wife, for many years afterwards. A sharp tongue and nasty temper meant that as soon as a man had his fill of her charms, she was sent packing from one house to the next. Repeatedly failing to bag a loaded husband, having lost all hope by the time she was thirty-six, and crushed by her poverty-soured mother's gibes along the lines of *What happy-go-lucky fool's gonna have you, leftover of forty men?* Hürmüz settled for the **Albanian carter Recep**, married him and moved into his ramshackle wooden house in Fatih's Malta neighbourhood.

Life in that dump was no bed of roses for grasping Hürmüz, whose designs on the dead pasha's yalı had come to nought. If Recep earned three pence with his cart hauled by a pair of horses, one blind, the other lame, he pissed two up a wall in some sleazy stand-up bar and came home drunk as a skunk. Her only hope was for him to die as soon as possible so that she might inherit that hovel; it was still a roof over her head. But when it came to avarice, the carter's **marriageable daughter Safiye** could teach Hürmüz a thing or two. Stepmother and stepdaughter were at it all day long, and badgered Recep too. Hürmüz wanted to get her hands on the wooden hovel, and Safiye wanted her father to divorce Hürmüz. But Recep enjoyed his third wife's playfulness in bed. Despite all his daughter's efforts, he didn't divorce Hürmüz.

At long last, Safiye accepted defeat and married **her chronic suitor Offal Seller Bünyamin** who'd made a habit of banging at the door to proclaim his devotion whenever he got drunk. But she didn't forget to nick her stepmother's bundle containing the pasha's ruby ring, the illuminated hand-written Koran with the pasha's photo inside and a few bits and bobs of no value. She had no idea what was in it; she'd stolen it just to spite Hürmüz.

The bridegroom thumbed through the pilfered bundle, found the ruby ring and placed it on his finger. The new bride of no more than a week tried to wrest it back, won a good hiding as a reward, and thus learnt that love was no barrier to a beating, and love ended when you got what you wanted anyway. Once he'd placed the ring on his finger – never to be removed, even when he was chopping liver – Bünyamin paid no attention to anything else Safiye had brought along as her dowry, not even so much as taken the Koran out of its pink satin sleeve. The ring now gone, Safiye hung the pinched Koran – sleeve and all – on a nail she'd hammered above her bed.

The stepdaughter whose life she'd made a living hell now out of the picture, Hürmüz (still unaware of the theft of the bundle) charmed Recep to make the house over to her name. He had weak lungs; she'd get the house when he died, he already had one foot in the grave. But she never got to enjoy her dilapidated home. At the age of forty-five, she perished in the awful 1918 fire that devastated the districts of Laleli and Fatih. As for Recep, who'd been boozing in some den in Pazartekke during the fire: he forgot Hürmüz just like that, and married for the fourth time within three months, regardless of his age, and moved in to his new wife's rented place in Atikali.

Left penniless after the death of the husband who'd beaten her regularly twice a day for years and years, Safiye had to seek shelter with her son-in-law **Kemal who ran the Nemlizade Han teashop in Sirkeci**. She didn't have the heart to sell the ruby ring she'd slipped off his finger before he'd breathed his last; instead, she hid it in a tiny pocket she'd sewn into her drawers When **her cold-hearted daughter Necla** asked, *Dad had a ruby ring, what happened to it?* Safiye nearly lashed out, *Who says it was his?* She bit her tongue and replied, *Been years since that no-good dad of yours sold that lovely ring and pissed it up the wall!* Too lazy to insist, Necla never asked about the ring again, and Safiye kept it safely her drawers for years.

Kemal, who had six mouths to feed in his three-room house, shoved his mother-in-law in the old coal store that was little better than a dungeon, its walls blistering in the damp. Safiye hammered another nail above her bed to hang the still unopened Koran which shielded the Pasha's photo. Every morsel that passed through her gullet was begrudged by the son-in-law who 'cut' tea with sodium bicarbonate and served stale coffee in his two-square-metre teashop. Scared of being turned out to the street in her old age, Safiye worked her fingers to the bone and kept her head down, and was told off by her lazy daughter if she didn't. It was the second day of the Cyprus Peace Operation, 1974, when she'd thought, *I'd better wrap blue paper around the sitting room light* to comply with the blackout, fell from the chair and broke her hip. Kemal wouldn't keep her at home. He rushed her over to the Hospital for the Poor, and promptly forgot about her. For three months no one visited as she lay there and her hip refused to heal; she died cursing her daughter and son-in-law.

That curse worked, and quickly too. First, the landlord evicted the family with the four kids. Earlier, when Necla had lifted Safiye who had just broken her hip to undress her, the ruby ring came to light; instead of taking care of her mum, Necla had raised hell, *You said dad sold it and pissed it up a wall! Why did you lie?* and pocketed the ring. They sold it and rented a flat in Fındıkzade. Yes, it was small, but it did have a nice garden at the rear where a mulberry tree bore fruit the size of knuckles. Just when they'd settled in, one of his customers thought about counting the tokens he'd bought from Kemal and found ninety-five even though he'd paid for one hundred. *It was a mistake!* he swore blind; to no avail. Fed up with his bicarbonate tea, stale coffee and rudenesss, the tenants in the office block had him sacked.

Teashop Kemal and his wife moved dozens of times after that. Their kids grew up in the meanwhile, and each and every one turned out to be useless. They only dropped in once in a blue moon, and then only to either beat up their mum, or exchange blows with their dad when he refused to hand over money. Husband and wife were living in a single room of a good size in a Greek house with a shared toilet in Aynalıçeşme when Necla contracted cutaneous tuberculosis and died in agony. Kemal died soon afterwards. His useless sons raided Kemal's one-room pad for money. They found what little was wrapped in a handkerchief and hidden inside a pillow, left the room and never went back. Before long the building was sold to a chemicals company. The estate agent wanted to clear the building, so they engaged the **devout Scrap Dealer Gazanfer who had a warehouse in Dolapdere.**

Gazanfer had started out by picking through rubbish; now he had a warehouse. He inspected the entire building and told his men to sift through every single thing left behind by the tenants, from the filthy mattresses through to the loo pitchers, sort them, stuff them into sacks and take them over to the warehouse. There was lots to do; once those odds and ends were cleared, the doors, flooring and windows, including the frames, would be removed; it would all be sorted, the building would be gutted, and handed over to the interior architects commissioned by the chemicals company to transform it into a head office.

On the ground floor, Gazanfer spotted the pink satin sleeve hanging on the nail above the bed Necla had died in, and recognised it as a Koran. He couldn't touch it, since he hadn't washed. Going to the revolting shared toilet, he washed in the knee-deep filth, returned, removed the illuminated hand-written Koran from the sleeve, kissed and touched it to his forehead. He was flicking through it, hoping to find some money, when he came across the Pasha's picture. With no time to inspect it in depth, he glanced at it and placed it back inside the Koran. He told his men to load up and make for the warehouse, took the Koran he didn't know was handwritten, got into his black Murat Kartal and drove off to the accompaniment of the busted silencer, making an unholy racket.

When he got to Dolapdere, he saw **his black-browed, silky-skinned apprentice Memet** dribbling a ball outside the warehouse. The boy was only nine. He'd been thrilled to find a busted football in the junk and pleaded with the tyre repairman next door, *Chieef... Please Chieef...* to inflate it. A cheerful, kindly soul who'd played left back for Kasımpaşaspor for years, the former footballer didn't have the heart to make the boy beg. He inflated the filthy football and patched the tear with a piece from an inner tube for good measure.

Scared by the exhaust spewing jet-black fumes, Memet got jittery and lost control of the ball. It rolled towards the road. Gazanfer – who'd never enjoyed his own childhood, and hated children anyway – deliberately ran over it, making sure Memet saw him. The kid was nearly as badly deflated as the flattened ball. Gazanfer hopped out, and in his customary rage looking for something to lash out at, he gave the boy an almighty slap as if he hadn't done enough already, *Screw you and your family too... Like you have nothing to do inside, ya' git!* Memet was used to getting beaten; it hurt, sure, not as much the squashed ball though. Handing over a handful of coins Gazanfer told the boy, *Go get me kokoreç in two half loaves... and make sure he puts plenty of hot pepper too, off you go!* Memet trudged off towards the kokoreç cart for the grilled offal delicacy, swearing his head off.

The scrap dealer hadn't entirely overlooked the possibility that the Koran might be valuable. He mulled for a while *Shall I show it around, or not?* and eventually decided to hang on to it. He'd been wanting to get a copy of the Holy Koran for the shop for some time, just never got round to it. The illuminated hand-written Koran that was the Pasha's wedding gift to his greedy wife Hürmüz, and had stayed in pristine condition since it had only been removed a few times from its sleeve for over a hundred years, was placed on the shelf next to cheap religious volumes in Gazanfer's office separated from the warehouse by a glazed partition, books such as *Forty Verses and Forty Hadiths, An Illustrated Prayer Guide, The Faith That Everyone Needs,* and *I'm Learning About My Religion.*

Had the Koran commissioned by Kalemkâri Beardless Kasım Pasha in 1875 of **Slowhand İsmail Efendi** and **Hafız Ömer Çelebi**, famous calligrapher and illuminator, respectively, of their time, ended up with Haymon Yener instead of Gazanfer, it would have been auctioned with an opening price higher than what the scrap dealer made in a year, and collectors would have fought over this Koran with the immaculate cover and untouched pages. But the exquisite book of priceless calligraphy and illuminations stayed on the filthy shelf of a filthy warehouse.

When Memet brought the kokoreç, Gazanfer was staring at the Pasha's portrait. It looked like an important person. He might save it and hang it up somewhere at home. The Pasha's piercing gaze and authoritarian bearing were impressive. Leaving the picture at the edge of the desk, he attacked his kokoreç. As he chomped, dribbling grease, he pointed at a heap of several *Doğan Kardeş* magazines, *Hayat* magazines from 1961–62, schoolbooks in Greek that had belonged to a pupil of the Zoğrafyon Lycée, and a mouldy box piled high with nondescript books and an array of printed papers, and said to Memet, *This lot's gonna go to Mr Haymon, don't you forget.* He wasn't all that great in the literacy stakes; he knew nothing about the value of such stuff, nor cared to learn. It was enough to send word to Mr Haymon whenever he got hold of anyting in these lines.

He finished eating and went to the tyre repairman's shop next door to wash his hands. Caught by his jacket, the photo fell by the pile he'd just pointed at. He was washing his hands with dishwashing detergent in the trough made out of a shower tray when the exhaust repairman from three doors down dropped in. He knew about Gazanfer's busted silencer, and had brought over a replacement. Gazanfer was haggling when Mr Haymon's man came to the warehouse. He was carrying the pile Memet had pointed at, when he spotted the photo on the floor, thought it must have fallen by mistake, picked it up and popped it in the box. That is how the photo shot by Cosmi Sébah reached Haymon Yener.

Many days passed before Gazanfer remembered the Pasha's picture. He asked Memet. Black eyes wide open under those black eyebrows on silky dark skin, the boy said, *I never saw no picture nor nothing,* giving his boss yet another chance too good to miss: a single slap with the back of the hand. Memet stood stock still, waiting *Any more?* His heart sinking a tiny bit when he saw those eyes filming, Gazanfer murmured, *Thrashed the kid so much he doesn't feel it any more.* He'd gone too far, and decided it would be best to make up to the boy. Just then he heard the call to afternoon prayers, postponed making up to Memet and trundled over to the Imperial Judge Mosque whose muezzin he knew.

Whilst Gazanfer performed afternoon prayers, still bemoaning the loss of the picture he thought was valuable, Haymon was sorting through the box he had emptied. He was delighted at the Photo Sébah mark on the picture, but couldn't read the faint old script on the reverse. Setting it aside for his godfather, he sent to the shop in Aslıhan Arcade a box full of greeting cards, doctors' visiting cards, wedding invitations, commonplace postcards with cityscapes, menus of once famous restaurants, theatre and concert posters, handbills, and magazines.

Energised by deciphering the inscription *Likeness of Kalemkâri Beardless Kasım Pasha,* Stavro had made straight for Ottoman periodicals section of Beyazıt Library, where he'd found an item on the Pasha's suicide, after which he'd consulted historian friends and done his homework. He returned to the gallery the next day, elated, with the satisfaction of having learnt something – Haymon's lukewarm reaction notwithstanding.

In actual fact, Stavro had been harbouring a secret hope as he went through his godson's inventory – and offered priceless information. He was hoping to come across the photograph he'd left behind when he moved to Istanbul all that time ago. He would recognise the Sabuncuyan signature straightaway, and *The Clock Tower and the Town on a Snowy Day* still remained fresh in his mind's eye like it was yesterday.

The best image of Stavro's hometown – that he missed more and more – had been hanging in Ardıçoğlu Mansion, which had sustained heavy damage in the great earthquake that had also destroyed the lovely Clock Tower built in 1886. Extensive repairs would have rescued the mansion. But the Turkish family had it knocked down to make way for a six-storey block of flats, a horrible eyesore.

Sabuncuyan's *The Clock Tower and the Town on a Snowy Day* vanished during the Ardıçoğlu family's move. As if in validation of the candle theorem on the correlation between ageing and memory, Stavro recalled more of the past as he forgot more of the present. He would get lost time and again between Bronze Street and his own place on Kurtuluş Road, but remembered as if yesterday the moles on the faces of his youthful dalliances, or the parties in the men's reception room where the photo used to hang.

For a while, whether this photograph actually existed was debated by the handful of people interested in the history and culture of their city. There was no such photograph, purported some, since no photographer called Karnik Sabuncuyan had ever lived there; just a farcical legend concocted by some Armenian charlatan claiming kinship in the hope of bleeding them for money and stuff. This man they cast apspersions on, those would-be re-writers of the history of the city – *It was one hundred per cent Turkish!* – was none other than **Musicologist Michel Simonian, grandson of Karnik Sabuncuyan**, and he knew precisely who his grandfather was.

A close friend of Nemlizade Hayati Bey, one of the founders of the hospital, Karnik wasn't content that fame had spread to neighbouring cities. He wanted to repeat his success in the Imperial Seat despite its troubles due to the war that had just broken out in the Balkans. He would establish a modern studio in the ground floor of the Nemlizade Han, for which Hayati Bey had commissioned a Levantine architect. The plans were drawn up, cards printed bearing the name Photo Saboundjian-Stamboul, and new equipment ordered from Paris. He was hopeful; it was wartime, yes, but his professional future would assuredly be bright.

Come 1915, however, it all fell apart. The baleful winds sweeping through Anatolia, which ripped thousands out of their homes, did not spare this unassuming Black Sea city. Smiles vanished. Displaced Armenians trudged along the roads, wretched, miserable, as their neighbours lamented behind closed doors, and others less scrupulous seized the opportunity to seize abandoned properties. Temporarily shelving his dreams of becoming the best photographer in Istanbul, Karnik left the studio he had never got round to opening, and went to Paris with his family. He wasn't planning on dying there; he thought he'd go back one day and pick up where he'd left off. But it wasn't going to be possible anytime soon, he realised very quickly and painfully.

Karnik was nothing if not hardworking and resolute; he would have carried on in Paris. Except it was already teeming with famous photographers; he never managed to break through. Over the years he gradually lost hope. He lived for a long time on the proceeds of his property (thanks to the intercession of Hayati Bey, who had made sure he'd got a fair price despite it being wartime), lamenting over fate's repeated tricks, until his death.

Nıvart, who'd had to focus on saving her family since leaving the Black Sea, and consequently forgotten about the wonderful photos she used to take, laid her husband to rest in Paris on 2 September 1939, one day after the pall of blood and fire over Europe that would be known as the Second World War broke out.

What revived public awareness in Karnik many years later was his grandson's visit to Istanbul. Michel Simonian – a specialist in academic studies of ethnic music – was the youngest son of Karnik's daughter, who'd married a Lebanese Armenian. Michel had come to Istanbul for a fortnight to research local music under the auspices of a UNESCO-supported project. He met many musicians, both famous and obscure throughout his stay, compiled folk songs in Armenian and Turkish, and gave a local music seminar to a small, open-minded audience at the Conservatoire.

If he hadn't met **the china doll beauty that was Arsen Melkonyan** on the last day of the seminar, he would have returned to Paris on the following day and the interview that was to cause such controversy in the city would never have been published.

But the pretty twenty-two-year-old with the luminous skin who spoke with tilted her nose up in the air had come over at the end of the seminar and asked in flawless French if he had seen much of Istanbul. Michel was smitten. She looked as delicate as a new leaf; he wanted to sweep her up and swing her in the air. Explaining that this was his first visit to Istanbul, and no, he hadn't done much sightseeing at all; he asked if she would accompany him. It was beyond her wildest dreams. She was equally keen to spend time with him; she liked his colourful delivery, the way he forgot about the world as he played the *duduk* and the *oud*, his style and manner and everything. They explored Istanbul for a week. Michel fell madly in love with this girl half his age.

On their fourth day together, when they were having aubergine pastry and *hünkârbeğendi*, Sultan's delight lamb stew with aubergine purée at the historic Pandeli Restaurant in the Spice Bazaar when, resisting the temptation to reach out and stroke her long, slender fingers like a bird's wing, he asked if she played any instruments. The athletic Arsen, who owed her French to the Lycée Notre Dame de Sion where she'd captained the gymnastics team, wasn't in the least bit musical. *But my great-grandmother taught music at the Mıhitaryan Armenian Lycée, and she played the violin beautifully,* she said, before adding what she'd heard from the family: after Lerna Hanım had been assaulted by Headmaster Serop Efendi one day, she'd given up teaching then and there, and never touched a violin again.

Michel Simonian would never know that he owed his existence to Serop Efendi's temporary attack of insanity. If only the devout and solemn headmaster had not eaten the fly agaric stew that lunchtime, instead of going insane, he would have taken Michel's grandfather Karnik by the hand and escorted the young orphan back to Meram, where the lad would have stayed, and therefore never gone to that Black Sea town in the provinces, never married Nıvart, and Michel would never have been born.

Blissfully unaware of this particular turn of fate that had not taken place, Michel lost himself in Arsen's china doll face as he sipped his lunchtime rakı. Except this new love did nothing to quell his unease; quite the opposite.

He was very unhappy with **his Dutch wife Femke** whom he'd once fallen as suddenly for, much like he was with Arsen now. They had been the ideal couple, their love had been the toast of their friends and hailed as an example to hopeless others; yet, for some time, they had been trying to figure out what had gone wrong. Or more accurately, Femke was bending over backwards to understand and rebuild their love that was her only raison d'être, and a sympathetic Michel supported his wife's efforts. Realising they could no longer avoid the truth (that unhappiness filled their souls like a fug) they'd sent **their sixteen-year-old son Eric** to his grandmother in Amsterdam. In his new school, the lad hoped his parents would sort out whatever was troubling them and return to those happy days of old.

Michel and Femke had moved to a two-storey house with a garden in the suburbs of Paris in the same hope, and the regimen of opening up to each other and rekindling their love helped. They'd spent a wonderful week in candlelight, with flowers, lots of music and lovemaking. Michel believed he'd fallen in love with Femke all over again as he stroked her ageing skin with a fondness he'd deny had anything to do with pity.

He would have taken her along on this UNESCO trip. But she was convinced they really had rekindled their love; and since everything was back on track, and an absence due to a business trip would only make the heart grow fonder, she'd refused. She'd driven him to Orly and sent him off with a kiss on the lips.

As the aircraft took off, a deep unhappiness settled over Michel. All that stirring music, candles, wine, the diet of love that had filled their week, everything they'd undertaken to save their marriage as if following doctor's orders, along with stilted communication that lacked spontaneity: in short, none of that was going to help one little bit. His heart sank at admitting he was unable to fall in love with his wife again. As the aircraft landed at Yeşilköy Airport, he was thinking it would be cruel to pretend, that it was best to tell her upon his return, *It's not working, it's just not going to work… Best not to hurt each other.*

What brought on his cruelty was his sudden infatuation with Arsen, though. He was planning on coming clean the moment he was back in Paris and breaking up with Femke, before returning to Istanbul to be with his young girlfriend. But by second day with Arsen, Femke had flown his mind. The future looked entirely different.

He rang his wife, citing lots of flimsy pretexts for his delay by a week: the seminar had attracted a great deal of interest, he had to attend a number of meetings for future projects, Istanbul was wonderful, he wished she were there, but not to worry, they would soon come here together, they would enjoy this magnificent city, et cetera, et cetera, et cetera. Femke wanted to believe him despite the faint stab that she felt; but the moment Michel replaced the handset, he'd already forgotten about his wife. He was lost in the dreams of a future with Arsen. They might live in Istanbul for a few years, flitting over to Paris now and then, Femke would get herself sorted in the meanwhile, Eric would go to London for university, and so everyone would be fine one way or the other. Even if things were to turn out differently, he was determined to leave Femke. That was the first step he had to take if he were to change his life.

Which is what he did. The moment he was back in Paris, within the hour, he blurted out he wanted to leave. Femke's mumbled suggestions of repeating the same romantic regimen only hardened his attitude and he confessed to having fallen in love with a young Armenian girl named Arsen in Istanbul. It all sounded much more like an ecstatic declaration of love than a guilty admission. He wanted to avoid the clichés such as, *Let's give it another go; we belong to each other* that would only string it out. Hurting Femke might simplify things; if she broke it off, there would be no going back.

They had a dreadful argument. Femke accused her husband of the worst kind of treachery, of stabbing her in the back, and flung a wine bottle at his head, and Michel slammed the door as he stormed out. He went to a hotel and grabbed the phone as soon as he entered his room to ring Arsen. He said it was all finished with his wife and he'd come over to Istanbul the moment he'd sorted things out. He'd come to realise he couldn't live without her; they would live however she wanted and their love would last until death. Arsen nearly went crazy with happiness. They spoke for so long that the receptionist thought Michel had left the phone off the hook.

In the meanwhile, having realised she had lost for good the husband she still loved deeply, Femke stepped into a hot bath and slit her wrists with her husband's razor blade.

The next day, Michel arrived in his minibus to collect his stuff (and his ethnic musical instruments in particular) and discovered her in a bathtub full of blood-red water. He was devastated by Femke's blood-drained face, now indistinguishable from the colour of the bathtub. He'd been too cruel.

Eric rushed over from Amsterdam. Unaware of the events of that tragic night, he tried to console his dad, feeling, in the over-emotionalism that is natural at that age, like they'd swapped places, putting his arm over his dad's shoulder to say they'd support each other, as if he was the senior of the two.

Crushed by his guilt, Michel blamed Arsen for his crime. He hated her, as if she'd tricked him. Femke's grey-blue eyes and sweet smile filled his mind, Femke, who had always been at his side, through the ups and downs of youth, in the best of times and the worst too, as they'd matured. Michel banished the image of Arsen who was desperately trying to fill the void left in his mind by Femke, and banished that image violently. It didn't occur to him to write her a brief note to say he was ending it. It didn't occur to him that he was about to destroy yet another heart.

With no idea where he lived, so going out of her mind at the lack of news, Arsen had stopped eating. Refusing to leave the house in case *Michel might phone*, she sat by the silent telephone for days. Three weeks later a dry, loveless, sad letter arrived, naming their age difference as the insurmountable obstacle.

Once Michel was over the shock, he'd gathered his wits and had written those couple of lines to eradicate any possibility that Arsen might fetch up and find him.

Unaware of the tragedy Michel lived through, and believing he had toyed with her heart, Arsen slit her wrists just like Femke had. She'd read the letter in tears, smashed her glass against the wall and stabbed her own wrist. Her mother, who had been concerned about Arsen's depression, raced over and grabbing the screaming and shuddering girl, rushed her over to the Taksim A&E.

Three weeks earlier, (on Michel's last day in Istanbul, to be precise) when they were still on cloud nine, he'd met a journalist by chance. The resulting interview published in the *Hürriyet* would reverberate around the Black Sea city. At the time, in the first flush of new love, yet dreading the prospect of facing Femke on the following day, Michel was looking for an easy way out.

Galatasaray Lycée graduate interpreter-cum-journalist Osman had already set up his tape recorder to interview Michel who'd turned out to be an expert in ethnic music. The interview on music demonstrated a modicum of political flavour and touched on the Armenian diaspora's condemnation of Turkey.

Michel spoke of growing up on his grandfather's lap; the photographer had left his mark on the Black Sea city, and had even described to his grandson the panorama he still regretted not keeping a copy of, his famed *The Clock Tower and the Town on a Snowy Day* . Based on the information provided by Michel, the journalist included Karnik Sabuncuyan's biography in a small inset. There was a fundamental error in the biography, however. Unable to remember his grandfather's birthplace, Michel had just said, *He was a Black Sea native, born and bred.*

The mention of this small Black Sea city in a major newspaper, and in such a prestigious manner too, naturally rekindled the legend of Karnik Sabuncuyan. His name suddenly assumed a historic significance, and a few citizens set about flicking through family albums *Wonder if Sabuncuyan photographed our family too?* The interview put quite a few noses out too. The group who labelled Michel Simonian as a charlatan: There never had been a photo showing the city in the snow and the Clock Tower and what have you, such claims were based on an attempt to erase from public memory the actions of ASALA, the Armenian terror organisation who'd been assassinating Turkish diplomats around the world.

Türkan Kaymakoğlu, however, who had first learnt the old script, recalled both the photograph that bore the title *The Clock Tower and the Town on a Snowy Day* in old script at the bottom, and the rosewood frame.[5] She'd started collecting historic photographs of the city after settling back into the Kaymakoğlu Mansion in her retirement, and subsequently decided to create an archive. Any attempts to repudiate the photograph were scotched at once: it had hung on the wall in the men's reception room of the Ardıçoğlu Mansion. In fact, a photograph taken during the banquet given by Ardıçoğlu Totodaki Bey in honour of İsmet Pasha who was visiting the city clearly showed *The Clock Tower and the Town on a Snowy Day* on the wall behind them; this photo of the National Chief was published in the *The Coast*.

Anticipating political payback, **the future District Mayor Cumhur Eryıldıran** had taken it upon himself to prove her claim. He was still quite young at the time, not yet a mayor or anything. That exalted station might have crossed his mind as a highly remote possibility, but he lacked the courage, experience and networks to embark upon the political stage.

It would have been a gross injustice to attribute those efforts solely to his political aspirations. Cumhur ran four shops in the fish market and two fishing boats, and would continue to do so during his term as District Mayor; with a degree in Ethnology from the Faculty of Languages, History and Geography in Ankara, he had always been very keen on culture and history. Whilst the Metropolitan City Council contented itself with superficial cultural activities *for appearances' sake*, Cumhur happily allocated budgets to free-to-attend events such as folk song festivals, drawing courses for women and novel reading drives. It had taken him years of roaming mountain villages along the Black Sea coast all the way to the border; but his 480-page *Black Sea Songs and Their Tales* was at long last finished after adding just one more song or tale he'd encountered. Four rejections later, he decided to self-publish this authoritative tome on ethnology, which is how it was entrusted to printer Kamer.

At the time the legend of Karnik Sabuncuyan initiated such controversy, a newly qualified Cumhur had just returned home; he was compiling his book, running fishing boats, and sounding out political circles. With the help of a former flatmate, he'd located the newspaper mentioned by Türkan Hanım in the National Library's periodicals department. True enough, *The Coast*, once one of the most popular newspapers in the city until folding in the late sixties, unable to compete with the circulation figures of national papers, did show İsmet Pasha on the front page, and *The Clock Tower and the Town on a Snowy Day* was clearly visible on the wall behind him, rosewood frame and everything. That being a time predating microfilms and scanners, Cumhur Eryıldıran had photocopied the newspaper instead, and delivered it to Türkan Hanım.

Having proven the existence of the legend of Sabuncuyan, Türkan showed the photocopy everywhere; this was the photo she was looking for. Many years later, her old friend Huma İpekören sent word that she'd found the photograph in question, and Türkan, who had a head cold that day, had despatched her driver Hamdi Tutuş to fetch it. But then the driver ran over the old physician Nurettin Kozanlı's wife Midwife Mualla,

Türkan forgot all about the picture and dealt with the accident. It was only after Hamdi was diagnosed and hospitalised, quite a while later, in fact, that she visited Huma Hanım personally, and was hugely disappointed at the offering. It was nothing more than a news clipping. The ninety-seven-year-old Türkan, whose mind was as sharp as a razor, realised her friend, who'd only just turned seventy, was losing her grip. It was more upsetting than the failure to find Sabuncuyan's famed photograph.

The news clipping she took just to avoid hurting the poor woman showed a colour photo taken from the highest point in the city on a snowy day. It did feature a clock tower, true, just like in Sabuncuyan's photo. Except it wasn't the lovely tower erected as a tribute to Abdülhamid II, later destroyed in the great earthquake; it was the tasteless replica erected as a replacement.

Türkan Kaymakoğlu collected and saved many other Sabuncuyan photographs, though. Give him his due: but for Latif Tibuk, the city might never have seen these fabulous sepia photos. Before relations between the two had soured, Latif would borrow landscapes and building photos bearing the mark Photo Saboundjian in Latin script and publish them, accompanied by a short blurb, in a small column entitled 'Once Upon A Time' on the back page of his *Popular News*, thus silencing aspersions cast on the legend of Karnik Sabuncuyan.

After Latif was caught with Moldovan Anya, however, Türkan had distanced herself from the star of this *utterly deblorable* incident. At first she'd sided with, and wholeheartedly supported Asiye Tibuk. But when the glowering Asiye took him back as if nothing had happened and posed for heaps of photos, she too fell from grace with Türkan. The retired judge not only stopped seeing the family, but also refused to lend any more photos. And despatched her steward to ask for the return of those Latif still had.

In perpetual awe of Türkan Kaymakoğlu, Latif went to the mansion carrying a box of the finest chocolates. Of course, it wasn't about 'Once Upon A Time'. He wanted to make peace with this old lady who still called the tune in the city. Her attitude to the leading citizens set the standard for the rest. If he failed to regain her friendship, this distance could cast a pall on his business affairs. Not to be taken in by a box of chocolates, of course, Türkan pleaded an indisposition and refused to see him. Leaving with his tail between his legs, and still fuming, he replaced it with a selection of amateur shots taken on digital cameras; 'From Our City' soon died a death.

Türkan was as confident as Stavro of eventually locating *The Clock Tower and the Town on a Snowy Day*. They might both have one foot in the grave, but for them, this particular Sabuncuyan masterpiece could have been the validation of a fabulous golden age. Their search was in vain, however. No such photograph existed, not any longer, that is.

The Turkish family who wanted to knock the Ardıçoğlu Mansion down and replace it with a block of flats had left behind loads of worthless stuff as they moved to their temporary place. They'd also told their **cleaner Gülayşe Döngel** to take whatever she wanted. At the sight of the junk still there, and with a *Hurry girls!* Gülayşe fetched up with her sisters. They plundered. Grabbed everything, from coal buckets with broken handles to cracked gas lamps to dented copper sieves to rugs with the nap beaten out. They didn't leave a single pin. They'd have taken the doors if they could.

As her sisters scavenged, their mouths watering, Gülayşe's eye fell on *The Clock Tower and the Town on a Snowy Day* in the rosewood frame. The frame, rather than the picture. It was hanging quite high, but that wasn't going to stop her: she took the trouble to fetch the rickety stepladder from next door, removed the picture and threw it onto the floor, where it was soon trampled by the dirty shoes of the other sisters who'd been pawing ripped cardigans, broken coffee tables and cracked jars. Later, as Gülayşe was placing her wedding picture into the rosewood frame back in her own home, the demolition crew arrived, and oblivious to the beauty of even the ceiling roses, began swinging sledgehammers at the walls. A thick cloud of dust settled upon Karnik Sabuncuyan's legendary photograph and *The Clock Tower and the Town on a Snowy Day* perished in the rubble.

Polishing their rosewater puddings off with unsweetened Turkish coffees at the Three Brothers Patisserie, the Medical Director asked Türkan whether she'd been able to locate the photograph she'd been looking for all these years. It was a throwaway question. He thought he might be able to offer a few words to the conversation instead of listening agape to the old lady talking about the Internet. This question reminded Türkan of the members of the hospital founding board. She spoke about the Karnik Sabuncuyan portraits in her archive, portraits of these gentlemen she had an enormous respect for; and how it would be right and proper to upload them onto the website. In fact, he could even use them in the book she'd heard he was about to write. This last comment suddenly alerted and excited the Medical Director who'd been nodding restlessly up to that moment. Loath to trouble the old lady, he said, *I'll have them copied and returned to you.* But she – ever abreast of the latest in every field imaginable, two feet in the grave notwithstanding – replied that she'd already had them scanned by her secretary, and although it was possible to e-mail each jpeg individually, there was no need to waste time, and added that she would record the photos onto a CD that she would send over.

Amongst the photographs on the CD, in addition to the members of the board, was the hospital conceived of in 1898 and opened in 1902, also shot by Karnik Sabuncuyan. The group posing in front of the new hospital consisted of Governor (and Hospital Board Chairman) Hüsnü Simavi Bey, members Kalustyan Ara Bey, Ardıçoğlu Totodaki Bey, Nemlizade Hayati Bey and **Yelkencizade Rahmi Bey** as well as **the first Medical Director of the hospital: Turcophile Alain Latour** recruited from France on a salary of ten gold liras a month. They were all handsome, all charismatic; moreover, that they were all extraordinarily dedicated and patriotic was indubitable. Eyes welling up with nationalist fervour at this stirring image, the present Medical Director decided that the book he'd occasionally found too daunting to attempt was nothing less than his debt to these noble philanthropists.

Back in the day, the city's only healthcare institution was a wooden mansion serving as a rudimentary hospital for the poor and the old. The healthcare professionals consisting of three doctors (one Russian, two Turkish) and two pharmacies (one run by a superannuated Greek, and the other by a cross-eyed Armenian) failed to meet the city's needs. Serious illnesses resulted in a quick death for the poor; as for the rich: anyone who reached Istanbul survived, and the rest perished on the roads. Residents sought a cure in folk medicines that occasionally caused horrifying deaths. Notables (led by the Governor) acknowledged this great need and source of grief.

In the meanwhile, commanded by Sultan Abdülhamid II to erect a Children's Hospital in Istanbul as a tribute to Hatice Sultan, his daughter who had died of diphtheria aged eight months, work had begun on a modern facility based on Berlin's famous Kaiser und Kaiserin Friedrich Kinderkrankenhaus. Conscious of the unlikelihood of any help from the August State, and aware of the splendid hospital currently in construction in the Imperial Seat, Governor Hüsnü Simavi Bey lamented the situation in his own city so far from Istanbul.

His first step was admitting, *Best build your own hospital!* This *Meet your own needs* attitude of the Ottoman subjects would later be embraced even more enthusiastically by the new democratic republic's citizens: one hundred years after Governor Hüsnü Simavi Bey, a nation too scared to ask the state for the services they had every right to demand (and happily tugged forelocks in gratitude if by some random chance any were to be offered) would support the 'Build Your Own School' campaign with astonishing alacrity. Nay, not a single person would stand up to ask, *Why the heck are we paying taxes if we're going to build our schools ourselves?*

Thanks to the munificence of His Imperial Majesty the Sultan and a generous scattering of Ottoman Treasury gold, the Hamidiye Etfal children's hospital was built and opened within the year; in the meanwhile, the squad led by Governor Hüsnü Simavi Bey delighted in their accomplishment: the completion of their hospital in four years in a city that was a hardship area compared to Istanbul. It was commissioned without any financial assistance from the majestic empire, and it was practically perfect. Which is why everyone who had contributed posed with such proud smiles in the photograph shot by Sabuncuyan to mark the opening ceremony.

The French surgeon Alain Latour was indeed a Turcophile, not that blowing it out of all proportion was called for. He was more interested in the monthly salary of ten gold coins – much more than he could ever make in his own country – than in any sentimental attachment to Turks. The smile that had brought tears to the eyes of the Medical Director Demir Demir was caused as much by Latour's emotional response to the welcome he'd received as the thought of working in this backwater for a few years to hopefully save up enough for a house and vineyard in Toulouse where he would embark upon oenology.

To be fair, surgeon Alain Latour discharged his duty well: he was never anything other than totally dedicated to his profession; he saved countless patients from certain death and ran the hospital like clockwork. The strange thing was, despite his original *I'll return in a few years,* he served for twelve years the city that had taken him to heart. In 1914, he left for home in tears when war broke out and the hospital was closed down. His earlier enthusiasm for winemaking in Toulouse staunched after all that time on the shores of the Black Sea, and unable to find a position in one of the great hospitals in Paris, Latour settled in Marseilles. He carried on as an unassuming surgeon, constantly comparing the Mediterranean with the Black Sea, and admitting a preference for the harsh climate and the wild waves of the latter; until his dying day, he never stopped missing the fishermen friends who conversed in shouts, smoked like chimneys, and whose grumpy exteriors hid genuine affection.

The Medical Director thought this historic hospital deserved three or four hundred pages on coated paper, a leather-bound book with a sleeve. Despite Printer Kamer's assurances *Don't you worry, Sir, the print costs're on me,* the estimate was still daunting. The stock, colour separations, binding, this, that, and the other all would add up to a considerable sum. The Medical Director needed a sponsor. Strictly speaking, it wasn't yet written, but he'd planned it in a broad outline. He thought a sponsor would help with his motivation.

He would relate the hospital's history in chronological order. The first page would feature the photo of the Governor Hüsnü Simavi Bey, who had led the drive to found the hospital, followed by the photos of the other board members; this series would naturally have to conclude with his own photo, as not only the latest Medical Director, but also as the author.

However, having inspected all his photos, he'd failed to find a single one he liked. The only one that was anywhere near passable was a twenty-year-old passport photo, where he looked quite handsome, even formidable. True, it would have been better if he didn't have a moustache, but those were the years when a moustache was a *sine qua non* for a man. But using a twenty-year-old photo would have been quite ridiculous. But then again, he was getting on; he no longer looked as good.

He could avoid the topic no longer when the resident nerd Emrah asked for a photo for the website: *For some reason* he seemed to look older in photos. Never one to let an opportunity pass by, Emrah replied, *Just get a new one, Mr Medical Director Sir, and I'll sort it out on Photoshop.*

What this Photoshop lark was, the Medical Director had no idea. But he trusted Emrah. If only he'd known that the kid – whose belt loop featured a clang of keys on a cheap Fenerbahçe logo key ring and who'd yet to do his national service – supplied the addicts with dope and pills, he'd haul him over the coals. *That* was the real reason why work on the hospital's IT systems seemed to drag on and on, and why Emrah had become a permanent fixture. It really should have been obvious. A little curiosity on the part of the Medical Director was all that was needed: how on earth had the kid managed to buy a car when he'd only got his licence less than six months earlier, or afford to smoke forty red Marlboro a day? Another curious point was how uncomplaining the caretakers in Substance Abuse were, yet they raised merry hell if they were ever assigned elsewhere. Fixated on this book he would write, however, the Medical Director was oblivious to all this.

He would put into his book – after those precious portraits, obviously – the opening ceremony photograph, again, another Sabuncuyan piece. The next page would have a single word headline: *History*. Then the actual text would follow. He'd start *The year was 1898* but had no idea how to continue. He made a few attempts:

'The year was 1898! Governor Hüsnü Simavi Bey said, "Gentlemen! Let us levy forty para on each bale of tobacco and thirty on each merchant's despatch note, so that a suitably fine hospital may be erected in our fine city!" The residents took Governor Hüsnü Simavi Bey's wish as a command.'

That was the sum total of what he'd managed to write. And *that* was lifted from an account of the hospital's history he'd found – again – in Türkan's archive, in a newspaper that had been published for three and a half years in the 1950s.

Still stuck, he was seeking inspiration in the portraits of the hospital's founders Emrah had printed off the Türkan's CD, staring in particular at the face of the Governor Hüsnü Simavi Bey: despite the fez, a western gentleman if he'd ever seen one with that European-style goatee, tail coat and necktie. Every time he looked, he likened the handsome Governor to Abdülhak Hamit Tarhan and gave into the temptation to murmur the famous song with the great poet's lyrics: *Darkness prevails everywhere, yet divine light fills that abode / Is that sunset, or a grave, oh Lord?*

Hüsnü Simavi Bey was, indeed, very handsome, and he married four times. He divorced his **first wife Ayşe Edibe** on grounds of sterility. She'd just not conceived in two years of marriage, which ruined his prestige – an intolerable situation, one he could no longer entertain. It had been an arranged marriage, at any rate; and he found her dull, lethargic and so utterly lacking in femininity that he simply didn't want to sleep with a wife whose face he'd only seen after the wedding. Eventually he sent her back to her father's home on the pretext of childlessness. A mortified Ayşe Edibe was terribly offended. She was sure she wasn't sterile, and thought she'd been treated unfairly. Unperturbed by the convention that *no daughter of an agha would sink so low,* she married the younger son of her father's steward and by bearing him a chubby son before the year was out, proved she wasn't sterile; the Governor had done her wrong.

If his **second wife Headstrong Gülcemal** – a love match this time – hadn't fallen pregnant immediately, the Governor's devastated prestige would have been all but impossible to salvage. Aspersions on his masculinity had swept the city when Ayşe Edibe had a baby before Gülcemal. Even the fact that his second wife's belly looked ready to burst had made no difference to the women's whispers; everyone wondered whom the baby would resemble. It was only when the Governor's son with Gülcemal turned out to be a dead ringer that the poor fellow regained his old swagger.

Gülcemal owed her moniker to a childhood and adolescence spent riding horses, wearing her big brothers' trousers and flat caps to go to the coffee house, never once hesitating *I'm not a man, I'd better shut up and sit where I'm told,* or shying away from a punch-up; yet those wilful and androgynous airs hid a highly feminine and fertile physique. By some inexplicable instinct, the Governor had recognised that latent fecundity, and turned a deaf ear to insinuations about her boyishness – as if they had anything to do with fertility. He was proven right. Headstrong Gülcemal softened after becoming a mother; gone were her boyish airs. She bore another son eleven months after the first one. Two girls and another boy followed.

Governor Hüsnü Simavi Bey divorced Headstrong Gülcemal, mother of his five children, when he fell in love with the barely **fifteen-year-old Esma** with puffy eyes. To be honest, he didn't want the divorce; he did offer to *set you up in a house of your own, where you can live with your children; and I'll come from time to time.* Such a proposal was utterly abhorrent to the only daughter of Uzunoğlu Yakup Bey, a leading local merchant; Gülcemal would never submit to such injustice. Refusing to listen to another word of her husband's conciliatory efforts (he had hoped to effect this split without much unpleasantness) she returned to her father's home, not wanting to be married to this man any longer. The former rebel was wretched; Gülcemal just couldn't forgive her husband for marrying Esma in a hurry – *like he was chased by the cavalry!* – the moment *they* had divorced; she cursed him night and day.

The Governor then swung into action when the bride twenty-seven years his junior contracted yellow fever on the first day of their marriage. Lamenting the lack of a hospital in the city, he brought the subject round to yellow fever at every opportunity whenever he was in the company of other notables, and insisted on the necessity of building one. Sadly it was too late for his bride. He never got to enjoy his puffy-eyed Esma, and Esma never got to enjoy her youth. The girl who, unbeknownst to all, had conceived on her wedding night, was interred before the month was out.

Hearing of her successor's death agonies, Gülcemal had donned her cloak and rushed out to stand outside the mansion where the Koran was being recited over the dead body; raising her arms up to the skies, she started yelling at the top of her voice, *O great Allaaaaah!* She yelled constantly, a tragic voice rending the air. The women who'd been reverently listening to the Koran ran to the windows to watch the half-crazed woman on her knees, her cloak slipping off her head, screaming, *O great Allaaaaah! O Thee whose purpose defies man!* She never once uttered Esma's name, just spoke of destiny and divine justice.

No one made any effort to stop these heartbreaking cries reaching all the way into the room where the dead body lay covered with a white sheet and pressed down with a knife so it wouldn't swell. Headstrong Gülcemal yelled herself hoarse, *O great Allaaaaah! My Almighty God!* Eventually (having heard she was screaming the place down) her father Uzunoğlu Yakup Bey and her eldest son rushed over and half sweet-talked, half dragged her back home. She fell asleep, exhausted, yet swinging between a guilty conscience and peace; in the meanwhile, witnesses to the great Governor's sobs were astounded at how quickly Gülcemal's curses had worked.

Marginally appeased by Esma's death, but still loath to forgive her husband, Gülcemal went crazy at hearing her father had donated acres and acres for a modern hospital. At the time she was running an ivory comb through her glorious locks still wet from the bath. She pricked up her ears at the whispered name of the Governor. The female servants had sided with Gülcemal from the off, and had no idea why Uzunoğlu Yakup Bey might wish to give land over to his former son-in-law. Scared of their master, they tried to hide the news, but Gülcemal's blazing eyes dragged it out. She staggered, and then shot off like an arrow.

It was late in the evening, her hair was wet, it was snowing heavily, but nothing would prevent her from marching over to her father's horse-dealing office in a caravanserai dating back to the Seljuks. Any other woman who'd dare to stride between dozens of merchants of the grubbiest, filthiest ware, with no fear of molestation would have imperilled the reputation of her husband, father, big brother or whichever male was responsible for her. But this was rebellious as well as cantankerous Gülcemal. Had any one there dared ask, *Sister, what are you doing out at this time?* she'd have slammed him against the wall, and no messing.

She dived into the office and brought her father to book. *Say you'd discovered you really need it, say whatever, take that land back!* she demanded; why should her father contribute to a good deed that her former husband would tot up? Uzunoğlu Yakup Bey was equally adamant: *I've given my word, no going back now.* He saw her side, and he hadn't forgiven the Governor for divorcing his daughter and breaking her heart either. But he loved his homeland, he had a good reputation, and he was aware of the city's desperate need for a hospital.

At any rate, there was no way he'd risk losing his townsfolk's regard, or risk judgments along the lines of *He begrudged the land just because his former son-in-law heads the thing;* so when Yelkencizade Rahmi Bey mumbled on about this delicate matter, *Your former son-in-law daren't ask you in person… but the city does need a hospital… and the most suitable site is your land…* Uzunoğlu Yakup Bey stared wordlessly and interrupted before long so the poor fellow wouldn't have to cringe any more, *Yelkenci, who are we to deny what our hometown needs!* And promptly donated the piece of land stretching along the coast for the hospital.

Years passed; Gülcemal never married again. Her children grew up, got married, and she became a grandmother several times over. She eventually forgot about the hurt of being abandoned for a fifteen-year-old, and never saw the Governor again, neither at the weddings of her children, nor at the births of her grandchildren. True, she kept cursing him well after his death *My hands are going on be on his collar even in the hereafter!* But this curse no longer had the power to sear her heart, just empty words she kept repeating.

By the time the hospital was opened, with a ceremony blessed by prayers and recitations, the Governor who'd quickly got over the grief of the untimely death of his third wife had already been married to **his fourth wife Nezaket Hanım** for two and a half years. He'd already had a sixth child, and a seventh was on the way. He had made enormous efforts to create a hospital named *Hamidiye* as a tribute to the sultan; but he wouldn't live long enough, however, to see the name change to *Gureba* – Hospital for the Poor, in 1908.

A month before the proclamation of the Second Constitutional Monarchy, the Govenor had a sudden, acute pain in the abdomen at some ungodly hour of the night. Thinking her husband had overdone the anchovies fried in butter and the corn bread, Nezaket Hanım heated a brick on the stove, wrapped it in several towels and laid it on his belly. All it did was to speed his end.

Governor Hüsnü Simavi was in agony towards morning; forcing himself to wait until the first call to prayer, he headed to the hospital to see the great Medical Director Alain Latour. But Monsieur Latour was out. He'd settled well into this city he'd originally come for a stay of a few years; so, taking advantage of the day off on Friday, he'd gone fishing with a few fishermen who'd become his firm friends.

Enticed by the exuberance of the Black Sea, the Frenchman had learnt a good deal of Turkish, although not well enough to distinguish between the accents varying from village to village. Gestures worked better than words when it came to communicating with his strapping friends who threw in a net and hauled up a mountain of anchovies. To look at him, no one could tell this fellow with the bright blue eyes and thin, blond beard was a *Marseillais*. Like the fishermen, he sailed wearing a leather waistcoat and black hand-knitted beret, and loved drinking at the meze table laid out on the deck. He loved placing the turbot on the deck still alive, chopping the mirror-bright fish, dipping the fillets in corn meal and frying them in hot butter; so much so that his hands were covered in hot butter and chopper scars. Patients who'd seen their state close up would think twice about entrusting themselves to those hands.

Thoroughly mistrustful of the chatter of **the newly appointed young Doctor Fishbone Seyfettin Efendi**, the Governor, now in excruciating pain, had commanded the orderly, *Go, look for Alain, fetch him wherever you find him… Tell him I'm dying, tell him to hurry!* Having learnt that the surgeon was out fishing, the orderly leapt into a small rowboat; in the meanwhile, the doctor dubbed Fishbone Seyfi by the orderlies on account of his skinny build was emphatically concurring with Nezaket's diagnosis of gas pains: the stomach had rebelled at having to digest two panfuls of anchovies dipped in corn meal and fried in butter. This promising graduate of the Imperial School of Medicine was a real wit too. He tried a number of pleasantries on the man undressing for an examination, but the suffering Governor was in no state to laugh.

The orderly and the boatman looked for the happy surgeon on the vast Black Sea. Luck was on their side; they saw the vessel just where the folks at the fish hall had guessed it would be. As they approached, the Governor went into an attack of shivers. Witty physician Seyfi was puzzled by the profuse sweating and trembling, now that he'd given the fellow an enema, and never mind the yells. Meanwhile, the orderly spotted Alain Latour hauling in tons of anchovies along with the other fishermen, hopped onto the fishing boat, and exclaimed, *Fellasdyingehcomeover!*

It took quite a while for Alain Latour to figure out what the orderly was saying, even with the help of his fellow fishermen. He made it to the hospital, but the Governor had expired barely ten minutes earlier from a burst appendix. The hot brick laid on his belly had worsened the inflammation, and he had spent his final minutes in agony due to the enema given by Fishbone Seyfi.

The Governor Hüsnü Simavi Bey died groaning in excruciating pain in the very same hospital that would never have come into existence but for his own efforts. The Governor's death was the first in a series of sad events in the destiny of the hospital and its founders. Thanks to his Turkish friends, Ara Bey might have been spared the Armenian Displacement in 1915, but he died heartbroken and all alone after his daughter, son-in-law and two grandchildren had emigrated to Paris. No amount of pride in his involvement in the foundation of the hospital could rekindle his interest in it now; all he wanted was a quick death. And he got his wish.

Just like Ara Bey, Ardıçoğlu Totodaki Bey also died longing for the old happy days of friendship, alone in his mansion where *The Clock Tower and the Town on a Snowy Day* hung on the men's reception room wall. Life had palled after the Balkan Wars; once he'd sensed a decline in the heartiness of the greetings on the street, he withdrew into the mansion, withdrew from the city's social life. He, too, joined wholeheartedly in the progressive exuberance that was born with the Republic, but he didn't live long enough to see the tenth anniversary of the new regime of his homeland. After the Events of 6–7 September, only Stavro remained in Turkey; his four other children had all settled in Athens by then. An entire generation had to pass away before his children would shake off the *Turkish migrants* treatment. Many years passed; it was only in the early 1990s that the family's sad history was forgotten. By then, there was no one who remembered the family's roots went not to the Aegean but to Anatolia, to a small city on the Black Sea.

Yelkencizade Rahmi Bey's end was the most tragic of all the founders. Having gone all out to keep the hospital going even after it was closed down during the Great War, Rahmi Bey was arrested by the Ottoman Government on charges of treason for having joined the Nationalists; he died in a dungeon of a broken heart, without even appearing before a court. Yes, he certainly had sympathised with the Nationalists and been looking for ways of actively supporting the War of Independence, but he also knew that keeping the hospital going in these troubled times was equally crucial. To be branded a *traitor* – albeit by the Ottoman Government – had cut him to the quick, this venerable gentleman who loved his country more than anything.

His death left the hospital bereft of patronage. Flitting between the British and the Americans during the war, the hospital was transferred to private management after the proclamation of the Republic. Now renamed the National Hospital, it resumed service to an exhausted nation fresh out of a great and honourable war.

His sketchy knowledge about the hospital's history limited to main headings, once the Medical Director started research in earnest, *lack of source material* popped up on his agenda. Writing a history based on a few newspapers in Ottoman he'd asked Turkology undergraduates to transcribe, and some unreliable tales told by the elderly, was going to be impossible. As uninteresting as its recent history was, there existed plenty of documentation on the past thirty years of what was originally constructed as a general hospital, and reassigned as a mental health institution soon after the new building was commissioned – thereby obviating the need to build a twin block to connect to the blind façade. At the very least, a colossal archive lay before him in the new script. Local press offered information along the lines of *X new unit is commissioned in our hospital… Professor Y visits our hospital… Purchase of X instrument at great sacrifice…* The Medical Director was not aware that a good book required serious research into reliable sources, and that he would have to read every single book about the city; in short, that this would be a long, arduous and painstaking effort.

Not that anyone actually expected him to produce a book of historiographic precision. If he had put his heart into it, and looked up architect Çetin Kansız (for instance) to ask why he'd built it with its back to the sea; even that little snippet would have made his book interesting. But the Medical Director knew nothing about writing books.

To give him his due, it's not like he didn't try a variety of methods *In the hope of catching something of interest.* A few months back, he had asked his secretary Nemişo to draw up a list of all the guest speakers who had graced the conference hall. The idea was to interview important speakers to glean their thoughts and feelings about the hospital. Unable to believe his ears at her cheeky *What for?* he snapped at his secretary of this many years, *Just get on with your work… Never you mind what for!* Torn off a strip, this time she whinged, *Where am I gonna find it though? Not like anyone keeps track of who goes into the conference hall or comes out or anything…* The Medical Director guided her once again, *Don't we announce our events in* The Black Sea Herald, *Child? Doesn't this little trick occur to you?*

Unconvinced as to the need for this book, Nemişo had for months been pretending to draw up the list that she was equally unconvinced as to the need for. She should have finished it long ago. All she had to do was to flick through the bound volumes of close to one thousand issues of *The Black Sea Herald* the Medical Director had summoned from the paper's archives, look up any lecture announcements, and note down the name of the speaker and the topic. All she could manage, in reality, was a maximum of one volume a day. She would lift a thick, heavy volume onto her desk, open the first few pages, find an announcement (provided one was there) and just as she was about to note down the necessary details, her eye would catch a headline along the lines of *Young Bride Runs Away with the Gold Given at the Wedding* or *Stampede at Famous Singer X's Concert on Town Square*, and she'd drop everything to read the rest.

In the meantime, the Medical Director got into trouble when, during an interview with *The Black Sea Herald*, he blurted out his intention to write the hospital's history. No one had heard of his intention until that moment… and now everyone knew.

When the interview he'd originally given to praise the increasingly higher standards at the hospital was published with the headline *Medical Director Demir Demir Writes a Book*, his wife Sevim was quite upset, *The whole city knows but for me! Shame on you!* She didn't stay cross for long, though, mollified by the Medical Director's childish enthusiasm and well-wishing phone calls from friends and family.

But the real trouble started once the crunch came. Sevim thought he'd take up a pristine white exercise book and sit down to write neatly using his Mont Blanc fountain pen as she dreamt of the dedication she was sure her husband would include in the foreword: *Wholehearted thanks to my dear wife Sevim Demir for her boundless support during the time it took to write this book. Sevim, but for you, this book would never have happened!*

It was precisely her presence in his life, however, that somewhat hampered the poor fellow.

When he attempted to bring home the filthy wads of documents he'd unearthed in the archive next to the boiler room, Sevim nearly had a fit, *There's no way I'm letting this germ-infested junk into the house!* she shouted, as her obsessive-compulsive disorder took over. Forget the dedication; she just wouldn't listen. No amount of pleading worked; *Look Sevim, I have to look at these, and think of my endless thanks in the foreword…* there was no way those grubby carrier bags would get past the threshold. To be fair, she did have a point: untouched for years, those files were thick with dust, not to mention the mice tracks on the covers.

Forced to schlep all the official documents back into his office, the Medical Director ordered a cabinet. Odd-Eye Sipahi, who'd taken three and a half months to complete the neuropsychiatrist's order all those years ago delivered a lovely cabinet within the week. So the Medical Director started working in his office, except, the daily business of the hospital rarely allowed him much time to write. In the end he had to have photocopies made of every single document. Those reams of paper caretaker Cumali had hauled on his back were only allowed into the flat once Sevim had satisfied herself of their cleanliness, and the Medical Director was able to start working at home in the evenings. Or more accurately, skim through the photocopies.

Because he'd not inspected the wads in detail, he'd had thousands of photocopies made. But the piles of documents in a corner of the sitting room proved to be disappointingly limited to appointments, personnel records, payrolls, supply lists and other similar official correspondence. He wasn't quite sure what he expected to find anyway in that mountain of paper. There wasn't even a single line worthy of inclusion in his book. So he flicked through the patient files. They looked quite haphazard, quite incomplete; all the same, they might at least offer inspiration he thought, and carted some home. The official documents had cost such a lot in photocopies – too much to meet from the float in good conscience, so he'd paid for them himself, at least in part. Which now precluded photocopying patient histories.

The Medical Director had a blazing row with his wife on the morning of 14 February. Sevim might be obsessive-compulsive, but she loved going out. The previous night she'd attended the Lions Club dinner at the five-star Diamond Hotel; yes, she did find the ballroom kitsch, but at least the hygiene standards were quite high. All the same, she had eaten before going out. It was quite late by the time she'd returned, stiff from having sat with her elbows on the table all evening. She undressed in the entrance hall and made straight for the bathroom without a glance at the lounge-dining room. Dead on her feet or not, she had a long bath, dried her hair and got into bed. Her husband had been studying patient histories with reading specs perched on his nose all night long, and noting down a few interesting titbits in his squared A4 exercise book; she hugged him and fell asleep straightaway.

In the morning, she awoke, well rested, but flipped when she saw the grimy patient files on the dining table. A greasy black coating of dust marked by filthy boot prints had smudged everything and ruined the lovely tablecloth she'd bought in Prague. The Medical Director's teacup was still on the table (so he'd been drinking tea as he worked on these revolting things!) and the teapot was resting on a hotplate on the coffee table, his black fingerprint marking the Virgin Mary's face.

She screamed at the top of her voice, *Are you trying to drive me crazyyy Demiiiir!* Shaving in the bathroom, his razor slipped, and cut his chin as he heard her scraming. He hoofed it to the lounge-dining room to find her yelling and sobbing, *You're doing it deliberately, aren't you? Doing it deliberately to drive me crazy!* His hands slick with the blood from his chin, he yelled back and she returned the favour. The escalating shouting match flared up in earnest when the subject of Sevim's abortions came up, utterly unrelated to the original topic.

She'd fallen pregnant three times, and each time, the Medical Director had asked her for a termination claiming the timing was wrong as he was on the verge of yet another professional milestone just then. On the third occasion, her womb was torn due to medical incompetence, she was left unable to conceive, and the couple had accepted a childless life. Outraged at the dirty files piled on the table, Sevim launched into a tirade, *I gave up my career for you, I had three abortions, nearly lost my own life and all for this?* The Medical Director, who'd had enough of years of bitching (as if it wasn't he who'd spent hours cajoling her into a termination every time she'd fallen pregnant) exclaimed, *Like I told you to get an abortion! You shouldn't have!* She couldn't believe her ears. Grabbing the 'Virgin Mary Holding the Infant Jesus' icon she'd been using as a hotplate, she flung it at his head.

And she did it with such violence that it smashed through the window, flew out, fell down to the pavement and smashed in two: the 19th century Tbilisi painter Guram Chaliashvili's cinnabar icon painted in a flash of religious fervour cracked down the middle. The baby face of the infant Jesus fell on one side, and the Virgin's sweet countenance on the other.

A few hours later, the concierge went out with a broom and picked up the shards of the shattered icon. He turned the broken pieces over this way and that; but to him they looked like nothing much, so he threw them in the bin. And that was the end of Guram Chaliashvili's lovely work of art.

The icon had missed the Medical Director's head by a whisker; he was fuming. It suddenly dawned on him that this row was the perfect excuse to give up on the book he'd made no progress with. He grabbed the files and heaped them up by the door. Then made straight for the bathroom. His chin was still bleeding, so he deliberately pawed the washbasin, mirror, cabinet doors with those messy hands: everywhere he could think of. He washed his hands; the black water smeared the washbasin. Sticking a plaster on his chin, he dressed neatly and went to the hospital, still trembling with rage.

He had no idea that a Black Wednesday lay in wait for the city… and him. Hamdi Tutuş, now a regular due to the stress and violence triggered by his neurotic feelings of guilt, was sitting in the security hut once again. Spotting the Medical Director, he came out and asked for identification, shouting, *Oy! Where the bloody hell d'ya think you're going without so much as a by-your-leave?*

The root of Hamdi's feelings of guilt had eluded his doctor Âlim Kâhkeci until about a year ago. The driver, once the gentlest of souls, had been spending the majority of his time praying and reciting repentance for sins not yet committed. But one day, something really bizarre happened, finally opening the eyes of the hospital's most senior psychiatrist to the origins of Hamdi's condition. That was only the third time in his life he'd missed Friday prayers, the first being the birth of his daughter Zehra's.

It was a semester holiday. Whingeing non-stop about her ridiculous homework, Zehra had picked up two Ömer Seyfettin volumes of short stories to read and summarise – in a perfunctorily simplified edition on the pretext of rendering them more accessible to the young generations – at the irritable bookseller Özcan Durna's Road Bookshop and come over to her father's office. Âlim was going to drop her at the English tutor's for her private lesson before proceeding to the mosque. He finished his rounds and returned to his office to see the alarming sight of Hamdi Tutuş in tears. Zehra looked equally dazed. *Daddy, I swear I did nothing. I was reading, he said 'What'cha reading?' and began crying when I told him…* she explained, trembling, staring at Hamdi in horror. Âlim read her the riot act; she should never mingle with the patients. He was about to lay into Hamdi Tutuş as well for entering his office and sitting down without leave, but the man was shaking with sobs.

Further questioning revealed it was the story entitled *Curry Comb* that had caused Hamdi to burst into tears. That's when it suddenly dawned on Âlim that some fraternal trauma lay at the root of the man's guilt. He got so excited that he forgot he had to go to prayers. The anorexic social services expert Buse Göçer had just dropped in to enquire about the documents of a newly committed patient; Âlim asked her to put Zehra into a taxi from the stand outside the hospital, issued strict instructions to Zehra to ring her mother as soon as she had arrived at the tutor's home, and sat down facing Hamdi.

In his gentlest possible tone, he set about asking questions along the lines of, *You had a brother, didn't you, Hamdi? But you must have been very young then, Hamdi, right?* and digging a little deeper, he finally learnt about the two-year-old-brother that a desperately envious Hamdi, then only five himself, had pushed into the well and killed. Âlim changed Hamdi's medication at once.

Weeks of psychotherapy brought Hamdi round to confront this childhood incident, at least in part; however, instead of improving his condition, all it achieved was to aggravate his sense of guilt. Holding himself responsible for every ill in the world, he tried to punish himself by banging his head against the wall or cutting himself, which only led to even worse incidents. He was discharged time and again as cured, and returned each time with a new problem.

On that day, he'd taken advantage of the guard's absence and settled into the hut, staring at the gate to prevent some random stranger from entering the grounds. Failing to recognise the irritably frowning Medical Director who was stomping in an uncharacteristically hunched gait, Hamdi attempted to ask for identification, then recognition hit and he panicked unnecessarily and wanted to apologise. He was grabbing the Medical Director's hands and waist, beseeching, *Pleeease pleeease forgive me!* in tears, whilst the other man's *All right Hamdi, let go… there's nothing to forgive!* fell upon deaf ears. Hamdi wouldn't let go; he followed the Medical Director all the way to the entrance, where he started to bang his head against the glass door, forcing the Medical Director to call for help. As he was led away by the caretakers, Hamdi was still yelling, *I didn't recognise you Mr Medical Director Sir; I swear I didn't… never have asked if I did, would I? Pleeease forgive me; just say the word and I'll be your dog!*

Freed of Hamdi's grip, the Medical Director made for his office; he came across Neuropsychiatrist Nebahat in the hallway. He'd have sneaked off, pretending not to have seen her, but caught sight of the cake. He'd missed breakfast after the row with his wife, the cake was studded with walnuts gleaming like gold, and he suddenly felt hungry, so he asked her for a slice.

The stumpy neuropsychiatrist made the still seething Medical Director a delicious cup of vanilla flavoured filter coffee, placed two slices of cake on a paper plate, added a plastic fork and brought it all over. She then sat down facing him. Coffee and cake polished off, the Medical Director calmed down a little.

The two old friends discussed the unfortunate death of the retired literature teacher Miss Zarife. That she might never make it had been pointed out by her physician, the young surgeon Kerem Savul: *The only person who'd dare open his patient's brain was Yaşar Mustaki; sadly we lost our master years ago!* Despite the caveat that the probability of success was no higher than fifty per cent, Zeki had decided to take his wife to

Wisconsin, to a hospital he'd found after searching high and low. He would sell his rented flat – well under its value if need be. But they never got the chance. Zeki, whose command of English was quite poor, was busy with an on-line ticket booking with the help of a nephew (a pupil at an Anatolian lycée) when the poor lady took a turn for the worse and was hospitalised after a violent bout of vomiting. There was nothing more that could be done, though, and she died a few days later.

With a rather disingenuous, *I knew it was a tumour as soon as I looked at her, but Âlim Bey, bless him,… just wouldn't listen to me,* Nebahat seized the opportunity to badmouth her colleague. When she attempted to follow that up with how her ex-husband was similarly obstinate, the Medical Director concocted an excuse to leave lest she launch into that same stale old story. He was hoping to shake off the pall cast by the row with Sevim that morning, but had no idea that it would pale in comparison to what lay in wait for the hospital – and him.

The moment he stepped out, he came face to face with Tuğba, Dr Âlim's wife. Poor thing was ashen, stammering, barely able to talk sense. She was in such a state that she hadn't even noticed her headscarf had slipped to reveal her glossy auburn locks. Before the Medical Director could even ask, *What's the matter Tuğba Hanım?* she said she'd come to enquire whether it was possible to hospitalise a colleague of hers as an emergency case. She'd been unable to reach her husband on the phone – he was in a session with a patient – and leapt into her silver Toyota to get there as quickly as possible. It took quite a while for the Medical Director to figure out that the patient in question was Ayşe Nuran Serbest, the harelipped gynaecologist who'd grated on his nerves when she'd flung her tea at his face.

The previous evening, the young nurses at the Maternity Hospital had organised an alcohol-free party to welcome the newly appointed and **truly gorgeous Gynaecologist İskender**, a real heartthrob for the female staff. Ayşe Nuran was also invited, though the nurses didn't think she would come. Extremely conservative (so a real pain when it came to such parties, and in particular inside the hospital) Ayşe Nuran had had to bite her tongue all this time, since her lack of managerial status precluded her from banning events of this type. But she was tempted to go this time.

More accurately, she was tempted by İskender's looks. So the doctor who grumbled whenever someone mentioned a party astonished everyone by settling into the best spot.

She planted herself at one side, nursing a glass of orange pop as she watched the pretty young nurses enviously. Her eyes never left İskender all night. The handsome gynaecologist – and didn't he know it – flattered his fans, enjoying his conquest of all these hearts in the space of just a month. He glanced at Ayşe Nuran with what the poor girl thought was a sneering, scornful smile before turning to chat to one of the real lookers. She was wrong. He wasn't sneering at all; if anything, he'd barely taken notice of her. Her harelip had not been overlooked. On the contrary, he'd spotted it on his first day. Mocking was the last thing on his mind, though. Instead, he had recalled procedures carried out with nearly perfect outcomes by a plastic surgeon friend, and wondered how he could mention it without offending this shapely, attractive woman.

Ayşe Nuran's mind was in turmoil. Anyone else with that sneer she'd imagined on İskender's face would have received the full blaze of her fury, and she'd have made the party hell for everyone there. But his looks had tied her hands. She could neither storm off, nor attack him. She just stood there until the party came to an end.

As might be guessed, Ayşe Nuran had felt hideous that night and paced in her tiny room until sunrise. The next morning she went into the bathroom to wash up, saw her face in the mirror and slashed her harelip with a razor blade.

Scared that her daughter just wasn't coming out of the bathroom, Faika asked for neighbours to help and broke down the door, to find a raving Ayşe Nuran bleeding buckets from her mouth. The washbasin, the mirror, her clothes: she was covered in blood all over. Waving the blade at everyone, she was saying she'd torn out the lips she hated, but since her mouth was in pieces, no one understood a word.

It took all they could to take the young woman to hospital. The doctor who'd stitched the slashed lips to the best of his ability pronounced the wound to be terrible. It would certainly leave a scar, and even with plastic surgery, Ayşe Nuran's face would look worse than before. Faika's heart sank.

She was thankful her daughter was still alive, but the worst wasn't over. The mild sedative had proven inadequate and Ayşe Nuran had to be tied to the bed after clamping the nurses' arms with steel-grip fingers (giving them dreadful bruises in the process) and ruined the dressing, hitting her own mouth wherever she could. She was screaming the place down. Faika called Tuğba for help; she knew the gynaecologist's husband was a psychiatrist. A horrifying scene confronted Tuğba at the hospital: two hulking male nurses were struggling, and failing, to restrain the girl strapped to the bed. Her mouth was in shreds and still bleeding.

Unaware that the cake he'd eaten was spiked, the Medical Director listened to Tuğba and said, *Bring her over in an ambulance; we'll admit her straightaway.* His mind was beginning to slow down though, and he was puzzling over his increasingly sluggish strides.

An eventful day awaited not only the Medical Director and the Mental Health Hospital, but the city too. The skies had grown misty and grey as if in anticipation. It was bitterly cold. Pedestrians hunched their shoulders as a sporadic stiff wind jolted the branches.

Having alighted from Hooknose Şahin's minibus, Girlie İsmet was about to enter the Arcade Market. He'd got up with the morning call to prayer, had a ritual wash and hanged himself with the clothesline from the beam of the raised grain store. But the beam collapsed, he fell down without even putting his neck through the noose, went straight through the rotten floorboards and ended up on the dung heap. Wiping the fresh ordure off his face, having failed to kill himself in the morning of 14 February he tucked his father's double edge steel knife with a blood groove into the pocket of his long parka and went out. Shivering in the minibus with the broken heater, he stroked the edge of the blade with icy fingertips all the way.

He entered the Arcade Market for the first time since that sickening night in the summerhouse miles from the city, and saw the burping wholesaler, bug-eyed broker Hidayet, and Remzi all sitting on rattan stools outside the latter's two-square-metre-shop where he repaired umbrellas, pressure cookers, teapot handles coffee mills and the like. They were breakfasting on Kurdish pastry spread out on the filthy coffee table, stuffing their mouths, licking sugar off their fingers, and refilling grubby teacups from the teapot boiling on the camper stove at their feet.

İsmet's heart was thumping in his mouth. He checked for his knife and strode towards this hateful trio of evil. A vile grin spread on Remzi's face. *Wo-ooow! Where the hell have you been, girl?* he exclaimed, but before he could add, *Long time, no see…* İsmet drew the knife and ran him through in the neck.

He ruptured the carotid. A jet of blood flooded the wholesaler's eyes, splashed Hidayet and stained the snow-white caster sugar on the pastry. The waddling wholesaler was in shock. Hidayet was screaming as Remzi thrashed about on the floor. Shopwindows, walls and floors, everything was covered in blood within a minute. Everyone bolted out of the photocopy and computer repair booths, the trousseau boutique and the china shop. At the sight of İsmet holding the bloody knife, they all ran back in and locked the doors. The trousseau seller had drawn his handgun from his belt. Ready to shoot if that crazy İsmet turned towards him.

The pirate DVD seller Talip, who, since the time he'd beaten Remzi to a pulp for stroking his arm had ignored the geezer's presence in the arcade, was shocked. The tragically pathetic expression on İsmet's face hinted at a possible motive, though, so Talip watched without stirring.

Staring at their own fate, the wholesaler and Hidayet had run to the other exit. But it was blocked. Five minutes earlier a lorry delivering beer to the bar down in the basement had drawn up close to make it easy for the two delivery boys to carry and stack huge crates, effectively cutting off the exit. The boys had scuttled off at the sight of the rivers of blood, leaving the barrels. The wholesaler and Hidayet tried to leap over, knowing İsmet's knife was coming, but crashed into each other and fell. They were both running for dear life, each ready to sacrifice the other to İsmet's knife to save his own skin. İsmet caught up with Hidayet first and stabbed him over and over again in the belly. He didn't stop stabbing until he'd plunged the knife into the back of the wholesaler, who'd slipped and fallen on his face when he tried to scramble to his feet.

Umbrella seller Remzi bled to death on the spot as life spurted out of his neck. Hidayet and the burping wholesaler were in the throes of death. İsmet tried to withdraw the knife in the wholesaler's scapula, failed, and instead kicked it in all the way with his heel. He then took a deep breath, grabbed one of the discounted t-shirts hanging outside the tacky casual wear shop, wiped his face and hands of blood, tossed the t-shirt over Remzi and strode out. The arcade folk stood shellshocked.

As İsmet rocked up to the Nation Tea Garden and ordered a medium coffee from the waiter who had frozen in ashtonishment at his blood-covered clothes, the burping wholesaler died. If Talip hadn't thought to call 155 Police Emergency, and an ambulance hadn't arrived within half an hour, Hidayet would certainly have followed suit.

It was a day when the sirens never fell silent in the city. One ambulance was transporting the gynaecologist who'd slashed her harelip to the Mental Health Hospital, a second was rushing Hidayet over to the State Hospital, and a third carried the bodies of Remzi and the wholesaler to the morgue as police vehicles searching for İsmet added to the clamour filling the air.

There was a traffic jam as the ambulances passed by the Three Brothers Patisserie. Beckoned by the sirens, everyone nearby was at the windows. Wondering if a bomb had exploded somewhere when they saw three ambulances and police cars, some people rushed to switch on their TVs. The commotion also roused guest speaker Ülkü Birinci, who'd arrived earlier that morning to deliver his lecture *Love: Self-sacrifice? Or Self-preservation?* and was currently snoozing, head against the backrest of his chair at the patisserie. The staff milling at the door were asking passers-by what was going on. His interest piqued, yet still sleepy, Ülkü Birinci laid his head back to resume his nap as soon as traffic cleared and the sirens vanished into the distance.

He'd arrived on the morning flight; in want of a good breakfast before going to the hospital, asked the taxi driver for a decent spot, and was brought to the Three Brothers Patisserie. Ülkü walked in like a zombie, having boarded his flight without any sleep at all, thanks to an all night chat with **nickname Honeybuns**. After enjoying a cheese pastry baked to golden perfection and downing a strong cup of tea, he opened his laptop, but fell asleep before he could take a look at his still sketchy lecture.

He'd started chatting with Honeybuns at about eleven thirty. He wasn't quite sure of the sex, but this virtual person insisted she was *a woman, and what a woman!* At precisely midnight Honeybuns said *as of now* it was Valentine's Day, that this was also her twenty-fifth birthday and repeated, for the third time, that sex was her favourite thing in life. This virtual friend proceeded to use colourful obscenities he'd never heard before, and her fantasies swept him off his feet. Promising to chat again, Honeybuns signed off on grounds of having to go to work; Ülkü glanced at his watch and panicked: two hours to his flight! After a hasty wash, he rushed to the airport. The time had just flown by, and his lecture still wasn't ready.

He did want to take a look at his lecture once the ambulances and police vehicles had gone, but was unable to prevent his eyelids dropping. He gave himself another half hour's snooze, after which he would attack his lecture with a clear head … but was woken up this time by some noises grating on his nerves. He glanced around, grumbling, and found quite a commotion in the patisserie, with the arrival of a TV crew. Tables were being dragged, armchairs pushed, the cameraman was looking for angles, the gaffer was trying to light the scene, batteries were lugged, tripods opened … the noise just wouldn't stop.

Ülkü was still rubbing his eyes when the proprietor's son **Serhat who could easily pass for a cocaine baron** got into a heated conversation with the documentary director Çiğdem Taşpınar, who was puffing away at her super slim Davidoff. The long-legged, middle-aged director wore a pair of jeans ripped at the knees and a reporter's waistcoat; her close-cropped silver hair featured a long ponytail in the nape.

The perfectionist director who'd been forced to finance *Bosnia's Weeping Women* out of her own pocket, having been shafted by that shyster Frenchman Vincent Barratier (who was the cause of her split with environmentalist Menderes Bakış, father to Barış) had run out of money despite all the critical acclaim and screenings at documentary festivals around the world. Struggling to make ends meet and sick of looking for financing for her projects, she had eventually made for a big news and documentary TV channel.

She had arrived a few days before for *Road Tales*, a thirteen-episode documentary she wasn't exactly dying to shoot. It wasn't a very original a project, to be honest; just a familiar formula. All the same, she made a good job of it, leaving no detail unexplored. On the day of her arrival, she had shot the baking of the sucuk-and-egg pide at the Draw Black Sea Pide Shop, and driven the chef round the bend when she made him repeat it twenty times. And now she was in the Three Brothers Patisserie, one of the oldest establishments in the city. Once she was done talking to Serhat, she planned to go into the kitchen and shoot the preparation of their particular specialty: rosewater pudding.

Setting her sights on the corner where Ülkü Birinci was sitting, Çiğdem asked Serhat to move his customer. Sharp in a black pinstriped suit and red shirt with the collar out, the look completed with heavily gelled hair, the young boss complied, thrilled at the prospect of facing the camera to tell the story of how his grandfather's modest pudding shop had grown into the most exclusive spot in the city. He prodded Ülkü in the shoulder to wake him up and told him to move to another table. Ülkü hated being prodded, and he was quite grumpy from lack of sleep too; so he bristled, *I'm not getting up!* He grumbled on and on, sneering as he made dismissive gestures. True to his Black Sea blood, Serhat flared up at once, *What'cha mean you're not bloody getting up!* and grabbed Ülkü by the collar. Seeing the anger on the younger man's face and reluctant to risk a fight, Ülkü yielded to Çiğdem's gentler intervention, *Sir, it was I who made the request, if it's no trouble, that is…* and pretending to have just noticed the TV crew, he gathered his belongings in a show of gracious assent, *Oh, so you're shooting… You should have said…* By which time Serhat's hot temper had cooled as fast as it had flared, and he hugged and kissed Ülkü as if they were old friends.

Serhat was plying Ülkü with teas, coffees, pastries and cakes to make up for his earlier rudeness when the Medical Director, who had definitely given up on the idea of writing his book after the quarrel with his wife, received a visitor. District Mayor Cumhur Eryıldıran had come to announce he awaited the Medical Director's book project with bated breath and was prepared to fund all printing, distribution and promotion costs. He even brought along several books written on the city, having flagged any mention of the hospital's history with post-it notes.

With impeccable courtesy, Cumhur Eryıldıran then spread out photocopies of news clippings, black-and-white photos taken at the foundation laying ceremony where an ecstatic Undersecretary Cevdet Pektaş had posed with the Minister of Health at the time, and colour photos of the half-finished building under construction shot in the eighties.

Rebuffed by the Metropolitan Mayor Tacettin Başusta earlier, and still seething over the row with his wife, the Medical Director had said to himself *Curse that bloody book, and the hospital too!* Now faced with the industrious, though less important, Mayor's enthusiasm, he regretted having announced to the whole world that he was going to write the hospital's history, but it was too late. He had no idea how to get out of this business that he was clearly not cut out for.

What really occupied his mind just then wasn't the goodwill of this unassuming mayor, though; it was the tremendous physical and mental strangeness he felt. It never occurred to him that Nebahat might have spiked those two thick slices of cake with lashings of dope; he was busy trying to figure out what was happening and recall all his vital organs and possible symptoms, whilst slouching lower in his seat *Oh my Goooood… what's wrong with me?* suddenly came out of his mouth. He didn't feel bad, he wasn't sick, but he felt peculiar, as a detached part of his mind regarded with perturbation this unusual state that he was obviously enjoying at the same time. He was rapidly losing control of his thoughts.

Then, quite out of the blue, he burst into a detailed account of the quarrel with his wife, including the matter of the abortions, thinking he was wrong to do so all the while, and wanting to shut up, but he couldn't. Listening to the increasingly slack-mouthed Medical Director's revelations of the most inappropriate minutiae of his private life, the District Mayor wondered whether the fellow was drunk so early in the day. It was all very puzzling, and more than a little unsettling too.

You might like to check your blood pressure… It could be low or something, suggested an apprehensive District Mayor, triggering a violent outburst from the Medical Director still going on about his wife's abortions three decades ago. Tapping his temple, he exclaimed, *Sick, sick! The missus is obsessed with hygiene, sick up here!* He was right on one count: Sevim was very, very sick at that moment.

Guest speaker Ülkü Birinci had dozed on and off until noon, drunk all that bottomless tea and coffee offered by Serhat, left the Three Brothers Patisserie and jumped into a taxi to go to the hospital. They had barely covered one hundred metres when the city's streets rang with the siren of the fourth ambulance. The taxi driver took advantage of the opportunity to tailgate the ambulance carrying the Medical Director's obsessive-compulsive wife Sevim.

After her husband had stormed out, a plaster over the shaving cut, Sevim cried and cried, mulling over her three abortions and lamenting her childlessness. When she entered the bathroom, she went berserk: his pyjamas were strewn around the place, surely infested with germs now that he'd grabbed those grubby files, and the place was covered in bloody fingerprints. This intolerable scene prompted her to pour an entire bottle of hydrochloric acid into the bathtub and another into the toilet pan, and after dousing the washbasin and the floor with bleach and other powerful cleaners, she set to scrubbing vigorously. Before long, overcome by the toxic fumes of these strong chemicals filling the tiny bathroom, she vomited.

Instead of going out for some fresh air, she then tried to clean the mess before finally twigging that she could be dying. She crawled to the flat opposite where she threw up at the feet of the neighbour who'd opened the door. The neighbour rang the Medical Director at once. But having said good-bye to the District Mayor who'd been impatient to leave (*The Council is your Council, Mr Medical Director, I'm at your service whenever you want…*) the Medical Director had sat down with schizoaffective İsmail Çeliktaş for a boisterous game of backgammon that would put Ofli Durali to shame. A panicking Nemişo rushed over to alert her boss – who was by then too woozy to pay attention – only to be scolded, *I'm playing backgammon, Lass, can't you see?* an outburst that left even the patients gaping.

Unable to raise the Medical Director, the neighbour called an ambulance, which drove Sevim to the State Hospital. As she was wheeled in for urgent treatment, Ülkü Birinci, who had reached the Mental Health Hospital in no time at all and was being introduced to the Medical Director, who had just abandoned the backgammon game as being too tiresome, and whose spontaneous guffaws incongruous with his evident maturity seemed puzzling at best. Ülkü wanted to review his lecture in the green room; so handing his guest over to Nemişo, the Medical Director set off for Nebahat's office for another slice of cake, singing under his breath *Darkness prevails everywhere, yet divine light fills that abode / Is that the sunset or the grave, oh Lord?* That's when the Paediatric Psychiatrist Faik Abacı was alerted to the state of the Medical Director.

Faik had been sorting the samples left by the pharmaceutical rep İlhami, who'd been waxing lyrical about a new medication with a clinically proven high success rate in treating hyperactivity and attention deficit in children (all the while moaning about the spot baldness ruining his scalp), when Nemişo turned up, pleading, *Doctor, something's wrong with the Medical Director, please please will you take a look, I beg you!* Faik left his room and blocked the still singing Medical Director's way. Nemişo recounted the Medical Director's weird behaviour and then rang the State Hospital to enquire about Sevim's condition

Faik Abacı took the Medical Director by the arm. The fellow was acting strangely. Pulling him into the first room he spotted on the ground floor, Faik checked his blood pressure and listened to his heart; he couldn't detect any immediate danger.

The Medical Director was sitting on a filthy stretcher in the room stuffed with broken stretchers, chairs with broken wheels and other pieces of equipment awaiting repairs. He said, *Don't get it, Faik; your auntie Sevim drove me crazy in the morning, I wonder if that's why I feel so strange?* All he wanted to do was put his head down and rest. He did intend to go back to his room for a nap, but collapsed onto the stretcher instead. He set to wondering why he felt so dizzy even though he hadn't had a drop to drink or anything, wondering why, despite the mild nausea, he didn't actually feel that bad. His pulse could have been considered normal and his breathing was regular, if a little elevated. Faik instructed Nemişo to *Cover him up with a blanket and let him sleep it off for a while. We'll take another look when he's woken up.* By the time Faik was back his office to enquire about Sevim's condition, the Medical Director had fallen into a truly deep sleep.

In the meanwhile, sitting all on his own in the vast green room, Ülkü Birinci was sipping his medium Turkish coffee brought by Earless Ziya as he glanced at his lecture that he didn't think mattered all that much, but had to pad out a little to spare his blushes at the lectern. That's when he overheard the banter between Foulmouth Sister Zerrin and Matron Servinaz Ceviz, who'd sneaked into the supplies room next door.

Designed to allow for partitioning by Çetin Kansız (the architect who'd sited the building with its back to the sea) the huge green room was still a single space. Except for a section at the entrance, that is: when the medical supplies store on the ground floor had proven inadequate, a long and narrow room had been knocked together. With nothing between them but a paper-thin chipboard wall, Ülkü heard the women as clearly as if they were right next to him.

They were discussing Sister Zerrin's birthday, which happened to fall on the 14 February. Her new boyfriend **young actor Ozan Çağlar** – who'd finally been appointed to Istanbul after working at the Trabzon State Theatre – had rung to announce that it would have been out of the question to leave her alone on such an important date and that he was coming on the evening flight. Ozan was no oil painting, neither was Zerrin – despite being strangely sexy; they had met six weeks earlier and had sex that very first night.

After finishing a performance of Haldun Taner's *I Close my Eyes and Do my Duty* to an empty house, Ozan and his colleagues had gone to the Trabzon Dedeman Hotel resplendent in outlandish New Year's Eve decorations. Sister Zerrin was also there. When she met **her actress (and matchmaker) friend Pelin** – whose greatest dream was predictably to play Ophelia like most actresses, yet whose concept of stage literature had barely reached Shakespeare – they hugged with much screaming and yelling. They'd met a year earlier when Pelin was recovering from a myomectomy in a private hospital where Zerrin occasionally moon-lighted. Like most ugly women lacking sufficient excitement in their own love lives, Pelin loved matchmaking. Noticing Ozan's interest in her friend's sex appeal, Pelin invited the nurse to their table, sat her down next to Ozan and made sure they hooked up.

Zerrin didn't return to her table after meeting Ozan; her three mates were also single, they'd all forked out in the hope of meeting someone at the New Year's Ball in Trabzon, and ended up having an awful time. They didn't meet anyone, but what really rankled was that Zerrin did, and she'd never even come anywhere near them afterwards. They were really cross. They didn't like the *prix fixe* menu, the singers hadn't dropped by their table: all that money they'd shelled out for a New Year's Eve in a chic hotel had been wasted. The next day they hopped on a coach without waiting for her, in a real huff like it was all Zerrin's fault. But Zerrin didn't give a hoot as she woke up and stretched luxuriously in Ozan's bed near noon.

As Ülkü was padding out his lecture with inane additions, Zerrin lit a cigarette in the cramped store and spoke about the anticipated romantic dinner followed by bone-crunching sex with the gallant Ozan who'd come over all the way from Istanbul to celebrate Valentine's Day and her birthday. Much more playful since having killed her husband, Matron Servinaz listened in giggles.

Eavesdropping on this chat about love, sex and Valentine's Day, Ülkü was grinning from ear to ear, until something Zerrin said froze him to the spot. He went bright red as if the transcript of last night's shamelessly erotic chat were making the rounds in the university senate, as if everyone was pointing at him. What Zerrin had said was – having done with the love stuff and moving on to bitching about the kitchen staff – *I've had it with this Hacer Abla... That bitch yells all the time, like the wail of a torn cunt!* Cold sweat poured down his back, terrified they might come face to face and recognise each other: *Was this the woman he'd been chatting with all night?*

He had been thinking of his chat mate as an expert when it came to fantasy, but not that great in the written word; putting together a rare obscenity and a birthday date, and suddenly sure the Honeybuns of his fantasies stood right there, right behind that chipboard partition, Ülkü fretted about how to deliver his lecture and bugger off as soon as possible to avoid meeting her.

He needn't have, since virtual person Honeybuns and Zerrin had nothing at all to do with each other. The profanity had been coined by **Foulmouth Cevriye**, next-door neighbour to Zerrin who'd adopted it enthusiastically; it had done the rounds and reached Ülkü Birinci's chat mate Honeybuns.

It hadn't been a long route. **Cevriye's even more foul-mouthed daughter Designer Gönül** had been working for a dressmaker in Istanbul for years and years. **Designer/Dressmaker Piraye** (or, as she insisted, a *couturier* of a *maison*, certainly not a seamstress running a workshop) was quite chummy with her designer. She loved dipping into the vast vocabulary of profanities cheerfully used by the plain but merry Gönül.

Piraye, also a master of the rather more exotic expletive generously applied whether in curse or praise, had passed this particular one on as soon as she'd snapped it up. Thanks to a couturier friend who dressed TV stars, it reached that bohemia of creative glitterati called Cihangir where it referred specifically to singers with awful voices; its lightning-quick espousal by the entire district had been nothing short of miraculous.

Ülkü Birinci's Honeybuns was an unemployed advertising copywriter who'd had a nervous breakdown after a particularly awful menopause. Although she loathed the world of advertising that so relentlessly ground you down, she still continued to look for work in the same industry, whiling away the hours in Cihangir cafés to sound out the snobbish advertisers there.

Of course she knew how to write beautifully; she just liked using poor Turkish in chat rooms for a bit of a lark. And when this so-called Zebb – who'd said he was a professional basketball player – had corrected her, she'd laughed up her sleeve, guessing he had to be a teacher or an educator of some description. Last night, she'd used this idiom picked up in Cihangir cafés to refer to a famous pop singer whose latest album blasted out everywhere she went; Ülkü, whose brain was addled by hours of erotic conversation, had replied in the chat lingo he took such pride in, *Wtffff????* *Awsmmmmm!!!!* A language of minimal *wvls* and repeated final letters thick with tons of exclamation marks, question marks and emojis.

It was only after the nurses had left that Ülkü managed to think with a cool head. The woman behind the chipboard partition couldn't have been Honeybuns. Such an impossible coincidence would defy the reality of life. And even if she were, they could never recognise each other's faces: they had never exchanged real photos or turned their webcams on.

As Ülkü allowed himself to relax a little, the city was experiencing a true Black Wednesday. Gunshots coming from the reasonably decent four-star hotel next to the Three Brothers Patisserie on the Atatürk Boulevard, followed *again* by police and ambulance sirens had unsettled the residents *again* and caused a commotion yet *again*.

Wearing an astrakhan coat and matching kalpak, Türkan was exiting her Mercedes outside the patisserie when she noticed Asiye Tibuk descend from a taxi and enter the hotel next door. The old lady had been having problems with walking just this last month, but there was nothing wrong with her mind. She guessed what was about to happen at the sight of the pistol the Councillor Latif Tibuk's wife had pulled out of her handbag and was tucking into her belt like a man. Türkan stood rooted to the spot. Her driver tried to take her by the arm and lead her into the patisserie, but she signalled him to wait, squinted, and stared at the hotel door.

Rosewater pudding shoot finally over, Serhat was chatting with his *Çiğdem Abla* who was eating some beansprout-cum-walnut concoction from the patisserie's pretentious fusion kitchen, bending over backwards to assist his big sister who'd given him this opportunity to go on TV.

Spotting the latest arrival, he exclaimed, *Çiğdem Abla, it's Türkan Hanım you should interview!* One of Turkey's first female judges, Türkan knew everything about the city; she had to be at least one hundred and three, or even four, exaggerated Serhat, and she was worth a documentary in her own right. Fed up to the gills with suggestions offered during documentary shoots, *It's this you have to see… it's that you have to shoot…* etc., Çiğdem Taşpınar didn't pay the slightest bit of attention. But she pricked up her ears when Serhat said, like he'd seen it with his own eyes, *She's got such an archive of old photos, Abla, you'd go crazy if you saw it… all at least a hundred years old…*

She'd found nothing worthwhile in three days of shooting, and she was especially disappointed with the state of historic buildings ruined by bad restoration. This lady with the archive might be worth meeting. Delighted to be of help, Serhat leapt up to his feet and waited at the door for Türkan to enter. But she kept staring at something in the distance instead of coming in, so he went over, mumbling…

He was just about to say, *Please come in, M'lady*, when what Türkan had been expecting happened. First one round was heard, and then seven more in quick succession. Çiğdem Taşpınar bolted to Serhat's side at the first bang and everyone was already at the windows. *That's gotta give me something*, said an inner voice, and grabbing **her good-natured Bosnian cameraman Damir**, she ran to the hotel.

The scene that greeted her was as follows: lured by the besotted Latif Tibuk, Moldovan Anya (who had re-entered the country illegally, defying the expulsion order) was covering her naked body with the duvet and screaming in horror at the sight of ramrod straight Asiye Tibuk who had fired eight rounds without blinking an eye and now waited for the police. Çiğdem parted the crowd in the hallway and entered to hear Asiye tell Anya, *Enjoy: he's all yours now,* pointing at her husband with her pistol.

She had only shot her husband, not Anya; five of the eight rounds had hit Latif's milk white, hairless legs, and the others had lodged in the foot of the bed and the wall. Her intention was to maim her husband, not kill him, and she had succeeded. Latif Tibuk, meanwhile, despite being in agony, was trying to attack the cameraman just like the first time. Except he couldn't move with a shattered kneecap and blood pumping out of his calves. All he could manage was tug at the duvet to cover his nakedness, yelling, *Stop filming, ya' bastard, stop filming!*

In the meanwhile, the three-hundred-and-fifty-seat hall was filled with an audience almost exclusively consisting of the medical students forced there by their lecturers. Yawning right at the start of the lecture, they all got on Ülkü's wick; *Love is neither sacrifice, nor self-preservation. Love, actually, is nothing more than this!* he exclaimed, aiming his laser pointer to a bare female breast projected on the screen. In the meanwhile, ambulances and police cars were back on the roads again, beckoning the citizenry once again to the windows for the nth time today. The news that the victim was the Councillor, and that he was shot by his wife, caused quite a tumult. Except the city's Black Wednesday wasn't done yet. The really big one had yet to come.

The Medical Director snored under the blanket Nemişo had placed over him in a room in a quiet section of the ground floor of the Mental Health Hospital, whilst an intubated Sevim sobbed and sobbed in the State Hospital on the other side of the city: her husband was aware of her situation, but had refused to come. Believing it was all over between them after the quarrel that morning, she'd called her brothers in Ankara, explained – her voice breaking with sobs – she'd been poisoned whilst cleaning and immediately added she wanted to divorce the Medical Director. It was unthinkable for her to continue to live with a husband who had refused to come to her side just because she'd thrown something at his head in the morning, even as she lay in her death throes here in a shabby room in the State Hospital. Panicking at the news of their big sister's poisoning, the two brothers hopped into a car and set off. *Sevimsweets* had to be exaggerating; surely their brother-in-law would have arrived by the time they got there, and everything would have been sorted out.

Sevim wasn't the only person crying in the State Hospital. The families of umbrella seller Remzi and the wholesaler who'd succumbed to İsmet's double-blade knife with a blood groove lamented, tearing their hair outside the morgue as the wife, sisters and elderly parents of the seriously wounded Hidayet flocked to the hospital, scrambling to find some AB-negative blood from somewhere.

In the meanwhile, back at the Mental Health Hospital, harelipped Ayşe Nuran Serbest, heavily sedated by Âlim Kâhkeci, her dressings changed, given an antibiotic against any potential infection and strapped to a bed just in case, had fallen into a deep sleep. Faika was crying at her daughter's bedside when Gynaecologist Tuğba Kâhkeci approached. *Tough times lay ahead,* she said, *I'll take you home; you should rest and come back in the evening.* The hapless woman allowed herself to be convinced and set off to get a change of clothes.

İsmet was captured at the Nation Tea Garden as he ate a double cheese toastie and drank an ayran. He went like a lamb to the station for questioning. The Superintendent sympathised with the father who'd rushed over: this was Bard Seyit, his favourite on the TV show *Duelling Bards*; he'd even voted with a text message for Seyit! Offering detailed information about İsmet's prospects, the Superintendent recommended Seyit engage a good lawyer. Years of experience in the job suggested İsmet wouldn't get off easily; they might like to wangle a mental instability report.

Things seemed to have calmed down as Ülkü Birinci was starting his lecture – but this was only the lull before the storm, as it would turn out. High on the thin slice she'd indulged in after feeding two doorstoppers of her weed cake to the Medical Director, the neuropsychiatrist had mellowed so much, grown so merry that within half an hour she was offering *Mere slivers* to a few of the young nurses only too happy to ignore the warnings of their bane Matron Servinaz. Nebahat wouldn't rest until she'd handed it all out. Orderly Cemali, who, being resigned to his job at the hospital, had embraced it with renewed vigour lest he was given his walking papers, Earless Ziya who'd grumbled as he wiped the vinyl before Ülkü Birinci's lecture, Nemişo who'd been talking about the Medical Director's weird behaviour to the entire hospital, and even Barış Bakış, who had been frantically writing in his *Hospital Diary* for quite a while without leaving his room: they all enjoyed the yummy crunchy walnut weed cake.

By two o'clock, quite a few members of staff had consumed at least a bite. The last one was Odd-eye Sipahi, who'd come over to take measurements for a bookcase for Dr Âlim Kâhkeci as thanks to his wife, Gynaecologist Tuğba, for making sure his sister had a private room in the State Hospital during labour. Tuğba had shown Sipahi's sister special attention. Odd-eye grabbed half of Earless Ziya's slice and swallowed it without even chewing. The cake-eaters all burst into laughter for no reason, not a single one twigging the reason for that *Weird feelin'*.

Barış had been wandering aimlessly, diary tucked under his arm, when he was invited into the neuropsychiatrist's office where he, too, had his share of the cake. He asked for the time out of the blue. Nebahat wore no watch and couldn't be bothered to check her mobile phone; her perception of time now totally out of kilter, she made something up, *Twenny pas' five…* Thinking she'd said, *Twenny pas' one…* Barış left to return to his room saying, *Oh, well… loads of time yet,* tucked his journal under the pillow, went to bed still fully dressed and pulled the duvet over his head.

In fact, it was ten to three, and he was supposed to meet Gülnazmiye Görgün behind the hospital at three. On tenterhooks, and circumspect with it too, he needed her help to escape, but his plans had nothing in common with those of the psychologist who'd been reassuring him, *Don't worry, we've got lots of money!* He wanted to find the imaginary wife he believed was betraying him with his left hand, so he was going to meet Gülnazmiye, wrench her handbag away, hop into a taxi and set off for a showdown with his wife in Ankara's Bahçelievler district, where he thought she lived. Gülnazmiye might refuse to hand over the handbag, in which case, he would string her along until nightfall and then strangle her in some corner.

The three o'clock meeting was the final stage in Gülnazmiye's plan to rescue Barış from the hospital, a plan that had been in the making for months and that involved a diversion she personally would create. She had tried to take her boyfriend out twice before, through more regular channels, only to be thwarted at the gatehouse thanks to the Medical Director's instructions for the lad *to be confined to the hospital premises lest he'd get into trouble.* No amount of baklavas and cigarettes offered alongside plaintive tales of *Enver Abi, he's my patient, see… He needs a bit of fresh air, I'll bring him back in half an hour, I swear…* had done the trick. **Guard Enver, a keen audience for the religious parables** told by his new mate Hamdi Tutuş, as the latter hung thin strips of orange peel on the electric heater grille, wouldn't be swayed. *Go bring a piece of paper from the Medical Director, and then take him where the heck you want,* said her Big Brother Enver, sticking to his guns. So it had to be an irregular channel.

She was sure the only reason her boyfriend had been sectioned was to allow his mother to shag her Romanian lover to her heart's content. So her first priority was to persuade him to run away with her. Which turned out to be surprisingly easy. Oblivious of his obsession with an imaginary wife, all Gülnazmiye could see was those wonderful water-green eyes sparkling with enthusiasm. She had packed a suitcase with necessities such as clothing, cosmetics and jewellery, in readiness when the time came to rescue her boyfriend.

Having sold all her furniture, she'd been curling up on a foam mattress on the floor for the past week with only a thin duvet for warmth. She'd wheedled small amounts of money out of everyone: her dental technician big brother in Adana, her big sister (a mother of three with a wealthy farmer husband) in Konya, Matron Servinaz Ceviz, and her friends. She'd also taken several loans, including a consumer loan ten times her salary. All this came to a considerable amount of cash that she'd stuffed into a massive dark green fake leather handbag she now carried everywhere. She'd even stopped paying rent since deciding to run away with Barış, so whenever her landlord rang from Germany, where he lived, yelling and screaming (which was quite often) Gülnazmiye fabricated another lie.

Istanbul was dangerous, she thought, since her uncle and his sons lived there; she might meet any one of them at some unexpected place – an unsettling prospect. So it had to be Izmir, where no one knew her. She would certainly be fired and her family would take off after her, not that any of this occurred to her. She didn't have a shadow of a doubt that she would be snapped up with a super salary by the first hospital she fetched up at. She had even come to believe her own lies, *I had to pay for the funeral costs, that's why I was unable to pay the rent;* she could swear her mum had died in a traffic accident, instead of still struggling to make ends meet on a modest widow's pension in Ankara.

This love that had begun as an immature dream, a hopeless desire, had grown into a reality that she now accepted as truth. On imaginary telephone conversations in the middle of the night, she told Barış to be patient, that very soon they'd *be just the two of* them, that she'd sort it all out. Explaining all the while that she loved him very much, very very much, more than he could ever imagine.

There was talk in the block that she'd gone bananas. **Her next door neighbour Uncle Hacı** – who closed up his roastery around nine at night, came home, demolished an entire loaf of bread with his meal, tearing chunks off to dunk in the sauce, performed his night-time prayers and went to bed – was disturbed by the sound of conversation coming from Gülnazmiye's flat.

The first time he heard it, he thought she'd taken a man in (not proper at all, a young woman living on her own, at any rate!) and turned up at her door with a furious, *Think this is a whorehouse or what!* Pushing aside the girl who'd tried to bar his way, he'd scoured the flat. Of course there wasn't a man. He had no idea what he'd heard was Gülnazmiye's imaginary conversations with Barış and his loathsome mother Veda.

Thinking the sounds were coming from the TV, he stormed off saying, *Turn this thing down next time!* But he heard the same conversation again the following night, and pricked up his ears. It didn't sound like the TV, though. No, no: it was Gülnazmiye who was shouting. She was really losing it, quarrelling with Veda and smashing plates and pots and whatever else she could get hold of, screeching, *You can't coop Barış up in a loony bin just so you can shag your lovers whenever you want!* Uncle Hacı got even more worried when she emptied her flat, having sold her TV set to a scrap dealer and fridge to a student.

Yet part of her mind remained razor sharp as she fine tuned her plan: they would leap over the wall behind the hospital during the mind-boggling commotion that she would create, hop onto a coach and would be halfway to Izmir before the dust had settled. Even if someone twigged they'd run away together, they would have got there and disappeared without a trace. She was ready.

Just then, with a *Loads of time yet!* Barış had got back to his room upstairs as the fire started in the bedding storeroom on the ground floor; Gülnazmiye had doused a heap of mattresses, blankets and duvets with a tin of solvent, struck a match and proceeded to the medical supplies store at the other end of the hallway, carrying three more tins. The bag stuffed with cash was on her shoulder. She poured a full tin over the door of an unused room, and another into the locked medical supplies storeroom through the gap under the door. She didn't think she had been seen, not that it mattered to her anyway.

In the meanwhile, paraphasia sufferer Blue-eyed Maviş was wandering in the hospital. Her big brother Kamer, who handled all the hospital's print work, was head over heels in love with **Ceyda at Accounts**. In a bid to see her more often, he'd reduced his output to a trickle and so was dropping in all the time, bringing his blue-eyed sister for Ceyda to fuss over, *Oh, you sweetie… What a poppet!*

That was the day he'd intended to open up to Ceyda (who didn't seem totally uninterested either); for there could be no better date than the 14 February to ask someone out. So he'd suggested a cup of coffee at the café opposite the hospital: a relatively trendy spot popular with undergraduates with a menu featuring macchiato, cappuccino and espresso that contrasted with the kilim patterned cushions and the arabesk music. Would the girls in Accounts look after Maviş for a while?

The accountants all knew Kamer was potty about Ceyda – of course they hinted they would cover for her, and look after Maviş too. Kamer and Ceyda went to the café. The couple hadn't even left the building when the accountants started chattering about Ceyda's luck: she'd found love *and* money – Kamer was a great catch – and this led to a discussion about the luck of Valentine's Day.

Bored of sitting with accountants who didn't get what she said, Maviş went walkabout and got lost in the labyrinthine hospital. She was standing at the bottom of the second staircase (a later addition to the building) when she saw Gülnazmiye tipping liquid from a tin over the wooden doors.

Given Maviş spent the majority of her time at the print works since only her big brother could make sense of her speech, she knew all that was to know about flammables like solvent, and she had a very keen sense of smell too. She knew at once what Gülnazmiye's intention was, panicked, and started running around in the hospital yelling and screaming what sounded like gibberish. She couldn't find Accounts, but got to the Exit; she told Guard Enver Abi that Gülnazmiye was setting the place on fire. Except her *lighter... cloud... gone... dribbling... in the air...* made no sense. Enver knew she was the printer's sister; so taking her by the hand, he led her to the canteen and bought her an ice tea to cheer her up, as she burst into tears, frustrated by her own inability to communicate. He kept repeating, *Your brother'll be here by and by; come now, sit yourself down and drink your ice tea,* but couldn't make her stop. Eventually, sick of trying to describe what she'd seen, Maviş sat down on the bench outside the canteen and started drinking her ice tea. If only Enver had been able to make sense of her speech, or even looked for her brother instead of taking her to the canteen, the disaster would not have reached the proportions it did.

Earlier that morning, bulging green bag on her shoulder, Gülnazmiye had entered the ironmongery next to Uncle Hacı's roastery, bought four tins of solvent and come face to face with her neighbour on her way out. Seeing the contents of the clear carrier bags, Uncle Hacı asked why she needed all that solvent. Cool as a cucumber, she replied, *I'm gonna paint* and strode off. She was acting really strange, but he still didn't twig and forgot about her within minutes.

It took quite a while before she could find Barış to tell him to meet her at three at their usual spot; in the meanwhile, she'd secreted the tins under her desk, wrapped in pages of *Unnerving* she'd been buying every quarter in the hope of seeing the article – *Types of Relationships in Narcissist Personalities* – she'd written on the day she'd fallen for him. If the tins had already caught Uncle Hacı's attention, then they could easily raise other eyebrows too.

Barış had once started a fire by pouring eau de cologne on his bed; inspired by that incident, Gülnazmiye decided that setting fire to the hospital was going to be a superb way of rescuing her boyfriend. The solvent flared up the moment she threw a lighted match and soon all the mattresses, duvets and blankets caught fire. Doors and walls coated with several layers of oil based paint doused with solvent flared up next. In no time at all, the fire reached the door of the room where the Medical Director slept, destined never to know he'd been introduced to pot.

Unaware that her husband had died of the toxic fumes filling his mouth and nose and lungs well before his body had fried in the blaze melting the ground floor doors in fireballs, Sevim stared through her tears at the serum dripping into the tube, still unable to believe what had happened after all these years of marriage.

An hour before striking the match, Gülnazmiye had gone to her usual pharmacy in the shopping district to ask, *Can I leave this here for an hour?* dropped off her suitcase, done her make-up in their mirror and adjusted the new bra that accentuated her lovely breasts, before hastening back to the hospital, stuffed handbag on her shoulder. Now she sat waiting for her boyfriend, impatiently checking the rapidly growing fire and her watch in turn.

The city rang with fire engine sirens this time, far more ear shattering than ambulances or police vehicles. The ground floor was all but gone and the fire had already reached the first. In the mayhem inside, people were trampling over one another to get out. Anorexic Buse Göçer (who, too emaciated to be anything but perpetually cold, still flaunted plunging necklines as if she had a bosom to show off instead of a rack of ribs) had brought a portable gas heater from home. There was no one in her office when the tank exploded, but the noise was enough to tip spaced-out heads over the edge. Never one for cool composure, Nemişo was now hysterical; she had got out before the staircase was seized by the flames and was frantically trying to say that the Medical Director was stuck on the ground floor, but putting two words together was beyond her stoned mind.

Alerted to the situation, District Mayor Cumhur Eryıldıran and Metro-politan Mayor Tacettin Başusta both came rushing over. Every apparatus of the state was mobilised – from County Hall through to Police HQ and district councils – and the news had even reached the Ministry of Health. Local correspondents of national media outlets rang head offices to pile it on really thick: the 350-capacity hospital suddenly housed 700 as estimates of casualties rocketed before any concrete numbers were available. Ticker tape ran on news channels, announcing fears of one hundred dead at least.

The solvent Gülnazmiye had poured everywhere on the ground floor had caused a fire of mind-boggling proportions. Officials talking to the Fire Brigade Commissioner were trying to figure out what could have started such an enormous blaze just as Hacer Abla was trying to leave the kitchen, coughing and choking, when the industrial size LPG tanks exploded one by one. She died on the spot.

The sirens of fire engines converging from nearby districts filled the small city. Friends and family of the staff and patients had run over, watching the fire brigade's efforts in a panic, screaming, crying and lamenting. Scared of loonies ever since his head had been smashed with the backgammon board by schizoaffective İsmail Çeliktaş, Ofli Durali had also run over to join the rubberneckers. At the sight of the flames shooting up into the sky, he went out of his mind.

The previous night he'd been badly beaten by the night watchman Tahir at Substance Abuse – and Durali had no idea Tahir was off his head on dope. Durali had been cleaning when Tahir had trampled over the freshly mopped bit. Not brave enough to say openly, *Don't step on it!* he'd grumbled under his breath, *Eat shit ya' bastard!* But Tahir heard, and roared, eyes wide open. Durali tried to run away, sod the mop or the bucket. But couldn't. Tahir was bored. He blocked Durali's way and gave him a good hiding. Durali managed to get out of the hospital by the skin of his teeth, went home with a black eye and a ripped shirt, and told his wife he wasn't going back to the hospital ever again. He really had no intention of ever setting foot there again. First thing in the morning he rang his friends, telling them he'd resigned and was looking for a new job. He was planning to take revenge on the desperately hated night watchman Tahir: he'd write to the Medical Director and tell him Tahir was smoking dope in the hospital. But watching the fire, it dawned upon him that he too would have been inside if he hadn't been beaten up by that filthy dopehead. He'd have kissed Tahir if he could at that moment.

It was mayhem outside the hospital. The police were struggling to control the friends and family of those stuck inside. The husbands of the nurses, the wives of the orderlies, and the mothers, fathers, and children of the administrative personnel had all rushed over, making the disaster far worse with their screams. Pothead carpenter Odd-eyes Sipahi was also watching. He was well stoned, and had no doubt that the cake he'd eaten was spiked. He thought he would tell the police. But he'd only taken one step when his imagination whipped up by the dope reached gigantic dimensions and he succumbed to paranoia: what if he told them about eating spiked cake, and was found guilty, arrested, and even sentenced to death? He mistook the policemen's efforts to control the crowd; he thought they were trying to capture him. Terrified, he ran away from the burning hospital. He was panting, nearly choking by the time he got home. Telling his wife not to open the door to anyone, he locked himself up in the bedroom.

Faik Abacı's shy wife Gülümser dived into a taxi to get to the hospital, hoping to find her husband safe and sound, as Gynaecologist Tuğba also drove over. But her parking was so sloppy that one of the policemen dropped everything to look for the owner of the silver Toyota blocking the fire engines' way.

Earless Ziya's wife Munise had been shopping. She'd looked for shoes for the children, decided she couldn't afford them and hoped they could make do for another year. She was standing by the chestnut stall when fire engines went past one after the other. It never crossed her mind that the fire might be at the hospital as she remembered how much Ziya loved chestnuts and splashed out on a cone of chestnuts and set out, her heart filled with love. At reaching the disaster area and seeing the fire, she broke into a run, yelling, *Ziyaaa!* and flinging the cone to one side as she tried to get inside. But the firemen grabbed her in time and sent her behind the tape.

Ziya thought he was hurrying, when, in fact, under the influence of the spiked cake, his movements had slowed down horribly. Even though his mind was capable of thinking about intervening, he couldn't work the fire extinguisher it took him ages to lift. Instead of leaving, he kept trying to make it work, coughing and choking in the smoke, until a fireman dragged him outside. When she saw her husband emerge safe and sound, Munise fainted in relief.

Fuses and bulbs blew, cables melted, and the power went. Nylon curtains and plastic blinds were melting, tables, chairs, tonnes of paper, doors, window frames, walls, beds and cupboards in the floors were burning like torches: water sprayed constantly by the fire brigade had no effect. Dense, lethal smoke filled the whole building. Once the wooden railings caught fire, the stairs became inaccessible; it was impossible to see your hand in front of your face.

Patients in the secure unit, in particular, were under threat; the flames had not yet reached their wards, but dense smoke already filled the rooms. Breaking doors that normally needed special handles carried by the orderlies, the firemen were trying to take the patients out and struggling with those who resisted. Hampered as they were by the labyrinthine plan of the four-storey building, the lack of a fire staircase didn't help either.

If the rear façade had a few windows on each floor instead of being an entirely blind wall, it would have been so much easier to evacuate the building. As it was, there was a stampede towards the windows on the south façade. Some people leapt out of the first and even second floor windows without waiting for the fire brigade to hold life nets. Tahir, the pothead night watchman, who had supplied Nebahat and beaten Ofli Durali black and blue the previous night, was amongst those who leapt from the second floor; breaking both legs.

The real catastrophe took place in the conference hall where Ülkü Birinci had just been speaking. Although the fire had not yet reached the top floor, fifteen people were trampled in the stampede towards the narrow door of the windowless hall. A female medical student died of injuries to the head and an elderly gentleman who was whiling away the wait for his MR scan had a fatal heart attack. Ülkü Birinci stood rooted to the lectern, horrified by the pandemonium at the door. Convinced he would die here, he longed for a heart attack before the fire reached the hall, and broke into howling gibberish as he succumbed to claustrophobia in the cavernous space.

In the end, it turned out that the majority of the patients had been rescued. No effort had been spared to evacuate the secure unit; patients plucked from the fire had been put into a police minibus and sent to the State Hospital where they would be taken care of, or, more accurately, where they could not be taken care of. One of the psychiatrists there had to drug them all quite heavily.

Now some of the patients were watching the fire from the outside, mingling with the bystanders, as others had already slipped into the streets. Two schizoids roamed for a while before entering the stadium and starting to kick a discarded football. Another arrived at the ugly tower erected to replace the Clock Tower that had collapsed in the great earthquake and started forcing the door; he wanted to climb to the top and watch the fire from there. Patients sauntering in pyjamas and stopping dead to stare at shopwindows mystified what few townsfolk who still remained unaware of the fire. Of the criminals awaiting to be certified insane to dodge prison and rescued by the fire brigade, five scarpered. One hotfooted it to the coach station and set off for Istanbul. Another was sure he'd be captured, so he went to visit his family.

Sirens rang constantly as eleven ambulances carried the injured to the State Hospital and the city's three private hospitals, mingling with the constant horns of the taxis pressed into service as ambulances by the families of the injured. The sirens of the fire engines coming from neighbouring districts spread everywhere.

Türkan heard Asiye had shot her husband; she'd yet to hear about the fire when at first she was puzzled by the vehicles screaming down Atatürk Boulevard. She was sitting at her usual table at the Three Brothers Patisserie, reflecting upon the second class status of women in this country as she sipped the coffee Serhat had brought over with his own hands. She felt really sorry for Asiye, who had chosen to bloody her hands instead of getting a divorce; she would certainly visit her in prison, using her power and prestige if need be. Just as she was about to ask Serhat, *Son, what's with all these fire engines; is there a fire someplace?* the old physician Nurettin Kozanlı turned up and sat down at her table without so much as a by your leave. Türkan was bemused. Nurettin rushed through the greetings and launched into an appeal for intercession with the Medical Director.

His pathetic face looked even more crushing than ever. Back hunched, a two-day-old beard, a few strands of hair sticking to his scalp and sunken cheeks, he looked much older than his real age; his unwashed clothes exuded an awful stench. At the sight of the budding tears in those dreadfully sunken eyes, Türkan had to resist the temptation to reach out and touch the hand that was nothing more than dry bone. Nurettin was explaining he hadn't been able to pay the rent on his surgery for months, that his old friend of this many years had stopped talking to him over a trifle, and that he was ready to forget it all to make up. He had dropped all pretence at pride now; he really needed the Medical Director's patronage. Thoughts of helping this poor physician secretly flashing through her mind, Türkan promised she would pay the Medical Director a visit as soon as was humanly possible and ask him to bring an end to this rift. Just then, the flames were licking the Medical Director's body.

Faik Abacı and the pharmaceutical rep İlhami were amongst the first to run outside. Panicked at remembering the Medical Director sleeping in the densest part of the fire on the ground floor, Faik grabbed the Fire Brigade Commissioner by the collar, begging them to rescue the fellow. The Commissioner said it was impossible. By which time it was already too late anyway; the Medical Director's body was incinerated before the two men had finished arguing.

Neuropsychiatrist Nebahat Özdamar (she who'd doped the Medical Director with her cake and caused him to lose control, and thereby die in the fire) was very lucky. She was making herself a very strong pot of filter coffee when she'd noticed the smoke and shuffled out in her slippers without bothering to warn anyone else. She went as far away as possible, and then returned when the fire engines had arrived. Planting herself at the boundary of the safety cordon next to her fellow fate-mate Şaban Sekban, she asked anyone and everyone why the Medical Director wasn't there to take care of things, screeching at the top of her reedy voice to accuse him of incompetence – a terrible manager who had abandoned his hospital in its darkest hour (as the body of the man in question was burning to cinders).

Hamdi Tutuş, who'd been blaming himself for failing to recognise the Medical Director early in the morning, had escaped the fire since he'd returned to the security hut after freeing himself from the orderlies. But when his feeling of guilt returned at the sight of the flames enveloping the hospital and he burst into paroxysms of bawling, trying to hurl himself into the fire, one of the policemen (well done in by then) slapped him hard, exclaiming, *Who's gonna deal with you, you bloody maniac!* Thus floored, Hamdi calmed down and shut up, thinking he'd now paid for failing to recognise the Medical Director in the morning. He withdrew into a corner, forgotten by the orderlies, and made straight for the city cemetery to look for the grave of the brother who'd been giving him nightmares since Hamdi had pushed him into the dry well in the garden. But it was an impossible task: firstly because his brother had been buried in the village and not in the modern cemetery. And secondly, even if Hamdi went to the village cemetery, he'd never find the grave. That brother had died fifty years before; his name was forgotten a few years later, and his grave had long since vanished.

Having noticed the Medical Director's absence, Âlim Kâhkeci was working flat out to rescue the patients and assisting the Fire Brigade Commissioner. He spotted his wife, waved an *I'm all right*, and turned to lead the firemen to the rear to show them which walls they could knock down, when he suddenly remembered Ayşe Nuran Serbest strapped to a bed in a second floor room. There was no one with the hapless girl who'd been so hard to restrain. He asked the firemen for help, but it was too late; the heavily sedated harelipped gynaecologist had suffocated before any firemen could reach her.

As the crowds watched the fire outside the hospital and from their windows, a violent fight was taking place at the window of an accounting firm directly opposite. Çiğdem Taşpınar, although not actually a news reporter, was excited at this extraordinary turn of events; and having rung her news station and promised to send stunning footage of the fire, she'd rushed over with cameraman Damir, glanced around and picked the best angle. A short chat later, and with the manager's, *Come in, please do,* they dived into the office that was suddenly a key spot.

Just then, the **Channel SS Reporter/Cameraman Muzo** also turned up. He, too, wanted to shoot the commotion in the hospital garden and the waving of the flames in the windows from this angle that commanded the best view. Çiğdem Taşpınar, in the meanwhile, was talking to her station to arrange for the report to make the evening news.

The national station logo on Damir's camera really got Muzo's goat. He couldn't stand these big-headed big channel employees. *Off to the* next-door office with you, mate. *This place belongs to a friend, we always shoot here,* he said, shoving aside Damir, who'd seized the most fantastic spot by the window and was now busy focusing. Surprised by the rough shove, Damir glanced at Muzo, but carried on in silence since he spoke no Turkish.

Muzo blew a gasket when Damir didn't react, and without so much as a reply. *Who does this arsehole think he is? What right's he got to grab the best spot just because he's working for a big station?* Yelling, *Am I talking to the wall or what here, mate!* he shoved Damir, much more roughly this time. Taken aback at this second baffling attack, Damir paused, put his camera aside and placing both hands on Muzo's shoulders, he shoved back. He was a big, strapping fellow; it didn't take much effort.

Muzo took a few steps back to keep his balance, and banged against the manager's desk, knocking over the dry flower vase, giveaway plastic clock and copper pen holder. Incredulous at this treatment and watched by the astonished accountant, Muzo launched himself into the air, intending to head-butt in return, missed when the Bosnian bent down to plug in the battery, and slammed with his full weight into Damir instead.

Ignoring the accountant's protests, they laid into each other; kicks and punches flew freely. Çiğdem had gone outside to hear the editor better on the phone; she returned to find the two cameramen rolling around on the floor. Attempting to intervene, she barely escaped a couple of punches. The office was wrecked, the accountant hit the roof and roared, *My fault for being nice and letting you come in to shoot! Bugger off, I'm not giving you no permission, no nothing!*

But nothing could stop Muzo and Damir. The poor accountant was scuttling around the office, lugging an enormous LCD screen that had cost a pretty packet. By the time Çiğdem managed to break up the fight, the most crucial scenes of the fire had been and gone, and by the time the two cameramen had dusted themselves down and gone back to work, everything, including the flames, was obscured by a thick, black smoke.

An earlier foray into funeral videos having proven unprofitable, equally disillusioned with wedding videos due to the cutthroat competition in the sector, unable to repay the loan for the camera shop, his credit cards cancelled, broke and reeling under the strain, Tolga had been roaming around the city aimlessly; hoping *Perhaps if I could shoot the fire from a different angle, I could sell it to a station.* Spotting the throngs at the front, he'd grabbed his camera and gone round the back.

The fire had just started, and the windowless rear wall was stopping it from spreading to this side. Tolga climbed to the top of the half collapsed garden wall and started adjusting his camera when he caught sight of Gülnazmiye waiting for her lover. She didn't seem scared by the fire at all; if anything, she looked totally unfazed. He zoomed in watchfully. When she delved into her bag for her cigarettes whilst waiting for Barış, Tolga saw that the bag was full of cash. He couldn't believe his eyes.

Watching the fire from afar, Gülnazmiye Görgün was beginning to get worried, and started murmuring, *C'mon Barış! C'mon darling, come on now!* It never crossed her mind that he might be burning. Unable to figure out why her boyfriend wasn't coming, the more she wound herself up, the crazier she got. Out of the blue she got the idea that Veda Alkan had tricked her son. Any other possibility was out of the question. That horrible bitch must be in there, trying to turn Barış against her; otherwise her one and only love would have turned up long ago. Gülnazmiye had to stop that slapper, that common whore who'd locked her son up in a loony bin just so she could screw that bent Romanian to her heart's content; it was up to her to rescue her boyfriend from his mother's clutches. Leaving the green bag stuffed to the gills with banknotes, she shot off like an arrow.

The moment he saw her shoot off, Tolga leapt down from the wall, glanced around, went to the bag and gingerly opened it. He couldn't believe his eyes. The bag was really stuffed with money. Abandoning the fire, he grabbed the bag and hightailed it. As he was running away, camera in his hand, green woman's bag over his shoulder, Gülnazmiye was running towards the entrance where the flames were dancing, yelling, *Barış, don't believe your motheeeeer! You're not maaaad, just don't belieeeeeve her!* She was thrashing about, biting and kicking the policemen trying to stop her, yelling nonsense like, *Let me go! I'm gonna go in! I'm gonna kill that common whore!*

By the time two policemen had managed to clasp Gülnazmiye firmly by the arms, Kamer (who had asked Ceyda out and made a date for the following day) had located his sister Maviş, still babbling incoherently.

He was hugging her tight when Maviş related in floods of tears that she'd seen Gülnazmiye torch the place. The printer was horrified. As he walked over to tell the Fire Brigade Commissioner what he'd heard from his sister, Tolga was hopping into a taxi, trembling all over. Every once in a while he opened the bag he was clutching on his lap, just a crack, to guess how much money was in it.

As Gülnazmiye collapsed like an empty sack, exhausted from struggling with the policemen, sharp cameraman Tolga went home and locked the door. He'd dipped into the bag for a fifty for the fare and been overwhelmed by guilt over the theft. But it vanished when he got home. Emptying the bag he'd stolen, yes, stolen, he counted the wads quickly, and couldn't believe his eyes. It was enough to cover his debts, not a penny more. He was annoyed at that: Just a bit more and he'd have bought that leather jacket he'd set his sights on.

Barış Bakış was awakened by the smell of smoke when the flames reached his floor; he got out of bed to keep his appointment with Gülnazmiye, opened the door and saw the fire. He stood and listened to the roar for a while, then shut the door before the smoke started filling his room. Turning towards his bed, he pulled out his *Hospital Diary* from under the pillow. Found his fountain pen, neatly wrote *Today is the 14 February, Valentine's Day... They're all mad, wifey!* replaced the journal under the pillow and went to bed.

Barış was one of the twelve fatalities in the fire.

Notes

1   Wealth Wax: Varlık Vergisi, ostensibly enacted to raise funds in case of entry into the Second World War, it was levied mostly on non-Muslim citizens. Arbitrarily high assessments and demands for payment within a fortnight inflicted financial ruin on countless people, and those who could not pay were sent to the East as forced labour. 11 November 1942 – repealed 15 March 1944

2   War of Independence, also called War of Liberation: 1919–1922; following the end of the Great War, the Ottoman Empire was divided up amongst the Allies, leaving a small inland region of Anatolia to the vanquished state. The Nationalists, led by Mustafa Kemal – later Atatürk – defeated the occupying Greek forces and overturned the Treaty of Sèvres. The Republic of Turkey was proclaimed on 29 October 1923.

3   Mehmet Celal Bey, 1863–1926: Ottoman statesman, who, as Governor of Aleppo first, and Konya later, defied deportation orders, thereby saving thousands of Armenian lives. He was one of many statesmen dismissed for refusal to follow similar orders.

4   Events/Riots of 6–7 September: Organised mob attacks targeting Istanbul's Greeks, triggered by the fake news that Greeks had bombed the Turkish Consulate in Thessaloniki (the house where Atatürk was born), caused indiscriminate damage to non-Muslims and their property.

5   Atatürk's script reform enacted 1 November 1928 moved the language from Arabic script, which did not suit the sounds of Turkish, to Latin. Literacy rates doubled in the following seven years.

Translator's Notes

Turkish is phonetic, with a single sound assigned to most letters.
The letters pronounced differently from English are:

a = shorter than the English a in *father*

c = j in *jack*

ç = ch in *chat*

e = e in *bed* (never as in *me*) but en = an as in *ban*

ğ = 'soft g' is silent; it merely lengthens the vowel preceding it

ı = schwa; the second syllable in *higher*

i = i in *bin*; never as in *eye*

j = s in *measure*, or the French j in *jour*

r = r in *read*; at end of syllables closest to the Welsh, as in *mawr*

s = s in *sing*

ş = sh in *ship*

ö and ü = like the corresponding German umlaut sounds

y = English y in *yellow*

Turkish and Armenian given names are generally stressed on the final syllable, so *al-TAY, kar-NİK, ne-ba-HAT*, whereas Greek and Jewish given names are stressed on the first in two syllable names, and on the penultimate in multisyllabic ones: *SA-ra, to-to-DA-ki*, etc.

Standard Turkish spelling has been used for all proper nouns.

Honorifics follow the first name: *bey* (sir), *hanım* (lady), *abi* (elder brother), and *abla* (elder sister), for instance.

Historical figures who appear in the narrative

Abdülaziz 32nd Ottoman Sultan r 1861–1876; 1830–1876

Abdülhak Hamit Tarhan Turkish poet and playwright; 1852–1937

Abdülhamid II 34th Ottoman Sultan r 1876–1909; 1842–1918

Ahmet Hamdi Tanpınar Turkish writer and poet; 1901–1962

Alexander Solzhenitsyn Russian writer; 1918–2008

Andy Warhol American artist; 1928–1987

Augusto Pinochet Chilean general and dictator; 1915–2006

Ayhan Işık Turkish actor; 1929–1979

Brad Pitt American actor; b 1963

Caliph Omar Second Caliph r 634–644; b 584

Cosmi Sébah Ottoman photographer, elder brother of Pascal

Cüneyt Arkın Turkish actor and film director; b 1937

Dimitrie Cantemir Moldovan soldier, statesman, and chronicler of the Ottoman Empire; 1673–1723

Ebüzziya Tevfik Ottoman journalist, writer, publisher, and calligrapher; 1849–1912

Egon Schiele Austrian artist; 1890–1918

Enver Pasha Ottoman Committee of Union and Progress statesman; 1881–1922

Feyyaz Kayacan Fergar Turkish writer; 1919–1993

Friedrich Nietzsche German philosopher; 1844–1900

George Clooney American actor; b 1961

Grumpy Virginia Comedian Seyfi Dursunoğlu's (b 1932) drag queen persona

Gülriz Sururi Turkish actress; 1929–2018

Haldun Taner Turkish writer and playwright; 1915–1986

Halide Edip Adıvar Turkish writer and activist; 1884–1964

Hatice Sultan Abdülhamid II's daughter who died at eight months

Hüseyin Rahmi Gürpınar Turkish writer, civil servant and politician; 1864–1944

İsmet İnönü Pasha Turkish general and the Republic of Turkey's second president 1938–1950; 1884–1973

James Joyce Irish writer, poet and teacher; 1882–1941

Jean Pascal Sébah Ottoman photographer, son of Pascal; 1872–1947

Karl Marx German philosopher and social revolutionary; 1818–1883

Kemal Tahir Turkish writer; 1910–1973

Kenan Evren Turkish general, leader of the coup of 1980; Turkey's seventh president 1980–1989; 1917–2015

Leonardo da Vinci Italian polymath: architect, sculptor, inventor, painter; 1452–1519

Leontina Vaduva Romanian soprano; b 1960

Louis Conrad Rosenberg American architect and printmaker; 1890–1983

Macit Akman Director General of Turkish Radio and Television 1981–1984; b 1922

Max Fruchtermann Austro–Hungarian/German publisher of Istanbul postcards; 1852–1918

Mazhar Osman Uzman Turkish physician who founded the first modern mental health hospital in the country; 1884–1951

Mehmet Celal Bey Ottoman statesman, Governor of Konya; 1863–1926

Melek Görgün Turkish actress; b 1949

Mikhail Bulgakov Russian doctor, writer, and playwright; 1891–1940

Mithat Cemal Kuntay Turkish writer, poet and lawyer; 1885–1956

Mstislav Rostropovich Russian cellist and conductor; 1927–2007

Musa Eroğlu Turkish folk musician; b 1946

Müslüm Gürses Turkish singer and actor; 1953–2013

Nâzım Hikmet Turkish poet, writer, director; 1902–1963

Niko Pirosmanashvili Georgian painter also known as Niko Pirosmani; 1862–1918

Omar Khayyam Persian mathematician, astronomer and poet; 1048–1131

Ömer Seyfettin Turkish writer; 1884–1920

Orhan Veli Kanık Turkish poet; 1914–1950

Ottmar Zieher German publisher of postcards; active 1897–1908; 1857–1924

Özcan Deniz Turkish singer, composer, actor, writer and film director; b 1972

Pablo Picasso Spanish artist; 1881–1973

Pascal Sébah Prolific pioneering Ottoman photographer; 1823–1886

Polycarpe Joaillier French photographer who, together with Jean Sébah, formed Sébah & Joaillier in Istanbul; 1848–1904

Refik Epikman Turkish painter; 1902–1974

Reşat Nuri Güntekin Turkish writer; 1889–1956

Sadegh Hedayet Iranian writer and translator; 1903–1951

Sait Faik Turkish writer; 1906–1954

Seçil Heper Turkish singer; b 1946

Sezen Aksu Turkish songwriter and singer; b 1954

Sibel Can Turkish singer; b 1970

Turgut Sunalp Turkish general and later MP; 1917–1999

Vamık Volkan Turkish Cypriot psychiatrist; b 1932

William Shakespeare English playwright; 1564–1616

Yahya Kemal Turkish poet and writer; 1884–1958

The Author

Born in Adapazarı, AYFER TUNÇ was first published whilst still an undergraduate at Istanbul University Faculty of Political Sciences. In 1989 she won the *Cumhuriyet* newspaper's Yunus Nadi Short Story Prize. She took up writing full time after serving as editor-in-chief at Yapı Kredi Publishing House between 1999 and 2004. In addition to her work on TV scripts, Tunç has written several novels and short story collections, many of which have been published in other languages. *The Aziz Bey Incident*, a collection of short stories, was published by Istros in 2013.

The Translator

Born in Izmir, FEYZA HOWELL has a UK Honours degree in Graphic Design. Experienced in various aspects of international business including advertising, design and TV, she has always drawn, written and translated. Several of her English translations have been published in the UK to date. Feyza Howell is married, has a son and lives in Berkshire.

First published in 2020 by
Istros Books
London, United Kingdom www.istrosbooks.com

Copyright © Ayfer Tunç 2020

First published as *Bir Deliler Evinin Yalan Yanlış Anlatılan Kısa Tarihi*
Can Yayınları, 2009

Translation © Feyza Howell , 2020
Cover design: Kerem Yeğin
Typesetting: Davor Pukljak, www.frontispis.hr

ISBN: 978-1-912545-07-0

Printed by Pulsioprint, France/Bulgaria

The publication of this book has been funded with the support
of the TEDA programme of the Ministry of Culture and Tourism of Turkey